BREATHLESS IN BOMBAY

St. Martin's Griffin

NEW YORK

BREATHLESS in BOMBAY

Stories

MURZBAN F. SHROFF

BREATHLESS IN BOMBAY. Copyright © 2008 by Murzban F. Shroff. All rights reserved. Printed in the United States of America. No part of this book may be used or reproduced in any manner whatsoever without written permission except in the case of brief quotations embodied in critical articles or reviews. For information, address St. Martin's Press, 175 Fifth Avenue, New York, N.Y. 10010.

www.stmartins.com

Book design by Gretchen Achilles

Grateful acknowledgment to the publications in which these stories first appeared in a slightly different form:

"Dhobi Ghat," in *The Louisville Review*. "Traffic," in *Natural Bridge*. "The Maalishwalla," in *The Minnesota Review*. "Haraami," in *Wisconsin Review*. "Busy Sunday," in *Southwest Review*. "The Great Divide" (under the title "This Old Guard"), in *South Dakota Review*. "Meter Down," in *The South Carolina Review*. "Love in the Time of AIDS," in *Gulf Stream*. "Babu Barrah Takka," in *The Best of Carve*, Volume 5. "Jamal Haddi's Revenge," in *The Mochila Review*. "Breathless in Bombay," in *The Gettysburg Review*.

LIBRARY OF CONGRESS CATALOGING-IN-PUBLICATION DATA

Shroff, Murzban F.
    Breathless in Bombay / Murzban F. Shroff.—1st ed.
        p. cm.
    A collection of 14 stories.
    ISBN-13: 978-0-312-37270-5
    ISBN-10: 0-312-37270-1
    1. Bombay (India)—Fiction. 2. City and town life—India—Bombay—Fiction. 3. Bombay (India)—Social conditions—Fiction. I. Title.

    PS3619.H775B74 2008
    813'.6—dc22

                                                                    2007038265

First Edition: February 2008

10   9   8   7   6   5   4   3   2   1

CONTENTS

✦ ✦ ✦

DEDICATED

to the unparalleled love

of my grandfather

SAVAKSHAW

and all that he stood for:

fair play, integrity, and

dignity in the face of adversity

IMMEASURABLE GRATITUDE

✦ ✦ ✦

To Jeroo, my mother, who dreamt a bigger dream for me than I did, and who gave me the strength, the confidence, and the means to pursue that dream.

To Fali, my father, whose punctilious nature and sense of perfection are manifested in the genetics of this book and in the numerous reworks and shading that saw it to its published end.

To Jimmy, my maternal uncle, who lit the spark of literature for me a tad too early in life, and of whom there is more in this book than one can ever imagine.

To Firoza, my wife, my companion, who created for me the tranquillity and the space to write.

To Porus, who with the kind support of his Guide nurtured all that is correct in this book.

To Neville, my jolly-hearted friend, who promised me that the only book he would read in his life would be mine and who never lived to see the end of this book.

To Vistasp, young firehorse, who read all my work voraciously and responded unfailingly.

To Mansoor, gentleman farmer, who drove me out of my urban cubbyhole to a larger, more earthy sensibility.

To Abhi, my transatlantic pillar of support, who helped my manuscripts reach their destination.

To Jaideep, my firebrand friend, who backed me unstintingly in my views.

To Chris, man of God, who took my familial concerns as his own.

To V. B. Plumber, for her insights and her guidance.

To Madhur, Dilip, and Param, for their prompt and prolific support.

To George Witte, for his invaluable contributions.

To Daniela, my editor, who with her conviction and her care stood for me at the end of a long journey, stood like a rock.

There are others who have been a significant part of this work, if not directly, then by the very quality of their friendship and the generosity of their nature. I would like to share that writing is not the easiest of vocations; it is often a thankless task and almost always induces fear of failure and doubts of personal well-being. At such times, it is not just important but essential to have friends like Julie Brickman, Ben Fountain, J. Robert Lennon, and Melvin Sterne, who, being writers themselves, are happy to share their space and encourage one of their own. I am grateful for having known these rare friendships. They provided the terra firma on which I survived, actually thrived.

INTRODUCTION

✦   ✦   ✦

A host of mine, several years older than me and staying at Kemps Corner in South Bombay, once related this incident in between expressions
of outrage. "Do you see?" he asked, pointing to groups of poverty-
stricken families camping below the Kemps Corner overpass. "Do you
see those migrants there? And that police *chowky* at the side?" I nodded,
not knowing why an all-too-familiar sight should be the reason for his
anger. "You are not going to believe this, but I saw them store some of
their belongings inside the *chowky*. That was when I was out on my
morning walk, and at that time the *chowky* was deserted, but later, when
I passed it in the evening and I saw policemen there and the belongings,
it simply got my goat. I walked in and demanded why the cops were
turning a blind eye to the encroachers, why they were permitting *these*
people to use our roads as their home, cooking, eating, washing, and
defecating there? And how they could encourage them by giving them
space in the *chowky*? And do you know what the cops told me? '*Kai,
sahib,*' they said. 'Let them be, no? They also deserve to live. Where they
will go if we throw them out? How do they affect our lives in any way
by being here?' No hope," my host spluttered. "Take it from me, son;
this city has gone to the dogs. Soon will come a time when you and I
will have to move out and make way for these slum dwellers."

That got me thinking. About the fate of Bombay. About the enormous divide of classes, so latent and yet so real. About the deterioration,

which was too glaring and too rampant to deny. And about my own relationship with the city, which was one of love and one of hate. Love for its sense of history and security and hate for its failure to provide us a decent standard of living: clean roads, clean water, clean air, and of course a clean system of living without the constant despair of bribes and corruption. After forty years of living here, in Bombay, breathing its air, dodging its traffic, gorging its food, sipping its alcohol, admiring its feminine beauty (which I hold to be the most fetching and beguiling in the world), I needed to put my relationship with my city in perspective—not just for myself, but for my readers who might trust my opinion, my perspective, or, if not that, at least my intentions.

I confess Bombay has never failed to fascinate me. To walk along the streets of Colaba and to be wooed by peddlers of all trades, all motives, always imbues me with a measure of excitement. Could I possibly be a tourist in my own city? Could I shed my identity as easily as that? To sit in Café Leopold and watch the world go by; to sit on the parapet at Apollo Bunder and see the sailboats tossed on the coruscating waters; to walk past Jehangir Art Gallery and see the drug addicts huddled over their foil, while long-bearded artists stare at them disapprovingly for their failure to take life's disappointments on the chin; to walk along the Gothic colonnades of the Ballard Estate and relive the solidarity of a lost era of architecture; to walk along Marine Drive and see the couples, their backs to the city, their heads huddled, and a universal sun casting its light on them; to walk past the Asiatic Library and see young students crouched over their textbooks in the lamplight, while the more fortunate squander their wealth in bars and pubs and gourmet restaurants—all these are aspects of home and aspects of life that only Bombay can provide. And as easily as it does this, it takes me to Banganga, and to a day and age when Lord Rama might have pierced the earth with his mighty arrow, so that he might entice the Ganges to pour forth into a reservoir, and just as easily Bombay transports me to the simplicity of another day, another age, when I mix and mingle with the crowds in the sweet, gaudy temple-town atmosphere of the Mahalaxmi Temple, and just as easily it silences me, as I discover an ideal nook to watch the sunset—off a remote lane near Warden Road.

Bombay, my city of life—books have been written about it, songs have been composed, and collections have been compiled and anthologized. So what did I have to say that was any different? Well, for starters, I had to answer my host—people like him, people like me, who had stayed too long in the city and loved it too intensely to appreciate what was happening to it now. To go into details of Bombay's deterioration would be arduous and unnecessary—what happened during the great flood of July 2005 is evidence of a city abandoned by its rulers, a city left to find its own methods of survival. What then has been the lure of this city that inspires writers like me and a population of twenty million to stay and toil and dream?

To find the answers, I did what I am best at: I walked the streets; I met people. I studied their dreams, their lives, their preoccupations, their regrets, and I understood the motivation that drove them just the same. I savored the street life of Bombay as easily and as voraciously as I had indulged in its high life, and I did so with the intention of remaining rooted, of simply carrying home an answer that was convincing to myself and to my host.

And this is what I found:

The story of Bombay is the story of struggle and sacrifice. Perhaps there is no other city in the world where the struggle spills so vividly and unabashedly out onto the streets, for that's what people are here for: to make the journey, to realize their dreams—and the outward anarchy is only a reflection of their deep inner struggle, the churning that leads to a finer, more realized self. People here are not ashamed to be seen toiling and slaving out in the open. The barber does it. The cobbler does it. The *chaiwalla* does it. The *bhajiyawalla* does it. The *vada-pavwalla* does it. The vegetable vendor does it. The *fruitwalla* does it. The fisherwoman does it. The ragpicker does it. The hawker does it. The encroacher does it. The eunuch does it. The beggar does it. The cop does it. The tout does it. The *dhobi* does it. The *maalishwalla* does it. The *victoriawalla* does it. The *taxiwalla* does it. How many trades? How many dreams? How many journeys can a single city take and deliver?

The more I thought about it, the more convinced I became—Bombay is indeed the city of evolution, the wrenching out of all desires, a miracle of coexistence and acceptance—and this is what I have attempted to capture in *Breathless in Bombay:* a series of journeys, through the mental lives of its citizens, their conflicts, their betrayals, their realization, and their redemption. Even with the jet-set achievers of Bombay, I saw a struggle that was all too palpable. It was there in their need to be seen in the media, their need to be acknowledged by the city.

Breathless in Bombay is a shadowing of many lives, many conflicts. It is Bombay by foot, by train, by taxi, by victoria. It is Bombay as lived in the heads of its people. *Breathless in Bombay* is the Bombay of today, with its burning issues, its swamping chaos, and its underlying sense of responsibility that never fails to deliver realization at the end of a journey. I am grateful to her, my Lady of the Seven Islands, for leaving me breathless with all that she has in store.

DHOBI GHAT

◆ ◆ ◆

MATAPRASAD MAHADEV, fifty-three, dark, and fiercely mustached, was in a thoughtful mood as he sat cross-legged in *dhoti* and *chappals* on the floor of the luggage compartment of the Churchgate-bound local. Next to him was his *khep,* a soft white cloud of a parcel that held the clothes of his customers in a firmly knotted bedsheet and announced his occupation to be that of a *dhobi.*

The train, being a "fast," rocked and rolled and sometimes threatened to leave the tracks. The clickety-clack of the wheels was loud and slicing; after a while it settled into a rhythm, which made Mataprasad drift into reverie.

The compartment was empty. As it was a Sunday and close to lunchtime, it was considered an inappropriate hour to travel—unless of course you were like Mataprasad, for whom Sunday was delivery day, as busy as Monday for the general order of the human race.

Mataprasad had delivered three *kheps* that morning: one in Tardeo, one in Bombay Central, the last in Bandra, from where he was making his way back by train. It was a shame he had to travel so far these days, but then what to do? Work was work, and there was not enough to come by these days, damn those washing machines: front loading, top loading, tumble wash, bungle wash, whatever!

The washing machines had put the *dhobis* out of business. Well, almost. It was all right initially when the machines were expensively priced, when the housewives had shied away from those fancy push buttons, flashing lights, and beeping sounds. The women had wondered whether the machines would get rid of all the sweat and grime that came with Bombay humidity. Would the clothes be damaged with all the slapping the machines put them through? Not quite sure, the housewives had decided not to dispense with their *dhobis* yet.

Hilda Pestonji, his old customer from a Parsi colony at Colaba, had dragged Mataprasad in for a demonstration. She—a glum-faced, good-hearted dragon of fifty-two, an obeisant lover of fads and diversions—had led him to the bathroom, and there she'd press-started the enemy into action.

Through the transparent lid Mataprasad had watched the trickle of water till the tub filled, then the spin rinse, back and forth, back and forth. Oh, what speed! He could barely see the clothes. The whirring noise made him fret. Was this any way to treat clothes? he thought, and here, if there were a button missing or a collar frayed, he would fetch an earful. Yet this machine bashing around the clothes was considered fine. How strange, he thought, people were happy to bury their prejudices just so that they could be seen as modern. He stood in silence, wondering if this were a conspiracy between the clothes manufacturers and the *machinewallas.*

Another thing that angered him about his squat-legged, motor-driven competitor was that no individual care was given to the garments. They were treated alike in a bundle. Now, how would that remove the sweat? And the dirt that slid under the cuffs of shirts and the hemlines of skirts? He said to Hilda Pestonji, "Just think, sister, can a gadget go into armholes and seams? Can it bully the dirt out? Can it compare to the strength of human hands? You know how much work it takes to get the sweat out? Believe me, hand wash is the best!" "Nonsense," she scoffed. "There is nothing wrong with the machine, Mataprasad. Do you think people all over the world wear dirty clothes? You are simply finding fault and not seeing the good side. See, the clothes are washed already. No waiting for one week; no giving up Sunday mornings, counting, taking stock of what you deliver and what you take. I can wash while I cook and can watch television at the same time. No *jhanjhat*! No *khitpit*! And no chance of clothes getting misplaced." Mataprasad had sighed. How to argue with a woman whose mind was made up? How to fight that swell of chest that would go around proclaiming to the neighbors: "See, I bought a new washing machine today. Very advanced it is, and what a blessing! I don't know how I managed all these years"? How, in other words, to fight a machine that never strikes back, that just takes over man's life quietly, with new, new promises every day? But then who had invented this machine if not man himself? So man fights himself, puts himself out of business. And it doesn't matter as long as there is a new toy to enjoy.

But this was not the paradox occupying Mataprasad's mind today. This was not why his eyebrows furrowed and why he plucked at his mustache, a greasy black and white caterpillar bristling with arms, legs, hair, life, anything that hid a lip.

The mustache brought to his face a startling masculinity, a sense of authority, grim and sharply defined. All he had to do was stroke it and it came to life. It got people's attention, made them sit up. This was important when you were head *dhobi,* officially in charge of a *dhobi ghat* with eighty-nine families and their problems.

The train picked up speed. Lines of tenements flew past. It being Sunday, Bombay slept or was frozen before the television set. Overhead, the handgrips swung in unison; like gongs they hammered at Mataprasad's head. The train seemed to toss him, make light of him and his *khep.* His thoughts returned to the morning: the meeting at the *dhobi ghat* where so much was discussed and where some trouble had appeared and settled in his mind, a burden bigger than his *khep.*

THE *GHAT* WAS AN ARID HILL, brown and rocky, with green shrubs near the top. Behind it were two new skyscrapers: tall, thin birds of prey. At the foot of the *ghat* was the washing area: long, cement tanks grouted into the ground, and parallel to the tanks were the tubs, where the clothes were soaked before washing. A few feet away from the washing area was the *basti,* where the *dhobis* lived in small, dingy houses. The houses faced each other, in rows, with long narrow lanes in between—just enough space for a single person to pass by. In the houses, there were no doors, windows, or vents—only curtains, drawn back at all times.

The houses were made of old wooden boards and sheets of asbestos, plastic, and tin. The rooms were cramped and dark. There were stacks of clothes everywhere. White clothes. Colored clothes. Old clothes. New clothes. Outer wear. Inner wear. Daywear. Nightwear. There'd be kurtas and kaftans, frocks and *baba* suits, school uniforms and cotton saris, curtains and linen, napkins and towels, and old kitchen rags yellow with stains. The clothes would be stacked in lots, on the floor, on bunks, on a wooden platform reserved for ironing.

Mornings, an hour after sunrise, the *basti* would spring to life. Curtains lining the doorways would be flung open. The *dhobis* would emerge, yawning, stretching, and snapping the sleep out of their bones. The more religious ones would pray to the sun, or they'd chant and sprinkle water outside their doorsteps to ward off evil energy that had accrued during the night. The men would gargle at their doorsteps in the narrow lanes. Scooping water from stainless-steel buckets, they'd splash their faces, hands, and feet vigorously. The soapy water would collect and run in a steady stream, making the lanes wet and slippery. On finishing, the men would carry the dirty clothes outside. They'd be followed by a musty stench because the clothes would have been bundled up for days. The men would collide in the lanes—a clash of *kheps,* a conflict of burdens. One of the two would have to give way, and he who'd squeeze past on the merit of being older would invariably comment on the size of the *khep*—its value—that the other *dhobi* was carrying. Immediately there'd be a quip back about the size of the customer's pocket, which was shrinking. Yes, everybody knew that— *so why rub it in, brother?*

The separation of the clothes would have been done earlier by younger members of the family. The colored clothes would be separated from the whites, the heavy garments from the light ones. The stained ones would be set aside for special treatment. Otherwise the memsahibs would be unforgiving; they'd rail, rant, and threaten to switch to washing machines. Mataprasad had a saying for such stains, the ones that need a longer soak and intense scrubbing. "Ah," he would say to the younger *dhobis* who would sweat over them, "ah, trouble is a stain that doesn't wash easy."

First, the clothes would be soaked in wooden tubs called *bambas.* They'd be immersed in soapy water while the *dhobis* chatted about customers or about the scarcity of work and the rise in prices. After a while the clothes would be taken to the rinsing tanks, which were marked for three levels of water: low, medium, and high. The level would be decided by the *dhobi* as per his load, and the water would be released on request by a *mukkadam,* who would maintain a logbook of accounts. Each level had a different rate, starting with 40 rupees, going up to 120 rupees, and this would have to be totaled and paid to the municipality at the end of every month.

The actual washing was done in the rinsing tanks, but before that the clothes would be scrubbed against a grinding stone, the *dhoolayi patthar.* The act of scrubbing was called *dhona,* and it was a real sight to see the *dhobis* with their strong, sinewy arms raise the clothes like exuberant lassos and slam them against the grinding stones. While they did that, they'd sing quaint songs that they had inherited from their forefathers. The songs inspired the *dhobis,* brought to their labor a speckled unity, a magnetism that locked them like ants to a hill or bees to a hive.

Washed, the clothes would be taken up the *ghat* for drying. It was the women who'd go up, sure-footed like mountain goats, their saris knotted at the waist, their hair twisted in plaits, baskets of sweet-smelling clothes resting delicately on their hips. Within an hour, the hill would erupt in a blaze of colors, tents of wet clothes flapping like joyous birds on bright nylon strings, flapping, fluttering, threatening to leave their place and fly into the sun.

While the women would be hanging out the clothes, the men would watch from below. Some men would recline on *charpoys,* pulling dreamily at their *beedis;* others would be soaping and washing themselves in the tank water they had paid for. One of the men would call from below, "*Arrey,* woman, how much do you wring that garment? It's not your husband's neck, you know?" And she—the one spoken to—would turn and say irrepressibly, "Good thing, no—otherwise he'd be dead by now." The *dhobis* would laugh. The women were becoming bold now. It was the effect of those television serials they were watching.

Their eyes narrow with the glare of the sun, their skins wet with soapy water or sweat, their heart and muscles pounding with a rejuvenated flow of blood, the *dhobis* on the *charpoys* would call to Mohan and Sohan, the *chaiwalla* boys, who'd rush up and pour steaming hot *chai* from an old kettle into palm-size glasses. The air would be sharp with the smell of bleach; the breeze would bring its own fragrance—of freshly washed clothes wafting down from the *ghat*—the sun would rise and glower down on the clothes; the clothes would soak in the warm rays eagerly, gratefully; the women would tiptoe down, taking care to avoid the burning hot rocks that could scald their feet; the men would stretch, yawn, and dream of lunch and of a good sleep thereafter.

Outside, the city would be oblivious to this piquant little community holding its own, frozen, by its own choice, in time. Outside, cars would rush to well-appointed destinations; buses would honk fiercely, admonishingly; taxis and two-wheelers would dart out of their way; signals would flash and fail; cops would arrive; men in cars would roll down their windows and peer anxiously, then look at their watches and make frantic calls on their cell phones. Against this, the *ghat* would bask in its own space, its own serenity. Life here had its own language, pace, and traditions, which were part of the city's history of livelihoods. It was Mataprasad's dream to keep it so.

THE MEETING AT THE *GHAT* began harmlessly enough. Mataprasad sat under the banyan tree, flanked by two colleagues, Ram Manohar and Kashinath Chaudhary. Between them they made up the *ghat panchayat,* managing the affairs of the *dhobis* and their families. There was no question of an election or a change of leadership ever. Everyone trusted their judgment, their ability to resolve matters, swiftly, decisively, the same day.

That Sunday, the smaller matters were taken up first: the allocation of time slots at the rinsing tanks, the cleaning of pipes that brought water to the tanks, and the replacement cost for two leaking *bambas,* which would amount to six thousand rupees and which they'd share equally.

Someone suggested switching from Ariel to Finex. The new washing powder bleached as it washed; it would bring down operating costs dramatically. But then someone pointed out that the new product scalded your hands. What use was a washing powder that did not respect the tools of your trade? The *dhobis* nodded in agreement. The makers of Finex were condemned unanimously. The new product was never to be brought up or discussed again.

Kolsaram, the coal merchant, was acting up with his rates and with his late deliveries. He was charging six rupees per kilo, when all over it was five. He had to be told to pull up or they'd look elsewhere. The ironing couldn't pile up like that. The *kheps* couldn't be delayed. Worse, they couldn't allow Kolsaram to hold them for ransom. Ishwarilal, the head *istariwalla,* was told to call in other suppliers and begin negotiations right away. That should teach Kolsaram a lesson.

Lacchman Dubey rose. He was a dark, fat *dhobi,* with a shock of gray hair, a puffy face, small eyes, and a hard belly that protruded unabashedly. He was facing a serious problem, he said. Every morning someone was littering outside his doorstep, someone with malice in his heart, for they all knew how pious he, Lacchman Dubey, was; he'd have just finished his *puja* then.

Mataprasad suppressed a smile. Lacchman Dubey was unpopular with the kids. He'd chase them from the place at the back of his shanty, where they played their games of cricket and *kabaddi.* He'd run after them, catch them, and cuff them with a little extra strength. Or he'd confiscate their ball, pushing his fingers into it so that it became unusable. And he'd hold their ears and make them do *baithaks,* up and down a hundred times, till their knees ached and their breathing turned hard. But the children of the *ghat* wouldn't do something so mean. At most, they'd burst a firecracker outside his door, nothing beyond that.

Mataprasad knew who the real culprits were: the stray cats that lurked at the garbage dump on the main road. They were the ones who brought their excretory habits to Lacchman Dubey's door.

Solemnly he said, "I don't think this should bother you, Lacchman Dubey. It is a well-known fact that anyone as devout as you on the road to spirituality is bound to have obstacles in his path. That is God's way of testing you, to see if you get flustered and show intolerance to your fellow beings. By being upset, you are playing into the devil's hand. You are weakening your *puja,* stopping your own progress. You should show more forbearance than that."

"Yes, Lacchman Dubey," the other *dhobis* agreed. "Leave the culprit to his own deserts. A holy man like you should remain unmoved."

"If you say so, brothers," Lacchman Dubey said. He sat down feeling pleased and understood, oblivious to the smiles, the snickers, the warm eyes twinkling with mirth.

Kishore Sahu, an elderly *dhobi,* rose. He had a complaint about his son-in-law, Daman, he said. Why was Daman still staying with him when he had promised to leave once he got a job? And now the couple was expecting a baby. Was Kishore Sahu expected to look after the baby, too? How could he afford that on eight *kheps* a month? How could he feed four mouths on that?

Mataprasad asked Daman why he had failed to move out. He was working as a delivery boy to a jeweler. So did he not make enough to live on his own? To burden his father-in-law at his age was such a shame.

Daman rose—a thin, worried youth in his twenties. His eyes were gaunt and melancholic; his face was etched with worry lines; he mumbled as he spoke. He confessed he was making two thousand rupees a month and was desperately trying to find a *kholi* somewhere, but everywhere they wanted a deposit. "How do I raise thirty thousand rupees?" he said. Plus, there was an extra charge for water, electricity, and personal protection—yes, that, too. And some of the tenements were so shabby. Just enough space to crawl in, water one hour a day, and long queues and fights, and rats, mosquitoes, and dogs with disease, and in between huts places serving illicit liquor. How could he live there after living at the *ghat*? If only Kishore Sahu would give him more time.

Kishore Sahu said, "Tell me, brothers, how much more time am I to give? It's been two years since their marriage. Would any father-in-law tolerate as long? Would he support his daughter's husband? And where *is* his self-respect? And why did he get married if he could not support his wife and child? And why be a burden on my head?"

"It's not . . . not like that," Daman said. There were expenses he was facing that were heavy. His wife's pregnancy had turned complicated. The baby had moved into an awkward position. To guard against the risk of losing the child, regular tests had to be conducted; the baby's movements had to be observed. His wife was prescribed massages three times a week and was advised to do yoga, for which she had to attend classes. All this cost a lot more than what he could afford, more than what he earned. He was already in debt, having borrowed from his employer and from two colleagues. There'd be more expenses when the baby was born. All this weighed on him, crushed him, left him feeling sad and defeated. He knew he was a burden to his father-in-law, but how could he help it? He was trying to look after his family. He was trying to keep his job and his child. What was more important: his child or his self-respect? And who could he turn to if not his father-in-law, whom he considered like his own father?

To everyone's horror, Daman started crying. He raised his hands and said, oh yes, he was trying, but it wasn't enough; even the Gods seemed to be against him in his fight to bring a child into this world, and—if things got worse—he was ready to kill himself. He blurted his sorrow in between sobs, and promptly all the *dhobis* rose to their feet and said no, *that* was not the way. What madness to speak like this, to think like this, when God had conferred so fine a gift on him? Kishore Sahu felt ashamed. "Why didn't you tell me this?" he said, turning to Daman. "So much responsibility you are taking . . . I never knew."

"I was scared," Daman said. "You might have insulted me and said it was my fault. You might have said, 'You don't even know how to make a child properly.' How I would have felt then?"

The *dhobis* laughed. Yes, indeed, this was Kishore Sahu's style; he was capable of saying that.

Mataprasad leaned over and whispered to Ram Manohar and Kashinath Chaudhary, who heard him intently, nodding from time to time. When he spoke, it was in the clear voice of a leader.

"You can't throw them out, Kishore Sahu. Not at a time like this, when the parents are fighting to save the child. And you cannot expect the boy to hunt for a house when he has so big a burden upon his head. The *ghat panchayat* understands that you have expenses to meet, that the times are hard, you cannot have extra mouths to feed when your own business doesn't amount to much. But, surely, in your life you have seen worse. You remember how you came from the village, driven by dreams and hunger, and how you did not find work for days? It was the *ghat* that gave you food, shelter, and the means to build your house. This same *ghat* will stand by you now, Kishore Sahu. It will see that you receive a thousand rupees every month from the *dhobi* fund. This should help to ease your burden. Then, when the child is born and brings luck, the parents will move to a better place, leaving you to your own life."

"*Arrey wah!* How can that be?" Kishore Sahu exclaimed. "If there is luck, I must share it, too. How they can forget me then?"

Everybody laughed and agreed. A family that comes through the bad times must stay to enjoy the good times.

"How much do you owe by way of debt?" Mataprasad asked Daman suddenly.

Frowning, Daman did a finger count and said, "Three thousand to the office and four thousand to my colleagues. That would be the full sum, Mataprasad." A murmur went through the crowd. In these hard times that *was* debt.

Mataprasad leaned on his side to confer once more with his colleagues, while Daman stood fumbling at his kurta.

After a while Mataprasad spoke. "You may borrow four thousand rupees from the *dhobi* fund, Daman, and pay back your colleagues with that. But you will swear never to raise your hand again before an outsider. As for your employer, you can ask him to cut from your salary every month till you have paid back every rupee. That way you will feel the pinch of your folly and yet free yourself from debt."

"A thousand blessings on you, Mataprasad! A thousand blessings on the *panchayat* members! And to you, my brothers here," Daman said, with tears in his eyes, for he knew that the fund was a result of their collective effort, their quiet contributions that helped overburdened *dhobis* out of a mess. In a voice that was choked and raised with emotion, Daman said, "My child, my future child, knows not how many fathers he has, what a big family there is to welcome him. I will tell him that when he arrives. And I will also tell him that he has to obey all of you, all you sons of the *ghat*. And even if we go elsewhere to stay, he must return to visit you and to give you a full account of his life. And he has to make you all very proud of him—for all that you have done and for helping with his arrival."

The *dhobis* cheered. They insisted Daman was going nowhere. How could he, now that he had appointed them fathers of his son?

Making his way through the crowd, Kishore Sahu came up to Daman and embraced him. His son-in-law was okay, a little nervous but okay. The *ghat panchayat* had shown him that. It had also shown him that the *dhobi ghat* would stand by him as it always had. And soon he'd be a grandfather to a brave little boy, a child *dhobi* whom he'd dunk every morning in the rinsing tank and teach how to swim and sparkle under the morning sun. Things did seem better once expenses were met, once the tension was removed and you knew for sure you had help at hand. Kishore Sahu clasped and raised his hands to the *ghat* in a gesture of fervent gratitude.

Ram Manohar rose. He was the official treasurer, the man who understood money at the *ghat*. Everybody fell silent. The peace of the Sunday morning washed over them. The sky appeared higher than usual, white, ethereal, and aloof. "Brothers, dear brothers," he said, "I won't take up much of your time, for I know that you have deliveries to make. But I would like to draw your attention to the dwindling state of our *dhobi* fund. As you know, over the last few months things have not been so good. We have not been able to contribute because we've all had difficulties, our growing personal expenditures, which are like the morning sun. They never fail to rise, huh."

A ripple of laughter followed. Ram Manohar waited for the laughter to subside before continuing. "I request you brothers, should any of you come into some extra money, please come forward to contribute. Think of your needy brothers, the elder *dhobis* who are unable to manage heavy *kheps* because of their age and who have no sons or daughters to help." He sat down, and Mataprasad, who had remained seated, said softly, "Friends, I would also like to caution you that this year we will not be able to make elaborate arrangements for the Ganesha festival. We will have to conduct our festivities on a much smaller scale, so don't be disappointed."

The *dhobis* clicked their tongues and looked down at their feet. To lack the funds to appease the Gods was a matter of shame—but what to do? Such was life. That's what it had come to.

Someone shouted the name of Lacchman Dubey. "*Arrey,* Dubey," he said. "Where is the money you got for that land you sold in your village? The government must have paid you well. Are you saving it up for your third marriage or what?"

The *dhobis* laughed. Lacchman Dubey was an easy target. He hated spending.

Lacchman Dubey got to his feet. "*Arrey, bhai,* why would I want to sit on it if it was in my pocket? The sad thing is, it is only on paper. You know our government. They say they will give it only after all the formalities are complete. That, too, in the form of bonds, cashable after seven years."

"No problem, Lacchman Dubey; we can always take a loan against the bonds," Ram Manohar said, with a gleam in his eye. "It is good to know they are there for an emergency and that we can use them—with your blessings." The other *dhobis* agreed, fixing their twinkling eyes on Lacchman Dubey.

"I don't know about that, Manohar *bhai,*" Lacchman Dubey said shrewdly. "The bonds will also have my brother's name on them, so I'll have to ask him first. On my part, I will be happy to offer them as security, but I don't know about him. He is such a finicky, tightfisted fellow."

The *dhobis* shook their heads and said what a shame that someone like Lacchman Dubey, with his largeness of heart, had to have a skinflint as a brother. Lacchman Dubey nodded sheepishly and sat down, looking resigned yet palpably relieved.

The *mukkadam* rose and pushed his way through the crowd. He was a tall, serious man in his fifties, bald almost, with a tuft of hair in front. His shirt was out, his sleeves rolled down; his dark face glistened with sweat. "Friends," he said, "I was at the municipality yesterday and my contact there tells me that we are soon going to face a water cut. We should be getting the notice in a week or two. So I thought I would warn you. You can decide what to do."

"What sort of a cut, *mukkadam*? What percent? And how long will it last?" Mataprasad asked.

"It will be quite heavy, Mataprasad—fifty percent of what we get now, and, according to my contact, the cut is going to stay for a long time."

The *dhobis* stirred. *Hey Ram!* Fifty percent? That was too much. How would they cope? How would they manage? If they didn't deliver the *kheps* on time, it was over to the washing machines.

Turning to the *panchayat* members, the *mukkadam* said, "It can't be helped. All the water is being diverted to the new buildings coming up in the area. They get priority over us."

"So why should *we* suffer? Why should *our* water be cut? As it is, our work is less, and with less water how shall we manage?" The voice was shrill with panic. It was followed by a wave of indignation, murmurs of disbelief and anger. The sun appeared like a dot in the sky, sharp, fiery, and precise. The *dhobis* felt its heat on their necks and shoulders and mostly in their minds.

"Relax, brothers," Mataprasad said. "Don't behave like old women and run the minute there is a crisis. We will try and manage, and if we can't, I am sure the *mukkadam* can arrange for a little hand *maska*. We know how well that works with our friends at the municipality."

"Alas, no, Mataprasad," the *mukkadam* said. "Not this time. My friend says there are orders from the top. These builders have great influence. They have to get their buildings up in time. I am afraid we will have to bear up."

"*Arrey,* what bear up, *mukkadam*? It is easy for you to say. You don't have to face customers. You don't have to face their anger. You just sit on that arse of yours, turning the water on and off the whole day— that's all you do anyway."

"Why are we keeping him if he can't do his job? If he can't even get us our quota of water?"

"Enough, brothers," Mataprasad said. "There's no need to vent your anger on the poor *mukkadam*. If we can't get water from the municipality, we will buy it. We will call for a tanker daily."

"How will that be possible, Mataprasad?" a *dhobi* called Roshan Lal quipped. "The tanker pipes are not long enough to go through the *basti* and reach the rinsing tanks. Besides, by parking on the main road the tanker will create a traffic jam, and we will have to face the wrath of the traffic police."

"I wonder why God has given you a head, Roshan Lal, if you can't use it," Mataprasad said. "So what if the pipes don't reach? We shall form a human chain and carry it in buckets. We can get the women to help, which will be good for them, because it will leave them less time for gossip. As for traffic jams, don't worry about that. The *mukkadam* will take care of any cops that come by." He looked at the *mukkadam*, who nodded promptly.

"Yes, but the cost for the tanker will have to be shared," Ram Manohar said hurriedly. "We can't afford to pay from the *dhobi* fund. Not until we get some more funds in."

"But that will mean hardly any profit. What we are going to make God only knows! How are we going to feed our families? How will we survive?" groaned a voice in the congregation.

"Do not despair, brothers," Mataprasad said, trying to sound composed and cheerful. "The cut cannot last forever. If it does, we can always protest. We can take it up with the municipality and with the corporator. We can go all the way to Mantralaya, if necessary. Remember what our brother *dhobis* in Patna did? They refused to wash the clothes of the ministers when they were eyeing their *ghat* to build a bazaar in its place."

"Yes, but today who cares if we refuse to wash clothes, Mataprasad? They will laugh at us, replace us with washing machines. This is Mumbai, not Patna."

"There is nothing left, Mataprasad—nothing in this business. Why do you fool yourself? Why don't you admit it is all over? The *dhobis* will never enjoy the status they once did."

Heads turned. Standing in the aisle, at the far end of the gathering, was Shyam Pardesi, one of the few men who wouldn't be affected by the water cut simply because he wasn't a *dhobi*. Pardesi worked as a union leader in a packaging factory where the workers had been on strike, agitating for higher bonuses. The factory management had refused to give in to their demands, and Pardesi had been out of work for a long time.

"How come you are up so early, Pardesi? Was the liquor you had last night too mild or what?" Mataprasad said. There was an itching below his mustache, a tingling that did not augur well.

"You can say what you want, Mataprasad, but there are times when sitting and drinking at an *adda* has its advantages. That is why I am here—to share with you some excellent news."

The *dhobis* craned their necks and shifted. For a moment they thought that perhaps Pardesi was drunk, that he was reeling under some liquid daydreams or his unemployment had affected his mind.

"You may come here and say what you wish, Pardesi. You know ours is an open meeting," Kashinath Chaudhary said stiffly, concealing his disapproval of the union leader.

Pardesi came up. He was a slim, pock-faced man, in his early thirties. He had narrow, crinkly eyes and hair that curled over his ears and neck. Unlike the rest of the *dhobis,* who wore kurtas and *dhotis,* Pardesi wore modern clothes: a printed shirt, jeans, and a belt.

"Friends," he said, clearing his throat, "I don't need to remind you that things are not what they used to be. There was a time when we were among the foremost communities of Mumbai, when people couldn't imagine life without us, because the work we did was held in great esteem. In fact, there was a time when a whole lake was named after us—Dhobi Talao, as you know, was where we washed the uniforms of the British soldiers—and the *ghats* were given to us as our own proud places of work, as high points of trust and respect. Today, unfortunately, things have changed. It is the day of machines and gadgets. In our factory too many workers have lost their jobs, and who cares, really, whether the workers live or die? Now, you might say that I do not belong to your trade, that I am not a *dhobi,* but don't forget I *am* the son of one. My father, Namdeo Pardesi, raised me and my four sisters from the money he made as *a dhobi,* which is why I feel for the trade and for all of you."

"We don't have time for your *bhashan,* Pardesi. Leave that for your union meetings. Let's hear what you have to say. We have deliveries to make." The voice came from the center of the crowd, and it made the *dhobis* laugh. Mataprasad smiled, too, glad for the break in tension.

"Okay, friends, since you can't wait, hear me carefully. There is a chance for each of us to make good money, more than what we would ever make in our lifetimes. You have seen what is happening to the city today, and particularly to our area: construction everywhere—old buildings being broken down and new buildings coming up. A lot of this is under the city's slum removal plan, which allows builders to remove slums and put the slum dwellers up in new flats of 225 square feet each. In exchange for housing the slum dwellers free of charge, the builders get space to build tall buildings, thirty to forty stories high, which they can sell at a great profit."

"How does this concern us, Pardesi?" Mataprasad said. He was frowning now and knew not why but he felt a premonition, not on his upper lip but in his stomach and heart.

"It concerns us greatly, Mataprasad, for yesterday when I was drinking at Narang's *adda,* I met two men who are working for a builder, the same who built those towers there," Pardesi said, pointing to the two tall buildings behind the *ghat.*

The *dhobis* turned to stare at the skyscrapers. To Mataprasad's eyes there appeared something insolent about the structures: the way they rose in piercing defiance to the calm azure sky. He knew not why, but he felt the buildings were alive, their concrete embodied with some strange spirit that was waiting to swoop down on the inhabitants of the *ghat* and crush them.

"The builder's men were quite friendly and after a few drinks they spoke freely," Pardesi said. "They suggested they first get us registered as a slum. Although the *ghat* is a green zone protected against development, it can be de-reserved and brought under the slum removal plan. These things are easy to fix. All it takes is our understanding and our signatures. If we agree and give this place to the builder, within two years we can each own a house of 225 square feet. Going by the rate in this area, this comes to over rupees twenty lakhs. When I heard this, I was stunned. I thought why are we wasting our time in a dead trade? Why are we slaving and worrying about a future that seems bleak? Why are we not thinking like men of today and taking an opportunity? I say this is a God-given opportunity and it has come to us on a platter. So I said to the men I will speak to you and let them know. Of course, I will take my commission." Smiling, Pardesi turned to the *panchayat*. Their faces would tell him how his suggestion had been received.

"Have you gone mad, Pardesi? Has your drinking affected your senses? You are asking us to sell our *ghat,* our land, to betray our trade after all these years?" Mataprasad rose, a dark, steely-eyed colossus. He was followed by Ram Manohar and Kashinath Chaudhary. They rose and stood with grave expressions, legs astride, hands folded over their *dhotis.*

"What trade, Mataprasad?" Pardesi asked. "Shrinking *kheps,* water cuts, rising prices . . . how long will you struggle? How long will you endure? How long do you think your *ghat* will support you? Look at it! It is only a mountain of rock. Does it care whether you have work? Does it come to your rescue when the municipality increases your taxes or when it cuts your water? But now your *ghat* is trying to tell you something—that there is a value to it, if only you see it. It is ready to sell itself, to keep you afloat, Mataprasad. You and all these people here, who depend on you."

"So, for that you will have our *ghat* called a slum. You will reduce our trade to something negotiable, huh, Pardesi? Tell me, how much commission are you getting for this? How much are the builder's men paying you? And how did you even think that we would support you in this vile scheme?"

"Wait, Mataprasad; maybe we are being hasty. Pardesi *has* a point. Rupees twenty lakhs is a lot of money. If we invest it wisely, it can take care of our old age. It can buy us land in our village and pay for our sons' educations and our daughters' marriages." The voice belonged to Jodimal Vikas, a mild, elderly *dhobi* with a bony face and damp gray eyes. Mataprasad knew that Jodimal Vikas was finding it tough to get grooms for his two thirty-plus daughters. It was the usual story—the higher the age, the greater the dowry.

"What are you saying, Jodimal *bhai?* I know times are tough, but that is when we must be strong. We can't go selling the *ghat,* which has been like a parent to us." Mataprasad's voice was kindly, but a sense of despair had seeped in. Thankfully, it was evident only to his ears.

Sensing an advantage, Pardesi interjected. In an aggrieved voice he said, "I don't know, brothers, but when I spoke to the builder's men I was only thinking of your welfare. How was I to know I would hurt your feelings? How was I to know I'd invite such allegations and insults onto myself? Please forgive me if I have said too much or have spoken out of line." He began to walk away when a shrill, agitated voice rose.

"Wait, Shyam *bhai,* please don't go! We want to know more. Will the builder give us transit accommodation while the building is coming up? Will he buy back the flats once the building is ready? Will there be an agreement in writing?" Then, addressing the *dhobis,* the voice said, "I say, brothers, we give Shyam Pardesi a chance to share what he knows. He has brought Lakshmi to our door, and we are shooing her away. Why do that to the Goddess of Wealth? Rupees twenty lakhs is no small sum. We owe this not just to ourselves but to our children, too. How will we face them knowing that we had this opportunity and let it pass?" Mataprasad clenched his fists. His eyes narrowed as they fell on Daman—a new, inspired Daman, with his hands on his hips.

THE TRAIN HISSED and cut its speed. Beyond the tracks, small buildings whizzed past, buildings with shops below and grilled balconies above, and clothes hanging on crowded lines, blocking out the entry of air. Along the tracks, a woman washed clothes. Her sari was rolled up; her knees were bare and gleaming. Next to her, a girl bathed. She washed herself moodily, as if the whole ritual was a chore, a silly self-imposed ordeal. They both failed to look at the train, to take heed of its thundering proximity. Mataprasad saw them clearly, as he did the half-filled bucket before them.

MANY OF THE YOUNGER *DHOBIS* agreed with Pardesi. They felt why get sentimental about a hill? It had earned for them and was doing so now, giving them a benefit plan for keeps. In their minds, they dreamt of businesses like phone booths, photocopiers, and stationery shops, preferably outside a girls' college, where fresh-faced girls would flock to spend their allowances. They saw themselves with luxuries like motorcycles, cell phones, and movie tickets—all that had been denied them this far. Ram Manohar and Kashinath Chaudhary tried to maintain order, but it was impossible to curtail the babble of excitement, the doubts, queries, and dreams, which were being excavated and expressed freely.

Mataprasad tried to protest. Through clenched teeth, he tried to tell them what he knew—of the dismal conditions in the transit camps: no sanitation, no power, rationed water, the location some God-forsaken place outside the city where there'd be no opportunities for work and where they could easily be forgotten. He tried to tell them that he had been through this kind of thing, in his childhood, in his village, when his people were asked to move out and make way for a dam. They, too, had believed those promises of more land, of greener fields and higher yields, and then received nothing but the unchanging squalor of a transit camp. He tried to tell them that home was home and to abandon it for greener pastures was like cutting off your nose to spite your face—the consequences were indeed terrible. He tried to tell them that *this* was the mistake that had brought him to Bombay, in his teens, to earn and save, so that he could get his family out of the transit camp. But he had failed to do so. His younger brothers—the twins—had died, one from dengue, the other from typhoid. Distraught and depressed, his mother had lost her mind and wandered off into oblivion. His father had taken to drinking and died two years later, out of some kind of searing shame because he wasn't able to hold his family together. Mataprasad had realized the hard and bitter way that there was no point going back to the country; his life there was over. He tried to tell the *dhobis* that that's how they came to be his extended family; that's why he had tried to build them a village within a city, a home with traditions not unlike those of the one they had left behind. Had he not succeeded? Had he not built a community that was united and bonded by traditions? And weren't their homes exactly like those in the village: without doors, without locks, open to all who wished to enter? And now they were ready to trade it all away. For rupees twenty lakhs, which would disappear as soon as it came, giving rise to new habits and new temptations.

He could see the *dhobis* did not wish to hear him. It was Shyam Pardesi they wanted to follow. The union leader had spoken his way into a new job. The era of the *ghat panchayat* was over. The city had crushed the village, concrete had triumphed over mud, man had gained control over nature, and, like the ill-fated *ghat*, the *panchayat* had no option but to dissolve itself into the earth, to melt and mesh with the ways of the city.

THE TRAIN STOPPED. Mataprasad saw he'd arrived. He swung his *khep* over his shoulder and stepped out onto the platform. A *boot-polishwalla* struck his brush noisily against a foot stand. He did this many times over, an invitation for passersby to get their shoes polished. But, alas, Mataprasad wore only *chappals*. He had never known the comfort of shoes—too confining like the city. A gypsy woman in bedraggled clothes helped herself to water from a fountain. She collected the gushing water in a rusted old *Dalda* can. At the food stall near the entrance, some people stood, sipping *chai*, eating *vadas*, while near the ticket counter children begged and played intermittently. One of the beggar girls, a dark, sweet-faced ten-year-old, with hair falling over her forehead, came up to Mataprasad, and, rubbing her flat stomach, said, "Hungry, no?" And Mataprasad fished out a coin and, ruffling her hair, said, "Who is not, child? These days, who is not?"

Adjusting his *khep* into a convenient carry position, Mataprasad strode past a weighing machine. Its red circling disk and flashing lights invited him to weigh himself, to take stock of his burden. But ah, there'd be no correct measure for that, he thought. Nothing that would add up.

Walking out into the blinding sun, Mataprasad took the bazaar lane leading to the main road, which in turn would lead him home.

The bazaar was emptying out. The vendors were packing up for lunch. They flung damp sheets of jute over the baskets of fruits and vegetables to keep them fresh. Some of the vendors called out their closing prices, and some women stopped to consider them.

Halfway down the bazaar, Mataprasad came upon a fisherwoman. Her basket was heaped with sardines, and on top of the sardines was the most enormous kingfish he had ever seen. Its silver body, gleaming in the sun, seemed to be alive, breathing, and staring straight at Mataprasad.

His eyes narrowed. His mouth turned moist. Pointing to it, he asked the fisherwoman, "How much?"

"One hundred and twenty rupees," she said. "But to you I will give for one hundred," she added coyly.

"Why, sister?" Mataprasad said with a grin. "Do I look like your brother or what?"

"You want it or not?" said the woman with a scowl, a flush of red appearing on her face.

Just then Mataprasad heard a sound—a *meow* sound, once, twice. He turned. A bunch of stray cats were eyeing the fish. Their gray faces were locked in a snarl; their paws were taut and extended. They strained and they hissed, but they would not approach the basket. Mataprasad made as if to chase them, but the fisherwoman said, "Don't worry about them. You just say whether you want the fish or not."

"Aren't you worried that they will get at the fish?" Mataprasad asked curiously. "Then you will make a loss."

"No," she said. "You see this?" She shifted the basket slightly, to reveal small pieces of ginger cut and arranged in a circle. "This is what keeps them away. They can't bear the smell. No matter how hungry they are, or how tempted they get."

Mataprasad scratched his jaw and gave a low laugh. "You mean that's all it takes to protect your fish, a smell that the cats can't endure? Why, you are cleverer than I thought."

The fisherwoman blushed. "Go on now, saying nice things like that to me. I am not going to give it to you for less than one hundred. I am telling you that now."

Mataprasad thought for a while. It seemed a shame to bargain with one who had learned the tricks of guarding her business, of protecting her trade against greedy intruders. It was something Lacchman Dubey hadn't learned after all his hours of *puja*. Nor he, after all his sacrifices to build a village within a city. Nor the *panchayat* members with whom he had sat in council for years, thinking their position impregnable. This art of concealed self-defense: it was not something Mataprasad had learned, but which he could easily admire.

"Tell you what," he said to the fisherwoman, who was looking at him hopefully. "I will take it for one hundred and twenty. But you cut it, clean it, and put it in a bag for me. Then we are both happy."

TRAFFIC

◆ ◆ ◆

IT WAS THAT TIME of the day when everybody was scrambling toward something. The streets were in a scramble, the traffic was in a
scramble, and minds, unwittingly, were in a deep scramble, most of
them possessed by certain untoward events of the day, which had done
nothing to please or elevate them or lead them to believe in their luck
and invite a feeling of well-being. But then, the time was such—
twilight—a sullen, irresponsible glow, it made the air around the city
heavy; it weighed its gloomy pallor on the people, reminding them of
the baggage they carried: another day of abstract non-achievement,
simply the mediocrity they'd inherited or the luxury they'd not.

Vicki Dhanrajgiri was no exception. As she walked the streets of
Bombay, part of an enigmatic crowd, she was the queen of brooders.
Her heart weighed a ton. Her head throbbed with a million thoughts.
The thoughts pounded inside her mind, her black box, as she called it,
in moments of wry realization. She walked dodging the shuffling feet,
the onslaught of male shoulders, a colliding paunch reluctant to halt
its progress or to deflect in urbane city-slick courtesy.

Some of the collisions were deliberate: men taking their chances
and succeeding—bawled-out office boys pinching out their frustrations, or smart-alec Romeos with long hair, ear studs, tight jeans, doing sleight of hand, then melting away in a sea of shoulders. Did she
want to fight, scream? Did she want to run after them, get them

mobbed, as she had in her college days? Not for reasons as banal as these. Yet she felt frightened. A new fear this was, cold and confusing. It brought discomfort to her heart, confusion to her mind, and anxiety to her heels. She felt she must get away, the sooner the better.

Dodge and duck, dodge and duck—that's how she traversed the length of the pavement, which was endless, a conveyor belt of feet. She pretended this was a game going on. The fewer bodies she collided with, the more successful she'd be. Successful at whatever she was trying to outrun. Passersby thought her mad, slowed to give her a look. Good, she thought, this way at least they took notice; otherwise to be ignored on a day like this—*that* was unpardonable.

Twenty-seven and alone: it sounded unbelievable. This day, which twenty years ago would begin with promises, a house full of warmth and bustle, bright, squeaky balloons and loose, fluttering ribbons, and visitors with their hands behind their backs, winking broadly and saying, "Guess, guess what," and her father—a gentle, beaming giant— laying a trail of surprises all over the house, going, "Hot, hot, hot," or, "Cold, cold, cold," and she in tow, a flurry of legs, one shoe loose, yet oblivious, stupefied with the excitement of the day, and her mother in the kitchen, smiling, dropping crowns of icing from a nozzle onto a deep white fortress of a cake, while samosas hissed on the stove, curled, and changed color and sandwich paste lay open in jars waiting to be transferred onto slices of bread—this day had dragged by listlessly, a sad, grating burden even to herself.

In the morning, she'd opened the door to budget bouquets from people compelled to be courteous. People who relied on her for work: hairstylists, makeup artists, extras, and old character actors with dwindling fortunes and meager talents, Hindi cinema providing that kind of appeal, that kind of lure. One of the bouquets was from an old boyfriend, married since, but now on the brink of divorce. The flowers were an invitation to help with his rehabilitation, to salvage his pride, or his sex life, suspended as it were; but to her they were signs of desperation, weeds fit for the grave. She felt nothing discarding them, dropping them into the inviting dark of the dustbin—with the wrapper on, the gleaming noisy cellophane, and the card and wordings unread.

For lunch she had done leftovers: a broccoli and cauliflower bake and two cutlets with the chill of refrigeration embedded. She couldn't get the cold out of the cutlets, even after pressing 1.30 on the microwave, and she wondered if all things ignored hardened like that; frozen, would they turn bloodless and hard? It didn't taste good—this realization.

At regular intervals, there were phone calls. These she ignored, for among the numbers that flashed on her caller ID wasn't the *one* she was waiting for. The one that would make her heart leap, say all was forgiven, the storm had passed, a new year called for new beginnings. Could they begin afresh? Yes, yes, yes—she had the answers ready. It was difficult to think of anything else. It was difficult to still her heart and say things she didn't mean.

She looked at the man coming toward her. He was tall, gangly, complacent, like he didn't expect any more from life than what had been delivered. His face wore a silly acquiescence to suggest *married*! It gave rise to something in her, something like a sense of indignation. She quickened her pace, thinking that by walking fast she could convey that she, too, was married; she was hurrying home to her kids, their homework, baths, and bed. That done, there'd be dinner, chatter, washing up, locking up, a little television, then sly glances, an inquisitive silence between two adults who knew each other yet chose to negotiate. This followed by sex, still good after years, still on the sofa, fast, furious, and frenzied, lest the kids walk in, sleepy, surly, and full of excuses.

Once upon a time she'd dreamt of two little boys, two agile monkeys testing the limits of her patience, refusing to go to bed, refusing to succumb to shutdown time. She'd dreamt of shouting them down, warning them, bringing them down with a tackle, facedown, in deep pinioned sleep. She'd dreamt of two soft heads with damp hair tossed and breathing lightly and she like a conductor keeping time, aware of a wondrous expansion in her heart. But whom was she trying to kid? Where there were kids there was a husband, too, someone warm and dependable, on the sofa and in her arms.

The cars honked. The city rose and scattered the dust of twilight into her eyes. She blinked, to steady her vision, to absorb the invasion of concrete into her senses. It was just as well she was blinded by light, not by delusion, as she was all day long, sitting next to the phone, biting the whites of her knuckles, sweating each time it rang. The grim features of her apartment—the high ceilings, the long framed windows, the mosaic tiles, the biscuit-brown beams that held up the building—all these reminded her of a movie set designed to highlight her loneliness, a movie set in one of those black-and-white movies, stark, decisive, and unforgiving. It reminded her that she had been moved from the source of her happiness (his apartment) to a land of exile (her own) and that she had been brought to a point where to dream would be audacious, painful, and unreal.

NANDKUMAR CHAURASIA WAS AN ARTIST. He painted in black-and-white, saying he had a problem with colors. His themes were lean, spare, and Kafkaesque. "I am celebrating Kalyug," he would say, "the end of the world in all its glory." Vicki believed him. There was something about his work that told her he had been to an alternate world and that he went there many times over, like Coleridge, Dostoevsky, and Jim Morrison.

They'd met at a friend's over an evening of vodka. This was eleven months after she'd started working for a Bollywood producer, doing preproduction work like organizing props, meals, costumes, and locations and helping out with the casting of smaller actors. The screen tests she conducted herself, and the site visits, shooting them off on a digi-beta camera. Seeing her willingness to befriend all kinds of work, the producer had upped her to production controller; he'd given her the right to *contribute* to any aspect of the film and bought himself the right to invite her services on any task without paying extra. She made no great money, but she enjoyed the popularity that came from working with a top-heavy name. People looked at her with interest, invited her to their parties, listened when she spoke, and aunts and uncles showed her off as their proud connection in Bollywood. This gave her a background and something to do on holidays, which weren't too many to start with. Besides, she hated holidays. By evening she was usually depressed, not knowing what to do with herself. She wished she had a boyfriend. She wished she had someone to go for long walks with—to go for movies, take short breaks by the beach—instead of visiting relatives who took her visits for granted. Her relatives, sweet as they were, spoke to her the same kind of stuff each time—about how to get her life organized, how to save money, how to settle down with a nice, steady boy from a good family. They said this with an air of wisdom, like they were revealing to her a family secret and teaching her how to guard it. And yet the soaps they watched so routinely were all about homes breaking up, about the politics of marriage and domestic intrigue of the highest kind. She'd watch these with them, purely out of amusement or out of boredom, and she'd marvel at the flat, one-dimensional characters almost as boring as the men she met in Bollywood, the kind of men with a jaunty, churlish confidence, whom she just couldn't relate to.

The evening began with her and Nandkumar discussing the current state of Hindi cinema. It was deplorable, they said. There was a frightening lack of originality, a disgusting trend to rip off Hollywood plots, and a tendency to produce marriage romances as a safe *investable* trend.

On their second drink, they shot down a few of the big names. They agreed that there was a paucity of ideas, big budgets were standing in for small minds, and what was being sold was overproduced crap reliant on opulence and locations. The look was everything and the look was being bought: it was sprinkling stardust into star-struck eyes; it was covering up for unforgivable flaws like a lack of script, a lack of substance, and a departure from any kind of realism. The way they saw it, the youths were corrupted already; they couldn't think beyond choreographed song sequences and carnal close-ups. By the third drink, they'd nodded heads dissolutely and he was "Nandu" and she was "Vicks" and a gentle affection bubbled between them like a runaway brook. On their fourth drink, he was vehement—her boss was a plagiarizer, the biggest probably. He called him a cheap cut-and-paste artist, then paused and waited to see how she'd react. She giggled and said she knew that. She knew the movies her boss watched, the English ones from the seventies and eighties, from where he lifted his plots. She was surprised she'd confessed this to a perfect stranger and thought it was the vodka, a stiff new entrant brand from Goa. He smiled and said he knew *all* the sources, where each of her boss's films came from, and he proceeded to name them one by one. All she could do was nod. He was brilliantly right—and real.

A little later they discovered they had the same taste in cinema. They both enjoyed art films. They'd both spent weeks, months, at the film institute in Pune, and although they'd been there at different times, they'd stayed as long and got involved in campus politics. They'd both worn kurtas and *chappals* and smoked hash, watching films like Bergman's *Wild Strawberries* and Fellini's *Eight and a Half*. Nandkumar said he'd been agitated when some of the old classics were lost in a fire; he'd considered immolation to make the authorities sit up and take notice. She said she was glad he didn't. There were such few people who felt like this, felt that this was the only cinema worth watching, cinema that depicted real lives, real tragedies, without gloss and visual manipulation.

"Have you seen Kieslowski's trilogy?" he asked, his light gray eyes piercing and hopeful, as if were she to say yes he would go down on his knees and propose, or at least cry out with relief.

"About ten times!" she whispered. "Though *Blue* is still my favorite. I thought it was his best."

Nandkumar didn't say anything. Just knocked back his vodka and rose. "Give me your glass," he said. She surrendered her glass obediently.

"We have to toast to this one," he said solemnly.

"I will come with you," she said, following him into the kitchen where the drinks were laid out. This was at Anantrao's place in Juhu, his apartment overlooking the beach.

When they returned, Julie, Anantrao's wife, had turned the conversation to topics like video activism, censor board cowardice, and the surreptitious muzzling of issue-based documentaries. But they weren't interested. They knew all this, had brooded over it long enough. They were discovering an alternate orbit, quite by accident, quite by chance. He had moved to the window and was rolling a joint. And she was helping him, lifting and crushing the tobacco in her palm.

It was the first cut, he said, straight from the slopes of Manali. "*Asli malai,* cream of Manali, you mean?" she said, and he grinned and nodded, pleased that she knew its value, its worth.

They smoked the joint—a creased cannon, loaded to the brim, slow burning but effective—and they imbibed that zapped look, that translucent red absenteeism that showed up their innocence and their detachment, and she turned light and giggly and he maudlin and patient. Both felt frozen in time; both felt at peace and unhurried. The rest of the party was too agitated for them. They did not care to partake in the discussions, and no one minded, for Anantrao's place was such—a wanton world of artistic whims and vagaries, where everybody was allowed to do their thing, to carve out their space and retire into it without explanation or regrets.

Nandkumar invited her to his home the next day, to his one-bedroom apartment in a shaded lane in Bandra West, and there he showed her his paintings, his exquisitely poignant black-and-whites, which captured India in her rigor mortis, the truth as it existed in the villages—the exploitation, the isolation, the neglect, frozen on canvas in stark defining lines, in unsparing black-and-white.

"Our country is historically fated for rape," he said. It's been the mainstay of marauders. Mohammed of Ghazni, Bābur, Timur, and later the Portuguese, Dutch, French, and the British."

"And now us!" she said, holding up a book written by an NRI writer. "We are selling our culture and the West is buying. But it's still robbery, still rape. We are hawking ourselves, legitimately."

"It's worse in the arts," he said. "There's worse happening, if you know what I mean."

"Alibaug parties," she said. "Cocktails, conversation, Sunday brunches, and loud corporate sponsors . . . the real artists are staying away."

"You know . . . how?" he asked, incredulous. His heart was beating. Dots of sweat appeared on his brow. She'd realize later, once she knew him, that this was a sign of his blood pressure, his software reacting to a situation he hadn't anticipated, a defrag in his mind, which he couldn't fathom in the heat of the moment. Right now, it was the effect of the joint he had smoked before her arrival. He'd done that to calm himself, to compose his mind to the onslaught of a woman as agreeable, but it seemed to be working overtime; it was making him excited and uneasy at the same time.

He suggested a drink and she agreed, and while he got the vodka and the ice and cut and dropped slices of lime into their glasses, she began to ask about his motivations, the forces that drove and inspired him. She wanted to know about his concept of art and the role it should take on. While he answered, mulling over "take on," thinking how much he liked it, she took a cloth and wiped the puddle off the kitchen platform, which had formed because of the ice dripping. She held the wet cloth under a running tap, then wrung it out and put it on the windowsill for drying. She did this like she was familiar with his home, and he noticed this and felt a surge of pleasure. Everything, it appeared, was headed toward a logical conclusion. Everything, it appeared, was preordained and perfect. He hoped nothing would divert or stall the flow.

He found it surprising that she should show so much interest in his work. It was not as though he was known; it was not as though his work had appeared in galleries or had been reviewed in the press. It was not as though buyers were falling over to reach him or his work hung in their living rooms and conference rooms. His focus was different, he said. It was art as exposé, as consciousness. He believed in showing democracy where it ceased to exist, where it was stifled, thwarted, and twisted by the rulers of the nation. He wanted his art to be a call to conscience for the already sensitized and a shock to those who weren't. And, as of then, the only takers he'd found were musician friends wishing to liven up studio walls and unrecognized writer/poet friends wishing to conceal the craters on their walls at home. He was too naïve or too sheepish to ask for payment, and they were too broke or spaced-out to offer any.

"Do you know there are ten million tribals displaced since Independence?" he said. His eyes were watery and he looked at her bleakly. He had changed into shorts and a light white undershirt. (He'd asked whether she minded—too many clothes made him uncomfortable, he said.) He was squatted on the floor on a straw mattress that went well with the beige walls, and next to him were his paintings, looking like they'd been freshly framed. The light from above—from the gentle, swaying paper *kandeel*—was warm and diffused, and it made him appear brown, bloated, and shaven all over. Bloated because of the vodka, shaven because he was that—hairless, plump, and baby-smooth, like a seal washed up ashore. She could see he enjoyed being at home. And she enjoyed being there with him.

She gazed at the painting he was holding. It had tribal men being ushered into a police van and the face of a girl looking on. It was the face of a bride, barely twenty, just the side of her face and her eye—wide, gaping, disbelieving. In the background, small figures stood paralyzed. And in the foreground were cops with rifles. The doors of the van were open, to imply a deep, cavernous threat. It was all about detail, a lack of it, minimal strokes to achieve an optimum starkness of effect, and it carried a sense of isolation, like a holocaust imminent, like the men weren't coming back and their women would be left waiting forever.

She looked at the painting from various angles, lest she miss some oblique meaning hidden somewhere.

"They've disappeared," he said. "No one knows where. They were made to leave their cattle, crops, and fields; they were made to forget their identities and evacuate, for dams, power projects, and corporations. It's one big conspiracy and it's happening all the time, and we don't know it because we don't see it, and the payoffs are huge, and it's not us who are affected but the poor villagers, the poor farmers who have no clue why they are being shafted."

When she heard this, she felt like she was being dragged into another world—a Dantean world from which there was no return. Yet it was sweet, soporific, and numbing, like it was all she ever wanted. Like her soul had found its sphere.

There was one painting on the Bhagalpur blindings, one on Latur (the earthquake), one on Bhuj (the devastation), one on Orissa (the famine), one on the share bazaar scam, with a jowly modern-day demon dominating and shaking the stock exchange like King Kong incensed and people falling off, plunging to their deaths, while in the background politicians gave speeches, their fingers raised, their paunches stiff and bloated.

She stopped at two paintings that gripped her: that of a man sitting alone, drinking, before a stone wall, the face of alcoholism trapped in its own insurmountable prison; another of a giant excavator looming over a solitary hill with skyscrapers behind, the eradication of green zones in a fast-concretizing city. She clutched at the one of a sickle suspended like a noose, the story of a thousand farmers, killing themselves over failed crops and poverty.

With each painting, he had some tidbit of information for her, some fact she did not know, and she marveled at this hard disk of information in his head, and the magnitude of feeling in his heart, and the keenness of eye and the magic of hand that allowed him to capture all this, fluidly, lavishly. She had never met a man who she felt was so erudite, so sensitized. This made her feel warm and excited, as if she were on the brink of some impossible discovery, some uncontainable happiness that would well up and explode in her, washing away all her longings.

Partly out of euphoria and partly out of nervousness, she suggested a joint, the first cut, if there was any left. He smiled and said why not; it was great to meet someone like her, someone who had kept her bohemian traits carefully preserved, who hadn't sold out to the rigors of working life, which was death according to him, a state of abominable compromise.

They drank, they smoked, they waxed eloquent over the first cut, and they got nostalgic over the fifties phase in Indian cinema and the sixties and seventies in rock music. They ached for the world that did not know, did not see, and soared to a level where they saw nothing but their own thwarted version of life, and yet inwardly, distractedly, they grappled with an excitement that rose and licked at their hearts and minds. At 1:30 A.M. they hugged, kissed, and pledged. In that small room, with the paper lantern swaying, and the light throwing shadows about them, and the trees outside crossing their branches like devout soldiers taking a muscular oath, in that room a world opened up. A world bigger than what each of them had known. Or anticipated.

They sat down for dinner at 3:00 A.M. Before that he excused himself, saying he'd like some time to himself in the kitchen. She watched television while from the kitchen came sounds of vessels being banged around, and after some time she got a whiff of aromas that stirred her senses and made her realize how hungry she was.

He called her in to a veritable spread: a cheese and mushroom omelet, light, golden, and swollen; a *dekchi* of coconut fish curry, looking red and malignantly spicy; a stew of okra, potatoes, and capsicum served in a pan with wooden handles. There was also a bowl of long-grain basmati rice, and dal with a *tadka*. Her mouth was watering as she sat down. He smiled and pointed to the food invitingly, as if he'd guessed what was on her mind, as if the whole meal was one big conspiracy to delight her.

The table was small and rickety, with just enough space for the two of them. He apologized, saying they'd have to eat there, in the kitchen, because the smell lingered and got into the upholstery otherwise. She saw he had cut slices of onions on a plate and placed glasses of water next to their plates and near his own plate was a glass of vodka filled to the brim. She wondered how he had done all this, in the state of mind he was, and she marveled at him, this bachelor artist who seemed to have his life so figured out. His life and his art—in this sweet little den of his.

Eating silently, happily, she yearned to belong to his world. She yearned to see him shape his paintings with mighty strokes and his meals with the same instinct of cool, effervescent genius. She wanted to be a part of it. She wanted to sit down to dinners like this every evening. She wanted banter, chatter, and the warmth of home-cooked food, and then someone to hold her and lead her to bed light and dizzy; she wanted this over cold leftovers, take-out dinners, and the monologue of a television blaring. She wanted what she thought was achievable. And she whipped it to a fairy-tale conclusion in her mind.

CABS, SCOOTERS, CARS IN A RUSH; the signal: a steadfast green. Swirls of traffic sweeping in and merging. Then honking. Then cursing. That failing, empathizing. What to do? This was South Bombay, the rush hour. Everybody in a hurry to get home. Everybody in a sweat to reach their destinations. And some just to get away.

She was at that part of the road where the traffic kept coming, where people waited in queues, along the divider. She did not know why she had taken this road, why she was here at all, standing as part of a crowd. All she knew was she was out walking. And she was at a crossroad, waiting. And from there everything looked dangerous, capable of running her into the ground.

SHE'D MOVED INTO his Bandra flat, giving up her paying guest accommodation in Lokhandwalla. It was his idea, with him saying they'd save on the rent, the electricity, the phone bills, the loneliness, the commuting, now that they'd found each other. Yes, yes, yes, she'd gone, springing into his lap, straddling him, pulling at his cheeks, licking his nose, biting it, nibbling at the soapy-sweet flesh on his throat, then pulling back embarrassed. Before moving in she'd taken care to call the Salvation Army and dispose of clothes she'd outgrown. Things like her mattress, curtains, rugs, stools, freezer, chest of drawers, sofas, and a centerpiece—all this she sold to the *zaripuranawalla,* forgetting in her excitement to bargain. With the money she got she bought crockery and provisions for three months. She had no clue what his finances were: did his paintings support him, or was there an alternate source of income? She thought it would be premature to ask. Besides, their love was what mattered. There was a lifetime ahead to find out other things—and what did it matter what came up, as long as they were together?

She'd brought over a few of her personal things: books, CDs, curios, shells, beer mugs, coasters with happy-hour witticisms, and old *New Yorker* magazines, heaps of them. She had a thing about its covers, about the vibrant art that leapt out, the use of colors to depict an idyllic world. He read a few issues and said he preferred the cartoons; the wit was what impressed him, that and the non-fiction. The movie coverage gave him heartburn; it reminded him how many films failed to make it to Indian shores. And reading about the plays, he could envisage the scope of Broadway, the beauty of its spirited performances. He looked wistful when he spoke of the art exhibitions, and she swore in her heart that she'd save enough for a trip for the two of them. Those were the days when she could afford to dream. The dreams appeared distant but achievable. Like wooly white clouds they could spirit her away, unlike the dark thunderstorms of her black box, which only served to weigh her down.

She asked his permission to pin up posters of Bob Dylan, Pete Townsend, and John Lennon, sepia-tone versions in close-up, and he was delighted, for them he counted as his friends, his guiding lights from another age valid eternally.

In month one she bought a microwave, in month two a dishwasher, in month three a DVD player. She changed the faded blue curtains in the living room to a bright brown-and-maroon check. She put up plants in corners, plants with beds of sweet-smelling mud, and these she tended and watered daily. She bought three side tables and on these she placed lamps with soft ethnic shades. In the center, she placed a Kashmir rug—the warmth of rust, with a border of white tassels. On it, she placed a center table, with an exquisite glass top, resembling a palette. All these changes transformed the place. He was delighted with the centerpiece and said the house looked lived in now; earlier it had looked merely occupied. He smiled and said he felt almost married; this was as close as they'd get to it. Before she could ask what he meant, he said he was cooking them a dinner to celebrate. They would start with corn and cheese baskets, chicken croquets, a lime mousse salad, and all this would climax in a *desi* version of Chicken Xacuti. She sighed at the sheer incongruity of flavors, yet she knew that if anyone could make them coexist he could.

They worked at the meal together, and occasionally she'd stop and look at him for approval. She was glad to assist in the making of this splendid feast and felt proud that he allowed her to do so. Later, as she savored the flavors, the love of ingredients that came through in every bite, it seemed like all of heaven had moved in with them and that nothing could ever sully their dream. She noticed he liked to cook more than eat. He'd look at her while she ate, while she heaped on helpings and slurped at her fingers. He'd sit watching, smiling through hazy gray eyes. His own food would remain untouched, and when he'd nibble away it would be in between sips of vodka.

Mornings, she'd wake up early, her calls starting from 7:00 A.M.—an incessant ringing about actors, props, locations, dates planned and canceled. She'd rush from the bathroom, stammering out answers through a toothpaste-clogged mouth, and he'd groan and roll over, stuffing a mountain of blankets over his head, and he'd mole in and stay there hidden and catatonic. He'd sleep like this till early afternoon, till the sun would trickle in through the iron grills and warm his face, till his throat would parch, his stomach would cringe, and he'd feel like a piss from his distended bladder. Then he'd force himself to rise and, making himself a mug of coffee, would retire to the couch, with the newspaper, and while reading he'd smoke a joint. Then he'd decide whether to stare moodily outside the window, or to return to bed churlishly, or switch on the television and rail at the idiocy happening there, or simply fly to his canvas and vent—out of inspiration or anger.

Mid-afternoon she would call, and he would listen to some talk about some actor playing hard to get, or some location not working out, or some slut of a starlet offering herself to the producer. The producer was always willing, and she was sure that he was screwing in the office itself. She knew by the look of the girls who emerged that they'd been laid. There'd be a look about them to suggest they'd bagged a break. He would listen to her and go, "Hmm, hmm, hmm," and she'd know by that whether he'd had his coffee and smoke, or he was painting, or he was in the throes of a depression. She could make that out in the first few minutes, and she'd temper her talk accordingly, so as not to add to his chaos, not to disrespect the artist in the man. A few times she found him slurring his words, and she mustered up the courage to ask whether it was the vodka—that early.

She made up her mind to talk to him about it at the right time, without making a big deal of it. It was too early to start picking holes. She didn't want to appear a nag. She didn't want to sully her world, admit that the first crack *had* appeared.

Over time she discovered that he had a strange theory about working, earning, and spending. He believed that the pursuit of money was vulgar and vitiating; it led you to strange deceptions, strange delusions that strangled the real self, the soul of man. Real art must find its own outlet, he said. To market it was despicable. To go out and sell was nothing short of desperation. For an artist it would represent a fall, and for him, death.

She didn't ask how he got his money. She knew he lived frugally. He didn't go to restaurants or pubs. "Those places are not for us," he'd say. "They are for the mentally impoverished, who don't know what to do with their lives." He had a thing against restaurants, too, how they hyped up their prices, how they gypped on quality, and how there were fools who knew this and yet went—so empty and dead their lives were.

She missed her Koliwada prawns, her Hyderabadi fish, and her tandoori crab at the fish joints and her occasional drink at Cloud Nine in Bandra, but she said nothing. He was an amazing cook, and he insisted on cooking daily, but he wouldn't hesitate to ask her for money, saying he needed it for provisions. He did this after the twentieth of every month, and after some time she made it a point to leave the money out, so he wouldn't feel embarrassed. She'd leave two hundred rupees on the side table next to the phone, and sometimes a little more if he said the vodka had run out, or there was a score happening, some *primo* stuff from the foothills of Manali. The first cut didn't excite her anymore. She realized it was a daily habit for him, a means to shut out the world. He'd smoke at his window, or while painting, his joint in one hand, a glass of vodka at his side, his eyes glazed, his lips curled in a mock ironic smile.

NOW THE TRAFFIC HAD SLOWED, stopped, a burgeoning sheet of hot metal flowing in cool colors. Vicki readied herself to cross. In her state it was important not to be stuck; she'd been that way too long, and today was actually her way out. She mingled with the walkers and crossed obediently, looking over her shoulder, and it occurred to her why she was there among them, why she needed *their* presence, *their* panic, in front, at the side, shoulder-to-shoulder, and bottom-close, even that! She was scared of being alone. Being alone was being evil, which is what had happened back home—alone, unwanted, bypassed by life itself.

But would she have thought like this if she had continued living with Nandkumar, in his quaint Bandra flat, going mushy eyed over warm dinners and art films and turning a blind eye to his many obsessions, his artistic aversions that stood between them and a normal life?

THE MONEY CAME from his father in Deolali, his father who had settled there, gardening, golfing, practicing yoga, hobnobbing with officers from the army, his father, once a terror and now mellow, who'd abused him as a child, as a frustrated insurance man who couldn't get people to insure their lives easily and who'd vented his frustration on his son, because the boy was dyslexic but didn't know it and because a fortune had to be spent on getting him through school.

His father would do it with a cigarette, while his mother would watch and say nothing. She wasn't that kind of woman, that kind of wife who'd raise her voice. He wondered sometimes whether she'd felt anything, whether she had a voice that screamed and revolted from within, and if so, why she'd never exercised it, or why it had failed her when he needed it most.

He'd recollect how a remark written by a teacher on his report card would get him called to his father's room, the one he and Vicki were using now, where they slept, snored, and copulated, and there the old man would draw him into his arms, with a smile, and at the side the cigarette would be lying lit on the ashtray. He did not recollect his father smoking otherwise; he did not recollect him drinking or shouting them down; his was a slow, annihilating abuse, cold, clinical, and scientific, reserved for those he lived with. He didn't remember his father having friends ever; he didn't remember them visiting their relatives on festival days. Once in a while his mother took him to visit some cousins in Mulund, and before that he was warned what to say and what not; he was not to discuss his grades, his learning difficulties, or the fact that he had flunked twice.

In the ninth standard, when they started on the ICSE portion, the school had called them and asked that he be transferred to a special school for dyslexics.

His father was embarrassed. He threatened him with consequences if he ever gave out that he was in *that* school. According to him, *that* school was for delinquents, and what would the world think—that he'd produced a slow, non-functioning child? The good part was an art master who had spotted his talent, unearthed it among the confusing miasma of numbers and theories. Mr. Borkar encouraged him to partake in art competitions outside school; he pushed him to paint at home and in school, and to retain his sanity in a world of pain, ridicule, and torment.

In the first year of college, he won an art competition organized by a child-care organization, which promptly commissioned him to do their annual calendar for a sum of ten thousand rupees. He felt proud when he received the prize, and he felt sickened when his father was called onstage to say a few words on the future of the child. As his father walked onto the stage, he walked out of the auditorium and lit a cigarette, and after the first few drags he crushed it in the palm of his hand. The mark could still be seen: a dot of frail, pink baby-soft skin, a peephole into what lay beneath, a reminder of what had never healed, never would, and could rupture anytime.

When Vicki saw this, her heart went out to him. She hurt for the childhood he never had and for the monstrous disfigurements he had inherited. His reluctance to venture out, to face the world, to compete, to come through—all this had been taken away by the bogeyman of his childhood, by the man with the cigarette who kept asking why he couldn't be like the rest. Why he didn't understand. Why he didn't pass easily. Why he was such a failure, a miserable liability to them.

Nandkumar Chaurasia had no answers. Not then, not now. In his heart there was a perpetual dread that he *was* a failure. It had taken Vicki months to understand this, months of seeing him at close quarters, languishing on his soft, white bed, staring at the fan in smoked-out stupor, waiting for inspiration to drive him to his canvas, or something in the newspaper to send him to his palette, and when he got there he would weep tears of paint and shades of angst, and the victims he painted were not always the ones that mattered but the ones within, his own demons, and the women he showed sold or subjugated indeed had the face of his own mother.

Vicki realized he didn't mind taking money from his father. He said that was all the old man had to offer; it was punishment for his sins, redemption for his soul. He was only helping to save his father from a life of damnation, a private hell of remorse and retribution.

His mother had been kept in a home. She'd had two strokes, was reduced to a wheelchair, and had lapsed into a state of speechlessness, marked, diminishing, and more foreboding than in her earlier life. She remained like that till she died, till they placed her on the burning logs and her head exploded with a series of snaps. It reminded Nandkumar of the firecrackers on Diwali, which he could never enjoy. And the smoke reminded him of the cigarette circling before his face.

Vicki thought she'd be the good thing in his life. She dreamt that she'd give him back his lost childhood, and she allowed him to curl up night after night in her arms, in the folds of her body, all the way down to the burning epicenter of her soul. Where he'd been abused, places where he'd been hurt and damaged, she filled with love and devotion, a tenderness she never knew she possessed. She'd hold him, stroke him, shower him from head to toe with sweet, moist kisses, as if plucking and drawing the poison out, as if taking it in herself.

Her tenderness would give way to a torrid lovemaking, mostly silent, in the dark, and she'd note the rise of a slow, clutching panda anxious to prove himself. Not ready to disillusion this victim-child of an abusive father, she'd moan and groan away. She hated herself for doing this, for being this wily, thrashing woman, but if it served to enhance Nandkumar's confidence, if it made him feel as good as the next man, she was game. When they were like this, she'd dream of old boyfriends, old lovers, men she'd been with for a night, or for a month, boys at her college, and some later, who were there only to deliver, only to quench, and who made her feel empty and cheap thereafter. And she knew then that no matter what his failings were, in bed and out of it, it was *this* child she wanted, this responsibility she craved.

She thought she'd be his savior, his destiny. She thought he'd see it this way, too, and she allowed herself to dream fervently, to stroke his lush black head and his soft furry eyebrows, and his drooping vodka eyes, averted, uncertain whether he'd delivered at all, and she would sigh and bestow what she felt were kisses of lasting assurance. She never wanted him to know the truth. She never wanted him to feel he was a lesser man. She diminished herself on the altar of his love, gave up those womanly notions of fulfillment and reciprocal warmth. And she readied herself for a lifetime of sacrifice—whatever it took to keep the man intact.

While he'd sleep and snore lightly, she'd dream that she'd bring him luck; his work would get noticed and begin to sell. To do that, she took copies of his work, scanning and printing them out in large-size formats at her own expense, and these she showed to owners of art galleries who she knew were open to new artists. She didn't tell him, but she got these contacts from her boss, the Bollywood producer who was a big enough name to open doors, to call and invoke, if nothing else, some curiosity on her behalf.

Wherever she went, she got the same response: he is good, talented, excellent control, but people don't want to see angst on their walls, they don't want to face death and destruction; they want, well, wall art, or art that would enthrall and intrigue, or art that was solid and definitive, or art that was surreal and abstract. There was so much more he could do in figurative drawing, making it more defined and less grim.

One of the agents, a kindly old gentleman in whom she managed to inspire a paternal emotion, went to the extent of suggesting themes. Could he do a series on the heritage trades of Bombay: a *maalishwalla* by the beach, a *victoriawalla* under a streetlight, a *dhobi* buckling under his load—something to suggest his heavy debt? Now that would work. He'd be glad to represent that kind of work.

When she told Nandkumar about the agent's suggestion, he said, "Tell him to take his ideas to painters who are hard up for ideas." He said he was better off where he was. Better off in his own bed, under his own ceiling, smoking dope with his father's money, and dreaming up rebellions in his mind, rebellions that would never happen. She knew that as well as he did.

She kept trying, and he kept refusing, kept avoiding opportunities, as if the very idea of responding to them would imply a selling out, a beginning of the corruption process. She understood that there was an inborn fear of rejection, of being told he wasn't *there,* he was too indulgent, too dark and depressing. She understood that he couldn't operate without the fear of a cigarette over him. Its light and its threat.

Slowly, a change came over her. She found that she preferred staying late at work. The whole idea of returning home and finding him soaked in vodka or in depression filled her with a strange dread. Yet she loved and wanted him. Yet she kissed him warmly once she returned. Yet she melted when she saw that he hadn't eaten without her and he offered to heat her dinner despite his inebriated state. Looking at moments of closeness for inspiration, she tried to talk him into working, into pulling himself up. She tried to remind him it wouldn't be a compromise listening to what the agents were saying; it would be an investment for the future, their future, so to speak. She'd look at him with anxious eyes, wondering whether he thought of that as well.

But to all her pleas his defense was: "I can't sell out. I can't go and kiss ass, do things I don't believe in. They have to take me for what I am," and then slowly he'd add: "So must you, if you believe in me, if you believe in the work, and don't want to give up on us, all that we stand for."

And when he'd say things like that, when he'd transfer the onus onto her, a wild fear would spring to her eyes. Was this a threat? Or a challenge? She couldn't take any more responsibility than what she had already. Not because she didn't want to, but because it didn't seem to be working; it didn't seem to be getting them anywhere—to the possibility of a dream taking shape.

A few days before Diwali she saw him brood over a letter he had received. He read it again and again, pacing up and down the tiny passage along the living room, frowning, and smoking one cigarette after another.

"It's from the landlord," he said after some time. "It's an offer to convert this rented house into an ownership one. One hundred months' rent and it can become mine for life!"

She flinched at "mine" but chose to let it pass. "So what's the problem?" she said. "It sounds like a perfectly good proposition. Considering what an ownership flat would cost in this area, you stand to gain."

"I don't know," he said. "I don't know whether Dad will agree to pay. I suppose I had better go and see him. Do you mind? I will be gone a few days."

She was glad for the break, glad to see him off the next day, in an unreserved compartment of a train starting from Dadar Station. This was another of his quirks: he liked to travel with the masses; he liked the sweat, the suffocation, the rubbing of shoulders with the proletariat. He said he was as public as they were, the unfortunate product of an unfortunate birth, and that he did not wish to be any more removed from reality than what he already was.

With him gone, she'd come home early, play her CDs, fix herself a bubble bath, soak in it, and give herself to a world of creams, lotions, and other feminine cares that she had given up. She'd leaf through women's magazines, reading with interest the personal sagas, the personal advice columns, and the zodiac predictions that told her what the future held. Then one day she decided to invite her relatives over for dinner, her two *chachus* and two *chachis* whom she hadn't seen since the time she met Nandkumar. She thought this was a good time to tell them of her live-in arrangement with this sweet and not-so-steady boy from a not-so-great family. She spared them the details of his childhood but spelled out those of her own happiness at great length, requesting their blessings, and although they were a little hurt, they agreed to meet Nandkumar.

"Oh, but you can meet him right now," she said eagerly. "At least a part of him." She proudly brought out his paintings, thinking this was the best way to introduce him.

She was in the midst of showing them his work, explaining its deeper motivations and the details they would have missed, when there was a click at the door and he came in looking tired and disheveled. His hair was tossed, his cheeks were flushed, his neck was dark with perspiration, and his eyes had a vitreous look, a false alertness to suggest that some vodka had been consumed. "Ah," he said. "And what is this? A party in my absence! Something I should know about?" She flinched at his tone, for light as it was, it carried a hint of accusation. Her heart sank and a slight rage began in her. Why did he have to come in right now looking like this? Could he not have phoned her, warned her? He was so much more attractive in his absence.

"Oh, Nandu," she said, trying to sound pleasantly surprised. "This is my Ajay Chachu and my Vinay Chachu, and my *chachis,* Anjali and Gauri—you've heard me speak of them."

"Ah, yes!" he said coldly. "But I didn't know they were connoisseurs of art. I didn't know you were going to be holding a private exhibition while I was away. You might have at least asked me? Unless, of course, the idea was different—to wait till I was gone."

"Honey . . . it's not what you think. They asked what you do. I thought this was the best way."

"Best for whom? And with whose permission? Perhaps you could clarify, Vicks."

"Nandu, please, why don't you go in and freshen up? There is some nice food ordered. Wash up and join us. They are dying to know you, to talk to you."

"Wash up and join us," he chided. "Honey, I *am* shocked. What have you been telling your people: how obedient I am, how I need to get my instructions from you, or I fail to make it through the day effectively? Oh, please, we can do better than that, can't we, Vicki?"

"Nandu, please!" she implored, making eyes at him, desperate eyes, despite her anger, which was welling up.

"Go on; I am listening. I expect to come home to a bit of rest, a bit of privacy, and what do I find? My paintings on display before people who don't know a dot about art, who've probably never been to an exhibition in all their lives. Or have never stepped out of their homes to see what's happening elsewhere in the country, how the other half lives."

"Young man, you presume too much, and I don't think I like your tone. We see how wrong our niece was when she said all those nice things about you." This was her Vinay Chachu, firm, soft-spoken, almost like a father to her.

"I think he is drunk; I can get the smell. Maybe that's why he is being so rude." This was her Gauri Chachi, the observant one.

"I think, Vicki, you have made one big mistake. You will ruin your life if you settle with this mannerless fellow. Look at him, taking off at us like this. And for what? Just because we are seeing his paintings. *Cha,* who wants to see them now? All humbug they look like anyway." This was her Anju Chachi, the tactless one, the unsparing summarizer of all things unspoken, and Vicki's favorite.

Nandkumar dropped his bag, moved forward, and stood glowering at Anju Chachi. She met his gaze without flinching. He grabbed his paintings and leaned them against the wall. Then he said through clenched teeth, "Get out . . . all of you . . . and stay out. I don't want to see any of you here again."

"*Arrey,* don't think you can insult us and get away with it. Our niece is not going to stay with you long if you are so badly behaved. What do you think? She comes from a good family. Not like you, you bloody hooligan."

"Anju, please . . . let's go. It was a mistake coming here. We can see that now, Vicki," her Ajay Chachu said, turning to her. He got to his feet, and the others followed.

Vicki looked desperately from them to Nandkumar and to them again. She couldn't believe this was happening to her. Her little world, which she had planned so carefully, was crumbling, and it was all his fault. But how was she to know that he'd be back? How was she to know he'd feel this way about his paintings? But didn't they belong to her as well? Had she not taken them to heart, dreamt of their success, tried to give them a future? She found herself hating his paintings, hating his talent. His talent had created a wall between them. It had let her down before people whom she cared for. Oh, what greater humiliation than this? She felt a flood of tears build up, and she ran inside, while her relatives left and he slammed the door behind them.

For a long time she sat on the bed and cried, a stunned, brutalized pup, choked and horrified. She was sure that she had no family left; they wouldn't respect her anymore. Oh, why had he done this? What purpose did it serve? She couldn't even find the right words to reprimand him.

He came into the bedroom and without a word disappeared into the bathroom. When he came out showered and sweet smelling, he made a joint, lit it, and after the first drag said to her quietly, "Don't touch my paintings again. Don't ever make that mistake again, please."

His eyes were cold, penetrating, and unavailable to her. It was as if they had shut her out. She nodded helplessly. There was a new fear lining her throat. It left her speechless. It hammered at her mind, opening it to dark clouds that warned of a deeper storm in future.

PARP. A SHARP HORN BEEPED in her ear. She shrank back. Oh, her concentration was wavering. She was crossing once more and needed to be careful. There was no signal here, no cops to control or to direct the flow. The traffic was coming from all sides, an unplanned anarchy, a free flow of metal, the city left alone to find its own method, its own discipline, which just wasn't there. It happened because the cars were too many and the roads too few.

SHE TOOK THE NEXT FEW DAYS OFF, calling up work to say she was unwell. He stopped speaking to her, stopped cooking, too; not that it mattered, there was enough food left from what was ordered for her relatives. She didn't feel like touching any of it; eventually it all had to be thrown away.

A brittle tension hung between them, a sadness that bewildered her. He would slip away early in the afternoon and go spend the day with his musician friends at the studio, where he'd smoke pot, drink vodka, and listen to the music of his youth. He'd return home late at night, wretchedly drunk. He'd crash noisily beside her, and within moments he'd be off, snoring heavily. While he'd sink into a sour sleep, she'd lie awake on her side, wondering how deep his poison was, how infectious its breath.

She didn't have to wait long to find out. The phone call came while he was out and while she was just beginning to get a grip on herself. She'd started taking calls, coordinating a few things from home, and had promised her boss that she'd be back at work within the next day or two.

The caller announced himself as Major Singhal from the Maratha regiment, and he sounded very curt and very angry. He asked for Nandkumar, and when she informed him that he wasn't there, he said with vehemence, "Well, madam, you just tell that young bastard that if

I ever find him in Deolali again, I will give him the thrashing of his life, a thrashing he will never forget. I will make him pay for what he has done to his father. He will wish he were never born."

"I don't know what you are talking about, sir," she said coldly. "If my knowledge serves me right, it is Nandu's father who has a lot to account for, for what he has put Nandu through."

"Young lady, I don't know what your relationship with him is, but since you are around while he is not, I would infer that it is one of significance." He paused. "I believe by your tone and confidence that you don't know what has transpired, what happened when he came to Deolali. There was an argument, and he has left his father with a broken nose and two fractured ribs. And over what: just because the old man refused to give him some money, which he wanted for his house. And why should he? Isn't it enough that he has given him an entire house in Bombay? Isn't it enough that he sends him money every month? Which father would do that for a thirty-year-old son? Hah, if I had a boy like that, why, I'd leave him to fend for himself, a no-good wastrel of a fellow. And I'd break his face if he as much as raised his hand to me. I wish you'd see, madam, how much pain the old man is in, and yet he chooses not to make a complaint against his son. He didn't even want to tell us, till we heard it from the old *maali* who had overheard the fight."

Vicki felt sickened. Something churned in her gut. Yet she said, "Are you sure, sir? Are you sure of what you say? I don't think Nandkumar would do something like that. He is not capable of it."

There was a pause on the other side. "Young lady, you are either foolishly in love or just plain foolish. I don't know you, but you had better wise up about him. That boy is a lunatic; take it from me. Who in his right mind would strike and injure his own father—and one so gentle, too?"

"Is Mr. Chaurasia gentle?" Vicki asked in a low voice. She felt a faint tremor in her voice. The carpet, she felt, was slipping beneath her.

"Gentle? He wouldn't hurt a fly. Of course, he wasn't going to relent over the money for the house, but why should he? He is retired, living on his pension and his savings; he has himself to think of." Suddenly the voice turned brusque and commanding. "Please tell Nandkumar from me, please tell him that we *know* what he has done, and that the next time there will be no warning. The army will do all it can to protect senior citizens. And we have our ways."

After he had hung up, Vicki sat brooding a long time. Was everything about Nandkumar a lie? Everything, including the bit about the abuse? She knew now why he'd returned in such a foul mood, why he had been so furious to find her relatives there, and why he had insulted them. He had come home expecting to find consolation—to deliver stories about his father's pettiness—and instead he had to make himself sociable. He couldn't take that, not with the vodka, the fear, and the guilt raging through him. Vicki wondered how far back the lie stretched, how deep the pus was rooted. The gangrene had set in and it could infect her, drag her down. For the first time since she had met him, she thought of leaving. But she just thought about it, never did anything, just sat and thought in the dark, till the streetlights came on and lit up the windows and the plants cast dark, ominous shadows on the floor. She waited for him to come home—drunk, surly, and unsure—and then she told him about the call.

He denied it. "What Major? What injuries? That old bastard is shamming. It's just his way to get pity, to make me look bad. He'd stoop to anything to get back at me."

"But why would he get back at you at this advanced age?" she asked.

He scowled. "How would I know why? Did I know why he tortured me with that cigarette? He probably hates me because I was slow and he can't bear it that I have overcome my problem and gotten over my fear of him."

"The Major said he was gentle, he wouldn't hurt a fly."

"That fucking Major wasn't there to see me grow up. He wasn't there when the old man was not so old and I was so very young, face-to-face with that burning stick. That Major wasn't there to see me get it—here, and here, and here." Saying that, he slapped himself on his arms, hips, and thighs. Then he started jeering. "You seem to have believed the Major, haven't you, Vicki? Oh yes, don't you try and deny it. I know by your tone that you *have* believed him. And I thought I could trust you. You were the only one who knows everything, and yet you choose to disbclieve." He sighed. "I guess it is too much to ask to expect total trust. Times like this show how wrong you can be. How misplaced your faith in the one you love."

"It's not like that," she said. She didn't know what to believe anymore. She was tired of him, of the dark, swamping chaos in his soul, which seemed to envelop her, draw her into a plunging gloom, an irreversible illness from which she could not fight her way out.

"Ah, yes, I remember now. My father was saying horrible things to me before I left. He kept coming up and sticking that hand of his in my face. I couldn't bear it anymore. It reminded me of the abuse. Besides, I couldn't take his selfishness. So I pushed him away, nothing hard, just a shove to get him off my back. Then I left. But I remember him falling, and when I offered to help, he shrugged me off. I told him that *would* be the last time I'd be seeing him. Perhaps that is why he made up this story. He doesn't want to let go his hold on me."

He looked at her. His eyes were calm. To her they appeared grayer than ever, a mixture of shades they were trying to conceal. It was dark and silent outside. Only the occasional roar of an auto rickshaw, or the sound of footsteps scrunching on the gravel outside.

"I'll tell you what," he said suddenly. "I bet it was no Major who called, but someone my father put up to it. I had told him about you, how we plan to get married and have kids. So if he could let us have this house, put up the money for it, we could seal our future. But did he listen? No! It didn't matter, he said. Didn't matter what I wanted to do, what became of us. Now tell me, would any father say that? Does he have any right to call himself a father after that?"

A shudder of excitement ran through Vicki. Marriage? Kids? Had he really said that? Did he mean it? She looked at him, his eyes craving her trust. But why would he tell his father about them, she thought, when he had not broached the subject with her?

She drew herself up. "Why must you depend on him?" she said. "Why can't you raise the money yourself? Why can't you do it with your work, your talent? Why can't you be like the people you admire—the working class, who suffer indignities daily? Why must you be like one of those *amir baap ka betas,* one of those rich kids who get it all on a platter? Aren't your actions in direct contradiction to what you believe? And aren't you doing the same thing your father did to you? Aren't you feeding off his old age, the way he fed off your childhood?" She stopped. Her poison was out, all that she had gathered in the last few months, all that she'd swallowed and left unsaid.

Nandkumar looked like a storm had hit him across the face. He clenched his fists and said, "You bitch, you fucking bitch, you are saying this, living under my roof and sponging off me?" He came and stood close to her, so close that she could smell his anger, his heat. She shut her eyes, raised her hands to her face, and waited for the blows to come. In a perverse sort of a way she wanted it to happen, for that would tell her if he'd beaten the old man as well. After some time she knew he was no longer there, for she heard the bedroom door slam shut.

That night they lay back-to-back, ruptured souls pretending to sleep, each grappling with a private hell, a raging inferno in their heads, each seeing the chasm between them widen, for they could no longer face each other, no longer share the same breath, the same rhapsody of body rhythms, rising and falling, rising and sinking, finding its own level, its own depth. They could no longer do that, for one wore the face of a liar and the other the face of loathsome disbelief.

He began to show a strange side thereafter, especially when they'd meet with her friends. He'd wait for an evening to settle in, for conversation to flow—a book, a movie, or a play to be discussed—then he'd look for an opening, a comment borne of ignorance, or a loose comment somewhere, and he'd move in with a cold gray smile, and end up going for his victim, going hammer and tongs with the full flesh-and-blood faculties of his mind, and he'd enjoy seeing his victim squirm and lose his cool, and he'd come away feeling nice and triumphant, nice and bloated, a sense of achievement plastered all over his hot, drunken face.

Many were the evenings that ended like this, and many were the times she'd lead him away, a hazy, vodka-ridden figure unable to hold himself up. It appeared, too, that he enjoyed the idea of a storm, of a slow, seeping anarchy that whipped itself into something big and left the evening in tatters, and he made no effort to understand the people he hurt, or what their relationship with her was, or just her and her feelings, and there was no inclination to apologize later, to mend bridges burnt and damaged. In fact, he seemed to flaunt some kind of bravado, some kind of bluster not human at all, and he seemed to blame her for knowing such kinds of people. People, who, he said, they shouldn't waste their time on.

After some time her friends stopped inviting them. They decided she'd made her own choice, one that did not suit them, one that diminished her charm and wiped out the memories they'd shared. Besides, they had their own boyfriends and husbands to think of, bruised boyfriends and furious husbands, who did not forgive easily.

Her Anju Chachi and Gauri Chachi would call regularly on her cell phone and plead for her to leave him. What *was* her problem? Why was she staying? They'd find her a boy, a suitable boy from a good family, pleasant manners, pleasant looks, the kind who'd fit in with them, the kind who knew how to respect elders and would therefore respect her. And yet she could not leave, for she knew not what she'd be leaving: a dark genius or a poisoned child, a genius cheated out of opportunity or a child cheated out of love. There were two beings that crept into her bed every night, and she wondered who would win eventually, who would prevail and hold sway.

When she was on the phone with her aunts, there'd be a faint ironic smile playing on his lips, as if to say he pitied her. Casually she'd try to move out of range, and yet he'd be watching and smiling, his eyes riveted in a gloating sort of a way. When he did that, she'd feel a dark, hot unease, a sense of violation, a sense of losing her privacy, her control, and the house that had appeared so cozy earlier would suddenly become small and suffocating—a maximum-insecurity prison from which there was no escape.

She'd call her friends, not from home but from the office, and twitter how busy she was, how she missed them, how they *must* catch up once her film was done. She'd ask about their boyfriends, their husbands, and their work, and they'd answer sorrowfully, with a sense of awareness that she was flogging a dead horse, she was trying to keep alive something that had died one vodka-flushed evening.

They knew, and she knew, and so did her aunts and her uncles, and yet she battled this feeling that she must leave. That she must close the door and move on.

He threw her out one night after a fight. There was a *mahurat* of the film she'd been working on, a commercial film, a potboiler, with great drama, glitz, razzmatazz, filmy style, the kind of stuff he detested—which, he said, polluted the mind.

There was always excitement about such an occasion, and she had taken care to dress up. He had watched from the corner of his eye: she shading her eyes, patting her *churidaar,* rolling up her hair in a silken bun before the mirror. He watched her going through her box of jewelry—her cave of extreme vanities as he called it—and then applying a *bindi* dead center in her forehead. He watched from his bed, through eyes red from sleep and smoke, while the blades of the fan circled overhead and something churned in his head. Something unruly and unpleasant.

She'd made no attempt to invite him, knowing of his antagonism to the industry. And this made him resentful, for he thought at least she could have asked. He thought she was ashamed of him—of the fact that he was not working, not earning; he didn't have a job or a steady income like other men. That had to be it, he thought, for of late she had stopped discussing his work, too. It was as if it had ceased to matter.

It had started to pour as she left, and hearing the *peep-peep* of the car, she had blown him a kiss and rushed out to the "oohs" and "aahs" of her colleagues, who'd held open the door for her. In the car, she realized that he hadn't asked her what time she'd be back or said anything about her enjoying herself. She decided she wouldn't think about it. She'd try to enjoy herself, for she was glad to be out of the house, glad to be away from the iron grills and the giant branches that now appeared like predators waiting for her to fall.

At the *mahurat* the producer had gone out of his way to make her feel important. He had introduced her to famous actors, actresses, directors, and the press, saying the film wouldn't have been possible without her. She had glowed with excitement and felt sheepish—to think this was the very world she had reviled.

Happy to be out, happy to be fussed over and appreciated, she had drunk—Jack Daniel's with Coke, a combination that promised not to leave her with a hangover—and she had danced, a light, delirious creature unshackled after so long, drifting away from her identity of the last few months, the soul mate of a dead man walking, a dead man infecting all who came within the radius marked by him. While she did that, he drank, too, at home, pegs of vodka, first with limewater, then without, quick shots, one after the other, while the rain poured fiercely outside, and drummed against the shutters of his mind. Drummed loud and hard, in white relentless sheets.

After some time he smoked a stiff joint; then he played *Machine Head* by Deep Purple, swinging his arms to "Smoke on the Water" and "Highway Star," and after that he switched to the Doors' "The End," and then to King Crimson's "Epitaph," where he mouthed the lyrics: "The fate of all mankind is in the hands of fools." And he was sure that she was with some fool now, replete with the false graces that marked such occasions: the unctuousness, the simpering, the outstretched hands, the hugs and the kisses that went with the hype. He was sure that the world she claimed wasn't hers was hers all the same; otherwise why would she dress like that, why so much time spent over looking good, over false appearances, the superficial things in life? And, besides, she was no longer interested in his work.

He was sure she was doing this deliberately, this planned rebellion, this meeting of people he despised. He was sure she was trying to negate him, run a cigarette over old wounds, with no one to speak up for him, no one to cry, "stop." Oh yes, he knew all the signs of silent torture, which was why he drank more and more, and why he waited with inflamed breath, in his shorts, in his undershirt, looking like one of those street goons drunk during a festival, and which was why he'd gone out looking like that to receive her and he'd walked up to the car, the big white car with the big white hood, and, banging on it, said, "So, done your *darshan* to shit, paid your respects to kitsch?"

"Everything okay?" a voice from inside asked. He bent to see who this man was, who'd brought her home at 5:00 A.M., drunk and looking like she'd been screwed. He bent to see through the blinding rain, the sleek white sheets that came down and stung his neck, back, and shoulders. He peered and saw her boss, the producer, who looked angry, really angry, and she had sobbed and run inside, and he had followed, whistling.

He had thrown her out, calling her her boss's "in-house fuck." He said it was the right weather for a whore to be out, and he'd thrown her things out—first her records, then her mugs, then her crockery, her clothes, then her, out on the purple and silver streets, into the rain, which poured faster than her tears. She could scarcely believe that he was misunderstanding her so ruthlessly. He was tearing down everything they'd built, everything they'd cared and dreamt about.

Through blurred eyes, hair wet and swept across her face, she remembered seeing the shift of curtains, the silhouettes of faces watching from above. She remembered seeing them draw back when he'd carried out the glass center table and smashed it against the pavement. It had woken up the dogs and set them howling, and yet no one heard the screams in her heart. He'd thrown her posters after her, crushing them into a ball, and she wondered then with her Gods ruptured—his and hers—what chance did she have, what indeed?

She managed to get to Anantrao's place in Juhu, where she spent the next few days. Anantrao was sympathetic, but like most men, he chose to keep his opinion to himself; he saw no point in getting involved. An enraged Julie wanted to speak to Nandkumar; she wanted to set him right. But Vicki extracted a promise from her that she would do nothing of the sort. Julie agreed reluctantly and, turning her ire on Anantrao, warned him not to try any such thing with her.

After a few days, Vicki called up Nandkumar, but hearing her voice, he started abusing her, demanding to know why she was screwing up his life, why she wanted to wreck his world, which was better off without her. She said she wanted to meet him just for a while; there was something important she wanted to say; after that he could decide whether to stay with her or let her go. He refused, saying he didn't have time for another man's whore. She winced, pleaded one more time—it wasn't about her, wasn't about him, it was about them and what they had created—but he did not want to listen; he simply kept abusing her, kept accusing her of things she couldn't understand. She put down the receiver sobbing.

NOW SHE WAS ALONGSIDE THE TRAFFIC. She and the vehicles were headed the same way, to the same destination: the seaside stretch of Marine Drive. She quickened her pace and came to the horizon, which shimmered before her like some precious ore melted down. It shimmered and stretched like it was waiting to be minted into something rare, something beautiful for the twenty million residents of the city.

The traffic lined the drive bumper to bumper. Over the roofs of cars she could see the seawall; it was dotted with people who sat looking outward. The people sat and they dreamt. And the sky loomed over them, a giant tent, bright and dark in patches.

She crossed, cutting through the vehicles: buses, cars, taxis, two-wheelers, a victoria waiting patiently. She glanced at her watch. It showed seven. She'd have an hour of light to think through her plan, to decide how to do it and where—whether in the loneliness of her room or at the brink of some tall building, off its terrace. She wondered whether it should be by the rope or by the pill and whether she'd leave a note: "I, Vicki Dhanrajgiri, am doing this out of my own free will, and no one, known or otherwise, is in any way responsible for this." She wondered whether she should add something that would get printed in the papers and onto sensitive hearts and minds. Something about life being the main culprit, about dreams being unfaithful, about hopes and expectations being the great mantraps of evolution, chutes of deceit that ended only at death's door. No matter what she thought up, it all sounded trite and trivial. It sounded like something that had already been said, in books or in art films.

She found a spot in between a young couple and three white-haired men enjoying an animated conversation. She sat facing the traffic, not the water. Water had a way of taking you in, of making you forget the reality. It was deceptively like life itself.

Below her the ocean drummed its fury. Not hard. Not viciously.

Just a playful, lapping fury that was inevitable with power and size. She thought of the tsunami that had left so many cities in disarray, which had swept away endless lives, and she wished hers, too, could have ended like that. It would have been so much easier to face that kind of fate than to be stuck with the kind of thoughts that had assailed her in her crumbling bed-sitter of an apartment, on this day, her day of arrival, also to be, by an unpleasant coincidence, her day of exit.

Things seemed more defined now. The trick was to be out of the traffic—out of the chaos, the noise, the blare of horns, the rush of acceleration, the screech of brakes, the brinkmanship of cutting in and out, and the clever last-minute dodge to avoid hurt . . . no, none of that anymore. She smiled at the thought. Smiled because it was the only redeeming thought in an act of throwing in the towel, in an act where she still had a choice to save a life. A life that was starting in her as a seed. A life that was growing outward, more precious than her own. But which was denied a hearing, hence had no reason to be born.

Joggers slowed to catch their breath. Walkers stepped up their pace. An *ice-creamwalla* cycled past, ringing his bell. A *chana-singwalla* came and stood before some couples who were locked in conversation. He lingered, fanning the vessel that warmed the *chana-sing,* and he minded it not when the couples ushered him on the same way they would a beggar.

Two men came up and began feeling the trunk of a coconut tree. Both were dark and unshaven. Both wore *lungis.* One of them had a rope around his neck. The other had a knife tied to his waist. The men pushed at the tree and nodded to each other. Vicki looked at them curiously.

The man with the knife took the rope from the other and started to uncoil it. He loosened about four feet of it and gave the loose end to his partner. Then, strapping the rest of the coiled rope around his shoulder, he started to climb the tree. Up he went, in short, leaping froglike motions, his shoulder blades arching in and out like boomerangs. As he rose higher and higher, the rope around his shoulder unfurled, and the man below collected it.

A breeze started. The tree tilted over the road. Vicki held her breath. Would the tree snap? Would it bear the burden? What were these two up to? Her anxiety had left her now. She watched as a schoolgirl might have standing before a cage in a zoo.

The tree climber could scarcely be seen now. Through the rustling palms, Vicki caught a flurry of hands and feet clutching at a branch. She heard a hacking sound and the two men yelling to each other. She inferred it was some South Indian language she did not know. *Hack, hack,* went the man on top, and the man below would shout and tighten the rope. Then the sound stopped. A yell from above, a yell from below, and slowly a bunch of coconuts came into sight—a big bunch of around thirty coconuts, with the rope functioning as a pulley. As the bunch descended, the man below loosened the rope and the man above lowered it cautiously.

The coconuts landed. Soon after, the climber followed. Landing, he slapped hands in mid-air with his partner, and kneeling, he tore a coconut from the bunch. He held it to his ear and shook it thrice.

Smiling a lazy, indulgent smile—the smile of achievement—the climber began hacking at the coconut. Vicki watched his arm—a lean brown axe of muscle—get to work on the coconut. She watched the blade slash, the shavings fly, and the crown of wood appear.

The climber saw her looking at him. For a moment their eyes met. They locked in a chemistry of curiosity, of fascination, whatever it was that locks two people from different backgrounds, and then the man got back to what he was doing. *Khat,* the last bit came off, and the coconut trembled with clear sparkling water all the way to the top. Vicki saw the delicacy with which the man held the fruit. He could have been holding a child or an offering to his God.

Holding the coconut, the man came toward the sea. His *lungi* was tucked into his crotch. His legs were dark and hairy. He placed a leg on the ledge and was about to raise the coconut to his mouth when he saw Vicki looking. He struggled for a moment and then offered, "Coconut water, madam? Very fresh. Very sweet. You will enjoy. Please try."

Vicki looked at his wizened face, his lazy, smiling eyes, and said, "How much for one?"

"The first one is always free, madam. We have many more, which we can sell for profit."

"But something?" she said. "Some money? *Akhir, boni ka waqt hain,*" referring to the auspicious time of first sale, which she knew was important to them.

Meanwhile, the second man had gotten busy hacking at another coconut. From the corner of his eye, he watched his friend. His face had a sly look to suggest that he knew what his friend was up to: he was trying to lure this woman. Suspecting this herself, Vicki hesitated. "No," she said to the man before her. "You take something, anything—but not for free."

The coconut man looked at her and said solemnly, "Madam, why are you so stubborn? I am giving it to you in good faith, no? See what a great fruit this coconut is: it grows near the sea, near the ocean; it grows on salt water, which you and I can't bear to taste; and yet, when it comes to us, the water inside is always sweet, always delicious. And now, if our minds were like this, we took the bitter and we made it sweet, we would never need to worry; we can learn to live and trust each other." Saying this, he walked off and he joined his friend the rope man.

"Oh, wait, please," Vicki said. She was beginning to register what he'd said. "Please don't go. I am sorry. I didn't mean to insult you." She saw that the group of old men at the side had fallen silent. They were looking at her strangely, as if she were mad to apologize to this fellow. But to her he was a saint, a messenger of light, he was the one who had brought deliverance to her door, and she'd sent him away with her dark, stormy, and embittered mind. But to her relief she saw that he was coming back and there was a red and white straw sticking out of the coconut.

With both hands she reached for the fruit. She took it shyly, gratefully. She brought her lips over the straw, and clutching it, she sipped slowly, steadily, non-stop, all the way to the bottom. She sucked on it like it was the only coconut left in the world and her life depended on it.

THE MAALISHWALLA

✦ ✦ ✦

CHOWPATTY BEACH, BOMBAY, 10:30 P.M. The swaying palms cast sinister shadows on the sand, while in the background cars zipped uproariously along the sea road. Some of the motorists felt grateful to the Queen's Necklace: that shining, twinkling stretch of road along the coastline, which allowed them the freedom to race their cars, feel the wind in their hair, and in that dispel the frustrations of living in India's busiest, most hectic city.

Bheem Singh Bahadur himself pondered this reality as he spread out his thin red towel—shrunk by use and abuse—on the moist sand of Chowpatty Beach. He glanced at his customer, a stunted middle-aged man with sly lips, a straining belly, and an angular face that seemed to have gotten that way from having a conversation with itself.

Bheem Singh snapped his fingers, one by one, readying himself for the *maalish*. He looked at his customer and felt a strange sense of distancing. It happened usually when the men he *maalished* brought with them limp, slovenly bodies, distorted by excess food, excess liquor, and excess money. Bheem Singh knew the type only too well, but then, they were the kind who could afford the *maalish*—a slow, rhythmic massage, which gave Bheem Singh his living, night after night.

The man turned, faced the sea, and started pulling off his shirt; his fat quivered into sight. Bheem Singh's eyes wandered to the man's back pocket. It told the usual story: a vulgar bulge, the assertion of one too many credit cards and a bundle of notes, big denominations, too.

Lingering on the bulge, Bheem Singh felt resentment. Even if he worked twenty months at a stretch, he could never hope to have so much money. Not while he had so many responsibilities to meet on behalf of his family.

His mind drifted. To his village. His beloved Isthaanpur. Where life was lived in full earnest. Where the pace never changed, nor the balance of equations. Where the ribbing was earthy and affectionate. Where everybody knew what the other did and despite the usual stream of gossip in the quadrangle and the squabbles at the well, no one did anything unexpected, which got others on their guard. But Bombay: it was different. Demanding? Yes! Life sapping? Yes! You had to have alliances and a ready salute for those in power. There was always someone to bow to—like the *lungiwalla dada* in the slum where he lived, who claimed free massages from Bheem Singh, in addition to the eight hundred rupees he took as rent. Like the head *maalishwalla* who had allowed him into the coterie, after an initial deposit of twelve hundred rupees and an agreement that he would do no more than three massages per night. And that arrogant *policewalla,* who came to the beach every night, to rob Bheem Singh of his earnings. The face of the *policewalla* was different each night, the attitude always the same. The click of the stick demanded that money change hands. "*Haraami* police, *haraami* city! City of bastards," Bheem Singh brooded.

The customer had taken off his trousers and lay on the towel, flat on his stomach. He looked like a deformed eel, an amorphous mass of lethargy, and Bheem Singh—who enjoyed excellent physical health and was a strapping six foot three vertically and well expanded in the chest—could not help but feel a wave of contempt. Like all rustic men, Bheem Singh counted strength over riches: a good body was the first thing a man should have. But the customer had money and Bheem Singh had talent—so it seemed an acceptable transaction. Bheem Singh knew it was a rare talent that he carried between his fingers. He could massage his customers for hours, removing tension blocks, easing their nerves, and pouring the life back into their tired bones.

He knew his customers enjoyed his massages, though at first they'd haggle over the rates. He'd start by demanding thirty rupees, which would fetch the customer half an hour of *maalish,* not counting a scalp massage. They would try eagerly to bring him down to twenty, argue for a while, and eventually agree to twenty-five. But ten minutes into the *maalish* they'd ask him to take them up for an hour. That's when Bheem Singh would get difficult; he would ask for sixty, and he'd enjoy seeing the customer lose the negotiation. It was clearly a triumph of talent over will, of a pampered body shedding defenses of the mind. At the end of the massage, soothed into a charitable mood, his customers would even part with some extra baksheesh. So it worked well for Bheem Singh: this give-and-take, in this city of cold transactions.

It was Rathod Singh, Bheem Singh's father, who had first drawn attention to Bheem Singh's fingers. The boy was four years old then, and as they negotiated the small grassy pathway on their way to the paddy field his father had observed, "You have strong fingers, Bheem Singh. Like a wrestler. You mark my words. One day, you will hold the world between your fingers."

Promptly Bheem Singh had made it a point to clutch his father's hand tightly. He increased pressure every day, hoping his father would notice that his strength was growing. But Rathod Singh was careful not to comment. He did not wish to give the boy the wrong idea, fill him with undue pride. Rathod Singh knew Bheem would be strong, the strongest in the village perhaps. Wasn't that the reason he had named him after the famous Pandava warrior? Rathod Singh had wished that his elder son, Dalpat Singh, could have been as strong, too. But the boy was a disappointment. At eight, he seemed to prefer the company of girls. Behind the temple, he played hopscotch with them and joined in long, monotonous skipping competitions. Rathod Singh would have thrashed him for that—had the temple priest not intervened.

His *lungi* folded into his crotch, Bheem Singh dropped to his knees, to straddle the customer's prostrate form. With his brawny palms, he clutched at the customer's shoulders; his fingers negotiated the small bullish neck for tension blocks tucked away beneath the dollops of flesh.

Gently Bheem Singh navigated the neck region. He would find

the tension spots sooner or later; the customer's sigh would tell him so. Looking around, he saw other *maalishwallas* absorbed in their work. In the distance, the waves rose and fell, exhaling a faint December wind. The palm trees rustled and bowed deferentially, as though nature endorsed the diligence of man.

Bheem Singh thought of Dalpat as he began the massage. His brother was four years older, but since the time they were children he had relied on Bheem Singh for protection. Dalpat could never gain acceptance among the village boys. He could never take to their rugged activities and win their admiration and friendship. More than once, he had tripped and fallen flat on his face, especially when called upon to prove himself in masculine pursuits that so reliably bonded boys into gangs.

Bheem Singh remembered the time when eight of them had conspired to steal a goat from the old village butcher, Hamid Ali, with the intention of carrying it across the hill, killing it, roasting it, and feasting on it. All had gone as per plan, except that Dalpat had started retching as soon as the knife descended on the bleating neck. While the goat bled, Dalpat turned his insides out, making sounds like he himself was dying. The boys howled with laughter, and later Dalpat had sulked and refused to eat. This ungamely behavior had marred the mood of the occasion, and Dalpat was branded as a weakling, unworthy to be summoned for the next bold rush of adventure. But Bheem was popular. He was liked. And admired. And because the boys wanted his company, they had to include Dalpat, too.

The big test came when Dalpat was fifteen. The boys had planned to tie a rope across the river, linking both sides of the embankment, so that they could shimmy across and spy on girls from the neighboring village, who came there to wash their clothes, their vessels, and themselves. It was young Bheem, fearless as ever, who swam across the swirling waters and tied the rope to a tree on the opposite side. This he did to the cheers of his friends and to anxious protestations from Dalpat, who found it much too risky and not quite right. The boys ignored Dalpat. One by one, they climbed across with the help of the rope. When it was Dalpat's turn, Bheem noticed his brother was trembling.

Halfway through, Dalpat lost his grip. He was swept away by the current, and in an instant the boys could see his face bobbing out of sight—so great was the swell at that point.

Undeterred, Bheem dived in, followed by two other boys. By not fighting the river, as they were taught, but by accepting its natural superiority, the boys had gone after Dalpat, who, after struggling in panic and swallowing huge amounts of water, had given up the fight. Bheem caught up with his brother and, holding on with all the fervency of blood, had dragged him to the shore. There, with one crushing hug, Bheem squeezed the river out of Dalpat's lifeless form.

That night Dalpat broke into a terrible fever. The village *vaid* was called, and he covered the boy with leaves lathered with herbal paste. The family crowded around, while neighbors hung respectfully near the doorway. In other homes, the other participants in the adventure were chastised and even whipped by their fathers. All the boys cursed Dalpat and his weakness. Later they would brand him as a jinx and exile him permanently from their excursions.

After seventeen hours, the fever went down. The village *vaid* checked Dalpat's pulse for what seemed like an infinite amount of time; then he declared the boy was not to work or be exerted in any way. "He has the constitution of a girl in the body of a man," said the *vaid*. The family was to remember that and not coerce Dalpat into any strenuous activity. Carrying weight or working in the fields was out of the question. The boy had a weak heart. It would not stand up to pressure. The *vaid* could tell just by listening to Dalpat's heartbeat. As they heard this, the mother, Lajwanti Singh, raised her hands and thanked the Lord that they had been warned in time. Rathod Singh snorted and walked out of the house. Dalpat, lying in bed, saw his father's disgust. Bheem silently promised himself that he would take his brother's load in the fields. Such was his love for his brother.

After that day, Rathod Singh made no demands on his elder son. Though inwardly he scoffed at the idea of Dalpat not doing his share in the fields, he took care to see that he didn't force him. He gave all his attention to his younger son, who he claimed had been blessed with the strength of ten tigers. Once he told the boys' mother, lying next to him at night, that he knew why God had made Dalpat weak—so that all the strength could go into Bheem. Dalpat heard this and tensed in his bed. He did not sleep all night, wondering if that were true.

That year the Singhs enjoyed a bounteous harvest; they could sell their produce for twice the price expected. Rathod Singh smiled for two months continuously and bragged that even the heavens favored the strong. "It is Bheem's doing," he declared to the farmers who would congregate outside his hut after work. "He is so strong, he virtually forced the gold from inside the earth." Inside the hut, Dalpat heard this. He was proud of his brother but wished he had some of his strength, so he wouldn't be doing what he was doing now: stirring the rice in the pot.

The customer sighed and adjusted himself, and Bheem had to emerge from his reverie. He knew the massage was beginning to work; the muscles were loosening slowly.

Bheem Singh transferred the strength of the massage to four fingers. With the second and third finger of each hand and using his thumbs for a grip, he worked the sides of the neck, just below the earlobes. Then, with his thumbs, he massaged in between the shoulder blades. The customer allowed his body to go limp; in Bheem Singh's hands he sank into a cloud of trust. The palm trees swayed noisily, restlessly, then settled—night watchers once again. Bheem Singh established a rhythm in the massage, then returned to his thoughts.

The father was openly partial to Bheem, but this did not come in between the brothers. They remained as close as ever and shared secrets, all the dreams and heartbreaks of youth. Knowing that his brother lacked status in the family and in the village, Bheem continued to give Dalpat importance, asking him for advice through his growing years. When he decided to take up smoking, Bheem consulted Dalpat on which brand of *beedi* he should try. When, on *holi,* he downed his first jug of *bhang,* he asked Dalpat to keep an eye on him, and when Dalpat told him that he had spent too much time with Kaveri, the weaver's daughter, who had the fairest legs in the village, Bheem confessed to an overwhelming movement in his heart. Dalpat brushed it aside, saying it was the *bhang* making a fool of him. Bheem scratched his head and felt sheepish about it. Dalpat laughed. Lajwanti Singh, who toiled inside the hut, felt buoyant. It was a nice relationship her sons had, despite their father's stubborn ways.

By the time Bheem was in his teens, his strength had become legendary. His accomplishments were many, and the boys in his village looked up to him with undisguised admiration. He took part in all the village games and won unfailingly. He represented the village in inter-village competitions and brought back honor in sports like *kushti* and *kabaddi*. His strength was spoken of far and wide, and once, when a man-eating panther had terrorized the area, it was Bheem who was deputized by the government to lead the team of trackers. How they got to know about him and his strength was anybody's guess.

When the government team killed the panther and brought it back to the village, a special photograph was arranged. Bheem Singh was allowed to sit in with the officials who posed with the beast at their feet. That evening Dalpat Singh arranged a small celebration in the village square: a song and dance and joke-trading session between the younger boys and girls, after which he served steaming hot *khichda,* which he had made himself.

Intoxicated by his younger son's bravery, Rathod Singh drank more freely than he usually did. Then he joked publicly that at least his elder son, Dalpat, would make a good wife for someone. His friends—as drunk as him—roared with laughter; they bellowed with manly contempt. Dalpat, within earshot, felt an uncanny chill in his heart; his hand trembled while he served the *khichda*.

"Back! Now move to the back," directed the customer, pleased at the attention Bheem had given his neck and shoulders but worried that the other body parts would not get their dues. Obediently Bheem Singh shifted his attention. Placing his hands symmetrically across the spine, he pushed down, so that the entangled muscles went *crack*. The customer groaned, but almost at once a sinuous feeling of relaxation spread through his back. This *maalishwalla* knows what he is doing, thought the customer. What a gift he has. His thumbs pressed together, Bheem Singh started manipulating the customer's spine. The customer shut his eyes and slept.

This was important, this spine kneading. So Bheem Singh concentrated on it for a while. His work gave him pleasure, that he knew, but how he hated sharing his earnings with the *policewalla*. Especially the one on duty these days. He was the worst Bheem Singh had ever met. He humiliated the *maalishwallas,* called them *laundebaaz,* meaning "homosexuals." Not that they were all this way, thought Bheem Singh. He knew there were some who did offer extended services under cover of the night, but to brand them all was cruel and meaningless. The *policewalla* had a habit of coming up and prodding the *maalishwallas* with his stick. He would prod them in places of great irritation—like behind the ear, or in the soft part of the neck, or on their outstretched soles as they kneeled beside their customers. For Bheem, it was very hard to control his temper, but he knew that the consequences of such an outburst would be disastrous.

He worked on the spine for a while and then began to crush down on the muscles at the side. Not too much pressure, just enough to loosen up the back and ready it for a fresh routine of work. The customer slept on, a transient sleep, induced by those big, pampering hands. The smile on his face came from knowing that Bheem was applying the right amount of pressure. In the distance, the waves beat down on the beach. Thin, gray clouds moved overhead, eclipsing the moon. The *maalishwallas* plodded away, some silent, some jabbering, some throwing sneaky looks over their shoulders. Bheem Singh looked up at the sky. He wondered if he had spent too much time on this one customer. Maybe he needed to hurry up a bit.

The next phase of the massage was easy. The legs could be dealt with mechanically, because they seldom took on tension blocks. Bheem Singh began working on them, with a series of slaps, aimed and distributed over the sides of the thighs. Thin, weakened thighs, thought Bheem Singh. How could they be carrying the weight of that distorted body, that sagging stomach, and that heavy wallet? He was tempted to slap them hard, just to make his customer squeal, but he resisted the temptation. He knew if he took a little care there might be some extra baksheesh waiting.

On reflex, his hand touched the side of his *lungi,* where he felt something crisp. He compared the feeling of a few solitary ten-rupee notes to the wad his customer carried. Yet he felt good, for he knew that all his savings were lying safe in a bank account, and just that day he had made sure that his bank in Bombay would credit his bank in Isthaanpur, so that his family could withdraw money whenever they wanted. When the bank had asked him to name two family members who would have access to his money, Bheem found himself in a quandary. He wanted to name his mother, because she had brought him up and she always complained that Rathod Singh never gave her enough to run the house. He wanted to name Rathod Singh, because it would make his father proud, but he knew that owing to the same pride, his father would never touch the money. He wanted to name Dalpat, but Dalpat had no use for it. Well, that left only Kaveri—his beautiful, beautiful Kaveri, so teasing with her innocence, so childlike, pretty, and defenseless.

His arms would tremble with passion each time he held her, her soft molten form exuding small breaths of warmth in his embrace. And his heart—it would swell with burgeoning pride when he clasped her head against his chest. Yes, she would be the ideal beneficiary for his savings. Kaveri, his heart, his soul, his new bride, who made him forget he was big, dark, and clumsy. Bheem Singh's heart ached for her now, and he wondered when he would see her next.

Before his thoughts could return to his last trip home, during which he had married Kaveri, Bheem took the customer's right leg and placed it across his own shoulder. He began kneading the calves, to ease the tangle of nerves and send waves of pleasure and relaxation down to the feet. Knowing that this would take a few minutes, he allowed himself the luxury of a daydream. The dream within the dream, which had brought home his beloved Kaveri—to him, for life!

During that last trip home, so much had happened, in such a short time. He had arrived in Isthaanpur with gifts and stories, warm bear hugs, and loads of buttoned-up laughter, and they had indulged him for one night only. The next day, they broke the news. There was a proposal—from the weaver's side. It seemed the weaver had tried to get Kaveri married to Kalyan Singh, who kept accounts at the ration shop and who was in a position to favor them with more than their share of monthly rations. But the girl had kicked up a fuss. She had not eaten for two days and turned a deadly pale, till the father had to plead, persuade, and probe her state of mind. He asked her what she really wanted, if not marriage to Kalyan Singh. And bright-eyed and unflinching, as if returned to life by the very thought, she had mentioned Bheem, a childhood fondness for him.

The weaver had not found the idea objectionable. He liked Bheem and admired his strength greatly. He found Bheem to be one of those sensible men who had the courage to break away from the village and set themselves up in the city—where, eventually, they would make more money. Heartened by this thought, the weaver carried a proposal to Rathod Singh, his only condition being that the marriage should take place as soon as Bheem Singh returned home. It was not correct for a girl of Kaveri's age to remain single for another year.

When Bheem heard this, a fierce joy broke inside him. He went weak with happiness. How was it possible? he thought. Fair, fragile Kaveri wanting him, Bheem, who was so plain and dark? He did not voice his doubts—not to his parents, nor to Dalpat. All had been decided. He wasn't to say no. Good days were around the corner. The timing was perfect—otherwise a whole year would be wasted. Of course, after marriage Kaveri would stay in the village and help Bheem's mother with the housework. Dalpat, unlike during his early years, wasn't much help now. He had become lazy and indifferent, rendered so by his own inadequacies and by a biting bitterness about his ineffectiveness. Even Rathod Singh had given up on him and spared him his vituperations. It was just as well he had never maintained any ambitions about his elder son. It was his young tiger who did him proud.

In a daze, Bheem Singh had agreed to the proposal. He met Kaveri twice after that, and both times she had blushed and scurried away. Bheem knew it was her innocence that gave her flight, her silent admiration of him that took her to a safe distance from where she could watch.

Until the wedding Bheem walked, lived, and slept on a cloud. Nothing dampened his happiness. Not even the suspicion that Dalpat spent wasteful mornings at the local bar instead of spending time with him. His elder brother had not congratulated him, or teased him, or showered him with words of advice, as would have been expected. Nor had he shown any interest in the wedding arrangements. Instead, he seemed to remain in a sullen, inebriated state. Nothing noisy or offensive, just detached, inward, and brooding. Bheem wondered whether he should speak to Dalpat about it, but then it was the world that had made his brother this way. His father's scorn, his mother's overprotectiveness, the narrow-mindedness of the villagers, the contempt of the village girls, who, having been his playmates in childhood, called him bangle-boy, meaning effeminate. All this had twisted Dalpat's mind, angered him, led him to drink. If ever a brother understood his sibling's state of mind, it was Bheem's reading of Dalpat—his insecurities, his regrets, that had made him the way he was.

Bheem wasn't allowed to see Kaveri before the marriage. The elders didn't think it necessary. He saw her directly at the ceremony, and all through the rituals she refused to look at him. She stayed that way, hidden in her sari, which covered her face and veiled her shyness, and Bheem kept staring at her feet. How exquisite they were! And how fair! He wondered if she would mind if he held them to his lips. The thought made him glow with anticipation, and he quivered in a boyish sort of way.

His mind possessed with such thoughts, Bheem had gone through the ceremony in a trance. He didn't hear the priest's good counsel, traditional words of advice for a long-lasting marriage, nor did he hear his father's drunken laughter echoing through the celebration, nor the weaver's bragging about his son-in-law's strength. He missed the fact that Dalpat was absent at dinner.

That night Bheem Singh felt proud, privileged, and successful, and he smiled the largest smile of his life. Three hours later, when he crawled into bed, his large hands trembled as they reached for his wife's delicate feet. He raised them to his lips in an admission of surrender, and in that moment his soul left his physical body and it soared higher than a kite in a gale.

The waves on the beach had turned louder and noisier, and Bheem knew that it was high tide. It was surprising that the *policewalla* had not come around yet. Maybe he had found a new scapegoat, or maybe he was ill. Bheem Singh savored the thought as he lifted the customer's left leg and went to work on the sole, the last lap of the *maalish*.

In small circular motions, Bheem Singh began rubbing the foot. The customer slept on, oblivious to the swell of the sea, the waves thrashing their fury against the sparsely populated beach. Bheem looked up and saw a movement behind a tree: a couple struggling, grappling with each other. Bheem recognized it as a paid rendezvous, one of the many the beach was notorious for. The man was wanting more than what the open space could afford; the woman was struggling to fend him off. Bheem Singh saw her recoil. She came into sight, and he noticed she was young: barely eighteen or nineteen. Bheem shivered when he saw how fragile she was, how ineffectual against the man, who was holding her, pulling her, relishing his own strength and her captivity.

A dark uneasiness shot through Bheem Singh's spine. He felt cold. His hands trembled, and with great effort he regained possession of himself.

As he absentmindedly rubbed the foot of his customer, Bheem Singh's mind went back to Kaveri. To her feet: young and healthy. At first, when his lips had grazed her toes, they had curled with shyness. Then, slowly, they had relaxed, opening up to meet his kisses, his lips trying to find a hundred spots for devotion. Kaveri had not seemed to mind this adulation. It gave her joy, he could tell. By the way she looked at him. By the way she clutched at the bedsheet, with childlike hands and gleaming white knuckles.

Bheem Singh's simple act of devotion had served to reassure his bride that her colossus of a husband meant well. She had lost her inhibitions, her fears, her shyness, and that night, as one experimental touch led to another, the two came closer and closer. The girl gave herself to the man, and the man gave the full force of his tenderness to her, and he swore utmost devotion when all the energy in him flowed out into her. Bheem Singh felt blessed and heavenly, holding his bride while she slept. He watched the rise and fall of her breath and lay beside her, still as a leaf on a pond on a windless night. He did not move, even when he felt a mosquito sit on his naked arm, even when he felt a piercing prick and a burning scratchiness thereafter.

Bheem had stayed awake through the length of his wedding night. His eyes were wide-open with revelation and feeling, and his mind swam with thoughts of deep intensity. As dawn broke, he felt a sense of deprivation and fear, and he stayed rooted to Kaveri, who slept contentedly in his arms. Unlike him, she did not seem to fear the fact that this would be their first and last night together till Bheem returned to the village again—which would be next year. Yes, Bheem was scheduled to return the next day, and he hated the thought. Back to Bombay—the city of dark realism, of lonely, self-preserving nights and hot, oppressive days. Bheem refused to wake up, even when sounds from outside the curtained partition told him that the rest of the household were up and about their duties.

"No, behave yourself. Maintain a little shame at least." These words came from the girl under the tree. She was trying to fend off the demands of the man who had paid for her time. It broke through Bheem's daydream and brought back his panic. He wiped his brow, which was cold and moist, and ran his tongue over his lips, which had gone dry. The struggle intensified. The girl delivered a series of slaps to the man's hand. The man laughed, unaffected.

Bheem Singh felt a wave of fury against the man. How dare he force himself on the girl—so what if she was hired? Bheem Singh's hands shook with rage. His fingers dug savagely into the sole of the foot he was rubbing. The customer winced sharply, turned, and cursed him. Bheem Singh ignored him, keeping his eyes on the scene ahead. The customer raised his head to see what had distracted the *maalishwalla*. He saw the struggle, poohed his disgust, and went back to sleep. Bheem looked at his customer and felt sick. How could people be so blind? he thought. Here was a girl being molested in the open. Yet there was no one to stand by her. Not even he, Bheem Singh Bahadur, who was so worried about abandoning his work, lest he lose the money that was owed to him.

For a wild moment, Bheem Singh contemplated extracting a few notes from the customer's wallet, from the trousers lying at his side.

Bheem Singh could then save the girl from the man and give her the money, which she probably needed desperately. That was foolish, he realized, almost as soon as he thought of it. His customer would notice the theft when he paid him, and then there would be trouble. The head *maalishwalla* would expel him instantly.

Maybe he would just finish the massage, walk across, and give the man a hiding. He would shake him by the neck or catch him by midriff and squeeze the life out of him. Men like that deserved to have the life squeezed out of them, slowly—till they lived no more.

Bheem Singh turned the thought in his mind, over and over again, and he felt a huge relief. Ah, if only it were possible to let his hands speak—how effective that would be, how easy and instantaneous. He looked at the foot in his hands and almost gave a snort of contempt. How tempting it was to turn it, to snap the ankle abruptly—just to see this lazy, deformed creature squirm and howl in anguish. He looked ahead, to the side, where the girl had ceased struggling; she stood limp against her oppressor, while his hands navigated all over. On him—the oppressor—Bheem would use his hands slowly, and he'd watch, while the life hissed out of him, while his expression changed, and his body would slump to the ground, drained off its evil purpose. How grateful the girl would be. How eternally grateful!

But that wouldn't take away all the anger he felt, Bheem Singh thought. How could it? There was still so much injustice in this world, so much of accepted, accumulated tragedy. The worst was at home—in his village, his own family. Dalpat, casting eyes on Kaveri, just before Bheem Singh left. It was as if his elder brother wanted to show some foul intention. But no, he wouldn't! Surely he would re-member what they'd shared, those years of brotherhood, those days of closeness, and, if not that, then surely the swell in the river, the sweep of panic, the hand of death circling, and then Bheem's hand, a master-ful grip dragging him to safety.

But now it wasn't about hands anymore, or about courage, or about gratitude. It was pure custom, cold custom that allowed the elder brother to share the conjugal rights of the younger. That was how it had been for centuries, and no one was allowed to question it, let alone speak of it.

A gust of wind rose from the sea. It carried a little sand and scattered it into Bheem Singh's face and eyes. It stung and blinded him, making him wince, making him feel assaulted by a force he did not know. Bheem paused from the *maalish* and flexed the skin above and below his eyes. Upward and downward he rubbed and, feeling better for it, resumed what he was doing—bringing life to the crisp, deadened heel.

His mind returned to Dalpat. Surely he would remember how Bheem had stood by him, protected him, chasing away all those who teased him, so that they might leave him alone. Surely Dalpat would remember all that and the respect that Bheem had shown him—as much as any younger brother would show his elder brother. And when he'd remember that, surely Dalpat would blush with shame, he would stop right there, outside the curtained partition, and he would decide to leave Kaveri alone.

But, then, the question was (and this dawned on Bheem Singh slowly): did Dalpat respect himself anymore? Did he see himself as worthy, capable of noble thought and action? Or was he so steeped in humiliation, so doomed and denied that anything might appear a triumph over a lifetime of deprivation? And, as Bheem licked the bitter salt air off his lips, he realized why Dalpat had stayed aloof at the celebrations, why he was not his usual self with Bheem. It was not the liquor demon that stood between them but the demon of wretched tradition.

Sadly Bheem Singh replaced the customer's foot on the ground. He remained seated while the customer rose, swiveling his arms back and forth, back and forth, in a show of restored energy, his belly quivering impudently at the ocean. As expected, the customer paid Bheem Singh his full sixty rupees, and as a mark of respect to his talent, he dug into his pocket, fished out a five-rupee coin, and threw it at Bheem Singh, saying, "Baksheesh." Yet Bheem Singh sat unmoved. He did not bat an eyelid when the customer cursed him for his ingratitude. He just sat there, hearing the *boom-boom* of the ocean echoing unbearably in his heart and mind and sometimes deep within his stomach.

Bheem Singh did not know how long he sat like that, his eyes riveted on the waves rushing in and swallowing the beach bit by bit. He did not notice when the oppressor and the girl finished their business and moved away, or when a fleet of dark swollen clouds moved in and blanked out the stars. If he had looked behind him, he would have seen what was happening at the edge of the beach, where it met the city. He would have seen the head *maalishwalla* in conversation with a police inspector, who stood next to his jeep, flanked by two constables. He would have seen the officer give instructions to the head *maalishwalla,* who listened intently, nodding from time to time. He would have seen the inspector get into his jeep and drive off, leaving the head *maalishwalla* staring in disbelief, in confusion—and the head *maalishwalla* walk back, his feet dragging in the sand like they were sinking, like it was wet sand he was walking on. But Bheem Singh didn't see that. He only saw the dark of a horizon he couldn't fathom, the gloom of a night that had settled on his neck, his shoulders, his lithe, muscular spine.

A little later, a constable came around for *hafta;* he crept in on him as usual and tapped him with his *lathi.* Bheem Singh dug into his pocket, fished out the coin, and gave it to the constable. He felt no resentment when he did that, for—this is what he thought—what did it matter what he gave away when what really mattered would not remain his? The *lathi* creeping up reminded him of life. Just when you thought you had a little extra in hand, something to celebrate, to look forward to, you had to pay up.

Stretching out, he lay on his back. The sand felt cool and moist. He looked up at the dark, inky sky, which appeared to be parting slowly, layers of cloud moving aside to reveal deeper shades of darkness. Over the ocean, a lone star shone brightly; it appeared to be winking at Bheem Singh. He looked at it for a while, then shut his eyes firmly. Too much light could dazzle; it could fascinate and fool. Bheem lay like that, listening to the sound of his heart, the blood pounding at his temples, the ocean below, when he felt the presence of people surrounding him and watching. He opened his eyes to the sight of the head *maalishwalla* standing over him, and behind him were the other *maalishwallas* looking so tensed and worried. Bheem Singh sprang to his feet. If there was trouble, he'd better—

The head *maalishwalla* stepped forward and placed a hand on Bheem Singh's shoulder. It was a heavy hand, trying to be gentle. He looked at Bheem Singh with wet, searching eyes and spoke slowly and softly, a faint quiver in his voice: "I have news for you Bheem Singh. Bad, bad news. There is a garden coming up here at Chowpatty. The whole place is going to change. The trees are going to go. The food stalls are going to be moved. We, too, have been asked to go, as soon as possible. You will have to look for something new—maybe here, or maybe in your village."

THIS HOUSE OF MINE

✦ ✦ ✦

WHEN YOU'VE LIVED IN A HOUSE as long as I have, which is forty-odd years and some months, when you've laughed and sulked in every nook and corner, when you have looked out of its windows and seen the shingled roofs, the trees, and the cool, blue clouds drifting by like giant spaceships, when you've seen migratory birds come and park their colorful plumage on your windowsill, the songs in their hearts breaking loose over the sounds of city traffic, when you've skipped down its stairs, slid down its banisters, and leaned long enough from its balconies to catch a glimpse of passing cleavage, when you have rung the doorbells of old neighbors (long dead now) and fled, not waiting to hear them open their doors and grumble, "Oh, it's that *badmash* again; wait till we catch him," when you've kissed girls as curiously impatient as you, on the stairs, in your teenage years, for no other reason than the excitement of risky exploration, when you have dragged yourself up the same stairs, in the dark, confident not of the booze raging in your system but of the floor space you have navigated, when—in your later years—you have run up on your toes, purposefully, as a daily routine, to keep those seafood dinners from turning into arterial blocks in your heart, when you've done all this and more, and have done it in some strange way or another for forty-odd years and ten months, and when, on the third day of that tenth month, you get a notice from the housing board saying that your building is endangered, it is no longer safe to house you, then you know by the lurch in your heart that you haven't just lived in the house: the house has lived in you.

This is how I found myself thinking, on the third of October, the day the notice was sent to us and the neighbors began to pour in for advice and for resolution. They came one by one. First, the shopkeepers from the ground floor: Dinanath, Master of the Stores, potbellied owner of four proud shops, including the *kirana* shop that had earned him the other three shops; he was followed by his son, Gopinath, a pleasant-faced youth of twenty, wearing a white *churidaar* and a brown *khadi* jacket, smiling with the tranquility of one whose father has saved enough for him, he didn't need to slave for his daily bread; behind them was Ram Dulari, the plump-faced, bushy-whiskered milkman, now the owner of a sparkling new snack bar at the entrance; then the goldsmith, in his *lungi;* the flower vendor, in his undershirt and trousers; the tailor, in impeccable clothes, a walking advertisement for himself; the cloth merchant, fat and slovenly, who was always trying to proposition the woman who sold plastic household articles on the pavement. They crowded my doorstep shyly and insisted on leaving their footwear outside as a mark of respect. Making a garrulous entry was the owner of the math class on the ground floor: Professor Girish Kodial, young, suave, energetic, in his late thirties, who at once started talking about his trips abroad, his affiliations with universities there, and the affluence of his students here, whom he helped get overseas for a fat fee. His students would bring back degrees that might not get them coveted jobs but would certainly increase their value in the marriage market.

"See where math has taken me," Professor Kodial said excitedly, spontaneously, in a manner typical of a man of success. "It has placed me in a win-win situation. I make money from both ends—from rich students who can't get into institutions here and from universities that are not all that highly rated. I must confess, math has taught me to make the right calculations in life, taught me that one plus one need not amount to two. It can amount to four, though." He laughed. Then, for the umpteenth time, he said to me, "I want to come and sit with you one day. I want to see if we can do something together.

Math and literature can surely coexist. These non-applicable sciences can earn for us."

"Literature is not a science, but an art," I wanted to tell him coldly. "An art you can apply to life." But I didn't say that. I remembered I was the host. "Interesting thought," I said, and shut up.

Unable to understand our flow of English, the shopkeepers waited with bright, expectant faces, ready to take instruction, ready to be led and advised, in a language they could comprehend, which was to say Hindi or Gujarati. Out of shyness, they kept standing, even when my wife pointed politely to the plastic chairs and stools she had rented. She didn't want them sitting on her sofas, she had said to me earlier. She didn't want the sweat of these locals to get into her upholstery. She'd smell it for days, she'd said, twitching her nose disdainfully.

Soon after entered my residential neighbors: Olga Castellino, the Goan woman from the first floor, who would rave and rant at her husband, Olaf, when he went out shopping for sausages and came back instead red faced and happy, spiritedly whistling the songs of his youth; Olaf himself, bleary-eyed and disheveled, his shirt buttons open to his navel, his belly spilling out stodgily, Olaf in shorts and *chappals,* with frail, smooth legs, the looks of one who had long retired from work, who would rather be in Goa, breeding pigs and brewing his own liquor; Sohrab, the Parsi misanthrope from the second floor, tall, bent, with dark circles under his eyes from smoking too much pot through the day and mulling over too many regrets in life, while his wife, the pert-faced Angelina, worked out the whole day in front of the television set, listening to MTV or to a yoga instructor advocating poses of the body for fine, eternal health, Angelina, who made it a point to open the door to vendors, wearing nothing but skimpy shorts, who would address them in a haughty, delicate accent, just to make it clear that she didn't belong here, she belonged actually to a superior neighborhood, she was here purely by accident, purely by chance; Murad, the guy from the third floor, who worked as a clerk in a shipping company and, who, at least once a week had a fistfight with his younger brother, Nazir, now Nazarana, a friendly-faced homosexual who had recently stepped out of the closet, had done so by bringing home a boyfriend and announcing that a union, not a marriage, was in the cards and that anybody opposed to it could suck his you-know-what. Murad's wife was Farhana, a short, stout woman with stumplike legs and a sullen, withdrawn face. She was unfriendly, said hello only when she had to and mostly when she was alone, presumably because Murad didn't like her speaking to other men. I gathered Farhana didn't like her brother-in-law; she saw him as an impediment to them claiming ownership of the flat, long-standing tenants having that kind of right, here, in Bombay. She also saw Nazarana as an embarrassment. His effeminate ways were tough to explain to friends, relatives, and visiting clerics, let alone neighbors.

A motley crowd filled my living room that day—some sat on chairs; some kept standing. The shopkeepers sat after much coaxing; a humble lot they were. Looking at them, I saw we had nothing in common, not the same backgrounds, not the same Gods, not the same sense of dress or interests. And yet we were all neighbors, and we had a crisis that threatened to send us packing, to eject us from the comfort of a well-preserved life into the arms of an uncertain future.

I began by reading, then translating for the benefit of the shopkeepers, the eviction notice. Our building was among those slated for redevelopment. It had been examined, it had been inspected, and it had been condemned. We had a month to move to a new address: to a transit camp in Powai, miles from where we were.

"Is the landlord coming? Has he been informed?" asked the tailor, in Hindi.

"No," said Dinanath. "He went through an operation, a hip bone replacement, last week. He's in bed; he can't even walk." Dinanath knew this because he handled the rent receipts for the landlord, who stayed at Altamount Road, in a quiet leafy lane that exuded upper-crust elegance. The landlord had long back foreseen the deterioration of our neighborhood: the thickening of traffic, the escalation of noise, the density of vehicle fumes, the smell of hawkers cooking on pavements, and the proliferation of open-air urinals that had us holding our noses and running past certain parts of the street.

We discussed the notice. Our building was old but sturdy. There had been no tremors, no parts of it falling or crumbling—so where did this threat of eviction come from? Despite our varying backgrounds, we realized we had one thing in common—our fear of the unknown. Our fear of a government entity, which, as per the newspapers, had the best of intentions, but which remained just that: intentions. In a country of over 1 billion, it was easy to be moved and forgotten. There were several stories to this effect. Angelina took pride in narrating one about an aunt of hers, whose building at Byculla was declared endangered, and they had moved to Gorai, across the bay, and twenty-two years later they were still there. Angelina's uncle had passed away; her aunt had stopped working; her cousins, now in their twenties, had become fishermen, as they couldn't afford to go to college all the way from Gorai.

"*Arrey,* damn good," said Nazarana, grinning. "Now we can get fish at a discount."

"Well, they are distant cousins," said Angelina quickly. "But let me speak to my other cousin, Denzil, who is like a brother to me. He is a lawyer in the High Court, and very influential. He will know what to do about this notice." She began dialing on her cell phone, pacing at the same time. The shopkeepers looked impressed. Angelina *had* managed to convince them she was a product of high society. She was someone to be counted on, looked up to. A crisis of this nature was an excellent opportunity to reinforce that impression.

"That won't help," said Professor Kodial, smiling. "The best thing is to get the eviction notice changed. We can do so by shelling out some of this." He rubbed his fingers to imply money. We nodded. We knew he was right. He, after all, ran a flourishing business out of a residential flat. It must have taken some knowledge to get that fixed.

After a while, my wife served tea in paper cups. The paper was her idea, as she said we didn't know our neighbors' habits of hygiene. We didn't know where they ate, what sort of ailments they had. In this day and age of infections like hepatitis B and bird flu you couldn't afford to take chances.

While the neighbors sipped their tea and discussed—some in English, some in Hindi, and all in an excited babble—what should be the course of action, Olaf got to his feet and proclaimed, "Over my dead body will we go. Let's take on those bloody bulldozers. Let's show them." He said he knew activists in Andheri and Malad who had stood up to the demolitions. He would contact them, collaborate with them, show these bloody buggers just who they were messing with. Not for nothing had he played hockey for his club, and when some *ghatti* buggers had tried to force their way into the club premises he had wielded his hockey stick like a nunchaku and scared the hell out of them. That was thirty years ago, but if need be he could repeat the performance. He flexed his chest and shoulders and swung his arms. He staggered and almost fell. The flower vendor steadied him in time, helped him to sit down. Olga remarked wryly that he would first have to learn to stand upright without his morning peg. "What you mean?" Olaf said, rising again. "I can't face these bloody *ghatti* fuckers? Bloody . . . I will make them remember their mothers." We had to politely remind Olaf that most of the shopkeepers were also *ghattis*. We didn't want to risk offending them.

We agreed to visit the housing board the next day. We would go there in person, all of us. Murad pleaded his inability to join in. They were short staffed at work; he couldn't take a day off. We said that was fine; one person less wouldn't make a difference. Nazarana piped in and said *she* would be glad to represent the family. Everyone smiled. Murad glared at him. Farhana looked at him with loathing. Professor Kodial suggested we get an independent engineer to evaluate the building. The professor had a friend who was a builder; he would request him to send over one of his men. Dinanath said that might not be a good idea. The housing board officials might take offense; they would think we were challenging their authority. They could make life difficult for us and ours was an old building, so why upset them? Why take chances? Professor Kodial agreed with Dinanath. In any government interaction it was diplomacy that won the day. He said this as a caution to the women, so they wouldn't say something awkward at the board office. Angelina drew herself up. "Well, if you need Denzil's advice, let me know. He will do anything for me."

✦   ✦   ✦

THE HOUSING BOARD WAS SITUATED in an old building at Worli. The building had a dusty yard and two entrances: one in front, one at the back. There were scooters and motorcycles parked in front and cars at the back. Without looking up from his newspaper, the *chowkidar* at the gate gesticulated for us to go to the back entrance.

"How, sahib, how will we manage?" we asked an official to whose office we were directed. "We have our work here, our lives here. Our children go to schools here. What will we do in Powai? How will we commute from there daily?"

Sohrab, the pothead, spoke. "I have an elderly mother and an eighty-year-old aunt who I am looking after. They both need constant medical attention and their doctors and hospitals are in this area." He paused. His grief seemed real. He looked terribly deprived, I thought, probably because he was compelled to do without his morning smoke. Angelina would have made sure of that. And, just for the record, there was no mother and no aunt. They had passed away two years ago. All the official had to do was check his records. I don't think Sohrab realized that.

The official was a bland-faced fellow with a mop of gray hair, a trace of a mustache, and a small, round mouth that protruded. His eyes were small and impassive; they flickered restlessly. He looked rather young to be in charge of something as significant as evictions. He looked around distractedly, as though expecting someone more important than us.

Finally, he spoke. "That is the problem with these old buildings and this old system of rents. The rents are so low that your landlords cannot maintain your buildings. The buildings deteriorate and you, the tenants, do nothing about them until they become unlivable. In your case, our civil engineer has found the back portion of your building weak. It can collapse anytime. So we will have to repair it, and you all will have to move out until we do so."

"How long will the repairs take?" asked the tailor politely.

"Who knows?" said the official, leaning back in his chair, bringing his hands behind his head. "We cannot commit till we have broken down the entire back side. The demolition is handled by one department, the reconstruction by another. Each department has its own method and backlog. Who can say how long these things take?" He shrugged and looked away.

"Sahib." I coughed. "Is there some way we can do this? We have seen buildings with supports, railings, beams . . . and the residents continue to live there, while the repairs are going on."

We waited. We nudged ourselves and stopped breathing. Well, almost.

Dinanath pushed ahead, "Sahib, see what you can do. Everything is in your hands, we know."

Sohrab sniffed, once, twice. His nose was running. He looked afflicted. Without the warmth of his smoke, his sinuses were acting up.

Ram Dulari spoke. In his lowest voice he said he had just spent a fortune on doing up his shop—on converting it from a dairy to a snack bar. The move to Powai could put him out of business. How could he start afresh when he had a bank loan and installments to pay every month? Besides, what would happen to the interiors he had spent on so lavishly? He would be ruined.

The goldsmith said the wedding season was around the corner; he would lose out on orders. He had tears in his eyes, this man of indefatigable artistry, who listened to old Hindi songs on his transistor while he chipped away at his rings, earrings, bracelets, and pendants.

The tailor said he, too, would suffer if he wasn't in his shop during the wedding season. His customers would go elsewhere. That would be the end of his livelihood.

The official looked at them blankly. Below the desk, his one leg quivered impatiently.

"Ha, you think you are the only ones with problems? You know how much of a problem it is for us if your building collapses? Then everyone will come to catch our necks. No one will say we have obliged you. They will all say we have failed in our duty. No, it is better you move to Powai. We have a nice transit camp there. Nice greenery. Nice silence. Hundreds live there. They, too, had to adjust when they first went there. And so will you. It is just a matter of getting used to it. Powai is an upcoming area, so you can start a new business there. Food is good business. People feel hungry all the time." He looked at us and smiled. Beneath the smile, we could see his hunger.

Dinanath took the lead. "Sahib, do something," he said. "It is in your hands. Please advise. Please help. We are small traders. We cannot afford to start again."

Angelina thrust herself forward. "Please, sir, *oblige karo na?*" she said, in a slow, anglicized drawl. "I have already paid a big advance for my jazz ballet classes. That will all go to waste."

The official looked her up and down. His mouth was open. His eyes were still. Sohrab could see what he was thinking. Hurriedly Sohrab pulled his wife back.

Professor Kodial stepped forward. He said that perhaps the building had been inspected by some junior engineer who wasn't *so* experienced. Maybe if a senior engineer was to come by, he would get a different perspective. His findings might not be so severe. The professor looked at the official and smiled. "Surely, sir, you can recommend someone. We will be glad to leave the matter in your hands. And if there are any conditions to make the building safer, we will observe them." He locked eyes with the official, who nodded. We understood and trooped out quietly, while Professor Kodial extracted a thick brown envelope from his pocket.

WITHIN A WEEK WE GOT a notice saying that the eviction notice was canceled. The board had reevaluated our case, found the back portion could be reinforced without us needing to evacuate. Of course, they would have to place extra beams and supports. Additional beams of reinforced wood. The repairs would have to be rushed, in order to make the building safe for the monsoons.

The cost of the bribe was borne by Professor Kodial. When we asked him the amount and whether we could share it equally, he said not to bother: "It's the least I can do for our building. The land has given me so much." The shopkeepers looked at him with respect.

They made up their minds they'd no longer complain when his students crowded the entrance, when they ate their potato chips and crushed and left the empty packs on the stairs. His was true education, they thought. One that prepared man to protect himself against the system, taught him how to work the system inside out and win.

Olaf thought differently. "Why you bloody played into his hands, man, bugger?" he said to the professor after we left the housing board office. "These officials are dirty fellows. You can see it from their faces. Once you give in, they will come back. They are shameless, like beggars."

The professor smiled and proceeded to share with us what he knew about transit camps. Poor construction, cramped spaces, common bathrooms and toilets, and regular instances of theft. Besides, many of the rooms had been rented out unofficially to locals, and among these were goons who presided and collected protection money every month.

"*Cha,* what fellows, men," said Olaf with disgust. "Now, in the old days . . ." His voice tapered off. It was too hot for nostalgia, and besides, his throat was parched.

Ram Dulari sidled up to the professor and asked whether he could pay a small amount to the officials just to ensure there was no damage to his interiors during the repairs. The professor said he would think about it; we should be careful not to spoil them. Ram Dulari smiled and nodded gratefully. This math was interesting, he thought. It was easy to learn, and easier to practice.

THE REPAIR TEAM ARRIVED the day after we had signed the papers for them to get started. They drove beams through the building— through every floor, every apartment, through the stairway, all the way up to the terrace. They covered the exterior of the building, top to bottom, with long tarpaulins, which blocked out the air and the sunlight. They did this to ensure the debris wouldn't fall onto passersby below or onto the traffic.

Thirty to forty men worked away with hammers and chisels. They made gaps in the walls and in the ceilings and then filled those with cement. There was dust and rubble everywhere, and noise and dark-ness. A tall man in a white shirt and white trousers, wearing white shoes and swinging a gold chain in his hand, went from house to house introducing himself as Jayeshbhai Chokhani. He said he was the contractor appointed by the housing board to repair the building, and since his job was to keep us safe, he advised us not to venture to the back side. He said he hoped we would make his job easier by staying clear of the endangered area. Just to make sure, his men cordoned off the back with wooden boards. So, we could see nothing: no sacks of cement or workers going there. We could hear nothing: no sounds of breakage or the scraping of cement. The goldsmith—who used to live in his own shop and bathe and use the toilet at the back—made a deal with Olga Castellino. He agreed to redesign her mother's jewelry free of cost in ex-change for her letting him use their bath and toilet. Later Olga discov-ered some of her jewelry missing. She thought it was he who had swiped them. But no, Olaf looked unusually upbeat and cheerful. He had begun to whistle tunes like "Speedy Gonzales." He also claimed he had been lucky at *matka* daily. But that was too much to believe if you knew Olaf's luck.

For six months we lived in total gloom. There were times when the buildup of confined energy was too much to handle; we had to run out of our flats, onto the street below, just to take in a lungful of fresh air. Olaf, given to the sweats, started walking around naked. Olga swore she'd invite Nazarana home for plum cake if he didn't dress properly. She swore she would do it unexpectedly, without telling him, and Olaf promptly went back to his loose shirts and his bright spotted cotton shorts. He inferred there was nothing that would keep a woman happy. Nothing a man could do of his own free will.

Sohrab found his own way to deal with the noise and the darkness. He just mixed some more stash into his joints and said that he had risen above the problem. Angelina switched to the meditation channel and said it didn't matter to her; she had achieved perfect mind control.

Dinanath brought out his wares onto the streets, on mobile carts, from where he continued to sell, continued to do good business. Cleverly he painted the names of his shops onto the tarpaulin behind, his logos bigger and bolder than ever. When any municipality official questioned Dinanath about his encroachment onto the street, he gave the official free provisions and a small tip to look the other way.

True to our word, none of us ventured out back. At one point, all the workers flocked to the terrace and they chipped and hammered at the flooring and removed the mosaic waterproofing. It was imported mosaic, eighty years old, the kind you wouldn't get these days, the kind that had stood up to the Bombay rains for eighty years and that I believe had an excellent resale value in the market. The repair team replaced this precious mosaic with a light terra-cotta layer that, we suspected, would heat up the terrace in the summer. They left, after taking our signatures, saying the building was now safe. The amount spent on repairs would be added to our rent as a monthly surcharge. There was no mention for how long, how many months and years we would have to pay the additional amount. Come to think of it, they had failed to provide us an estimate for the repairs, and we had forgotten to ask for it—so glad we were not to have been evicted.

Two days after the repair team left, we all met and flocked to the back side. What we saw was some shoddy patchwork, looking like a map of the world where the continents had broken away from one another. Different worlds evident to different eyes. And each fairly unrecognizable.

SIX MONTHS LATER, we met again at my house. The fourth floor gave the best view, we all agreed.

Another problem, another discussion. Our wooden staircase was giving way. The steps were collapsing, and pieces of the banister were breaking, snapping off in our hands.

Professor Kodial said that the same thing was happening to the desks in his classrooms. Their bottoms were falling out. No one wanted to say the nightmarish words, least of all I, who had opened my bookcase one day to find the back portion eaten away. Pages and pages of my Steinbecks, my Salingers, my Faulkners, my Chekhovs, my

Capotes, and my Fitzgeralds—all hardcovers, mind you—were powdered dust.

Sam Firodia, the pest control expert we had invited to the meeting, shook his head, stroked his beard, and said, "Just what I expected. *Coptotermes formosanus shiraki.* The subterranean termite, the most evil of them all."

Sam proceeded to brief us on our new neighbors. "The most aggressive species of termites," he said. "Very dangerous, very persistent, and very difficult to dislodge once they get their teeth in and carve out their tunnels. They will build tunnels from anything: mud, paper, wood, even their own body secretions, like saliva and feces. They will pass from soil to wood without being detected, and will even infiltrate concrete."

I translated this for the shopkeepers, who looked at Sam Firodia anxiously.

"Will they eat cloth?" asked the tailor hesitatingly.

"No fear of that," replied Sam.

"What about foodstuffs?" asked Ram Dulari.

"They prefer wood and paper. *That* is their food."

"What about plants?" asked Sohrab, thinking of some newly acquired weed in his cupboard.

Sam answered all their questions patiently. Then, turning to me, he said, "I don't understand, in the first place, how they got into your building. Such an old structure would have solid wood, a solid foundation. I wonder how it came to be infected."

My mind went back to the repairs, to the days of no light, of being propped up by specially reinforced beams of wood. I wondered where the wood had come from and at what cost.

Sam said he would do the treatment but would not guarantee that the termites would be wiped out. We would have to get regular treatments done. We would have to be vigilant and observe.

"Sahib, I want to ask you one thing," said the flower vendor to Sam. "Does the smell of food attract these termites? Can *that* be the reason for the sudden invasion?"

"I know why he is asking this," said Ram Dulari with a sneer. "This *phoolwalla* thinks my food smells distract his customers from smelling his roses and his marigolds. He thinks that is why his business might be dropping, why people are buying flowers from other vendors. He is trying to make me a scapegoat. It seems he has some *keeda* against me and my success."

Everybody laughed. The flower vendor turned red and said he was just asking. Was it a crime to ask?

Sam Firodia left after agreeing to start the treatment the following weekend. We would have to check our apartments minutely before that. We would have to remove our wall units, our cupboards, our headboards, our sideboards, throw out all the infected wood, if there was even as much as a trace of termite dust.

Professor Kodial frowned and said that throwing out all his classroom furniture would cause great inconvenience to his students. How would they manage? Where would they sit?

Ram Dulari said he had some steel tables left from the time his snack bar was a dairy. The professor could buy these off him for a discount. The professor glared at him and said he was quite capable of buying new furniture himself. It was just that the timing was wrong; the exams were around the corner.

Just then Nazarana breezed in. He looked transformed. He wore a loose skirt, a bright top, his eyes were shaded blue, his eyebrows were trimmed and shaped, his cheeks were rouged lightly, and his arms and legs were shaven clean. His long hair was brushed to the sides, and in his ears he wore a pair of earrings, which he showed off as the goldsmith's artistry.

"He was *so* sweet; he knew just what I wanted," said Nazarana, smacking his lips at the goldsmith, who blushed, for fear of getting ribbed by the shopkeepers.

"I have some news to share with you," said Nazarana, breathlessly, to the gathering. Murad scowled and moved to the window, where no one could see his expression.

"I have changed my name. It will appear in tomorrow's papers. I am now Nazarana officially. And I am taking on my boyfriend's surname. So," he said with a flourish, "I am now Nazarana Himmatwalla. I have a new identity, a new life. I feel like a new person altogether."

Everyone congratulated her. The women went up and said maybe *she* could give them tips on how men thought. Was there any hope for men at all? Nazarana shrugged and said no, not unless they changed their sex.

Olaf, standing, looked at her uncertainly. "Bloody pansy," he exploded, "all wrong company you have been keeping. If I was your *fadder,* I would have given you one rap across your face. Then you'd have gone straight."

Tears sprang to Nazarana's eyes. Her lips quivered. She drew herself up, her face showing the strength and the softness of a woman. "It was my father's treatment of my mother that made me reject my own masculinity, by the way. I may have been a child then, but I know what he used to do—have *mujras* at home, get my mother to serve booze and snacks to him and his friends while the women danced, flirted, and humiliated her. That, too, in her own house."

Murad said that was enough. Nazarana had said enough against their father. Any more and there would be bloodshed.

We all fell silent. Each of us knew what was going through the other's mind. We had heard stories about the father, a muscular giant, slow and leering, for whom no display of masculinity was enough. We had heard how he would race his Triumph motorcycle on the old Khandala *ghat,* revving it up at hairpin bends, challenging less skilful friends to do the same. There had been an accident, and the parents of the biker friend who died had never been able to forgive Nazarana's father or to forget the incident. The father would do things like impersonate a police officer and accost underage girls at adult movies to extort favors from them. He would proposition women who came to clean the water tanks in our bathrooms; he would take them on the terrace, or at home, in the presence of his wife, a woman too scared to protest, too timid to question her fate or the limits of her marriage. And the building, our building, had seen all his misdeeds and misdemeanors, and it had helped Nazarana to bear her cross, until it had gotten too much. Until she had found her voice, spoken out on behalf of her mother, long suppressed and long dead. A family secret had left its grave, let out by one of its own.

Nazarana stuck her tongue out at Murad and ran out, just as quickly as she'd come.

Murad made as if to run after her, but Angelina stepped in his way. "Just you lay a hand on her, my lad, and you'll see," she said. Murad stood glowering, his fists clenched. Olga and my wife joined Angelina, and all three stood at the door, a sisterhood of instant impregnable support.

Murad snarled, made a hissing sound, and, brushing past them, left quietly.

Farhana, Murad's wife, drew close to Dinanath and whispered he would now have to tell the landlord to change Nazarana's name on the rent receipt; there was no point keeping the old name. I thought I detected a gleam of mischief in Farhana's eye. Maybe the ownership would be challenged in court one day on the basis of the name change. Maybe she had something up her sleeve I couldn't place my finger on. What did it matter? Right now I had other matters on my mind. The edifice of our building was collapsing. It was being eaten into, while we ate, slept, and dreamt.

Professor Kodial suggested we write a letter. We should put our complaint in black-and-white, addressing one copy to the housing board and one to the BMC, just so that we had it on record.

Angelina pulled out her cell phone. Enough was enough, she said. She had to reach Denzil. He would know what to do. He would file a public interest litigation on our behalf.

Professor Kodial asked her what was public about a termite invasion; he posed the question with erudite patience.

Angelina replied that the walls in her house were a public spectacle. There were tunnels running right through, where the termites had led their march of destruction. She would have to get the walls repainted before her fortieth birthday, which was when she was planning to throw a big party.

Sohrab looked up, surprised. "Unnecessary expense," he muttered, shaking his head.

"What is *your* problem?" Angelina said. "I turn forty once in a lifetime. Though, of course, my yoga instructor doesn't seem to think so.

He feels I have awoken some kind of inner energy from the base of my spine, which is going to keep me from aging."

Sohrab sighed. He had better go and meet this yoga instructor, he thought.

Dinanath said, "What is the use of writing a letter? These government organizations are too indifferent to respond to complaint letters. Maybe we should just sell the building to one of those private builders, under the redevelopment plan. Each of us would get an apartment or commercial space in the new structure."

Gopinath smiled. Somewhere in his mind he saw his four shops converted into one huge supermarket. Gopinath Superstore— he already had the name ready.

Someone spoke about the right to information. We should invoke it, ask how much the repairs had cost, insist on knowing the actual costs incurred. Someone said it wasn't easy to get the information out. These housing board guys were experts at dodging, at giving evasive answers.

We argued and discussed and managed to get a letter down that ran like this:

Dear Sir,

We regret to inform you that despite your long-drawn-out repairs, despite your reassurances to provide additional support and render our building safe, we now find a problem that is causing extreme discomfort and pain to all of us. The wood used by your contractor, Jayesh Chokhani, was undoubtedly of inferior quality, for we now find our eighty-year-old building infested, no, infected with white ants. As per the learned opinion of our pest control expert, who we invited at our own personal expense, this breed of white ants is, perhaps, the most dangerous. It can lead to an eventual rotting away of the structure, a deep-rooted disaster, which, thankfully, with timely intervention, we have managed to avoid.

We now request you, sir, to take note of this, to waive the monthly surcharge in our rent bills (in light of the destruction

we have suffered), and to impose a strict penalty on the contractor. We are bringing this to your notice as dutiful citizens
of Mumbai, as people who have lived all our lives in the city.
We hope you will take notice of our complaint and ensure that
no citizen of Mumbai is put through the indignity of seeing
the strong foundation of his/her home and his/her proud possessions reduced to dust.

Thanking you in anticipation of your cooperation.

Yours sincerely,

The residents of Chand Terraces, Mumbai

I offered to type out the letter on my computer the next day. Olaf
offered to take it around for signatures; he'd do so over the weekend,
so that we could send it off first thing on Monday morning. Olga began to say something, then changed her mind. It was a while since she
had seen her husband volunteer to do something productive.

7:00 P.M., SUNDAY, I had just returned from my walk when the doorbell rang. It was Olaf.

"The letter," he said to me simply when I opened the door.

"Why, that's quick work," I said.

"*Cha,* I don't waste time, man—never. When there is work, I do
it on the spot. They used to call me Speedy Castellino in the office.
The bosses all knew: once Speedy Castellino was on the job, the job
was as good as done. Not like these *ghatti* buggers, men. Can't trust
them with one important thing, huh. Now just see this letter. How
to send it?"

He held it out. The front page had the signatures of the three residential tenants, one tenant from each floor, and that of Professor Kodial. I turned to the back page and saw it was mostly full of thumb
impressions: some smudged, only half-clear; some showing a finely
etched pattern that seemed to grow lighter as it circled inward.

"Just see, no. How to send this? These *ghatti* buggers don't even
know how to sign."

He looked around, dropped his voice, and said, "I tell you what, just forget the back page. Tear it off and send only the front page. No one will know, man. It will be our secret." He crossed his heart the way a child would, the way we did in school to enforce our credibility.

I looked at him, looked at the letter in my hand, and said, "I can't do that, Olaf. For if I do that I will be no different from the housing board. I will have denied our building its foundation. I will have snipped at its roots. Tell you what my plan is. I am going to get photocopies of this, laminate it, frame it, and put it up at the entrance as an example of our unity. This, dear Olaf, is not a letter anymore. It is a piece of Bombay, as strong and as real as the ground we stand on."

"Eh. You bloody had a few drinks or what?" Olaf said, with a giggle.

I sighed and placed an arm around him. How to explain to this convivial neighbor of mine that I knew suddenly, after forty years, why we had all been thrown together? Why Professor Kodial's math class and the fingertip economics of the shopkeepers existed side by side; why Sohrab, the pothead, could pursue his narcotic dreams without fear of getting reported; why Angelina, for all her theatrical ways, could still find an audience that believed in her; why Nazarana, after a tormented childhood, had decided to live the adulthood of her choice, of her dreams, knowing full well the opposition she'd face from her family and the support she would get from her less judgmental neighbors. How to explain to Olaf why he, drunk and unsteady at most times, could once again be the young man of his youth, wielding his nunchaku and chasing imaginary villains out of the way, and why I, heartbroken at the loss of my beloved books, had chosen to diffuse my grief by writing a letter to the housing board. It was because we were all meant to experience and to understand the level of coexistence we were capable of. We were meant to understand that, in some strange way or the other, we were all driven by the same motivations, the same hopes, the same dreams and regrets. It was not just a matter of saving our property or our pride, but that of saving the validity of our entire lives: our past, our present, our future.

I knew it would take an infinite amount of ingenuity to explain this to Olaf. And since I didn't quite know where to start, I simply said, "No, Olaf, I haven't had a drink yet. But I was wondering if you would join me. I have a delightful brand of Jamaican rum I have been dying to inaugurate."

I opened my showcase, pulled out two copious rum glasses, and passed one to Olaf. I knew, at some point, my wife would breeze in, home from her mother's, bursting with recipes, ingredients, news on the best deals in the supermarket. I could see her glaring at me, frowning at the sight of Olaf, Olaf, with his feet up on the sofa, holding his glass out to me and saying, "Go on, man. One for the road that takes us home." I wondered if I could enjoy a similar experience with each of my neighbors. Something that each of us would savor and cherish. Something we could freeze into our hearts and minds, just in case the bulldozers come once again. They come without warning.

THE QUEEN GUARDS
HER OWN

• ◆ •

NARIMAN POINT, 7:00 P.M. The sun had set, leaving behind a crepuscular glow, a murky brilliance reluctant to fade. The glistening waters of the Arabian Sea, lapping against the gray stone wall, had turned dark and sullen and carried the portentous sound of the tide coming in.

Chacha Sawari, broad, short, and looking benignly refreshed in a *kurta-lehenga* as white and flowing as his beard, had to stop himself from smiling when he saw the Arab family cross the road. Behind the Arabs loomed their hotel—the Hilton, tall and remotely luxurious.

Chacha Sawari had just finished his prayers. Facing the ocean, he had prayed first to the God of his religion, who he believed was unforgiving when neglected, and then, somewhat fervently, he prayed to Rani Ma, the Queen Mother who gave him his earnings since he had been retired by the Bombay Syce Association, his license revoked for having cuffed a jockey who had whipped Badshah. Badshah, his beloved horse, whom he had groomed with his own hands, who he knew was his brother in past lives, who had gotten the crowd at the racecourse to its feet, unfailingly every Sunday, who had won against all odds and brought home trophies of all shapes, all sizes, and who now pulled the victoria at a leisurely trot along Marine Drive, giving Chacha a reliable source of income.

All through the prayers, the Queen Mother had remained silent. Her presence had been swamping and mysterious. She had heard him as usual and carried his request for a prosperous evening over the high seas. With the occasional gurgle of a wave she had assured him that his devotion had been noted: it would be reciprocated; all he had to do was wait.

It was a young British diplomat who had told him about the Queen Mother. The Queen's Necklace, it was called, for the fact that it arched along the sea, from Nariman Point to Walkeshwar, all along Marine Drive, and that every evening it sparkled, its buildings ablaze in a glow of neons. Every evening, the ample bosom of the Queen would coruscate—with the headlights of cars racing to and fro, with electronic billboards that flashed their messages, with streetlights that stood tall and proud, shedding their light like blessings. As if stirred by this luminous beauty, the ocean would growl, swell, and thunder at the retaining wall, the waters would turn dark and unfathomable like the night, and along the drive hawkers would arrive selling their wares, joggers would pause and breathe in the air, walkers would step up their pace, their last chance, before dinner, to shed calories, and lovers would squeeze palms and pledge with their eyes—eyes, not mouths—to remain united, and into the fold of Her Majesty's bosom Chacha would appear with his victoria, the sound of hooves drumming out an invitation to lovers, tourists, and passersby.

"Come, friends, hop aboard. The calash is down. Badshah's *darbar* is open. Don't be in a rush; don't be fooled. Don't be choked by the rigors of the day. Step aboard and feel like a Rajah. Feel the rhythm of Badshah's hooves. Your heartbeat was like that a long time ago. Feel the strength of Rani Ma. Feel her freshness and her breath. Throw back your head and feel like a prince. And go back home proud that you have an ocean left, a stretch of nature, in this squeezing juggernaut of a city. And mind you, no forebodings allowed. The Queen won't hear of it. *Yours is not to question why. A tilt of head and an open sky.* Yes, be her subject, loyal like me, and let the lady set you free."

As the Arab family approached, other *victoriawallas* narrowed their eyes and straightened in their seats. They tugged at the reins and tried to get their horses to lurch. But the two Arab boys had noticed Badshah.

They pointed to him excitedly—at the red crest on his head, his eyes, large, brown, soft and inviting.

The Arab family veered that way. Seeing them divert, other *victoria-wallas* lapsed into gloom; the pallor of the evening weighed in on them. The dull gray exterior of the Hilton stared down, birdlike, upon their crisis. It saw this kind of defeat every day. Nothing could be done about that. Badshah was a fine-looking animal, capable of tugging at anyone's heart.

The Arab father came up and asked, "*Kitna?* How much?"

"*Do sau!* Two hundred rupees," Chacha said, turning his back to him.

The Arab father frowned. His face darkened and he said, "*Cha!*" as if to say, "Too much." He said this out of habit, the way tourists do, as a safeguard against being cheated.

"Look at the animal, sahib," Chacha said, stroking Badshah affectionately, along the mane. "He is like your sheikh's horse—the finest pedigree on Bombay roads. He was a champion, not so long ago. He will make your boys enjoy the ride—that much I promise!"

Chacha spoke as much with craft as with conviction, for he knew that Arabs, like Indians, were partial to their sons; they spoilt their sons and were strict with their daughters.

The Arab made a face like he was about to retort something, like he was about to contest the comparison to the sheikh's horse but at the last minute he'd changed his mind.

Without looking at Chacha, the Arab gnawed at a corncob, which he held in his hand. The corncob was half-shorn, the uneaten part laced with masala. The Arab kept going *pooh-pooh,* spitting out the bits that were hard and underroasted.

The Arab gestured to his family to board the victoria. They flocked around the carriage, jostling and pushing one another. A strong incense-like fragrance rose off them; it drowned the aroma of peanuts roasting at the side of the road and the smell of the ocean, which was part fishy, part salty. Badshah snorted, not out of aversion to the fragrance but because he couldn't wait to get started. The first *sawari* always snapped the stillness out of his bones. Chacha patted his head, which was alert, gray, and intelligent. He did this to acknowledge that his old partner had brought him luck. The head bobbed with understanding. Chacha's hand went soft with emotion.

Chacha looked at the Arabs with fascination as they boarded the victoria.

The father—with his hooked nose, sallow complexion, wiry hair, and sharply crafted beard—had a rugged, impatient look about him. He was clearly the one in charge.

The mother was obese. She had thick, bloodless lips, jowls hanging, and small, hard, piercing eyes. She took her time getting in and occupied almost the full backseat. She wore on her neck a chain with a pendant the size of a shell. The pendant was studded with diamonds, a constellation of stars pulsating against the black night of her burka.

There were three daughters. Two of them were stout like the mother. They wore burkas that covered their heads but not their faces. They, too, had small eyes. Their fingernails were blunt and painted in fluorescent red, and on each finger shone a gold ring with diamonds. Their age, Chacha guessed, would be around twenty-one.

The third daughter was a beauty. She was a painting, a carving, a Noorjehan in the making. She had the softest eyes Chacha had seen. And features that spoke of unbearable purity. She was slimmer than her sisters and younger. Eighteen, at the most, Chacha thought. She squeezed next to her mother, who was chewing tobacco, putting her mouth through frenzied distortions. Her mother made no effort to accommodate her daughter.

The elder boy was around ten. He had a bony, bespectacled face. Seeing his elder sisters ensconced in the seat behind Chacha's, he looked unsure how to seat himself. His father ordered his daughters to move up. The sisters protested. The father let loose a barrage of Arabic, swinging his arms angrily. The corncob dangled from his hand, half-bitten and half-forgotten.

Grumbling, the sisters moved and made room for their brother. Their voices—harsh and indignant—made them sound old beyond their years. The elder boy blinked through his glasses and took to staring ahead calmly. It was obvious to Chacha he was used to them.

Chacha hoisted himself into the driver's seat. There he found another boy, no more than six. The boy had long eyelashes, curly brown
hair, and a mouth open and wary of the world. Chacha smiled at him
a lush, broad smile. His beard lit up with the smile. The boy stared
back sullenly.

The father was the last to get in. He pushed his way up and stood
like a charioteer, one foot on the seat. Chacha thought of asking him
to sit down but decided against it. The sight of the ocean always did
this to Arabs; it made them unduly excited. It brought them a world
larger than the dusty-brown landscape of the desert. It made them feel
like conquerors.

A crack of the whip and they were off, Badshah's fine red feathers
bobbing rhythmically, his hooves drumming against the concrete shell
of the city. Chacha returned the whip to its holder. It was only for effect anyway, an aesthetic touch to complete the picture of old-world
languor. Other *victoriawallas* looked relieved; with Badshah gone some
business *could* happen.

The victoria clattered along. With Badshah setting his own pace, it
went past the familiar sights of the drive: the elegant palms along the
promenade, the romantics with their backs to the city, the middle-aged
joggers desperate to leave their flab behind, the old men who came out
for their exercise and ended up discussing the stock market and failing
systems of social justice, the housewives who worried about getting back
to dinner and about the fate of characters in their favorite soaps, and fathers who bribed their children into silence with ice cream and cotton
candy while they dwelled on regrets about work. Silently it went past the
bhelpuriwallas, the *chana-singwallas,* the *chaiwallas,* the *makaibuthawallas,* all
who pushed hard to sell, and two *coconutwallas,* in *lungis,* who went
around with their baskets strapped to their chests, calling, "Fresh, freshly
cut coconuts for sale."

The evening traffic flew past: big, dusty BEST buses spitting fumes,
opportunistic taxis cutting into lanes, large crouching cars with stiff-
backed chauffeurs and impassive owners who read a lot behind tinted
windows. Occasionally a bike roared past: a hint of showmanship from

its rider, a squeal of delight from the pillion. Ah, noted Chacha, how these girls of today cling to their men, like long-missing pieces in a jigsaw.

In the backseat, the Arabs made conversation. They all spoke at the same time, and this baffled Chacha. Who was questioning? Who was replying? He was unable to tell. The only one quiet was the younger sister. She was veiled in beauty and silence, and Chacha imagined that when she spoke it would be in tones of measured softness. He adjusted the mirror and began to admire her lowered eyes, her delicate jaw, her soft, pink nose, and her mouth, so firm and fresh like a lily.

There was something about the girl that reminded Chacha of Zulfi. Zulfi, his six-year-old *beti* who wasn't his daughter in the real sense but more his in the way that people who aren't yours become yours, by virtue of a past-life association or by force of chemistry and circumstance. The image of the girl, the sanctity of her inner life reflected on her face, made Chacha think of Zulfi, the circumstances surrounding her birth.

ZULFI HAD BEEN SIRED by a man she didn't know. And in all probability she never would. It had taken only forty rupees to create her. And a whole lot of sweat and a whole lot of anger.

Zulfi's mother, Simran, was barely eighteen when she had been tricked by a foster uncle into coming to Bombay. The uncle had spoken about a job that would fetch five thousand rupees a month. "Imagine what you can do with the money," he'd told Simran. "You can use it to help your sisters marry, your brothers get pretty wives, and your father—his legs swollen with arthritis and gout—can get proper attention in town." Softly he had added, "Also you can spend money on yourself: on dresses, makeup, movies, jewelry, and ha, when you are smart enough, I can take you to see Aishwarya Rai at Film City. I know her makeup man; he is a good friend."

"Nothing like that happened," Simran told Chacha sadly, sitting, legs folded, on a large biscuit tin with a torn cushion on top, in the midst of a golden suffusion of hay in Badshah's stable, in Chacha's home, where they spoke so often, before her customers started coming in and before Chacha harnessed Badshah for his evening trot.

Sucking on a piece of sugarcane from Badshah's stock, Simran had told Chacha how she'd been brought to Bombay, how they had traveled for fourteen hours, hitching rides with truck drivers who eyed Simran slyly, who gibed her uncle about his "young-young" preferences. A few kilometers from Bombay, the truck had stopped; they had disembarked. The uncle led her to a *dhaba,* where he ordered *idli, dosa,* and *lassi* for her and a glass of beer for himself. While she was enjoying her meal, her uncle told her that a girl her age must keep her health up; she must eat well and look well fed always; her work would demand that. In between swigs of beer, her uncle kept glancing at his watch. "Once in a while he'd look at me in a funny sort of a way, as if he wanted to say something," Simran said. "Then all of a sudden he got up and began walking away. He joined some men who emerged from a *tempo.* The *tempo* looked like an ambulance. There was something final about it. My uncle spoke to the men and engaged them in a heated discussion. Then he came and told me I must hurry; they were leaving right away."

Her uncle had ordered her into the *tempo* while he waited outside, pensive and avoiding her gaze. She'd wondered what Bombay would hold for her. Would it make her rich? Would it fulfill at least some of her dreams? She never got to find out. After two hours of driving on the highway, the *tempo* turned into a lane, a bumpy stretch full of stones and shrubs, and it stopped outside a warehouse that could not be seen from the main road. The men led her in, and there they did things to her too shameful to mention. One by one, they tore at her heart, mind, body, youth, tore through every little part of her that was girl. After some time, it did not matter what they did, how long they hurt, and where. She stopped seeing their faces, that's all. "One thought I had in my mind," she told Chacha. "Why my uncle did this to me? What had I done to deserve this?"

A week later, Simran was brought to Bombay, to its red-light district, where she was put to work servicing migrant workers. Coolies, dockhands, factory workers, milkmen, *rickshawwallas,* taxi drivers, truck drivers: night after night, they came and unloaded their fatigue into her. They punished her for the crimes of the city, which she knew nothing about. Night after night, she thought of her family—her parents, brothers, sisters, all so unaware of what was happening. She wondered what her uncle would have told them. Would he spin tales of her well-being, and would they believe him—the trusting fools?

After a while, she began to see it differently. She said to Chacha there was no point dwelling on things that were out of reach. Even if she were rescued, what fate would she have? The villagers wouldn't accept her. Their family name would be in ruins. Her brothers and sisters would remain unmarried. Such was the shame she'd bring onto them.

To brace herself against yearnings of home, Simran took to black opium, which she kept, at all times, below her gums. Slowly, the village began to appear like a make-believe world, a transient place imagined by a child. Slowly, she began to forget. "It took time, but it was better this way," she said to Chacha. Better she accept her fate once and for all, better—for all.

Three years after she arrived at the *adda,* Simran developed a funny sickness. Waking one morning, she found the ground began to wobble; she could barely stand, barely hold herself upright. She was reminded of a *mela* she had attended as a child, a Ferris wheel that refused to stop, which went faster and faster, threatening to mash her brains out till, in one relieving whoop, she had thrown up, and the liquid had curled and slapped itself like exuberant paint onto the faces of others below. There was screaming and shouting, and her *baba,* who was standing below, had looked up and, seeing her slumped, had leapt onto the dashboard. He had said something to the operator that made him pull at a lever, and the next thing she remembered was being carried away, safe in her *baba*'s arms. But here there was no one to lean on. So she tried clinging to a bedpost or to a door, whatever was at hand.

When the madam of the *adda* saw Simran throw up her morning tea she told her to go easy on the opium. She swore that Yaqub Qureshi, that bastard pusher, was mixing *gard* into the opium. Simran checked with girls from other *addas.* They said that Qureshi's stuff wasn't as good as before, the *nasha* wore out too soon, but there were no side effects to complain about. She went to the doctor, who told her what the problem was—she was carrying a child.

She received the news with trepidation. What would she do with a child? How would she handle it? How should she prepare? She knew nothing about babies and how they grew.

For a while, Simran didn't tell her friends at the *adda,* for she did not know how the madam would react. During her free time, in the mornings, she began to slip away, befriending mothers from other *addas.* From them she wrenched details about childbirth and child care. The first four months she'd have to be careful, and later, if her stomach got too big, it would have to be cut open. She learned that injections were necessary for the child; otherwise it could develop a strange handicap in the legs. She'd seen children like that—one leg slimmer than the other, one leg frail and useless—they were the children who were unable to work but made good money begging. Most important, from now on, she'd have to insist her clients wear condoms. No condom, no sex—it was that simple, that straightforward. All this made sense to her. She began to feel grown-up and responsible. "I feel trusted," she said to Chacha, while he was grooming Badshah, rubbing his coat and tail. "Trusted to take charge, to give life and protect it." And Chacha had smiled, knowing full well what she meant.

As the weeks flew by, Simran began to feel a change in herself. She felt the cracking of a hard layer of topsoil, and below that she felt a tributary stir. It started as a trickle, drop by drop, then a flow gentle and clear, and soon, with consistent awareness, she felt a flood of emotions sweep through her. She felt she wanted to live again. She felt she wanted to fuss, feel, and belong, and what better than to a part of her? In a desert of longing, she would sprout her own plant, her own sweet little baby. She'd hold it to the sun and say, "Let it grow! Let it thrive! Give it a chance better than what you gave me. This is a wonderful, feeling part of me. Only if it grows can I feel hope. Only if it lives can I breathe again. Without it I am dead—dead like before."

And it was as if the heavens heard her, for though she could feel the seed become a shape, and though she could feel a warmth and a movement, and imagine in her daydreams the eyes, nose, ears, lips, fingers, and toes forming, though she could see all this and exult in it, her stomach stayed noncommittal, and with the help of loose cotton gowns she could keep the news a secret from the madam. By the time the swell began to show, it was too late. All the madam could do was curse and say, "Bah, another mouth to feed! Now make sure you work twice as hard."

So Simran had given birth to Zulfi, eight pounds of warm, thrashing humanity, sometimes cringing wormlike and sometimes eager and flitting, mothlike. Frail little Zulfi—when she cried it seemed her world was coming down, and when she was happy she beamed and spread sunlight all over. You could see the happiness in the eyes and smiles of the confined women. You could hear it in their laughter, warm, joyous, and rippling through the bars on the doors.

But how long would that continue? How long would the laughter remain bright and infectious? How long would Simran endure the loud, drunken men who came staggering in the dead of night, clawing at the half-shut doors? How long could she see her child woken to harsh banging, to heinous laughter, to the sudden onslaught of lights, to cigarette smoke in cheerless rooms, with no windows, no ventilation? If not that, then the clinking of beer bottles and glasses, loud bragging, slurred words, and songs delivered with lewd intent? Often Simran would confess her fears to Chacha, who'd fall silent, thinking it would be much worse when the child grew up, when she'd be made aware of her mother's trade. It is an unfair life, Chacha thought, that does not give a child the right to start afresh, with hope and with promise, like other children.

From Simran Chacha learned of the conditions in the *adda*.

A tiny, decrepit hovel, the *adda* reeked of poverty and dissolution. The sweat of laborers embedded in mattresses. The smell of onions left from dinner. Stale *beedi* smoke that hung like a cloud, coiling itself in the throat and nostrils.

Sometimes there was a urine smell from the toilet, the clogged toilet with a broken flush tank and moldy green pipes. Sometimes there was puke, stinking up the place from under the bed.

Sometimes there'd be disconcerting sounds: rats, scuffling below or scraping at the asbestos above. Or sometimes there'd be rows and rows of ants, crawling over spilt food and beer, and sometimes, actually, a centipede in bed.

The brothel was a few feet away from the stable where Chacha parked his victoria and lived with Badshah. The entrance to the stable was guarded by tall, heavy teak doors that creaked when they opened, and they opened to two thousand square feet of dazzling brown space.

The walls were of wood. The ground was bare, hard, and rocky. The roof was at a distance of twenty-five feet from the ground. Just below the roof was an open loft that ran all around the stable. The loft was aired by a bent, rusted wire mesh, coated with dark, moist cobwebs.

Zigzag wheel marks indicated where the victoria was parked—in the center. On the right side of the stable was a wooden cupboard, in which Chacha kept his clothes and linen. Next to the cupboard were two old chairs. On one chair was a pile of unwashed clothes, on the other a bunch of old newspapers, yellow and frayed and carrying reports of Badshah's victories.

In line with the furniture was an old dining table with a greasy two-burner stove. On this Chacha cooked his dal, rice, and vegetables. He'd yearn for a little chicken, but he barely had any money left after paying for Badshah's feed, the oats and bran his champion was used to.

On the left side of the stable were stacks of hay and some ground cleared to define Badshah's eating-sleeping-stomping space. There were chairs stacked along the wall, one on top of the other, sleek, black chairs with curved legs and backs, the kind found in Irani restaurants. An old red jukebox lent the only bit of color to the place; it leaned on three legs, a performer silenced by age. It had been discarded by the owner from whom Chacha had rented the stable.

In a remote corner, at the end, was the washing area, separated from the rest of the stable by a cement parapet. The washing area had an overhead tank and a brass tap around which was coiled a hose. This was Badshah's shower, long enough to reach him, and although he'd hate this weekly ritual, he'd endure it bravely. Once a week, Chacha would grin, tease, and run around Badshah, spraying him from side to side, like a schoolboy gone mad on *holi*. "*Arrey*, Badshah," he would say. "Which race do you want to win now? The Poonawala Millions, or the St. Ledger, or the Derby itself you will take? Don't come home without the prize money, huh, or Chacha will have nothing to do with you." And Badshah would neigh and rear excitedly, for these were not mere names to him but memories of an age when he had sprouted wings, when he had set pace and flown, king of the turf and king of all he surveyed, seeing nothing but the finishing line and Chacha's raised fist.

When Chacha lost his job at the racecourse and he heard that Badshah, too, was to be retired, he had dipped into his savings, bought him, and brought him here under a roof big enough for the two of them. In this there was no confusion, for there was no value for retired runners. They would end up in Matheran, trotting up dusty slopes, or at Juhu Beach, where the pebbled sand was bad for their legs. Worse, they'd be sold to horsemen who'd whip them, forget to feed them, and work them to the bone. But Chacha was different. He loved horses. He loved them more than human beings, and Badshah to him was nothing less than royalty, a winged creature who saw, absorbed, and understood everything, who deserved to be treated like a family member.

From what was left of his savings Chacha bought an old victoria. He oiled it, polished it, and hammered the harness in place. He tightened the spokes on the wheels and changed the seat and the footboard, and he fixed new reins and scrubbed the lamp at the side till it shone. Then he rented the stable from Hausangbhai Irani, broad-faced owner of A-1 Bakery and Restaurant.

Hausangbhai was a good man to know. His heart was stout, like the rest of him, and he was forever giving credit to his customers, much to the distress of his wife, Havovi. Haola, as he called her in moments of affection, was a plump-faced woman with the pink of Iran frozen in her cheeks. Years younger than Hausangbhai, she had borne him four proud sons, all broad and stocky like him, and shrewdly she had sent them to a school in the hills and then to a college in Pune, thereby avoiding interaction with the area. Haola would total up the money Hausangbhai was owed in terms of shoes sacrificed or saris bypassed in showroom windows or jewelry seen and admired but not bought. "But don't you understand, my dear Haola?" Hausangbhai would say. "A little debt gets people back. It is like the cycle of birth and rebirth. You keep doing wrong, and you keep coming back. Don't you see it is to our benefit only?"

Everyone knew and liked Hausangbhai, for he was always nice to people. He was never impolite, not to the whores who appeared in a sullen mood mistreated by some customer, or to the customers who walked in late bellowing for beer, or to the pimps who had been cheated by some madam or shortchanged by some customer and needed to drink and drown their anger. Times like this, Hausangbhai would nod to a waiter, and invariably something free would go from the counter, something to make up for life's harshness. Hausangbhai understood the ways of the area; he understood its burden and its sorrows, and yet its necessity to the order of things.

Hausangbhai had inherited the restaurant from his father, Meherwanji, who had arrived from Iran in 1948, a year after Independence. Meherwanji had landed off a steamer with four large trunks, his wife, Sera, and the world's finest recipes for berry *biryani,* Persian *kheema,* and confectioneries like butter cookies, cream puffs, and *mawa* cakes. There was also an African parrot, one-eyed Kaikaus, who sat unapproachably proud in a cage that Meherwanji carried. Later Kaikaus was uncaged and allowed to take his place beside Meherwanji, at the counter, where he remained alert and glaring, looking more like the owner than Meherwanji himself.

Renting the restaurant at first, then buying it, Meherwanji made an instant hit with his recipes. People would flock early morning, in hordes, for his *kheema pav,* and later, in the afternoon and evening, for his melt-in-the-mouth butter cookies, cream puffs, and *mawa* cakes. As the restaurant prospered, Meherwanji built four cozy rooms on top, where his son Hausang, and his two daughters, Arnaz and Farnaz, were born. For his first son, Kaikaus, Meherwanji could afford the finest almonds bought at ten rupees a kilo from Crawford Market.

When Hausangbhai was barely twenty, his father passed away. Two days later, Kaikaus died of a broken heart, and Hausangbhai, as a mark of respect, kept the restaurant shut for a week and had the funeral prayers recited twice: once for his father and once for dear Kaikaus.

Hausangbhai made every effort to keep alive the traditions of his father. He served berry *biryani* with berries brought from Iran. He served *kheema* made from minced lamb only. (Other restaurant owners preferred beef, which was a lot cheaper.) He served *brun pav,* with a lavish spread of butter. He also ensured that the cream for his puffs came from Parsi Dairy Farm, the butter was strictly Polsen, the oil strictly refined, and every customer could play two free songs on the jukebox. He did this for a number of years, till he realized that things were changing. He needed to cut costs; he needed to be cautious, if he was to educate his four sons, give them a life away from this neighborhood. Hausangbhai did not mind the pickpockets, the pimps, the whores, the touts, and the underworld characters who frequented the restaurant: them he could understand. What he did mind was the constables who ate for free every night, taking away huge meals for their families, the *municipalitywallas* who came for their bribes every month, and the food and the health inspectors who charged shamelessly to pass the facilities in the kitchen. With pressures like these, Hausangbhai found it difficult to make a profit. He also found it difficult to ask his customers to pay the long credit tabs they ran up, much to Haola's distress. At the end of the month, things became tight for the Iranis. They had no option but to ration the electricity, to cut down on the original ingredients of their recipes, and to forget about things like holidays, shopping, and long phone calls to their sons.

The stable had been bought by Meherwanji with the intention of starting a second restaurant. But a few months before he could do so, he had died, slumping over the counter, dropping a head full of rich white hair in full view of his customers, while Kaikaus looked on and squawked frantically. Sera, Meherwanji's wife, said there was no point starting another restaurant, for Meherwanji's spirit would linger at A-1. For many years thereafter the stable remained unoccupied; it was hired out occasionally as a warehouse to traders of cloth and then to workers from out of town as a lodging place. The workers used to smoke, drink, gamble, cook, and sleep there, and once in a while they'd sneak in some women for the night. Hausangbhai knew this and turned a blind eye. He said to Haola, "Boys will be boys, and that's fine as long as they know when to be men."

One night, when the *boys* were drunk, when they'd passed out on a surfeit of country liquor, the place had caught fire. Hearing the commotion, Hausangbhai had rushed out in his pajamas. He'd collected the whores, the pimps, the customers, and forming a human chain had flung buckets of water on the flames. This was after he had dragged his lodgers to safety, carrying them on his shoulders, while they slurred their words and threatened him in their stupor. After that, Hausangbhai had avoided taking in anyone until he met Chacha, until he'd spoken to him and realized that the old horseman could be trusted for all the white hairs he carried in his beard.

Hausangbhai agreed to rent the stable to Chacha at two hundred rupees a month, which could hardly be considered income. But, of late, an opportunity had presented itself. A builder by the name of Riyaz Padamjee, a tall, sallow-faced man with shrewd eyes and a mildly unctuous air, had approached Hausangbhai. "Name your price!" he said to Hausangbhai, referring not to the restaurant but to the stable. And he quoted a figure that made Haola dream of chiffon dresses, jewelry sets, and holidays in fancy hotels with her family.

In a low-lit corner of the restaurant, Riyaz Padamjee shared his plans with Hausangbhai. He said he wanted to tear down the stable and build in its place a three-star hotel. The location was ideal; the time was right; the licenses and sanctions he would get in a week. The hotel would send prices rocketing in the area, which would be good for the restaurant, too.

Hausangbhai was not the kind to be lured by money. He liked antiquity; he liked charm. He liked the irony that the prostitutes and a horse should be neighbors. Both were low in the karmic order. Both, in a sense, were beasts of burden. They had no ability to protest or to change their destinies. On the other hand, he boiled at these builders who were changing the face of Bombay with their gaudy high-rise structures, who were buying out the city with the help of corrupt politicians and greedy civic officials.

Stifling the snort of contempt rising in his throat, Hausangbhai told Padamjee he wasn't interested. The builder said he should think about it; such offers didn't come daily. "Besides," Padamjee said, wearing a slight ironic smile, "the place is dangerous: it has burned once and can burn again, in which case the fire department will seal it permanently."

Hausangbhai sensed the threat. Although he didn't say anything to Haola, he emptied out his heart to Chacha. "Bloody parasites," he said. "These builders think they own this city; they can do anything in the name of progress."

"But weren't you tempted?" Chacha asked. "I know, Hausang-bhai, things aren't easy for you. You have many difficulties."

"Maybe I am being foolish," Hausangbhai said. "Maybe I will regret it later, at some point. But I hate the thought of being bulldozed by these builders. I hate the thought of giving in to their greed." The two were sitting in the A-1 Restaurant late at night. The restaurant was empty. Hausangbhai was drinking beer, Chacha was drinking *chai,* and between them they had finished a plate of *kheema bhurji* and two masala omelets.

"I know what you mean," Chacha said, thinking of some people at the racecourse who bribed jockeys, doped horses, and rigged races. "But you have four sons to think about, and their future. Doesn't this worry you?"

Hausangbhai thought for a while before replying. Then he said, "Of course. I worry about it all the time. I worry what we will do when the boys want to settle down, how any girl will agree to marry them and come to a place like this—so I just hope that they will be intelligent and choose careers apart from this dying restaurant business, where either the taxes kill you or the bribes and, if not that, then the builders' threats."

That night when Chacha climbed into bed—his loft at the top of the stable—he did not sleep right away. For a long time, he stayed awake, rubbing his chest, running his fingers through his thick, white hair. Once in a while, he'd turn on his side and stare at Badshah below. Chacha, too, had his worries; he, too, would have to think ahead, to the time when Badshah would grow old, when he would not be able to pull the victoria and bring home the earnings that fed them.

But Badshah was his own, a part of him. He'd known him for years. From the time he was a colt, lean, restless, and sprightly. Chacha cared for him like no *syce* cared for his horse. In racing days, he would dry Badshah as soon as he came in from his workout, so that he wouldn't catch a chill. He'd *maalish* him daily, remove bits of hay and unwanted hair, check him for ticks, and clean his ears, so that he wouldn't catch an infection. When the vet would visit, Chacha would be holding Badshah, stroking him, while the vet would inject vitamins into the side of his neck. And Badshah would quiver, but he wouldn't create a fuss; he wouldn't rear and break away like other horses; he wouldn't make Chacha look bad in front of the vet. Caring for Badshah was nothing new for Chacha. But how had he come to develop so much affection for the girl-child, Zulfi? How did she, who was nothing to him, bound not by blood or by obligation, come to mean so much to him? As the victoria clattered along, Chacha tried to remember how it had begun—his attachment to Zulfi.

WHEN ZULFI WAS SIX MONTHS OLD, a terrible thing happened at the *adda*. It was 11:30 P.M. and the area was swarming with activity. The pimps were busy scouting for customers. The brothel doors were open. The disengaged women sat on the steps, laughing, applying makeup, gesticulating to passersby. On the side of the road, *kebabwallas* slid lumps of slimy, wet liver and balls of shredded meat onto long, black skewers, which they held over an oven of coals. Chanda, a young prostitute, was waiting for Sukhram, a *kelawalla* who had arrived in the city a few months before. It appeared that Sukhram was enamored of Chanda; he chose her always over the rest and would bring her gifts like bangles, beads, and flowers. He also spent more time with Chanda than the time he had paid for, and of late he'd gotten her a *mangalsutra* to suggest that he wished to marry her. This got Zarinabai Doobrasta, the madam of the brothel, agitated. "It's not good," she warned Chanda. "Not good to get so involved. Not good if Mussabhai knows."

The night of the incident was a busy night at the *adda*. It was a Saturday night, and a group of truckers had docked in at Cotton

Green. They had been on the road for over a month. They had delivered their cargo, collected their wages, and were flush with extra money, which they made by cheating on the gasoline, by driving on kerosene and urine.

The truckers were big, hearty men with deep pockets to match. They swooped in with bottles of hooch, *paan* in their mouths, fire in their eyes, and mischief on their minds.

The girls received them warmly; they knew if they did, the madam would permit them the next day off; she'd allow them a movie at the theater, with a beer at the intermission.

The truckers sat nuzzling the girls. The girls played up happily. They crossed their legs and bared their thighs; they showed their tongues and teased; they even struggled and moved away, to increase the heat and the longing.

But the truckers caught them and held them firmly. They fondled the girls and bit them on their arms and necks, or they pinched their thighs and slapped their bottoms. The girls squealed and understood: they were not to lose sight of what mattered, what was desired eventually.

The truckers had all the time in the world. At home, in their villages, they would have wives and children. They would have fathers who'd sit gazing at the sky, radios to their ears, predicting rain or shine, and mothers who'd cook and serve them and rub oil into their scalps with fingers of devotion. They would have brothers who'd work the fields and boast about the changing hues of the land and sisters who'd play hopscotch and blush at talk of marriage, and they'd have priests whom they'd have known since childhood and whose words of wisdom they would lap up reverentially, swearing there was no other way of life.

But that was there in the villages. This was Mumbai, queen of cities. *Dhamaal* city, *masti* city, city of chances and fun. Who'd be mad enough to stay sober? Who'd be mad enough to miss out? Who'd be stupid enough not to succumb? There was none so crazy or born so foolish. So they bellowed for food; they bellowed for music; they asked that some *naach-gaana* should begin. An old two-in-one was dragged out from under a bed and slapped and rattled into playing.

The truckers rose. They removed their shirts, bared their chests, and, unfurling their turbans, began to dance. Before that, they knocked back some hooch and made the women sip, too, which each did with a gasp and a grimace. In the back room, a child started crying. Zarina-bai signaled to Simran: "Tell the sweeper-woman to mind the baby. At the back, where she can keep an eye."

In this atmosphere, who should come by but Sukhram drunk, Sukhram resolute, Sukhram wanting to spend time with Chanda.

When he walked in, Chanda was sitting between two truckers. They were fondling her, nuzzling her cheeks, stroking her neck and thighs. And she was laughing, pretending to enjoy their attention.

The truckers' actions tore at Sukhram's soul. The music appeared loud and deafening, the dancing coarse and demeaning. He stood and stared disbelievingly.

After a few moments, he found his voice. "Stop!" he shouted. "Stop this madness; stop this vile behavior! I will not have this. I will not tolerate it. I will not see her like this."

The truckers looked up and howled. In the state they were in, they thought it a joke. "Oh, we are so very scared," one of them said, and drawing in his knees huddled up to Chanda. Pulling her close, he squeezed her breast and cupped it tightly. The others erupted into laughter.

The madam frowned. "Quick," she said to the boy who had delivered the kebabs. "Quick! Tell Mussabhai there might be trouble."

Sukhram looked around and his eyes fell on a hooch bottle, its stem fat and inviting. He grabbed it and advanced toward the truckers. "I warn you," he said. "Let her go this instant."

Chanda sprang to her feet. "No," she said. "This is madness! What are you trying to do? Can't you see I am busy? Come back later, toward morning, or first thing tomorrow. I promise . . . I will spend time with you. All the time you want."

"Shut up!" said the *kelawalla*. His eyes were on the truckers; he refused to look at her.

She felt hurt by his tone and frustrated. What did he expect—that she pledge herself to him? That she refuse other men? Did he have the muscle for that? Or the money? And did he know the consequences of such an action? Already she was seeing the dark face of Zarinabai Doobrasta. It was poised and ready for a storm.

From the back, one of the truckers tried to grab the bottle. Sukhram saw the movement and with astonishing speed turned and struck the trucker across the face. There was a sickening crunch, which, in the crowded room, sounded like a gunshot. The trucker reeled and fell on his back. He sprawled in a corner and spurted blood. In moments, his jaw began to swell.

Sukhram turned to Chanda and pulled her by the wrist. "Come!" he said. "We are leaving." She marveled at his strength and shrank at his breath, hot and pungent with alcohol.

Holding her, he started backing toward the door, the bottle erect in his hand. "I warned you," he said to the truckers. "I warned you, didn't I? Don't fool with her. She is my woman."

"And you?" he said to Zarinabai. "You have always despised me, haven't you? You knew one day I will take her away. You knew one day you will lose your hold and there will be nothing you can do. See—I am taking her now, under your nose. And what you can do, huh?"

And loudly he laughed, unaware that outside a crowd had gathered, that customers slid toward remote corners, that *paan-beediwallas* pulled down their shutters, that the *kebabwalla* blew hard to extinguish his coals, that vendors of fruits and vegetables wheeled away their carts, and pimps, diverted from their business, whispered bewildered, "Who is this? What is he trying to do? If he must die, couldn't he choose an easier way?"

As Sukhram and Chanda emerged, backs to the entrance, the street behind them cleared. A eunuch raised her sari to her face and spat in disgust, "What a madman! Would he do what he is doing otherwise?"

The truckers made as if to follow, but Zarinabai stayed them with her hand. Slowly, a smile appeared on her face. It was a smile of patience, a smile of hard-earned street knowledge. It was the smile of a clairvoyant who had known the outcome all along.

Chanda turned, and her expression changed to one of horror. She tried to cry out, but nothing came. Otherwise she would have warned

Sukhram before he was spun around and a searing acid flung in his face. Sukhram screamed. His eyes, nose, cheeks, and lips began to smoke and burn, smoke and wilt, and rivulets of flesh began to appear. Tears streamed down his face, and he screamed the scream of a tortured soul crying for deliverance. He could not bear it; he could not see; he could not live—oh, what agony this was! Sukhram ran blindly. He struck a lamppost and fell. The bottle in his hand fell, too. It rolled toward a forgotten corner.

As instantly as he had come, the attacker strode away. Those who saw him whispered to themselves, "Mussabhai! *Hey Ram*, to try this in Mussabhai's area."

Chanda ran inside screaming. Zarinabai gripped her by the hair and flung her on the bed, her face locked in a snarl. Sprawled on the bed, Chanda screamed and thrashed. The other girls moved to comfort her, but she lashed at them in fear. She screamed for her life, which she thought was in danger, and she screamed for Sukhram, who she knew was dying. She could hear his shrieks and his imprecations: "*Hey Bhagwan*. Take me please. Release me from this agony."

Chanda wished she could have warned Sukhram about Mussabhai, about his reputation, which no one dared to challenge. Not the girls whom he owned, nor the madams who worked for him, nor the policemen who bowed to him, nor the politicians who paid him to fix *bandhs* and riots. Mussabhai had his arm all the way to Dubai, to the dreaded don himself, and it was rumored that he had twenty-seven murder cases pending, not counting the ones unreported.

Twenty minutes later, three police jeeps appeared. In charge was a young inspector, who cordoned off the area and asked his men to pick up the bystanders. One by one, he questioned them. He slapped them hard, saying, "Who did this? Speak, you scumbags, or we will put you in jail. Speak, or we will pull your balls out! We will make sure you never fuck again."

No one spoke for fear of Mussabhai, knowing that nothing good would come of it. He, Mussabhai, would go underground, to some foreign country perhaps; his men would walk freely, they'd continue to extort money, and his dens would continue to operate and attract customers. Soon there'd be a payment made and the case would close permanently. And Mussabhai would return and walk the streets, dreaded and salaamed by all.

Yet appearances of investigation had to be maintained. So the whores of the *adda* were herded out. The inspector barked at Zarina-bai, "We want all your girls out at once!" To his men he said, "Round them up. A night in the lock-up will do them good."

A constable blew his whistle. Zarinabai stood at the door, comforting her girls as they emerged. "Don't worry," she whispered. "Say nothing! We have Mussabhai's hand over us."

As she stepped out with Zulfi, Simran had barely a few seconds to search out a friendly face. Her eyes fell on Chacha. Chacha, her friend, Chacha her confidant, who never judged her, never condemned her. "Please," Simran said, holding out Zulfi, who had begun to wail. "Look after her, just for a day or two?"

As he held the warm, struggling bundle, Chacha felt something stir—something rare, puzzling, and overwhelming. And he who held most human beings in contempt, he who had seen their fickleness at the racecourse and fortunes being made and surrendered and the horses who made them being willfully retired, he felt proud to take charge of a child. So small and unspoiled the baby was—and so fragile. It seemed unfair that she should be crying.

Later, when the crying subsided and Zulfi had shown fascination with Chacha's gossamer-white beard—she had clutched it with plump little fingers and squealed when Chacha contorted his face in make-believe agony—then he had known an even greater delight, a secret inward joy, which made him break into a song. He'd waltzed all round the stable, her in his arms, a ludicrous, shuffling Mary Poppins bloated on happiness. He held her to Badshah and said, "See, my angel. This is your Uncle Badshah. Like me, he is your protector. When you are older, you can dress like a princess and ride along the Queen's Necklace. Then everybody will see how pretty you are."

Even as he said that, Chacha shivered. Would Zulfi be permitted to do that? Or would she, like her mother, be initiated into the trade? *Hey Bhagwan,* he thought. Let this child know better. Let her have my luck, if there's any left. With this thought began a bond between child and man, a bond that gave Chacha the strength to look after the child, to warm her milk, not once but thrice, to wash her bottle in boiling hot water and burn an *agarbatti* to keep the mosquitoes away.

That night Chacha didn't sleep in the loft; he didn't sleep at all. He lay next to Zulfi, whom he placed on a mattress borrowed from Hausangbhai's wife. "Don't worry, O *victoriawalla,*" Haola had said. "When God places a child in your hands, he also gives you the means to look after it. If there's anything you need, don't hesitate to ask. Not for nothing have I brought up four sons."

Three times during the night Zulfi woke, and three times Chacha fed her, carried her, and patted her to sleep, speaking to her in a soft, lulling voice.

When Simran returned from the lock-up, he spoke to her seriously. It would be okay if she left Zulfi with him every night, after he returned from his *sawari,* once he'd cleaned out the stable and dried and fed Badshah. This way the child could sleep undisturbed and she'd see less of her mother's life. He looked at Simran anxiously, dreading her answer.

Simran couldn't believe her ears. Chacha must be an angel sent by God. He must be a saint in disguise. She bent and touched his feet, and she clasped her hands and thanked him, saying he had relieved her of so much tension. "Don't forget to remove her milk," Chacha said gruffly. "This outside milk is okay for a day or two, but not for long. And she wakes up three times at night, so make sure there's enough."

THE STEADFAST RHYTHM of the hooves, the rocking motion of the carriage, the fading light of twilight, and a faint breeze from the Queen Mother made Chacha drift deeper into thought. He sighed. It was bad luck that Zulfi was born in the red-light district. It was bad luck that she had to grow up in a neighborhood where childhood wasn't allowed to run its course, where innocence was considered a frailty and beauty an asset to be exploited without remorse.

Now that she was older, Zulfi was being noticed; she was drawing attention. The out-of-work *tapori* boys had started calling to her.

They tried to lure her with their promises of "we will give you this, but do this for us first"—things like singing, dancing, wriggling her hips, rolling her eyes, in exchange for sweets or sherbet. On the surface, it looked innocent enough, but later it would lead to things beyond an ordinary performance.

So far, between Simran and Chacha, they had managed to protect Zulfi. They had impressed on her to trust no one. "Be good, be courteous, but go with no one," they had said. And she had listened and obeyed and stayed a child—thank God for that!

But just that morning Amir Jawaab had visited the *adda*. He had business with Zulfi's mother, he said. And Zulfi was the business.

Suddenly the Arab boy at Chacha's side let out a squeal, forcing him to break from his thoughts. The boy stood and pointed to a man on the road, along the sea-face, who was blowing bubbles through a handheld object. The object was like a magnifying glass, except there was no glass. The *bubblewalla* pulled the soapy mixture from a bucket at his feet, and the mixture clung to the object like a thin, transparent film. The man smiled and blew in the direction of the passing victoria. The bubbles came forth like spaceships.

The Arab boy was fascinated. And seeing his son fascinated, the father, too, was fascinated.

Beaming, the boy pointed to the bubbles, and he stretched and grabbed at them as they came toward him. A gust of wind drove them overhead. The boy got excited and jumped higher. The victoria lurched. The movement startled Badshah, who, in his nervousness, quickened his pace.

The *bubblewalla* saw he was losing a customer. Smiling like a magician, he blew, and more bubbles appeared, a steady stream, behind the victoria.

The victoria rolled along. The boy whined to his father. The father's face darkened.

"Stop the *tonga*," he ordered in terse Hindi.

Chacha tugged at the reins. Badshah stopped. The father fumbled in his pocket and pulled out a wad of hundred-rupee notes. He thrust a few notes at Chacha and said, "Go! Buy it for him."

Chacha was affronted. He was a horseman, not a servant. But seeing the boy's face, he took the money.

Chacha walked over to the *bubblewalla,* who waited with a smile.
"How much?" Chacha asked, and the *bubblewalla* said, "*Teen sau!*
Three hundred rupees!"

Chacha shook his head. "Say the correct amount. You know that
is not fair."

"What do you mean not fair?" the *bubblewalla* said, frowning.
"That *is* the price. It is fixed."

"Why, brother, do you want to cheat?" Chacha said kindly. "A single transaction won't make a rich man out of you."

"What's it to you?" hissed the *bubblewalla.* "It's not your money,
going out of your pocket. Let the Arabs pay. They can well afford it!"

"No, brother, it doesn't look good for our country, to cheat a guest
this way."

"Don't tell me what looks good and what doesn't, you old scoundrel.
I bet you are overcharging them yourself. And what are you trying to
do—cut me out, huh?" Then lowering his voice, he said, "If you want
your cut, just say so. Why you are being difficult?"

Chacha was adamant—not a paisa more than hundred rupees. So
what if his customers were rich and could afford it many times over?
In his book, honesty had to be maintained.

Finally, the *bubblewalla* relented, but not before calling Chacha
names under his breath.

Chacha returned with the gadget and gave the remaining money
to the Arab, who pulled out a hundred-rupee note and held it to
Chacha, saying, "*Rakhlo,* baksheesh. Keep it, as a tip."

Politely Chacha refused the money. The *bubblewalla* eyed him resentfully.

Chacha returned to the driver's seat, thinking he would show the
boy how to use the gadget: how to twirl the object round and round
in the mixture and blow gently at the film till it became a steady, rising
bubble. But the boy didn't seem interested. He had found a new toy,
which occupied his attention. The whip dangled in his hand, left to
right and back again. He stood up, showing the whip to the passing

traffic. Chacha kept the bubble jar on the seat and tugged at the reins. The victoria resumed its journey.

The boy kept swinging his whip at the passing cars and saying, "Sultan." He squealed his invincibility to the skies, and his father bristled with pride, his mother grinned through tobacco-shot teeth, and his sisters nudged one another and looked at him adoringly.

The victoria clattered along. Behind it the first gray of night rolled in. The lights came on—in buildings, in flats, on the streets, and overhead, on electronic billboards. Headlights from outgoing traffic, headlights from incoming streams—they flashed and they blinded. In the center, on street poles, translights shone like soldiers carrying shields, poised to defend the beauty of the Queen. Slowly, Her Majesty donned her necklace. The ocean stirred approvingly. The clouds gathered and formed a canopy—a still gray blanket, or a fashionable wig. Chacha returned to his thoughts—as dark as the advancing night.

He thought of Badshah. His brother was aging. There were signs, small signs like him tiring after two stretches. He would wheeze on the way back, which was so unlike him. And last week, on a Bombay-by-night tour, Badshah had begun to shiver, breaking into a warm, trembling sweat. Of course Chacha had fussed and comforted him; he had wiped him down, while the tourists had disembarked for pictures, but there was a look in his eyes that spelt defeat, that said the race was run, the finishing post was in sight. Yes, it's time, Chacha thought. Time for him to retire.

But today Badshah appeared fine; his gait was sprightly. Looking at the red crest bobbing reliably, Chacha felt a surge of admiration. His mind went back to the days of old, to the classics Badshah had won. How the onlookers had cheered. How they had gone mad. How many fortunes had been made by Badshah and how many strengthened and multiplied. What a horse! What an animal! Unbeatable, unbeatable Badshah, uncrowned king of the turf. Oh, what would Chacha give to see him race again, to see him thunder home, warm, victorious, and welcomed by all.

The red crest also raised an unpleasant memory. It reminded Chacha of Amir Jawaab. Amir Jawaab, prince of beggars, thin, gaunt, and bearded, who wore a cocky hat with a red plume and strutted his successful career down the garish lanes of the red-light area. "*Sab bhookhe, sab bhikari, amir bhikari, garib bhikari, sab sale bhikari,*" he would say with undisguised conviction, daring anyone to challenge his theory, which held that all were beggars: the rich, the poor, all were wanting, all were craving; in some strange way no one was satisfied.

In an old empty garage, Amir Jawaab ran a school for beggars. With Ghulam, his stray dog, at his feet, whom he'd kick or feed depending on his moods, Amir Jawaab gave instructions to his students, aged between six and fourteen.

Amir Jawaab's day would begin at 8:00 A.M., after gobbling a masala omelet and drinking two cups of *chai* because he was too drunk to have eaten the night before. Then, munching on a pink-icing cake for a rush of glucose energy, he would walk the lanes, hurling his greetings to the madams, who were the only ones awake, brushing their swollen, acidic mouths in narrow doorways. "Good morning, Chachi; good morning, Auntie. May poverty stay away from your door. May the day bring you luck."

The madams liked Amir Jawaab and his bravado. They had known him since childhood, the bastard seed of Aminabai Maktoud. Amir was fourteen when they had taken Aminabai away in an Ambassador car. They took her at knifepoint, because they thought she told on Latif Chickna, a member of the dreaded Salim Bhangar gang from Nagpada. Amir never got to see his mother again, and no one—least of all the cops—bothered to find out what had happened to her.

In time, Amir learned to fend for himself, to get by on his wits, to switch careers depending on his needs. He tried his hand as a pickpocket, a car thief, a pimp. He failed in all these, landing each time in a police dragnet that seemed to dog his footsteps. Then he saw Amitabh Bachchan in *Naseeb* and knew that he, too, could act. He could convince people to part with their money. Time-harried Bombayites would be glad to get him off their backs and off their conscience.

Dressed in filthy rags, Amir Jawaab would tilt his head, twist his hand, make his fingers quiver, and stoop and walk with a pronounced jerk, throwing one leg before another. He would approach cars at signals, cars with softhearted girls and curious children and businessmen guilty of the wealth they had amassed. He would throw back his head, roll his eyes, and give a deep, low animal groan. His tongue would dangle in mid-air, a starving blue serpent, and he would continue rolling his head, groaning like some dying animal, till the occupant of the car would shift uncomfortably and release a generous amount of change into Amir's outstretched palm.

It didn't take him long to wise up to places of easy profit. He took his act to the gates of temples, where people arrived in a charitable mood, and to hospitals, where the relatives of patients prayed for miracles, and to wedding halls, where the families of the bridal couple were anxious to collect blessings for the to-be-weds. He knew which of his customers would succumb and at what point. Boyfriends wishing to impress their girlfriends, mothers waiting for their children outside schools, businessmen in their cars, locked in important discussions, and foreign tourists who'd never seen anything like this—all of them came under the spell of Amir Jawaab's act.

Working the streets, he got to know others like him, other beggars not as successful. At first, he'd give them free advice, telling them how to playact successfully. Then, realizing he had a talent and possibly could gain a following, he began a school for beggars. He started with street children, whose parents worked as daily-wage earners, pushing a handcart, toiling at a construction site, or watering plants in parks. The parents were glad to have the children off their backs and were gladder when they saw the children's earnings. They encouraged their children to attend Amir Jawaab's school, to listen carefully and learn his tricks. In some cases, when the parents landed jobs in the Gulf, they even left their children with Amir Jawaab, and he was fine with that. Children were lucky for him. The more dependent they became, the more they ended up earning for him. His flock grew; his income, too. But it was never enough, for there was so much money to be made in Bombay, if only you knew how to plead and persist.

That morning Amir Jawaab had dropped in at the *adda*. Zarinabai Doobrasta welcomed him warmly, saying, "Give me a tip, no, Amir Jawaab, for the *matka* bazaar?"

"Later," he replied, unbuttoning his shirt and rubbing the hair on his chest. "Right now I have business with Simran, business that cannot wait."

Zarinabai nodded and called to Simran.

The moment she saw him, sprawled on the bed, in flared green trousers, his shirt open to his navel, Simran knew it to be a bad sign. She knew he had come for Zulfi. Zulfi, who was a natural-born beggar, he said. Who would get his customers' hearts bleeding, empty their pockets in no time. Amir Jawaab knew an actress when he saw one. And Zulfi was the right age, too, when her mind could easily be molded.

"You should be grateful I have spotted her," he bragged to Simran. "Without me, what chance does she have? She will have to watch you dying, alone and unwanted. Or she will have to come into the trade herself. Working with me, she can earn for you and for herself. She can make good money for both of us. And she can see to you, when you are old and useless."

Simran knew this to be the truth. Many mothers had given up their children just to save them from a life of prostitution. But she had nursed a dream for Zulfi, a big and sacred dream. And she knew not whether it was possible or real, but it angered her to hear Amir Jawaab speak like this.

"Stay away from my daughter, O prince of beggars," she said to Amir Jawaab, raising a finger and her voice. "I will slit your *nunu* if you come near her. She is *not* going to join your school. She is *not* going to be your puppet, living on people's charity. She will study. She will educate herself. She will meet fine people, and look like them, and talk like them, and she will learn their habits and their tastes. I will see that she does that, no matter what it takes."

"Fool yourself, you insane woman," snarled Amir Jawaab, rising from the bed. "This is not you talking but your opium. It has filled your head with impossible dreams. No one makes it out of here; no one breaks the code. Haven't you heard? Haven't you seen? Now hear this carefully. Just the other day I heard Bhikoo Bhadva ask about some very young girls. He has a request from a sheikh who likes them young. And when the sheikh finishes with them, he puts them in the camel races. And you know what those are, don't you? Death sentences in mid-desert!"

Tipping his hat, the beggar-prince left, pausing at the door to remind Simran that he *would* be back and that would be the last time.

Seeing he was gone, Zarinabai clutched her head and wailed. "I don't even know what to play for the *matka* bazaar. How will I make up my losses?"

Ignoring her, Simran lifted her petticoat and ran full speed to the stable. Chacha—she needed to see Chacha. He would know what to do. Chacha cared. He cared deeply. He was God's own man. And he loved her child like mad, almost as much as she did.

"What is happening? Is this a horse or a donkey?" the Arab's voice broke.

Chacha awoke from his thoughts. What was wrong with Badshah? He was almost trudging.

Chacha tugged at the reins gently, then hard, and Badshah, after snorting twice, began to trot again.

A car with kids whizzed past. In it was a German shepherd, his head and neck out of the window, his long, pink tongue dripping. The Arab boy showed the dog his whip.

WHEN SIMRAN BROKE IN on him, Chacha was massaging Badshah's legs. He was applying mustard oil in a swift, downward motion. Although expensive, the oil brought Badshah relief; it prevented his bones from degenerating. Simran entered nervously, for in Chacha's presence she felt the shyness of a niece. She sat on her favorite seat, the old biscuit tin, fumbled in her blouse, pulled out a half-smoked cigarette, and managed to light it after a couple of aborted strikes.

"Amir Jawaab wants Zulfi," she said without looking at Chacha. "He says either he gets her or that Bhikoo Bhadva. I won't let them have her. I will kill them. Then I will kill myself. But I will not let their dirty hands fall on her. Why, that Bhikoo Bhadva, son of a serpent, wants to sell her to a sheikh who is a real animal—he likes to have his fun with young girls. You will help?"

Chacha did not look up. He continued massaging the leg. At one spot, he thought he felt a quiver, a kind of recoil, but then Simran's problems were more serious, so serious that he could not even turn his face lest the uncertainty showed. He continued massaging up and down, increasing pressure. After a while he stopped and said, "No . . . they won't have her. Not Amir Jawaab, nor Bhikoo Bhadva, nor that sheikh who comes to buy our children. Our Zulfi will go to a fine school in the hills, away from all this squalor. A fine lady she will be. She will speak English, write English. And she will wear fine clothes and have sahibs open doors for her."

"Promise! Promise me, Chacha Sawari," Simran said, jumping up and knocking the tin over. "Promise me that our Zulfi will never know the corridors of hell. That she won't have to live with criminals, and pimps, and madams, and drug addicts? We will be able to save her all that?"

Chacha Sawari cleared his throat and raised his hands to the sky, and just then Badshah neighed.

"See, even he agrees," Chacha said with a smile. "*Arrey,* Badshah, you will have to be there, too, on Zulfi's wedding, in her procession. Who will bring the groom otherwise? But make sure you don't run away with him—okay?"

They both laughed. They both felt released. The monotony of the stable seemed to bind them. And beyond that, there was a higher love, and a higher dream, which both knew was foolish and impossible to achieve. But they weren't going to admit that, for if they did, they would cease to see meaning in their own lives, and that wouldn't be good for Zulfi. She was young. Maybe there was hope. Maybe there was a better life waiting. Maybe there *was* something planned. They would have to wait and see. All they could do was hope. Hope and pray. And pray and hope. And share their hopes, and pool their prayers, and get by that way.

Maybe I call sell the victoria, Chacha thought. By now they had reached the gymkhanas, where during the day young boys practiced cricket at the nets and at night migrant workers played cards, sang, and wrestled their frustrations away.

Chacha thought of the last *victoriawalla* who had left the trade. Khote Singh Durgaspur had felled his horse with an almighty blow, pulled his turban firmly upon his head, and vowed that he would now live, work, and die only in the golden wheat fields of Punjab. The old *sardar* admitted he had paid a heavy price for leaving home, but now no more. No more *lassi* that tasted like urine. No more sparrows served up as tandoori chicken. No more sparsely buttered *parathas* being passed off as the real ones. No, he had had it with this city.

Khote Singh had managed to get four thousand rupees for his victoria. But that's because he was in a hurry to sell. Chacha would be a lot smarter. By selling it to a hotel or a heritage site he would get a better price.

Even as he thought that, Chacha felt a tug of guilt. Was he cutting his nose to spite his face? Selling a brother to save a daughter? What about Badshah? What would happen to him? No one, as far as Chacha knew, took care of old horses. Not unless they had their own farm and a steady income. Chacha had to think of his old partner; he owed him that much at least. And, as if he read Chacha's thoughts, Badshah slowed. He jerked his head three times. Then he stopped. Chacha felt the reins tremble.

"*Kya ho raha hain?* What is happening?" the Arab father exclaimed. "*Gadha vapas rukh kyun gaya?* Why has the donkey stopped again?"

With a litheness that mocked his years, Chacha jumped down beside Badshah. His old partner was trembling; his eyes were taut; he was trying to say something with his eyes. Once upon a time Badshah's eyes had been globes of fire; today they craved understanding.

"What's wrong, Badshah? What's wrong, old-timer? Are you tired? Do you want to rest? I promise you will, if only you go a little farther. Only till the beach, mind you. There I will get you a nice fat sugarcane piece. You will like that—won't you?"

Chacha was whispering, but the voice that came from the victoria was loud and demanding.

"*Kya hua? Gadha so gaya kya?* What has happened? Has the donkey gone to sleep?"

"*Gadha so gaya, gadha so gaya,*" the Arab boy chanted. "*Jaago gadha, jaago! Jaldi jaago, jaldi bhaago!* Wake up, donkey; wake up. Get up and start moving." The boy started whipping Badshah, a lash here, a lash there, and one that got him on the head.

The whip startled Badshah; it frightened him; it was many years since he had felt its sting. He neighed with disbelief and shock.

Chacha leapt onto the footboard and grabbed the whip, almost sweeping the boy off in his rage. He replaced the whip in its holder and, fists clenched, glared at the boy. It was a good thing he was so small; otherwise—

The boy started to howl, pointing at Chacha accusingly, pointing to the whip.

The women went into hysterics. The mother beat her chest and shook a fat finger at Chacha. The elder sisters patted the boy's head and tried to soothe him. The elder boy grinned at his brother. He made sure his brother noticed his delight.

The Arab father swung into action. Seeing his son upset, he sprang into the driver's seat, pulled the whip from its holder, and brought it down on Badshah's back. His face locked in a snarl, he lashed away with all his might. Badshah neighed and moved to and fro. But the lashes kept coming—on his back, on his sides, on his slender gray neck.

The victoria rocked from side to side. As the father lashed harder, the boy's sobs diminished. Chacha was paralyzed. He tried to say something, something like, "Poor animal, no, please, stop," but the father paid no heed. He continued to rain his fury on Badshah.

Cars slowed. Ocean gazers turned their heads. The locals in the *maidan* broke from their cards and chatter. Who was this crazy man? Why was he expending his fury on a mute animal? Chacha tugged at the Arab's leg from below. The Arab kicked him viciously and turned the whip on him. It stung Chacha across his face and made him cry out in pain. Badshah saw this and broke. Lashes, humiliation, pain—all this he could take in his stride. But how dare anyone hurt his master? He rose, gathering all the strength in his legs. He rose and neighed, and the victoria tilted. Its occupants screamed, and the man with the whip—the enemy—was thrown off guard.

Before the Arab could recover, Badshah reared again. He neighed and reared, and neighed and reared, and at the side the ocean growled. The tide was in. It was rushing in toward the shore. Badshah reared again, higher this time. Let no man misjudge him. Let no man abuse his master. Let no man think he'd let that pass. And let the skies be witness to that.

The victoria tilted farther and the Arabs landed on one another. The girls and the elder boy landed on the mother, and the father landed on top of them, his white robe sliding over his knees, exposing his hairy legs to the sky.

It took them five minutes to sort themselves out. Get a head out of a chin, an elbow out of an eye. Someone had lost his glasses; someone had gotten scratched on the face: it hurt, therefore the howling. The father had lost a sandal. By now a sympathetic animal lover had escorted it to the sea. The younger boy scratched and fought his way out. His mother howled and petted him. He tried to get away from her vigorous caresses. The elder sisters blamed him. The father threatened them with dire consequences; he used loud, vituperative language to get that across. The elder son groped for his glasses and clutched one of his mother's breasts instead. She slapped him hard. He looked at her dazed and dumbfounded.

Dismayed as he was by the sight of his toppled victoria, Chacha moved over to comfort Badshah. He held his head and stroked him, looking into his eyes. His old partner appeared sedate now, unaware of the chaos he'd caused.

The Arabs extricated themselves, grumbling and swearing. Up front, on the seat, the bubble jar had smashed. The soapy water trickled down and formed a foamy puddle on the road. The mother almost slipped on the puddle, but her daughters steadied her in time. She glared at them, as if their help was unnecessary. The father looked at Chacha, and his eyes went to the whip. But then he became aware of the crowd: too many eyes and all so hostile.

Waving his arms, raving like a madman about a lost sandal and about a dying and diseased horse, the Arab paced the road in search of a taxi. He flagged down two. The first taxi driver pulled over obediently. The second driver—a surly-faced opportunist—said he'd take them only if the Arab agreed to pay a hundred rupees, not a paisa less, for he would have to take his cab all the way round, in the opposite direction. The Arab agreed, for he could sense a collective unruliness, a unity in the crowd that could turn nasty. Barking instructions, he hurried his family into the waiting cabs.

With mixed feelings of rage and relief, Chacha watched them exit. He cooled down slightly when he saw the younger Arab girl. She shot Badshah an apologetic look. Then she looked at Chacha and her eyes went toward the victoria—to its tilted calash, its raised seat. Behind her, the father screamed. Quickly she disappeared into the taxi.

As the vehicles took off, the Arab spat at Chacha and, sticking his head out, raised his middle finger several times over. Chacha shook his fist and stood glaring till the taxis were out of sight. Then he turned to his victoria. Strange it looked, his fallen chariot.

"Come, brothers," he requested the onlookers. "Please lend me a hand."

Willingly they came forward: the *bhelpuriwalla,* the *chaiwalla,* the *chana-singwalla,* and the *ice-creamwalla.* Together they heaved and restored the victoria to its original position. Badshah shook his neck, as if shedding off a bad memory. The helpers asked Chacha what had transpired, and he poured out his outrage. Listening to him, they clicked their tongues and shook their heads disapprovingly; then they melted into the night.

Chacha saw there were footmarks all over the seats. He took a cloth and began wiping off the marks, rubbing in slow, swiping movements. He felt sad as he realized he'd missed out not only on the fare but also on the baksheesh he'd been offered earlier.

Of what use is money if this is what it does? he thought. If it makes animals out of human beings and reduces animals to slaves? He thought of all those who had cheered Badshah, who had bet on him and won each time. He thought about the bookies who had refused to give good odds, knowing Badshah was unbeatable, and the owners who led him in proudly and posed with his trophies. Where were they when Badshah needed them? It is better to be poor and grateful than to be rich and forgetful, he thought, giving the seat a final swipe, up and down, and at the sides, too.

A breeze had started, a sharp breeze with the sting of salt water. It made Chacha realize that he should be getting back. It was too late for another fare. Besides, he wasn't up to it.

There were people seated all along the seafront. They were looking into the dark, as if fastened on to some speck of hope that only they could see. They sat in silence, hearing the drumming of the ocean over their own heartbeat. None appeared keen to leave the bosom of the Queen.

Chacha looked to his left, at the Hilton, where the Arabs would sleep that night, in air-conditioned rooms, on soft, clean beds with sink-in pillows and rich quilts. He looked to his right, toward Chowpatty, the food stalls, where middle-class families tucked into plates of *bhelpuri, ragda pattice,* and *sevpuri* or mashed obsessively at bricks of frozen *kulfi.*

His eyes wandered farther—down to the beach, where children ran squealing onto the sands, their hands raised, and his heart ached for Zulfi. Six, and she hadn't seen the beach yet.

He looked at the place where he stood. Could he be center, dead center? If so, all would be justified; the Queen Mother would have spoken. Not quite, he realized. A little to the left would have been perfect, but it didn't matter, for nothing in life is precise, nothing perfect. It's up to you to tilt the odds. And if the odds tilt in your favor when you need them, then so much the better.

He walked over to Badshah and stroked his head. Bringing his palm lower, he opened it and said, "See, partner; see what Rani Ma has given you: your retirement bonus, and mine, too, and a life for *bithiya,* and freedom, perhaps, for *beti.*" And with that, he opened his palm just a little more, to show Badshah what he'd found in between the seats. And Badshah blinked, no different from how he usually did, for what was important to him was Chacha's voice, his touch, his presence, and not this silly little rock that twinkled and shone with a million eyes.

Chacha hoisted himself up, took the reins, and set off at a leisurely pace. Overhead, the sky settled into a canopy of darkness. Behind him, the necklace gleamed, a burning river of halogens. At the side, the ocean lapped, a quivering mass of velvet.

As he pulled out of the drive and took a right, Chacha began whistling a tune: "*Bekaraar karke humein yun ne jaaiye, aap ko hamari kasam laut aaiye.*" As he whistled away, it dawned on him that he was whistling not out of joy but out of a feeling of sadness, the poignancy of leaving his turf after a long and tiring race. The worst was he did not know whether he'd won or lost the race.

Turning his back on the drive, joining a narrow stream of traffic, Chacha wondered what had happened to his integrity, his honor, which he had spoken about so freely with the *bubblewalla?* Was it as fragile as the bubbles that were sent his way? Did it have to burst in the face of necessity? In the face of hardship?

He looked at Badshah, who was trotting along calmly. How long would his old partner pull the weight of their collective burden? How long before he collapsed at the side of the road, unable to hoist himself up? Chacha shivered, thinking of it.

He thought of Simran, the fire in her eyes when she spoke of Zulfi—and the hatred and venom she felt for Amir Jawaab and Bhikoo Bhadva. How long before she did something drastic? Before she killed them, or herself and Zulfi? She might—if Chacha's promise to her remained unfulfilled.

Instinctively Chacha's hand went to the bulge in his pocket. He felt a warmth and a promise there. The promise of three lives saved.

In his early days, Chacha had worked for a few months as a diamond polisher, before the flames and the dust had brought on an attack of asthma; then he'd been advised to work outdoors.

So he knew the value of what he held and the price it could fetch: Simran's freedom, perhaps; Zulfi's schooling for sure; and, with a little luck, a small plot in the countryside, where he could keep Badshah and maintain him the way champion horses deserved to be maintained. Chacha's eyes filled with tears thinking of the inevitable, Badshah's last days. But at least they would be under an open sky—with the clouds, the stars, and God as witness.

Stuck in a traffic jam—some commotion caused by a rich sahib having parked his car brazenly—Chacha wondered about Simran, how he'd negotiate her freedom. He would have to talk to Mussabhai. He would have to tell him what Simran and the little girl meant to him. He was sure that Mussabhai, too, would have a heart, somewhere, deep down, under that criminal mind of his. And why, Chacha was ready to make a payment; he was ready to pay the price for two lives that mattered. He would have to reach Mussabhai through Hausangbhai, good old Hausangbhai, whom everyone knew and liked. Thinking of Hausangbhai made Chacha feel hungry. He rubbed his belly and allowed his mind to dream. This time for himself. For his stomach.

IT WAS LATE BY THE TIME he pulled into the area. The power had gone and the only light was from the traffic. A cacophony of horns rose to greet him and beyond that a stunned, stupefied darkness. What foul luck, he thought, just when I thought I'd buy myself a meal and take something for Simran and Zulfi, too.

He decided to leave the victoria in a side lane. It would be too difficult to navigate in the dark. Using an old lock and chain, he tied it to a lamppost. He patted Badshah, saying, "Give me a few minutes, old-timer. I will see what the position is, when the lights are expected."

He sauntered into the area. Lights or no lights, it was busy as ever, a flame that could not stop burning lest it extinguish itself.

He went past the movie theater, outside of which waited groups of youth, smoking cigarettes, drinking *chai,* contemplating the women who solicited.

He went past the timber stores, unloading in the dark, and past the handcart pushers, who waited for a load, waited half the night, for a run, so they could earn and eat by morning.

He walked past the auto shops, dark and greasy and where there was always night, always some stolen part being bought or traded, and talk of vehicles being dismantled before they were traced. And past the *mujra* parlors, their music silent, their customers evicted onto long, frail balconies, and past the *mujrawallis,* flirting expertly with the customers, so that they might hold their interest till the lights returned.

He went past the *kebabwallas* crouched over their ovens, slapping marinades, stirring the coals, and turning the skewers in the nick of time. And past the *pav-bhajiwallas,* churning their vegetables on black, greasy pans, and around them their customers waiting, with gaunt faces and cavernous mouths.

He walked past the brothels, lit by candles . . . the women outside, on the steps, their faces tired and unsure. And past the eunuchs standing in clusters, their bones and lips gleaming.

He walked farther into the lane and heard someone call. It was Hausangbhai, sitting on the steps of his restaurant. Hausangbhai in his traditional nightwear: a white silken undershirt, cut at the shoulders, and striped green pajamas, loose and flared. In his hand was a bottle of beer.

"*Arrey,* Sawari, what are you doing strolling in the dark, like a young man bent on pleasure? Come and have some beer with me. Come and join me for berry *biryani*, if you don't have some mischief in mind, that is."

Chacha laughed, for it was not his habit to drink. But his mouth turned moist thinking of the *biryani,* its tender meat, its saffron rice, its roasted almonds, its cashews, its spices, and the onion rings, so fresh, tingling, and good for his sinuses. But no—Badshah was alone, facing the warm, blinding lights of the traffic, and he'd be hungry, too, after the ride.

So Chacha said, "Not now, Hausangbhai. I will wait till the lights come back . . . till I can bring Badshah in, and dry him and feed him. Meanwhile, if you could keep three packets of *biryani* ready, two normal, with normal spice, and one with less oil and less spice, why, I would be grateful." Then he added in a low, embarrassed voice, "And please don't mind, but I will pay you later."

Hausangbhai rose with effort. He was a big man with thick arms that poured out of his undershirt. His arms were dark and pimpled and had shrubs of hair sprouting up in places. He came toward Chacha, dragging his feet noisily, and, placing an arm around him, said, "*Arrey,* Chacha, what do you think? I am such a *baniya* or what, that I am going to ask you for money? We both know how much you love your *bithiya*. How much you dream for her and her future. You are a good man, Sawari, and I tell you what, you can stay in my stable as long as you like. You and that champion horse of yours. And don't you worry about any rent increase, huh. Or about my selling and asking you to go. No two-bit builder is going to scare me. I am not going to take his money or his threats. And if ever he gets tough, why, I will just speak to Mussabhai."

Hearing this from a man like Hausangbhai, a man so down on his luck and yet so strong, Chacha began to cry. He wept softly on Hausangbhai's shoulder—there, in the dark, out in the open—while all around people milled and moved around, conducting business as usual.

Hausangbhai let Chacha cry, for he assumed that the old horseman was weeping out some strange and terrible sorrow, which was deeply rooted and which needed expression. Probably he was crying for his *bithiya* and for the life she could not lead, or for his horse, whom he loved as much, or simply for a day that had proved too rough and too overwhelming. And Hausangbhai knew, for he had been through such days, when everything appeared bad and insurmountable, when fate itself drew swords against you and the hands of God seemed irrevocably crossed.

After some time, Chacha stopped crying. He looked up sheepishly and whispered to Hausangbhai, "Thank you, Hausangbhai, for being so kind. Thank you for your piety."

And Hausangbhai said, "*Chaal,* worry not, Sawari, come back, and I will keep your *biryani* ready, nice and hot, just the way you like it, and some *kheema,* too. And, if you don't find me here, you know where I will be—in the *biryani,* cut up and cooked by Haola for not charging."

And both of them laughed, and then there was silence, a hot, crazy silence, the kind that exists between men who had seen too much and who didn't need to say much, either, to be understood. If Chacha drank, Hausangbhai would have offered him the bottle. And they would have both sat drinking till the power came back, till Haola had gotten tired of heating up the food and retired to bed resigned to the ways of *men who would be boys*—and many bottles later Chacha would have reached into his pocket, pulled out the stone, and placed it before Hausangbhai's dim, disbelieving eyes, and the two would have chuckled over it, dreamt over it, and planned feverishly like rogues on a binge.

But since that wasn't possible, since Chacha didn't drink and he had Badshah to think of first, Hausangbhai looked up at the half-derelict buildings, the partial moon, the frail antennas, penciled against a pitiless, black sky and he said, "The power should be here any moment, any moment now."

And Chacha replied, stroking his beard, "Let's hope so. What more can we do anyway?"

HARAAMI

✦ ✦ ✦

HARAAMI: AN EXQUISITE HINDI WORD, explicit, therapeutic, and useful—because it is able to take multiple forms. Quite plainly, it means "of bad blood, ill descent." To use it as such you have to add venom. But *haraami* can also be delivered with affection, to describe a mischievous person—in which case you pucker your lips and say, *"Bahut haraami hain sala,"* meaning, "a real scoundrel he is, an affable rogue."

Rohit was a *haraami,* the harsher kind, spelled "low-down." He worked at the ad agency where I worked. He was tall, thin, good-looking, with a boyish face and hazy eyes. I soon realized that the haziness was induced by three joints of grass, enjoyed at different times of the day—one in the morning, one at midday, followed by a third, mid-afternoon or early evening, depending on the kind of pressures we faced. No complaints with that. Everybody in advertising smoked, except the accountants, the peons, the chauffeurs, and the managing directors. The latter preferred alcohol, which suited us fine, because we didn't want them hitting us for stash, bad enough that they'd monopolize half the nice-looking girls in the agency, get to sleep with them, too. But that didn't make them *haraamis;* it just made us dream of owning an ad agency, of having a permanent hotel room booked for extemporary stints in the sack.

Rohit was crying the day I found him. He was huddled over the phone, clutching the receiver and pleading into it. Transparent tears rolled down his face, onto the boss's mahogany table. It was just as well the boss wasn't there. The table had come at a price, rescued from an old solicitor's firm that had gone broke. No idea why Rohit decided it was *the* place to have a breakdown. Long back, a Chivas ad had legitimized tears for the sensitive male; it had shown a broken bottle of Chivas and a headline that read: "Ever seen a full-grown man cry?" Years later, the *Bombay Times* came in with their own version of the sensitive, emoting man—the metrosexual, they called him. He did everything the girls did: looked after his hair, his wardrobe, his toes, his complexion, his nails, his eyelashes. He even cried—like them.

I confess I was fascinated by Rohit crying. I wanted to ask him if he was a metrosexual, if he was *that* modern. So I waited for him to finish the call. Then I tapped him eagerly on the shoulder but chickened out seeing his face strained and damp with tears. "We can go somewhere. Talk. Can't be all that bad," I said, more concerned now and less curious.

We went to the spot behind the agency. It was a tiny corner off Warden Road, looking out onto the sea. Being part of a private road, it was undiscovered, quite scenic, and full of horizon. We sat there— on a jagged brick wall—gazing at the Arabian Sea, a quivering mass of silver, gleaming under the evening sun.

The tide was in. It scampered and rushed toward us. When it pulled out, it left all sorts of refuse on the black, oily sand: empty coconuts, a broken *chappal,* the cap of a Bisleri bottle, a Bisleri bottle, some plastic bags, frail and torn, and a tangled mass of branches. It calmed Rohit momentarily to see the turbulence of the waves, to see them gain height, speed, strength, roll over rocks, crash, and fizzle out in a foamy whimper. He dug into his pocket and pulled out a joint. It was crushed and creased. He checked to see it wasn't broken. It wasn't. He drew out his lighter, one of those cheap refillable ones, where the carriage could slip anytime. With his other hand, he smoothened the joint, using two fingers pressed together, and I saw he did this gently. Then he went *click, click,* with the lighter, a number of times before the joint lit. He had to pull hard against the breeze to make it start. He inhaled, and then he spoke.

"I am up shit creek, man," he said. "A few months ago I was sleeping with this girl I was seeing then. She had to leave the city suddenly—to stay with an old uncle who was ailing or dying, God knows what. She is back now, and says she's pregnant. Three months and a week up, and she's done nothing so far. Says she doesn't know what to do, where to go, whom to turn to? 'So, what can *I* do?' I said to her, but she is threatening to spill the beans to her brother. I know him. He has connections. He won't hesitate to get me beaten up. He might even get me knifed. I am sunk, man. I am fucked."

He started crying again, covering his face with the same hand in which he held the joint. The ash hung precariously, so I took the cigarette off him, from between his fingers. I took a few drags, long and pensive, and gazed at the setting sun. The sky had turned purple, an indigo blaze heralding the advent of twilight. The clouds, too, had changed complexion, more solemn and restful now. A fresh breeze had started: it fanned my face, lulled my mind, and sent the grass racing through my veins. I added my own clouds—of thick, rich Kerala grass—to the horizon. Then I said, "There's nothing to panic about. You've left it late, but maybe we can pull it off."

We? I knew in my mind it was the grass doing this: this assumption of ownership, this transference of power, from offender to helper. I looked at the culprit in my hand—this wand of brotherhood, this rock-and-roll energy at work.

"I know a doc—a good one," I continued. "She's a friend, strong, caring, and clever. Let me call her. I am sure she will work something out."

"Would you do that for me?" he asked, looking up. His eyes were red, mournful, searching. They craved assurance. "I mean, shit, man. Can we go and meet her, your doc friend? Maybe now! Maybe tomorrow—if you like!" His brow darkened. "But look, how much do you think the termination will cost? I can't pay the earth, you know. I don't make big bucks in this job."

"You won't need to. Like I said, she *is* a friend. She will help to make matters easy."

I returned to the agency and called up my friend. She lived up to the high opinion I had of her, for she volunteered to see the couple the next day. The color returned to Rohit's face. He gripped me by the shoulders and said, "Shit, man, you *are* a buddy. I owe you big; that I do!"

Doc saw us the next day. We—that is I, Rohit, and his girl—went to her clinic, a large consulting room above Aziz Antiques in Colaba. Her office was part of a nursing home. Tucked away at the end of a long wooden corridor, it had a high ceiling, half-swivel doors, a high bed, an old desk, some certificates on the wall, and a Confucian saying that warned against asking for credit. Outside was a sofa, which could seat four, and two chairs with Rexene upholstery. In between the chairs was a rack of outdated film magazines.

Doc, as usual, was bright and motherly. She was not much older than me, which served to reassure Rohit that she'd be easy to talk to. She filled the chair—a revolving high-back—with her presence while she heard Rohit patiently. She frowned when she heard how much time had lapsed, and I could tell she wanted to say something, an ad-monition perhaps, but changed her mind. Flashing a dimpled smile, she said to Rohit, "It's not all that bad. Relax. We have done worse. I can tell you that. We *can* terminate without risk, but you should bring her in fast—tomorrow preferably. I have a busy day, but I can take her between 8.00 and 9.00 A.M., if that's fine by you. She will need a few hours of rest thereafter, and you can take her home by three."

"Whew, thanks, Doc!" Rohit said. He looked at his girl, who smiled and nodded. Then he said in a voice that was low and respect-ful, "And how much will this cost, Doc? For my information."

Reclining in her chair, Doc thought for a moment before saying, "The room will cost eight hundred rupees. The rest of the expenses— the nursing and the operating costs—I can waive." She leaned forward and smiled. "Stop worrying," she said. "It was a mistake, okay? It hap-pens all the time." With that she rose to her feet.

I felt a surge of gratitude toward Doc. She'd said nothing about her own fees. But Rohit hadn't realized that. Before leaving, I thanked her. She squeezed my arm and said, "Don't be silly; it's nothing. But make sure you come as well. The girl seems fine, but the boy looks like he will go to pieces. Lucky for her, to have someone so caring." She said that wistfully.

At this point I contemplated falling in love with Doc. I knew I'd be on safe waters emotionally, but her looks were a stumbling block: something matronly, something pale, prosaic, and insipid about her. I sighed inwardly. The moment passed.

The next day, I took off work to accompany the couple. I must say I was impressed with the girl. Her name was Shyla. She was dark, big boned, and had great composure. "Look after my baby," she said with a wink before she was wheeled into the operating theater. Rohit, I saw, was a loose cannon. He could go off any moment. He kept playing with his fingers, and he kept licking his lips like an expectant father, like there was a life under question.

She went in, and his panic rose. "I hope she's okay; nothing happens to her. I will never forgive myself if anything goes wrong," he said, lighting a cigarette. Then, in a more guarded tone: "I hope your friend knows what she is doing." I felt like slapping him when he said that, but then he was deranged by his concern for the girl. I reminded myself of that.

Within an hour, she was out. She looked tired and compressed, a disheveled doll, yet managed a smile. They wheeled her to a room on the same floor. The stretcher trolley made a rumbling sound as it traveled down the long linoleum corridor. A short, potbellied nurse hurried after it, clasping the instructions file in her hand.

Doc came out and spoke to Rohit, who slouched as though he'd been through an ordeal. "That's a brave girl you've got there," she said to him. "Didn't cry once, when we removed it. I am worried, though, she might break later. Stay with her, will you?"

Rohit nodded and mumbled his thanks. Doc turned and walked off smartly. She was followed by a team of assistants almost as young as herself. My eyes followed her retreating form, her stodgy calves and boxy hips. I tried to imagine them twenty years later. Sadly, I could not. Nor could I imagine myself with her.

In the room, Rohit appeared nervous. He kept picking up objects, examining them, and placing them back. He opened the toilet door and looked inside. After a while, he moved to the window and smoked a cigarette. He appeared deep in thought. Noise from the road poured into the room. A nurse came and took Shyla's blood pressure. She was short, sour faced, and brisk in her movements. "No smoking!" she said to Rohit. "Why do we put up rules if you are not going to observe them?"

Rohit leaned and stubbed out the cigarette against the window ledge. He pocketed the stub, turned, and looked at her with a smirk. "No tip for this one," he said audibly when she left.

A gentle breeze came through the window. I looked out. A great part of Bombay this was: central, convergent, historic, reminiscent of a day and age when all roads led to the ocean, led to a horizon that was clean and fathomless. From where she lay, Shyla called out, "It's over, love. There's no hurt, no pain. I just feel a little raw inside. Empty actually."

"You need some water?" Rohit asked. I could see he hadn't recovered. He was restless and edgy, awkward in the way he kept pacing around. After a while, he stopped and swung his arms like a bowler. Something weighed on his mind, I could tell. He was trying to divert himself. Maybe he was one of those men who are ineffectual in a crisis. Maybe that's why he had this lovely woman, to give him strength. This dark, intriguing woman, who was attempting to sit up, to prop herself up, be brave and cheerful, after having dropped his child. She looked determined—I can tell you that.

I wanted to give them privacy, so I left. I tried to find Doc to ask whether she wanted to do lunch with me. I was told she was busy: deliveries throughout! I remembered her saying so, the previous day, when we had visited. She had left word, though, that if Shyla was in pain she was to be contacted at once. Should I disturb her? I wondered. I wasn't sure whether I was just feeling grateful or, in a subversive way, I wanted to explore my feelings toward her further. Enthusiasm being absent, I opted for my own company. A walk would clear my mind, get rid of the hospital smells from my nose.

I wandered out into the street, stopping before the secondhand books on the pavement. I had always found it fascinating how entire collections landed up here. One generation's pleasure became a burden for another. Hence, entire collections from father to son were sold for a song, and the vendors, knowing nothing about literature, would place a price on the books. They would determine the value of a Maugham, a Shaw, a Salinger, a Steinbeck, a Faulkner, a Fitzgerald. And they'd hold up a Jhumpa Lahiri, a Rushdie, a Seth, a Tagore, in the hope of tempting you. If that failed, the pirated versions came out. Toilet-paper versions with smudgy, castigating print. I walked away in disgust, an outraged bibliophile.

A fakir called to me. He was selling sandalwood figures, wood carved ashtrays, paperweights of Gods and Goddesses, beads, *malas,* trinkets, semi-precious stones, and some strange-looking herbs in bottles. All this was laid out on a cloth, while he himself sat, legs apart, on a wooden crate. I heard his sales pitch and was eventually drawn by a *chillum* with Lord Ganesha on one side and Lord Shiva on the other. Both Gods wore an expression of benign universal knowledge. Twice blessed, I thought, and asked how much. "Only two hundred rupees, sahib," the fakir said. "*Asli cheez hain.* Smoke it and you will see heaven." I looked at him, his grim face, his kohl-rimmed eyes, his thick matted hair, tied in a bun at the top, and the streaks of orange on his forehead. I looked at the chillum and saw Lord Shiva, his hairdo almost the same. Promptly, I abandoned all negotiations. I paid and thought I saw a smile spread across the fakir's face. The smile of unexpected gain.

I walked on, taking in the colors of Colaba, the magic of a neighborhood always on holiday, always on display for its shoppers. I stopped before a street palmist with drawings and charts in front of him. He looked learned, so just for kicks I thought I'd get my hand read. I dropped to my knees and crouched before him. He studied my palm, pinching the flesh to accentuate the lines. He clicked his tongue and assured me that I had no real flame in my life, only imagined ones. And he warned me that I was a failure when it came to judging people. I'd be unable to guess their deep inner motives. Amused and unimpressed, I paid and left.

A while later, I felt hungry. I stopped and considered the options.

Moghlai food at Delhi Darbar or Parsi food at Paradise? Finally, I settled for two beers, a Manchow soup, and a plate of wontons at Café Leopold. There, I had the advantage of scenery: friendly-faced white women, in loose-falling clothes, whose breasts and faces I could gaze at slyly. I relished this freedom and felt like a tourist in my own city. I thought of Doc, my imagined flame. Good heart, but the body had no power to impress, no ability to hold. It would feel like I was missing something in bed. I felt surprised at my callousness—to think such a base thought, despite her kindness—but what to do? That's how things were, how they stood.

2.30 p.m., I returned to the clinic. Shyla was alone. She was sitting up in bed, fully dressed. Rohit had gone to settle the bill. There was a faint smell of grass in the place. He had smoked here—now that was the limit, I thought. A crumpled newspaper with dark, oily stains told me that food had been ordered and consumed. Shyla looked drained. I asked if she felt well enough to go. She said she did. I wasn't so sure. At home, she would have to return to a facade of normalcy. How would she manage? I asked. "Well, yes, I have to pretend now that everything is normal," she said sharply. The strain was telling on her, I thought. I wished that Rohit would hurry back.

While we waited, Shyla maintained an uncomfortable silence. I got the feeling that she didn't want me there. She didn't want to speak to me or have me speak to her. I glanced at her from the corner of my eye. It appeared that there was a cloud over her head, a rain cloud waiting to break. She was frowning, and once in a while she ran her tongue over her lips, the way athletes do—before a race, before a marathon.

"Is there any pain, any discomfort?" I asked anxiously. I was feeling a little uninspired because of the two beers.

"Pain?" She scowled. "No, no pain!" she replied wryly, after a pause.

Just then Rohit entered. The bill was settled and he'd asked the *chowkidar* to call a cab. I picked up the suitcase that held Shyla's things, and we started for the elevator. It was one of those creaky jobs that made its way up slowly.

Shyla walked to the elevator with a slow, shuffling limp, gripping her stomach with one hand. When Rohit offered to help her, I saw her freeze. It was as though she couldn't bear the thought of him touching her. Maybe the crack-up had started, I thought. Maybe this was concealed hysteria or guilt. I could see that Rohit looked annoyed. When the ward boys came asking for tips, he shooed them away. Naturally, my sympathy was with him.

Shyla made it to the elevator on her own. Her stubbornness increased the tension. On our way down, I felt as though we were descending into an unknown hell, the abyss of her mind—dark, stony, and unavailable to us.

When we emerged from the elevator, atoms of tension formed a hard concentric circle around us and accompanied us to the exit. The afternoon sun felt like an invasion of our senses. We felt an inexplicable hate and, below it, confusion. Something like liquid sorrow lapped at our hearts and minds. Its source was unknown, but the silence it created was hard and unpleasant.

A cab waited. Rohit opened the door. He looked intently at Shyla, as she eased her way in slowly. He held his hand over her head, to prevent it from bumping against the roof, but she recoiled. First away from him, then with pain. Seated, she did not look sideways; she looked straight ahead at the road. Her eyes were vacant; her mouth, hard and determined.

Rohit slammed the door. "Aren't you going with her?" I asked, surprised.

Shyla looked at me. "Please . . . it doesn't matter," she said. "I can cope on my own." Her face softened and she said, "Thank you for everything. You have been splendid, but now I need to go." She told the taxi driver, "Walkeshwar!" I watched as the cab drove off.

"Why did you let her go?" I asked Rohit angrily. "You should have spent time with her. Taken her somewhere—to a friend's place, your place—anywhere she could have been with you."

A smile spread across his face. "Fuck it, man!" he said. "Am I glad to be rid of her! I told the bitch it was over between the two of us. I don't need this kind of crap in my life. Unnecessary mind-fuck it became. You saw how it fucked me up. You saw that, didn't you?"

It dawned on me then that it was fear of the brother that had sent Rohit to pieces. It was not the girl or his concern for her life. Nor was he concerned for the seed of life she had given up for him. I exploded and called him names. *Haraami* was only one of them.

Alone that evening, I blamed myself for my stupidity, my naïveté, my faulty sense of judgment. I felt scammed—by Rohit, by his tears, by the baseness of my sex in general. Male brutality or male cowardice: I didn't know what to make of it. Sex as achievement was terribly important to us males struggling through a less permissive age, struggling to prove our manhood, our attractiveness, but to transcend all boundaries of heelishness—to forget that if we penetrated it was because someone received. *Does she give?* It was a question we boys always asked one another. Now, how about: *Does she receive?* Or rather: *Does she find you worthy to receive?* And how does she accommodate your childish panting thrusts? Think the male ego can handle that? Rohit's did—all too comfortably. The baby face cracked, and in its place stood a smug, grinning escapist, a lily-livered contortionist unaware of his own hideousness.

Haraami, haraami, haraami: I screamed at Rohit for days thereafter. I couldn't stop calling him that, because he made a fool out of me, a complete sucker, and, worse, a party to cruelty. When my anger subsided, I asked him to give me Shyla's number. I wished to confirm that she was well. I hoped, by doing so, I could shed my guilt. "No use crying over spilt sperm," he sneered. "Besides, consolation sex is bad for your health. She might fall for you on the rebound." He refused to give me her number.

Three months later, just when I had given up hope of meeting her, Shyla surprised me with a call. "I would like to meet," she said, and suggested a coffee shop nearby.

I was beside myself when we met. I spat venom at Rohit. I swore enmity. I apologized on his behalf, on behalf of life, on behalf of all the males of the world. I said I didn't know of his intentions, else I'd have dropped her home, stayed in touch with her, been with her through her recuperation. She deserved better, much, much better: she could take that from me. That scumbag would get his desserts—by all the holy books, he *would* be sorted out.

I offered myself to her. I could be her friend, her confidant, if she wished. I could see her through this crisis. She laughed. "What crisis? That's over! It stunned me at first, but no more. And that's not why I wanted to meet you. There's something else, for which I need your help."

Edging closer, she lowered her voice and spoke confidingly. "You see, I have decided that love brings nothing but pain and disillusionment. How many married couples do you see who are still in love? That 'happily ever after' gambit is complete hogwash. I have decided I am going to marry for money." She paused, drew in her breath. "There is a proposal. A diamond merchant's son, filthy rich, with offices worldwide. I can do what I want, travel wherever, shop like crazy, start a business, close it, start another." She looked at me inquiringly, as if expecting a reaction. "I know it's soon, after what happened, but I have thought it through. That's what I want. That's what will make me happy. Mentally, I have accepted it."

"Oh, that's great then," I said, trying to sound light and agreeable. I wasn't prepared for such a cold-blooded recovery. Once again I felt let down by my sense of judgment.

"Yes, but for this to work, I will need your help. The boy's family is conservative. They are bothered about things like reputation. They found out about Rohit, but I said he was a friend, a *raakhi* brother actually. I said I had never been around, never known anybody intimately that way; my upbringing wouldn't permit that. This made them happy. They believed me. You see, they will not accept someone who they think is not pure, who is not a virgin. It could create problems later. So, could you ask your Doc friend to stitch me up? Just one or two, in the right place?" The last bit came out in a rush. Yet it was I who was winded, unable to express my shock or my surprise.

A YEAR LATER, I received the invite: one of those elaborate jobs, on handmade paper, with tassels, and a smear of vermilion for luck. I went, not knowing how I had come to be invited, considering that I had failed to do her the favor. I had failed to talk to Doc and arrange the deception.

The venue was sprawling: the Turf Club. There were people everywhere, important-looking people in fine suits and saris, in Nehru jackets, *shenvanis,* and designer *salwar kameez.* The men looked pleased, wealthy, and well fed. The women had jewelry dripping off them. The trees had lights. The men swaggered and walked around, looking for faces more successful than them. Occasionally they'd clutch each other. "Know who that is? Sureshbhai from Amsterdam" or "Saileshbhai from Antwerp!" And then, in lowered tones, "You know how much he is worth? The last I heard it was six hundred crores."

In the distance, music blared. Indipop and *bhangra* had the crowd swinging. Little children showed remarkable lightness of foot, with movements imbibed from MTV. The older girls swayed lavishly, their backs open, their hips lean and fluid. They'd been told that this was *the* place to invite proposals, *the* place to get a good boy from a good, wealthy family. So the girls rolled their eyes, undulated their hips, and moved their hands like temple dancers. The DJ smiled and upped the volume. Goaded by elders, prospecting males jumped into the fray. They entered briskly with a sense of purpose. They raised their hands, wriggled their shoulders, and danced *bhangra*-style to the beat. The girls turned and continued to sway; a little shyness came into play.

I waited in line to congratulate the bridal couple. My gift, a recycled Sega-of-Japan vase, felt inadequate in my hands. The couple stood on a stage. Behind them was a backdrop of gold. I tried to guess whether the gold was real, whether it was as pure as it looked, but of course it wasn't. It was just done up to look that way, to keep the crowd guessing.

Accompanied by their elders—their parents, uncles, aunts, grandaunts, and granduncles—the couple received the guests. Each time someone came up, the couple would bow and take their blessings. Shyla was the perfect bride. She smiled on cue, laughed on cue, even bent and touched some of the guests' feet. She did this many times over, and they—the guests—would pat her head and bless her, and at the side her in-laws would glow with pride.

I looked at her. She looked truly happy. Or should I say accomplished? My mind went back to the hospital, to the girl who had entered, warm and trusting, and she who had left, cold, confronted, and broken by life. My eyes went to the groom. He appeared plain and sloppy. And yet he looked so happy.

Just then a short bald man in a gray safari suit, flanked by gunmen, rushed past where I stood. "Some politician!" the man ahead of me whispered. The groom's father lurched forward to receive him, gesticulating frantically to the guests who were about to ascend the stage to move back. The guests understood and froze. If a custodian of the nation had made time for this, he must be given due respect. And besides, what an achievement for the host: to have persuaded the politician to break from his busy remunerative schedule and attend. "Wah, sahib, wah! You are truly connected. Truly bigger than we thought."

The bodyguards lowered their guns and eyed the women slyly. They let their eyes roll over the delicate waistlines curling into soft silken saris. Unknown to them, the women eyed them, too—for their bodies were rock-solid, not misshapen like their husbands'.

I took this in eagerly, this game of sanctimonious survival, and that's when I saw him: Rohit! He stood ahead in the line, tall and bemused. He was casually dressed, in a checked shirt, black trousers, and a jet-black blazer. No tie, and that stood out, made him appear cool and self-assured.

So, she had called him, her *raakhi* brother, sanctified by the laws of a festival that allowed a woman to take any man as her brother by simply tying a symbolic flower around his wrist. Seeing this, I remembered the legends of old: the noble Queen of Chittor, who'd sent Emperor Humayun a *raakhi,* requesting him to rescue her kingdom from the King of Gujarat, and long before that Alexander's wife, tying a *raakhi* to the wrist of King Porus—so that, if victorious, he'd spare her husband's life. Both times the *raakhi* had served its purpose, as it had done for centuries, later, uniting siblings, strengthening ties, transforming them into something sacred and unbreakable. But now the times had changed. Traditions were being twisted. They were being misused to serve different ends, different motives.

The cameras went flash, flash, flash, and the politician stood onstage, hugging the bride, hugging the groom. He was much shorter than them, and this allowed him the leeway to grip the bride by the waist, which he did firmly with his short, stubby fingers, looking very pleased and very photogenic. Through the photo session, the boy's family gave the broadest of smiles. Shyla stood erect and composed. The boy beamed oafishly. The women at his side touched their jewelry, drew up their backs, and looked into the camera demurely. The father barked at the photographer, "Come on; come on. Take some tight close-ups, some different angles. Make sure you get Sharma sahib in each and every frame, huh."

I looked at all this and wondered then who the real culprit was, who the real *haraami* in focus.

Was it the politician, the obvious one? Or the groom's father, who had insisted on a piece of hymen and paid this fabulous price? Or the groom, who had allowed himself to be the heir to such parochial thinking? Or the girl herself, looking so radiant and virginal, pleased that her past was buried and her future so well secured? Or, stepping out of frame but not out of line, was it Rohit, the *raakhi* brother, the man loosely dressed and at ease, inadvertently the architect of this sham?

By the time I stepped onto the stage, onto its red welcoming carpet, and into its embrace of warm, hearty camaraderie, I had figured out that *haraami* was a nice word to describe the world. It was a canopy for the human race, a comfort zone unto itself, an explanation for all of life's inexorable irrationalities. Maybe someday, after adequate observation, some lexicographer would realize this and invite its universality into the English language. Or some analyst would construct a theory around it. Or some evangelist would compose a song: "*Haraami!* That's you and me! No one escapes, don't you see?" Or, out of humble and retrograde acquiescence, I could end up meeting Shyla, for surely in her well-laid-out, functional marriage she'd need some diversion.

A DIFFERENT BHEL

✦   ✦   ✦

IT WAS A WARM SUNDAY EVENING, presided over by a slow-moving sky, when Nadir Ravankhot and his friends returned from their *shikaar* in the dark, distant Bhir Forest. As the dusky convoy of two Mahindra jeeps rolled in at the gates, the colony—a sedentary world of small residential blocks in a quiet part of South Bombay—started coming alive. Couples on their evening walk nudged each other and stepped onto the pavement. The volleyball game in the *maidan* was disbanded. The players—teenage boys in shorts and T-shirts—rushed to where they knew the convoy would stop: outside Nadir's house, M block, M-51 to be precise. The boys called to one another excitedly. They shouldn't miss out on the quarry the hunters had brought home, the spoils that would be transformed later into a mouthwatering feast. Seeing the jeeps, a twelve-year-old boy, his bicycle raised on one wheel, swayed and lost his balance; his feet shot out to collect himself in time. A teenage girl flirting with a boy her age lost interest in him; they both turned their heads in the direction of the approaching convoy. Boys playing cricket, girls playing hopscotch, middle-aged men discussing work, politics, or tax shelters under the new budget—all left their pursuits and looked at the jeeps. Men relegated to their balconies because of old age or arthritis called to their wives. "Look, he is back," they said gruffly, enviously. For all the killing Nadir had done, for all the times he had shot a deer, a rabbit, a wild boar, and twice even a panther—he had done so when *shikaar* was permitted, and later, when it was banned—still life had been kinder to him than to them. They didn't like that. Yet they felt the excitement.

There were two men in each jeep, each of them in their fifties. Nadir stood tall, towering, and red faced in the jeep his friend drove. His face was sunburnt. His eyes were small, hard, and alert. The hair on his head was light brown and receding, brushed back in waves to reveal a large, glistening forehead. His left leg was perched on the half door of the jeep. His rifle was in his hand. When the children of the colony came running up, he'd turn and train his rifle on them. He would pretend to take aim and shoot, and they would squeal and freeze, and he would roar with laughter. They'd know then he didn't mean to shoot. He was only playing with them.

"Can't say, though. Never can say with Nadir Ravankhot what might snap," said Hilda Pestonji. "He is not the terror he used to be, but still, when a man kills dumb animals for pleasure, knowing full well it is a crime, you know something is wrong. Something has never been right."

Hilda and her friends Gul Sinor and Roxanne Banaji were seated on a circular stone bench in the garden adjoining the *maidan.* The garden was secluded from the *maidan,* so that the elders of the colony could come here and sojourn in peace. The ladies met here every evening for a break from the routine of their lives: loud, noisy children; whimsical in-laws; husbands who liked their meals hot, on time; not to forget servants full of excuses, who needed constant supervision. The ladies believed this interaction kept them young. It also kept them abreast of what was going on in the colony: who was dating whom, who was leaving whom, who was trying to muscle into whose parking spot. Looking at the faces of the ladies, their well-preserved bodies, their youthful clothes—tight slacks, T-shirts, naughty boy shoes—you *would* believe they had succeeded in beating age at its own game. They scarcely looked their years, which were around mid-forties, except for Hilda, who was fifty-two, glum faced, and slightly stooped in her posture.

"Oh, Hilda, give the man a chance," said Roxanne Banaji. "He has paid for his sins long ago. Let us forgive now and forget." She smiled at Hilda, who gazed after the convoy reproachfully.

"The man was a brute and will always stay one," said Hilda. "After what he has done, how can we forgive him? If you knew him the way I do, you wouldn't hold such a charitable opinion."

"Then tell us, dear Hilda. Acquaint us with the sordid past of Nadir Ravankhot. Unlike you, we are latecomers in the colony. We don't know what he has done to earn this reputation. Tell us about his mysterious past: why it has everyone tight-lipped. What is *so* dreadful about him?" Gul Sinor's eyes fixed searchingly on her friend.

Hilda fell silent. Her lower lip dropped and her cheeks puffed outward. Her friends knew this to be a sign of contemplation. It was also a test of friendship, for there seemed to be a hidden pact among the older residents of the colony that the shenanigans of Nadir Ravankhot would never be discussed. Would Hilda break this pact? Would she deliver them the truth? It would be interesting to know.

Hilda sighed. "Very well," she said. "I will, with pain, recollect the times we lived in fear of Nadir Ravankhot. Listen quietly and don't interrupt until you see the *bhelwalla.*" Her friends nodded.

Hilda rose, stretched, and went and sat on the curve of the bench so that she faced her friends. Before sitting, she looked to see if the bench was clean and out of habit brushed the leaves and twigs off it. Gul Sinor brought her long legs up on the bench, crossed them, and sat in an erect yogic pose. With gray twinkling eyes she gazed at Hilda expectantly. Roxanne Banaji draped one leg over the other and placed her hands daintily over her knee. Fair, with liquid brown eyes, she was a picture of grace. The convoy rolled out of sight, taking its fans with it.

"I remember Nadir Ravankhot from the time he was fifteen and I was two years his junior," said Hilda. "His father was an accountant in Central Bank; his mother used to stitch vestments. They weren't well off; their house had a bleak, decrepit look about it. Passing by, you heard shouts and abuses. You heard terrible fights, for they were on the ground floor, where everything was audible. It was either Nadir yelling at his father or the old man telling the boy that what he was doing was no good; cutting classes and going to movies was not going to get him anywhere; it was going to land him in serious trouble. Not that the boy listened. He would play *matka*. He would drink at local bars. He would hang out with the *mawalis* outside the Strand Cinema, smoking *charas,* playing the flipper machines, and teasing coeds who came to see the morning shows. He would get bad reports from school; his parents would be summoned. It had no effect on him. He had flunked a couple of times and was already old for his grade. Once, during exams, he was caught cheating. He had sewn little chits of paper to elastic bands that, in turn, were sewn onto his underpants, and he would pull and refer to these through his half pants. A master noticed this and requested him to stop what he was doing. He smiled and told the master to mind his own business. He suggested the master look the other way if he knew what was good for him. The master—a short, overweight man— looked around nervously and saw what he stood to lose—the respect of other students who had stopped writing. He dragged Nadir off to the principal, who suspended him. The boy was not to come back to school for three weeks of the new term, which would begin after the holidays. After the bell had rung and the students had dispersed, Nadir gathered his schoolbag and approached the master. 'Sir,' he said. 'You have to walk to Churchgate Station for your train, right? You do that to stay healthy. But I don't think it will be healthy for you in the future. Anything can happen on the way.' He smiled and with a flourish whipped out a pocket comb, which made the poor master yelp in terror. The master knew Nadir's street connections. He sus- pected the boy carried a knife he wouldn't hesitate to use. After school reopened and Nadir returned from his suspension, the master would call a cab to the school gate and he would get a peon to ac- company him all the way to the station. Along the way, he would keep turning and looking back to see if he was being followed. Finally, it got to him so much that he gave Nadir additional points on his ex- ams, which the boy didn't deserve but which helped him pass that year. I got to know this from other colony boys who studied at the same school as Nadir.

"I think Nadir had a complex. It began in school, in the early days, when he saw other boys better off than him in status. He couldn't speak the way they did: fluently, in English. He couldn't dress like them or talk like them about clothes, cars, vacations, and birthday parties. It never occurred to Nadir's parents that a boy would need that as part of his acceptance quotient, his image. So Nadir decided to do things on his own, and he decided to throw his full weight behind it. With his height, size, and brute strength, he became a terror. He wouldn't hesitate to challenge boys older than him. He would provoke them to fight and take pleasure in beating them up. He and his friends, those guys he goes hunting with—Dara, Bailey, and Sheriar— they formed a nexus of terror. They called themselves the Four Aces gang and even got an ace with a serpent tattooed on their arms. Inspired by their friends from the Strand Cinema who would collect protection money from shopkeepers, the Four Aces began collecting *hafta* from boys in the colony who received their pocket money at the start of every month. Pointing to their tattoos, the Four Aces told the boys the serpent could protect them or crush them, depending on whether they cooperated or not. Depending on whether they paid up on time or not.

"One of the boys made the mistake of complaining to his father about Nadir's extortion racket. His father promptly whisked him before old Mr. Ravankhot, who, cringing with shame, heard the story. That night when Nadir came home, Mr. Ravankhot was waiting with his belt in his hand. Without a word, he lashed Nadir across his shoulders, his chest, his legs, until his arm hurt; he was unable to raise it any more. Through the flogging, Nadir stood still, smiling. He did not flinch or look down even when his trousers ripped and the blood seeped through. He wanted to show his father he was unmoved: the old man had no power to change or to control him. Some people who stayed near the fire temple swore they saw Mr. Ravankhot crying on the steps of the fire temple that night. He was that kind of a man, religious and emotional, softhearted to the core. The lashing had hurt him more than it hurt Nadir.

"Four days later, Nadir and his friends caught the boy who'd told on them and, seizing his schoolbag, they fled with it. They lured him into one of those quiet lanes opposite the bazaar. There they slapped him and kicked him, and when they were sure he could not put up any more resistance they took his schoolbag and emptied it out. They pulled out their peckers and pissed into it, saying he should think of *this* each time he opened his bag. They warned him from now on he would have to pay twice the *hafta*. Failing to do so, he would face some *real* shit.

"From the time he was in school, Nadir was fond of gambling. He would play street roulette and frequent dens like the Red Fox and the Blue Haven. He would hang out for hours, playing the slot machines, until he had exhausted his money. You might ask where he got it from, his parents being so poor. From what I have heard, he used to cheat Arab tourists at Colaba. He would sell them parrots in cages, saying that if they fed the parrots a special diet for a few months the parrots would start talking. He would sell the Arabs nuts, which he would get in wholesale quantity from Crawford Market. And he would charge a hefty amount for the nuts, too. He would also sell them a cage, saying it was made from special material to protect the parrot. You know Arabs? The fact that the boy spoke English, he seemed better mannered than the street touts, made them believe him. They parted with their money and waited for the day their parrots would talk back to them.

"Oh, he was a bad one, all the way from the start. He used to steal tires and fenders of cars and brakes and window shutters from the railway yard and has even stolen money from the donation box at the fire temple. There was no proof, but we knew it was him. He was seen by old Mr. Bharucha who had come for his early-morning prayers. Mr. Bharucha *had* wondered what a boy like Nadir, so defiant of authority, so devoid of spiritual inclination, was doing at the temple that early. But he was too polite to ask. Besides, Mr. Bharucha always hoped that the Lord, in his infinite mercy, might draw the misguided boy onto the right path. When the theft was discovered, the priest of the fire temple was so shocked that he held special prayers for the sinner, so that he would realize the gravity of his sin. Of course, we all knew it was Nadir. He wasn't seen for days thereafter, and it was rumored that he and his friends had rented motorcycles and taken off to

Lonavala, where they got drunk in some motel and did things best known to themselves.

"By the time he was in college, Nadir had earned a reputation as a thug, a *dada* of sorts. His services could be hired for a fee. A person standing for election to the college council could be persuaded to opt out; all it took was a visit from Nadir and his friends. Or a boy seeing a girl fancied by someone else could be persuaded to withdraw from the relationship, without as much as an explanation to the girl he was dating. This was not just in the college where Nadir and his friends were enrolled but across most South Bombay colleges: they all came under his sway. Virtually every week there was some street fight, some gang that Nadir and his friends messed with, messed up, and there'd be celebrations and liquor flowing. Two or three times Nadir got into a police *panga,* and the inspector from the Colaba police station came to see Mr. Ravankhot. The inspector had great respect for Nadir's father, whom he had met while investigating a fraud in the bank. Mr. Ravankhot had helped the inspector to narrow in on the culprits, who were his higher-ups in the bank. This show of integrity had impressed the inspector greatly, so he let off Nadir with a warning. Later Nadir was heard bragging to his friends, 'I refused to say I was sorry to the inspector, although Dad was expecting me to do so. For this Dad thrashed me badly. But did I care? No! Dad has no strength. He is not like my grandfather, who used to take part in Hindu–Muslim riots, siding with the community that was outnumbered. Granddad could tilt the odds with just a few punches. I take after him—thank God for that!'

"Nadir would do crazy things like incite African tourists who paced the backstreets of Colaba in search of hashish and women. He would take money from them, saying he would procure them their needs, and then he'd invite them to recover it by fighting him. Most times, the Africans would curse and walk away, not knowing the tourist laws in our country.

"Besides having great natural strength, Nadir knew karate. He would train every evening at a dojo, where full-contact sparring was encouraged. Yet after a while he was forbidden to spar with any opponent junior to him. He was also banned from partaking in karate competitions, his instructor having realized that Nadir relished the sight of blood. Invariably he would get carried away and cause grievous injury to his opponents. As with some of the larger prey he would kill later, he would be thirsting for the blood of his victims. And he would go all out for it.

"Over time, the exploits of the Four Aces became more brazen. One day, the four of them brought some poor, drunk *you-know-what* to the wall behind the pavilion, where they had a time with her. Then they threw her out, saying they'd report her for trespassing. The poor woman stood by the wall, shrieking her curses and sobbing. She had reason to be hysterical. The money they promised her would have fed her children that night.

"Another day, Mr. Kavarana from T block happened to be with the Four Aces on a crowded bus. He saw them standing in the aisle, rubbing themselves against a young girl, whom they had surrounded. They pretended it was the motion of the bus that thrust them against her. The girl was too embarrassed to complain, too scared to protest. Finally, she got off in disgust.

"Late one night, they were parked in a car at Apollo Bunder, smoking hashish, when a police van cruised up for inspection. Nadir bragged to the colony boys how the sight of the cops had done nothing to faze him; instead he had stepped out, gone to the back of the van, and hidden his *chillum,* his full-to-the-brim hash pipe, there. He stood there, flanked by the other Aces, who knew instinctively what they had to conceal, while the cops searched their car for the familiar drug. Before the cops left, Nadir had reached out and recovered his *chillum,* hiding it in the brawny folds of his palm. 'So much for smart-assed cops,' he said, wearing his characteristic sneer.

"I don't know if you girls remember, but there was a time in the seventies when a psychopath ran loose on the streets of Bombay. They used to call him the stone-head killer, for the fact that he would go around nude, braining sleeping pavement dwellers with a stone. The man was never caught, but so great was the fear he instilled that all citizens were ordered off the streets and there was a strict police vigil every night. You will never believe what the Four Aces did then. In a car borrowed from one of their mechanic friends, they went hunting for the stone-head killer, or so they said. On one of these expeditions, Nadir spotted a cop, who was alone, sleeping on a chair on a pavement. Nadir told Bailey, who was at the wheel, to stop the car. As the vehicle slowed, Nadir started disrobing. He whipped off his clothes one by one, right down to his socks; then, stepping out of the car, he walked up to the cop, shook him roughly, and asked, '*Bhai sahib, yahan koi patthar milega?* Brother, can you find me a stone at hand?' He did this with a straight face, a gleaming muscle of rock in the moonlight. You can imagine the poor cop's horror. He shrieked himself hoarse with terror, and even the sight of a car cruising up, stopping, the nude giant climbing in roaring with laughter, did nothing to assuage his nerves. This story became the talk of the colony. After this, it was established that there was nothing the boy Nadir feared. Not the stone-head killer, nor the cops, nor his own father or the one above in heaven."

"Good Lord, Hilda! I never knew all this. When I moved into the colony, all I was told was that Nadir Ravankhot was a wild one. He had a wild past, which was now behind him," said Gul, her gray eyes brimming with excitement.

"Wait; don't interrupt," said Hilda. She gulped twice and cleared her throat before speaking. "We had a girl called Franny Faraka who used to stay in C block. She was a bit of a mouse: shy, studious, prone to spending more time in the library, not into boys or into dating as we were. Each time they saw her the Four Aces would go, 'Frigid Franny, Frigid Franny, is there something we can do to warm your fanny?' On hearing this, the poor girl would turn red and step up her pace of walking. Once, in her haste to get away, she dropped her journal and ran, forgetting, in her terror, to recover it. Nadir went home with it and waited for Franny to approach him. But no—she preferred to copy out a whole year of notes, four hundred pages of text and sixty diagrams, if it meant avoiding contact with Nadir Ravankhot."

"But wasn't there someone who could speak up for her, a friend with the guts to approach Nadir, tell him off?" asked Roxanne, frowning. She could see herself in that role.

Hilda shook her head. "Franny had no friends, not because she was unfriendly but because there was no one on the same wavelength as her. Besides, she came from an orthodox family, who did not like her mixing with girls like us lest she pick up our modern habits. Also, her parents were poor. She was on a charitable grant, which came to her as long as she managed to secure a first place in college. With that kind of pressure, Franny had no time to mix around. All she did was spend time in the library or pray in the fire temple. She prayed that she would continue to stand first, continue to receive the grant, so that she could study and become a doctor.

"Nadir waited for a month before approaching her with the journal. Holding it out and staring at her cleavage, he asked whether it was true she preferred sex between the covers of a book to sex between the sheets. He also asked her whether she had cobwebs down there that were touching her knees. Then he turned and walked away to where the other Aces stood watching. They backslapped him and said, 'We've got to hand it to you, Nadir. In matters of daring, no one comes close.' This further emboldened him. He told his friends he would be the first to *leak into* Franny. They sneered at him, saying he was now shooting his mouth off. Extending his hand, he simply said, 'Your *hafta* commission against mine? I will prove to you it *can* be done.'"

"Oh, dear, don't tell me he did what he threatened," said Roxanne. Her brown eyes swam with worry. Her eyebrows furrowed in a deep, engulfing frown.

"What did you expect?" said Hilda. "I told you, didn't I, the man is a brute? He shouldn't be allowed in decent society."

"Go on, sweetie," said Gul Sinor. "Don't jump the gun. We want to hear every bit of it."

"Okay, but don't tell me to stop halfway. Unless, of course, the *bhelwalla* comes."

"Forget the *bhel*. I will buy you dinner at the Golden Dragon, if you go the whole hog. Tell us the full revolting details," said Gul. "I want to know what it is that makes this man such a fright."

"I think he looks a fright," said Roxanne. "What with those small, beady eyes and that bloated face. I can never get myself to speak to him, nothing more than a 'good morning' or a 'good day.' "

"Why, Rox, you *are* getting critical?" said Gul Sinor teasingly. "There is hope for you, after all. You might just make a super bitch, like the rest of us."

"Oh, dear, did I sound bitchy?" asked Roxanne, horrified.

"Hmmm . . . sort of, getting there. A start, you know?" said Gul Sinor, laughing. Then seeing her friend's distress, she quickly added, "Just kidding."

"Should I proceed?" asked Hilda stiffly.

"All yours, honey," said Gul, smiling. "Sorry for the diversion."

"Poor Franny: what she went through, really," said Hilda. "One day, an industrialist had come to the colony to address the youths on entrepreneurship. He was a real achiever, the head of a large industrial group, and a nation builder. A big crowd had gathered at the pavilion, and naturally, Franny was there to hear him. The crowd swelled to such an extent that there was barely a place to stand. People were craning over one another's shoulders, jostling to get a glimpse of the great man. Strangely, in that crowd were Nadir and his friends—complete misfits, you would think. Inching forward, Nadir drew close to Franny, who was standing with her hands cupped behind her back. You won't believe what he did next! He pulled out his pecker and, with his friends covering him, worked himself up to leak into Franny's cupped hands. In all the jostling and pushing, and with all eyes on the speaker, Franny didn't realize what had happened until it was too late. She felt something wet and sticky, turned, and saw Nadir and his friends slink away. She looked at her hands and fainted. People thought it was because of the crowd and suffocation. They took her home, where she ran a fever, became delirious. She stayed in bed for days, thinking she had been defiled, violated. She refused to leave her bed, refused to leave her house, and when she finally did, it was to visit the fire temple, where she clutched at the grills and broke down before the holy fire. There, with the flames as her witness, she asked for forgiveness, deliverance, her purity back. There must be something wrong with her, she felt, if she had been singled out for such humiliation. She stopped going to college. She lost interest in her studies. Her parents couldn't understand what was wrong. They pleaded with her to tell them what it was that had frightened her so. They even threatened her, saying she would lose the grant; she would no longer be able to go to college, complete her Inter-Science, and qualify for medical school, as was her plan. She didn't seem to mind that. It was as if she had lost her will to study, to listen, and to understand. Her professors came to see their model student. She refused to talk to them. She said it simply did not matter what she learned; life had taught her there were things beyond her control that didn't want her to study anymore. She didn't tell her professors there were voices that spoke to her at different times of the day, reminding her that she was merely an instrument in the hands of life. At night, she saw the faces behind the voices, one of them more clearly than the others. It was the leering face of Nadir Ravankhot, and it drove her farther under her blanket, into a shell she refused to emerge from. When she would venture out, she would feel the eyes of the colony boys on her. *They knew.* She knew that. They knew what had happened and they were discussing her. Her hands would burn; the heat would rise to her cheeks, to the spots behind her ears, and she felt all her dreams, hopes, and ambition were destroyed. The priest tried to speak to her, but she said that she was not worthy of his time. She had been *corrupted:* that was the word she used. He shook his head sadly and told her parents it seemed like a case of deadly possession; he would start on some powerful prayers that would dispel the spirit. After a month of prayers, her parents decided to call in a psychiatrist. Dr. Jal Unwalla spoke to Franny for an hour and then said to her parents he had no doubt she needed treatment and isolation. There was something in the environment that was worsening her condition. There was something that had soured her youth. The cause—whatever it was—had to be isolated from the effect; then maybe the effect would wear out. It could take days, months, or years. But that was her only hope, that and the treatment."

"How awful," said Roxanne. "A whole life gone to seed because of one man. But wasn't he punished? Didn't anybody get to know what he had done?"

"Someone obviously did," said Gul Sinor curtly. "Otherwise how would Hilda know?" She had abandoned her pose, brought her knees together, inward, locked her arms around them, and rested her chin on her kneecaps. From there, she looked at Hilda expectantly.

"Now you are asking me to reveal my sources, and that's asking too much," said Hilda. "Be a pet, dear Gul. Run to the entrance and see if you can spot the *bhelwalla*. I don't know why he is so late today. I have been dreaming about his *khatta bhel* all day. I just love the sour chutney. Sometimes I close my eyes and imagine the taste and I can actually experience it."

"Oh no, I don't like that chutney at all," said Roxanne. "I don't know how you can eat it. For me, it spoils a perfectly good *bhel*. I prefer the sweet date chutney. It is nice and thick and goes well with the crushed *puris,* the potatoes, and the dry vermicelli mixed in."

"Neither would work for me," said Gul. " 'Make mine spicy,' I always say. What's life without a bit of spice anyway?"

Gul strode to the edge of the garden, from where she peered over the hedge and called to a boy who was cycling, "Hey, fella! How would you like to earn yourself an ice cream? Just take a quick ride round the colony and see if you can spot the *bhelwalla*. Bring him here and get yourself a scoop from Kwality's. How does that sound?"

"Sure thing, Mrs. Sinor," said the boy, and pedaled away. "Just keep the money handy."

"These boys of today," said Gul, under her breath. "They won't do a thing without payment."

She walked back to where her friends sat lost in thought. The sun had set. The trees appeared dark and drooping. The chalk-yellow buildings looked bright and monotonous, barracklike, against a purple, inflamed sky. Lights had come on in the apartments. Television sets poured forth their soaps, and in the midst of that came a soft pounding sound from some speakers.

"You were saying, Hilda, how you got to know what happened to Franny," said Gul brightly.

"I don't remember saying any such thing," said Hilda. "I am allowed to keep a few secrets, am I not?" She pursed her lips stubbornly.

"Not if you consider us your good friends," said Gul solemnly.

"It doesn't matter," said Roxanne hurriedly. "As it is, I am finding all this rather upsetting. Just imagine what a harsh turn life took for this girl Franny. Did she ever recover? Did she get her confidence back, I wonder? She must have been so vulnerable to let things hurt her so."

"Yes, she was," said Hilda. "Franny was reserved but tender-hearted. She used to walk to college daily just so that she could save money and feed stray dogs milk and bread along the way. And what a mind! Topped our batch in ISC and would have become a doctor or a scientist—so bright she was. And helpful, too, always giving her notes and her time to weaker students, never expecting a rupee in return, although she needed the money desperately." Hilda's lips quivered. She wrapped her arms tightly around herself.

It couldn't be the breeze; there wasn't any, thought Gul Sinor.

Rising, she went and sat beside Hilda and placed an arm around her friend. "If this is upsetting you, we could talk about other things," she said. "We could talk about the bold and the beautiful."

"Yes, what's the latest on them?" asked Roxanne, taking the cue from her friend.

They were referring to a group of married couples in the colony who were having it out with each other's partners. The three friends had nicknamed them the bold and the beautiful for their ability to change partners without a thought to their marriages or to their children.

"There are things not easy to forget," said Hilda moodily. It was as if she hadn't heard her friends; she had entered a dark tunnel of thought through which she must pass, must grope and blunder on until she saw the exit, the light at the end.

"There are things he has done that make my blood boil, even today, after all these years," said Hilda. "One time, Nadir's parents had gone for a weekend to Udvada, leaving him alone at home. He invited his friends over, and they had spent the day drinking and listening to Hindi film songs. We could hear them shouting, singing, cursing, at times laughing hysterically. Around late morning, a Koli woman by the name of Gomti came around selling fish. She was a buxom thing, and it was no secret that many of the men in the colony had the hots for her. They would stare secretly at her curves, drink in her voluptuousness, but that is all they would do. Every morning, Gomti would go around the colony, calling out the catch of the day and its price. She had done this for years, fish being the main trade of the Kolis. As she passed the Ravankhot house, Nadir invited her in. Drunk and red-eyed, he bought fish from her. But when it was time to pay, he asked her to take the money from his pocket. He said his hands were greasy; he had applied some ointment after working on his motorcycle. She slipped her hand into his pocket only to find the bottom cut away. Her hand touched bare, flickering flesh. She screamed and ran out, forgetting to take the money he owed her. Standing outside his door, she hurled terrible insults at him, which drew the residents of the colony onto their balconies. She cursed him and his friends who stood there watching. She said they would all suffer; they would never have children, never know what it is like to procreate. For what he had done, he—Nadir— would become impotent; he would lose his powers of manhood. Knotting the end of her sari around her waist, her face blazing, she swore he would become a *chhakka,* a eunuch. She swore on her children, her Goddess, and the ocean that sustained her trade. No one thought of going down to pacify her, for it made no sense to get involved with an enraged Koli. Also, no one wanted the wrath of Nadir and his friends upon them. People stayed inside their homes, listening and trying to piece together the events that might have transpired. Later a mob of Koli men armed with sticks arrived at the gates of the colony, and they threatened to burn down the place if the culprit was not handed over to them. It took Dastoorji Dubash, the white-haired, white-bearded priest, to calm them. The culprit was drunk, said the *dastoorji,* employing his most dulcet voice. He didn't know what he was doing; he wasn't in his senses. The Kolis left after threatening never to come to the colony again, and much to the chagrin of the Parsis, who were great fish eaters, they kept their word. No Koli woman ever crossed the threshold of the colony again. Even when the Parsi women went to the market, the Koli women would up their prices, or they'd look away or turn to attend to other customers, making their disgust clear."

"Oh, dear," said Roxanne. "Imagine not getting to eat *patra* fish. I can imagine how difficult it must have been."

"Do you think Nadir got carried away with his own bravado?" asked Gul. "Perhaps he was so intoxicated on a sense of youth that he lacked the discernment to judge the consequences of his actions. I knew someone like that once: a friend of my brother's, who used to delight in phoning people and giving them a hard time. He would send people on fictitious interviews, phone and say they had won a huge prize, to come and collect it from some place far off. One of his favorite charades was to single out someone he did not like, and he would call up the Towers of Silence and get them to dispatch a hearse to this person's house, and he would follow it up with a call to the eye donation center, which would send a team to scoop out the person's eyes, believing him to be dead. The person at the receiving end would go hysterical, thinking someone actually wanted him dead, and this boy—my brother's friend—would feel tickled about it. He would chuckle over it for days."

"If you want to know about cruel pranks, hear this," said Hilda. "In K block lived an Irani called Bahadur Minocheri. He was a typical Irani, simpleminded, good-hearted, and candidly vocal about his feelings. He had a modest job, delivering milk every morning to the residents of the colony. He would do so on his bicycle, in his pajamas and vestment, unbothered as to what people might think of him. Minocheri had long ago decided that the rigors of a day job were not for him. He had tried his hand at being a cashier in a restaurant and a supervisor at the docks, but both jobs had ended in disaster. At the restaurant, when the BMC officers had come around asking for bribes, Minocheri had railed abuses at them and demanded why they were such *fokatchoddoos,* freeloaders who enriched themselves at the expense of those who tried to eke out an honest living. It had taken extreme tact on the part of Hausangbhai Irani—the young, broad-faced owner and a distant relative of Minocheri—to talk the BMC officers out of canceling his license. Likewise, at the docks, Bahadur Minocheri had a run-in with a customs officer who staked his claim to a few bottles of Chivas Regal. This was enough to incense Minocheri, who once again saw it as reason to expatiate on the beggarliness of the officer and on the fate of the country were there more officers of his sort in places of authority. It did not help that both jobs had come to Minocheri because his father had requested their relatives to *accommodate* his uneducated, good-natured son, and after these incidents the relatives had washed their hands of Minocheri. Drawing on his modest shares and fixed deposits income, Minocheri's father supported his son till he turned thirty; then he got him married to a girl from Iran whom he selected on the basis of a photograph. Thereafter, he persuaded Minocheri to leave Bombay and take up a job in an Arab country where he would earn a tax-free income and build up his bank balance. In Arabia, Minocheri had an idea. He decided to learn Arabic, with the intention of impressing the Arabs who, he was told, could confer great wealth on him. He spent all his evenings in his room—a small bachelor pad within a larger apartment—trying to spell out Arabic words in English; he tried hard to roll his words and utter them in the deep, throaty accent of the Arabs. His first courtesy to an Arab policeman, attempted after twenty-one days of practice, landed him in jail, and though Minocheri insisted he had only intended to ask the Arab how on that day his *life* was, the policeman told Minocheri's sponsor who came to visit him in jail that smart-aleck Minocheri had the gall to ask him how his *wife* was faring. Now this was a country where you don't as much as glance or talk to another man's wife, let alone ask about her. The policeman would have passed a five-year sentence on Minocheri, as per the powers conferred on him by the state, had the sponsor not been able to strike some sort of a deal that involved surrendering all that Minocheri had earned so far and seeing him off safely on the next flight to Bombay. On his arrival at the Bombay airport, Minocheri's father broke the news: Minocheri was to become a father himself. Even as he saw his son's joy, his father realized that Minocheri was unfit for regular employment—he could only be employed in some pursuit where there was no chance of him taking a moral or an emotional stand. So he struck a deal with a dairy at Marine Lines that Minocheri would collect and deliver milk on their behalf to the residents of the colony and for that he would earn a commission that would allow him to cope with the growing expenses of a family."

"What an interesting character this Minocheri sounds like," said Roxanne wistfully. "I wish we had more of his type around. Now it seems the colony is only for the wealthy. People are too prim and proper. The fun has gone out of our lives."

"You will be glad it has, my girl, if you let me finish what I have to share," said Hilda dryly. "Minocheri's father expired soon after he had fixed up his son, and three years later Minocheri's wife, too, died of some illness that Minocheri had failed to understand and get treated. The lot of bringing up his daughter fell to Minocheri, and because he was a loving man and because the child had no mother he was extra demonstrative with her. He would fuss over her, dress her well, take her every evening to Apollo Bunder on his bicycle, where he would buy her ice cream, balloons, boat rides, anything the girl wanted. Clearly, Minocheri loved her dearly, and she loved him with an equal intensity. 'Papa Jaan,' she used to call him. 'Papa Jaan, my hero.'

"The daughter grew up to be extremely beautiful. She had a fair complexion, red cheeks, dark eyes, and was well endowed in the right places. When she was in her teens, she was noticed by the Four Aces, and that was the beginning of trouble for poor Minocheri. They would phone him at odd times of the day, when he would be sleeping after his deliveries, and they would yell into the receiver, "*Minocheri, chodoon tori dikri ne,*" meaning, "Minocheri, should we fuck your daughter?" Or they'd ask if the milk he'd delivered that day was squeezed from his daughter's jugs and if the cream was from her you-know-what. On hearing this, Minocheri would charge out of his flat in his pajamas, screaming and shaking his fist at no one in particular. It went on like this for months, and though many of us thought it funny then, we had no idea what the poor man must be going through. Until one day an ambulance came beeping into the colony and Minocheri was rushed to the hospital, where he was pronounced dead on arrival. His daughter sat stone-faced through the funeral and through the four days of prayers. She sat, hands folded, eyes riveted to the place where her father's body had been placed for the last time, the bare, cold slab of stone.

"The day after she returned home, Hufrish Minocheri woke up at 5:00 A.M. She took her father's bicycle, went to the dairy like he had for years, collected four big cans of milk, and went about delivering these. People were surprised to see her that early, and to encourage her they bought twice the quantity of milk they usually would. Last of all, she delivered milk to the Ravankhot house, where Nadir slept, numb after a night of drinking. She poured out a liter of milk for Mrs. Ravankhot, who invited her in for a cup of tea, which she refused. Two hours into the morning, Mr. and Mrs. Ravankhot complained of severe pain around the chest and stomach region. It was a fierce, burning pain, they said, which choked the life out of them. They fell to the ground, writhing in pain and foaming at the mouth. Nadir, awakened to their cries, had to go running for Dr. Doongaji, who took one look at them and said, '*Baap re, baap*. This looks like a case of deliberate poisoning. We will have to call both the ambulance and the police.'

"It didn't take long for the police to figure out the source of the poison. Hufrish Minocheri was taken in for questioning, and she just smiled and asked if the Ravankhots were dead—all of them. When she was told it was just the elderly couple who were seriously ill, battling for their lives, she said, 'What a pity, but some punishment is better than none, and it is always the living who suffer more than the dead, the living who carry the cross.' "

"Oh God, Hilda. Don't tell me any more," said Roxanne. "I don't think I will be able to sleep tonight."

"I won't be able to sleep, not knowing what might have happened to Franny Faraka," said Gul. "I don't mean to probe, dear Hilda, but that gap in the story is obsessing and depressing me."

Just then a flippant voice came over the hedge: "Auntie, I have got the *bhelwalla*. The regular man wasn't there, so I got one from Apollo Bunder."

They looked and saw a scrawny *bhelwalla* perched on the carrier behind the young cyclist. He looked a sight, in his flared white *lehenga* and rubber slippers, balancing his aluminum vessel on his head and holding his stool high, so that it wouldn't scrape the ground.

"You certainly deserve more than an ice cream, young man," said Gul, drawing a fifty-rupee note from her purse.

"Don't be silly, Gul. You will spoil the boy," whispered Hilda.

"Well, rather spoil him than have him grow up to spoil others, like Nadir and the Four Aces," said Gul wryly. Her friends looked at her in surprise. Gul appeared affected by the story. This wasn't like her at all, for of the three she was the tough one, the one who could take spices.

The *bhelwalla* came inside the garden. He sat on the grass and began to prepare the *bhel*. He opened his vessel that had all the ingredients: the *sev*, the puffed rice, the *puris*, the potato disks, the finely chopped raw mangoes, the sliced onions, the pieces of tomato, and the cut coriander. From the side of the vessel he pulled out a newspaper, and twirling it round and round he made a cone of it. Using a steel measure, he scooped and poured two helpings of puffed rice and two helpings of *sev* into the cone. Into this he crushed a dozen or so *puris* and dropped some potato disks, some onions, some tomatoes, and half a teaspoon of finely chopped raw mango. Then he began to churn the mixture, stopping sporadically to add a little chutney—now some of that chili chutney, now some of that date chutney, now some of that mint and coriander chutney.

Hilda spoke slowly, as though with effort. "It's not that I don't want to tell you about Franny. It's just that it is too painful. I was in Franny's class in school and college. Every year, I would try and beat her for first place, and when I couldn't, when I realized she was more intelligent than me, I prayed and wished her dead. You see, I wasn't very pretty, quite ordinary, in fact, and dark, and overweight, and the only way I could enhance my self-worth was by standing first, and when that didn't happen, when I saw myself as second best and unable to change that, my hatred grew. It built up to something fierce in my head, something like a monster. That year, the year of the incident, our class was going on a cruise to Singapore. I was in love with a boy then, who, I knew, was going on the cruise. It was important I get on that ship, and the only way I could do so was by standing first, for that was my father's condition. My father was an army man. He set high standards for himself and for his children, and I knew that there was no way I was going to make that trip unless I stood first. As things went, the incident took place before the exams, and seeing how badly Franny was affected, I decided to make sure she wouldn't recover. I decided to tell everyone— especially the boys in the colony—what had happened. I was there, next to her, when she passed out. I had seen the fear in her eyes, the disbelief as she looked down at her hands and fell away, as if disowning them. When she recovered, she wasn't imagining that people knew. They *did* know, and they *did* speak about it—she could see it in their eyes and hear it in their whispers—and this is what humiliated her, broke her. Well, I got my rank, I got my trip, and though I failed to attract the boy, I did end up having a nice time. But when I returned to Bombay I found that Franny had been sent away to an institution, from where she would never return. The treatment failed to compensate her for the love of learning she had abandoned. The institution created a false sense of security. She got used to the privacy and isolation it offered. The drugs took their toll: she could no longer remember names, faces, equations, theories, all those things she had excelled in. One night, when an inebriated ward boy thrust himself on her, she did not even protest; she let him do his thing and leave. The next day she hanged herself from the ceiling fan, leaving behind a note that said no one was to be blamed for her action. It was her destiny, her karma—she alone was responsible; she had willed this onto herself by her actions in her past life. Why else would such things happen to her? If only Franny knew the real cause— not Nadir Ravankhot, not her karma, but me and my jealousy, me and my enormous hatred of her."

Hilda began to cry. She covered her face with her hands and began to sob convulsively.

Promptly Roxanne went and sat beside her. She hugged her friend warmly. Gul, rising, rested her hand on Hilda's head and began to stroke it lightly.

"Don't worry, love," said Gul. "We all do unreasonably cruel things when we are young. But we learn to forget and the world forgets with us. That is the kindness of memory. It allows us to forget, to overcome our shame. That is also the beauty of life, its regenerating power."

"Yes, just look at Nadir now," said Roxanne. "No one remembers what he has done. No one remembers his terrible past. He is considered a hero, and you know why, don't you? Because one day he used his influence with that local thug, Varun Paoli, to stop slum dwellers from stealing our water connection. He took the initiative to end our water crisis, which had us getting up early in the morning to fill water in drums and rationing our use. He ended our misery, and from that day on people's opinion about him changed. What was seen as *his* intimidating past became *our* collective strength. It takes just one little act of goodness—intentional or unintentional—to wipe out a lifetime of bad, and in your case you were young then; you didn't mean it. Don't feel bad, dear Hilda. It was a mistake and you have left it behind. Come, now, have your *bhel*. Should I ask him to make it nice and *khatta*—the way you like it?"

The *bhelwalla* had laid out three paper plates. The basic mix of the *bhel* was ready. Now it was only a matter of adding the chutneys that would decide the flavor: sweet, sour, or spicy.

Hilda daubed at her eyes with a small white perfumed handkerchief with roses embroidered in one corner. She looked into the warm brown eyes of her friend Roxanne, and she thought she saw a world of compassion in them, pools of reassurance in which she could dissolve her fears, her past. They were the eyes of a woman who saw no bad in the world, a woman who always tasted sweet.

Hilda looked up at her friend Gul. Cool Gul, they used to call her, for nothing could ruffle her. Gul was known to sparkle even under duress, and yet now she looked worried and pensive, and her fingers felt soft and soothing to Hilda, many years her senior.

Hilda looked at her friends and, managing a smile, said, "Know what? I think I will try a sweet *bhel* today. I will try a different kind of chutney. The sweet date chutney. Then, perhaps, I will have a new taste to imagine and remember."

BUSY SUNDAY

✦ ✦ ✦

GAMDEVI POLICE STATION, 11:30 A.M. I take my seat on the visitors' bench opposite Inspector Damle, the duty officer in charge of complaints. He is a robust-faced officer in his thirties, with smooth muscular arms, flickering eyes, and a mustache twirled like an army man's.

The visitors' bench is long and hard. There is no backrest; it is propped against the wall. To rest my back I would need to lean against the wall, which I don't do, because the paint on the wall is peeling; it would stain my shirt. Although I am first on the bench, I have to await my turn. The inspector is busy noting the complaint of an African man seated in front of him. The African has his back toward me. I can see his face only partly.

The African is stout, with a head like a bull, close-cropped hair, and layers of fat in the neck region. He appears uncomfortable with English. He keeps saying, "I beg your pardon," to the inspector, who, I notice, is patient with him.

Next to the African, on a chair, is an Indian, a weasel of a man with an air of self-importance. I realize he is some kind of aide because he acts as an interpreter for the African, repeating the inspector's questions slowly back to the African.

The African is some sort of a dignitary. I could tell that from his letterhead, which he handed to the inspector as a way of introducing himself. The inspector studied it, rubbed his jaw pensively, and passed it back.

The inspector asked the African whether he was a colonel, whether at some stage he had fought for his country. The African howled with laughter; he shook like a schoolboy possessed with mirth. Wiping his eyes, he replied that was his father's ruse; he had named him with great expectations. The inspector smiled and proceeded to ask him more questions.

Just then I was distracted by a video monitor on the wall, which showed what the prisoners in their cells were up to. The video shifted from cell to cell, jerking like a handheld camera. The camera would zoom in on the prisoners—from a long shot to a mid-close-up to a tight close-up—then to the next cell, and so on and so forth.

I saw some of the prisoners were eating moodily, others were playing cards, and two of them—bearded rogues—had struck up a yogic pose. I could swear they knew they were being watched. The picture changed to show a prisoner alone in his cell. He was asleep, in fetal position, fists clenched and held to his chest. I wondered if he had been beaten or tortured.

The African finished his complaint. He suspected he'd been robbed by some of his house staff. Some artifacts, curios, and medallions were missing. Also an African mask, a family heirloom he was attached to.

Inspector Damle assured him they'd get to the bottom of it. There was a heavy sentence for those who stole from foreign dignitaries. He'd use that to threaten the staff. The African shook his head. He said he just wanted his possessions back; he didn't want anyone punished. He was used to having things stolen. It happened all the time in his country. People there were so poor they took easily to a life of crime. They'd walk into homes and steal in the presence of owners who'd be watching television, eating dinner, or making love in their bedrooms. The idea was to pretend it wasn't happening. Let the thieves do their thing and leave. Make a fuss, and you could get shot. Seeing the inspector's shocked expression, the African chuckled. He said he was used to living with danger. Over time, he had begun to take a compassionate view of it, thought of it as charity: someone needed things more than you did, someone just forgot to ask or didn't know how to ask.

The inspector looked at him with warm, curious eyes and said, "You are a good man, Colonel." The African laughed. His whole belly shook. His aide wore a grim, disapproving face. He protested, saying this was not correct; the thieves should be punished severely—they'd set a bad example for the country.

The inspector turned to the aide and said the police would arrive at the house that afternoon. They'd line up the staff, threaten them, and give them time to return the valuables. If they didn't confess in twenty minutes, some rough handling might be necessary: a few slaps or two to loosen tongues. Two *havaldars* came and stood by the inspector's side. They stood with their hands behind their backs, listening intently. I could tell they'd be in charge of the investigation.

The inspector briefed the *havaldars* in Marathi. He had a plan in mind according to which they'd operate. As he spoke, every once in a while he would turn to the African and ask, "Correct?" and the African would nod enthusiastically, like a schoolboy called upon to partake in a secret venture. Before departing, the African held out his palms and made the inspector give him a five, then a ten. He caught the inspector's hands in a grip and swung them genially, left to right and to the left again. Other cops looked up from their work and smiled.

It was my turn next. Inspector Damle gestured to the empty steel chair, which made a grating sound as I sat. There was something wrong with the chair. I had to shuffle my weight and lean forward to steady it. Behind the inspector was a blackboard. Someone had scribbled on it that no officer of the law could ask for a bribe or a favor and, if anyone did, he should be reported to the Anti-Corruption Bureau. The numbers of the bureau were written down.

I began my complaint. It was not worth jotting down, I said, not worth official time, but if he—the inspector—could help me, I'd be obliged, for I had been cheated and knew not where to go.

Placing my elbows on the table, I began my story. My flat leaked every monsoon. The rain poured from the terrace into my apartment, trickling like one of those waterfalls on the Khandala *ghat*. It was a nuisance. Buckets everywhere, and me having to rush from room to room to see where a leak had sprung and where it had increased. To prevent this I had engaged the services of a *damarwalla,* who'd tar the terrace and make it waterproof. I chose a fellow by the name of Raju Gondva. He was short, plump, in khaki knee-length shorts, and stayed near the fire brigade, which was close to the police station. He looked honest, I thought. He had a big, brown face and a friendly disposition. His children—one girl, one boy, between the ages of six and eight— didn't look like urchins; instead they were clean and well dressed, which I thought spoke well of their father. Besides, I didn't smell any alcohol off him, which for a *damarwalla* was rare.

One sunny morning before the rain clouds appeared, Raju Gondva brought bricks, kerosene, and sawdust and began a slow fire on my terrace. On this he heated chunks of *damar* in an old vessel. He stirred the *damar* through the morning, until it turned thick and sticky, and all afternoon he applied it over cracks in the terrace floor and over my window shelters. He used a long pole wrapped with a cloth at one end for the application. He worked alone, he worked hard, and he smiled a smile of lazy contentment, the kind only labor can smile.

Once he finished, I inspected the work. The *damar* gleamed under the afternoon sun. He'd gotten the leaks covered. The splashes of tar—dark and severe—promised me a dry monsoon.

I paid Raju Gondva half the money due to him. The rest, I said, I would give him later, should the *damar* hold out against the first thundering Bombay showers. If it proved its mettle, there'd be baksheesh, a tip, no question about it.

"Please, sir," he said. "I know this is not the normal practice, but as an exception can you pay me the full amount? You see, I have to pay my children's school fees. I have to buy their books and uniforms. A new tuition year is starting, and I have no money left."

I looked at his face—the face of an expectant father bracing himself for rejection, for defeat—and something like pity came over me. I thought no father should cringe while there were men of conscience around. Besides, I knew where he stayed. I knew he had a family and kids. The money changed hands. Raju Gondva saluted me. His shoulders dropped and a boyish gratitude flitted across his face. Clutching the notes, he said, "Don't worry, sir. Any problem and I will be there." Then he went away, swinging his arms happily.

Three showers later, no sign of Raju Gondva. The flat leaked from all sides. The wood near the windows took on a dark, sagging texture. Plaster began to crumble from the ceiling and lay at my feet in clumps of white. My A/C panel began to peel. Running trails indicated where the leaks were heavy. I found myself placing buckets in every room and aluminum vessels on windowsills to collect the dripping rainwater. At night, the sound of the rain going *pitter-patter, pitter-patter* in the vessels drove me mad. I cursed Raju Gondva. I cursed myself. I still hadn't learned how to gauge my street brothers, to wise up to their smooth street-corner opportunism. A fool and his money invite partition. There was no running away from that.

Five times I went to call on Raju Gondva; five times I came away unsuccessful. I met his family: his wife washing clothes, his children studying, a big-bellied woman, in a sari, with thick, red lips and dark glasses, lying on a mattress. She said she was Raju Gondva's sister. She'd been operated on for a cataract two days ago. If Raju came, she'd tell him. Not to bother them otherwise.

On my sixth visit, the sister waved her hands and screamed at me, "Can't you see? He is not here. He has gone away. We don't know when he will be back. We don't know anything about him. Why do you bother us? Why do you harass us still?"

She had a coarse voice that broke from the center of the earth, and I found it embarrassing to be at its receiving end. The embarrassment was greater because they lived out in the open, in a compound off the main road, and there were people passing by every minute.

I turned to Raju Gondva's wife. She was young, in her early twenties. She was wringing out washed garments, pulling them from a bucket, and hanging them on a clothesline. I watched her work, silently, assiduously. She knew I was watching but pretended to be engrossed in her work. At the side, the children were doing their homework; they looked at me resentfully, as though I was intruding. The sister looked up and began to whistle, suggesting I should leave. I did so right away.

"So will you help?" I asked Inspector Damle. "I know I trouble you. I know it is a small thing, more like a favor, but who can I turn to for help, if not the police?"

The inspector reclined in his chair and rocked away, his knees pressing against the table. His khaki belly with the shining buckle loomed into sight. He swayed and stared at me. "What do you expect from us?" he asked guardedly, drumming with his fingernails on the buckle of his belt.

"Well, it's not that I wish to write a complaint—to put you through any such bother—but if you can send a *havaldar* with me, seeing him they will get frightened, and besides, it's right here—at the fire brigade—just around the corner."

"What do you do?" he asked suddenly. "What is your job, your line of work?" As though that might have some bearing on the cooperation he'd extend.

Now this was the tricky part, for I considered myself slightly worse off than Raju Gondva. I was not even seasonally employed. I was in the most uncertain profession of all times, that journey to the center of the earth where there might be treasure or plain rocks, where there might be pleasure or pain.

"I write!" I replied. "I am a writer."

"And your name?" he asked. He'd straightened up and was looking at me with interest.

I answered him, and after that he had no further questions. He called a constable, a tall, bland-faced *havaldar* with a *lathi* in one hand, and told him to accompany me and bring the *damarwalla* to the station; bring his wife and sister if necessary.

"Don't worry," the inspector said, leaning across, his palms locked together. "We will teach them not to mess with the press."

I groaned inwardly and nodded. He'd gotten me wrong, but I wasn't about to tell him that.

We walked to where Raju Gondva stayed. The constable appeared moody and listless, as if his duty had been trivialized; this was not why he'd joined the force. We climbed the steps to the compound, eyes following us: a *coconutwalla,* a *kelawalla,* a *mochi,* a *paanwalla,* all so curious.

The sister wasn't there, nor Raju, nor his children. His wife saw us and came up anxiously.

"See," I said to her, "I have come here many times, and I don't like doing this, but you people leave me no choice. I need to know where Raju Gondva is. When he is expected."

She looked at me, then at the constable, then back at me with slow, widening disbelief.

"How dare you?" she said, drawing herself up. "How dare you bring the police to our door? How dare you treat us like common criminals? What do you think—we will cheat you for a few thousand rupees?"

The constable pushed forward. He was frowning. Pointing his *lathi,* he towered above her.

"Look here," he said gruffly. "You'd better come along. The inspector wants you at the station."

"Wants me for what? First tell me my offense," she said. Her eyes were blazing. The end of her sari was tucked firmly around her waist, and she leaned forward, both hands on her hips.

She turned to me and said, "*Arrey,* sahib, what do you know about other people's problems? What do you know what my husband is doing? He is unable to come because he is holding two jobs. Yes, he works day and night to pay for his sister's operation. You know how much the cost was? Five thousand rupees! And we don't need any more bad luck than what we already have. So please leave. I beg you to go away and not insult us this way. Raju Gondva will come and do your *damaring* when he has the time. It's only a matter of an extra coat or two, so please be patient. Please wait."

The speech had tired her out. It was fatigue borne of outrage, a lioness spent defending her mate against people who'd come to trap them with unfair advantages of birth, class, and money.

"When do you think he can come?" I asked softly.

The constable tried to interrupt, but I stopped him.

"Sunday! He will have time on Sunday," she said. "First thing in the morning, he will come."

I nodded. A quiet understanding passed between us. She was grateful I had listened to her; I felt I craved her admiration in some way.

"Your *zabaan,* your word?" I asked, and she muttered, "Yes, yes," softly and clearly.

The constable frowned and said to me, "You come to the station and tell the inspector this. He will shout at me otherwise."

He was right. The inspector *was* annoyed. "You should have brought her," he said. "I'd have threatened her, given her a little *dhamki.* Then that husband of hers would have turned up at your doorstep. Now you don't know whether he will come and whether he will finish the job at all."

I said I did not wish to humiliate the woman, did not want to hurt her feelings any more than I already had. The inspector shook his head and muttered that *that* was the problem. The police were keen to attend to every complaint, but people took back their complaints, not realizing how much time was wasted. As I was leaving the room, I could feel his disappointment. I could feel his eyes bore into me sullenly. I had kept him out of the news, denied him an opportunity to impress the press. People like me were the problem.

SUNDAY ARRIVED: a calm, breezy day, no rain. I waited at my window. Below my building a bazaar was setting up. Taxis cruised in, their carriers heaped with crates of fruits and vegetables. The vendors called to one another and hurried forward to unload their wares. Old beach umbrellas clicked open, and under these the crates were emptied out, their contents displayed in baskets. The sun shone and withdrew. After a while it reemerged and shone brightly. It was a truant sun, the kind that would disappear and emerge and threaten to disappear altogether. When it was there, it pierced the skins of red-cheeked tomatoes, long, velvet *brinjals,* white, flowery cauliflowers, and leaves of coriander and lettuce, all washed and sparkling wet.

In loud voices, the vendors shouted out their prices. Women with small purses and big plastic bags stopped and bargained fiercely. The vendors held their prices. The women pretended to walk away. The vendors called them back. They returned. They were used to these daily charades, which helped them stay within their monthly budgets.

Sprightly urchin boys would run up and pester the women—should they carry their bags, take some load off? Five rupees per bag was not too much to ask.

On the opposite side of the road was a Shiva temple. At its entrance, devotees stopped to feed cows grass, which the cows ate lazily, pausing to swipe their tails at bothersome flies. Inside the temple, Nandi the bull stared at his Lord in stony wide-eyed devotion. His Lord looked on calmly, as was his habit, his universal stance in the order of things. Outside the temple, in a small shop, a bespectacled old woman sold flowers and *bili patta* out of a basket. "Come," she said. "Take some offerings for our Lord, who does not ask much, who delights in so little!" The devotees crowded around her and bought small baskets of flowers. Sometimes the women-devotees ordered *gajras,* soft, white garlands that they tied around their hair. Beggars with long, matted hair and dark, sullen faces paced at the gates of the temple. They looked expectantly at the male devotees, who, in white robes, tiptoed past, ignoring them. The beggars grumbled. This was no good, no good really. People were too busy praying for themselves these days. They just didn't have the eyes to see or the ears to listen.

I was watching this from my window when the doorbell rang. I opened the door, expecting to see Raju Gondva. But, no, it was his wife. Just her. With a sack.

"Where is Raju?" I asked.

"Sorry, sahib," she said. "He can't come. He was called to work suddenly. What to do? It is a matter of our stomachs, no? But don't worry, sir," she said, her face brightening, "I will do your *damaring*. I will finish the job Raju Gondva has begun. You won't need to complain again."

I saw a spark in her eyes, a jaunty challenge that made her look sweet and fetching, sexy and beguiling. At that moment, I pictured her in a different light—a lioness ready to give all for her mate, a woman in a man's world, with the potential to start a fire.

"Well," I said, letting my eyes sweep over what I hadn't seen but could easily imagine. "Will you be able to do it? It's a man's job—you know?"

"What a man can do I can as well," she said, and seeing my expression added hastily, "I have been with Raju many times."

"Yes, but still . . . ," I said. My mind was racing. I'd heard about these local women, heard that they were the best, for they expected not words, nor wooing, nor gestures of tenderness. Without that—the niceties of courtship—they had so much more to give.

My ears burned. The fire crept to my mouth. Perhaps it showed in my eyes, showed abruptly, because she looked at me and said, "I have come prepared, sir. I have brought my helpers."

Slowly, her two children came into sight. The fire went out of me, leaving my cheeks aflame, my heart pounding, my mind confused, and to tell you the truth, there was some relief, like I'd been spared madness.

Not liking the thought of little children being put to work, I was tempted to send them away, to insist on Raju coming, but then I thought of the next downpour: the water down my walls, the puddles, the constant carrying and emptying of buckets. There were months to go before the monsoon ended and there was no telling what damage it would do, how it would weaken the walls and the ceiling.

"Okay, but be careful," I said, unlocking the terrace doors for her.

The way up was dark and narrow. She had to grope before she found the switch. The children followed her. Every once in a while they'd turn to look at me.

Soon I heard a dragging sound, then some banging, and I knew the *damar* was being chopped. Soon there'd be a fire, too, and smoke curling over the rooftops.

I poured myself a mug of beer and settled down with the morning papers. The sun poured in through the windows and cast a glow in the living room. I could smell the *damar* burning on the terrace.

I went through the news: an exposé on builders who were trying to capture a *dhobi ghat* and one on politicians who'd given away tracts of public land to private companies. I read about a film on the Bombay bomb blasts being banned, because the accused felt it would interfere with the court judgment, expected now, twelve years after the tragedy. I read about two actors who were being sued for staging a foreign play without copyright permission. I read about their indignation and the producer's hot face-saving denial. I read about a girl being raped by a cop on Marine Drive and tribal girls being raped in Bihar as some form of caste-war vengeance. I decided to skip the international news page, which appeared to focus mostly on the new Pope, whether he was a Nazi sympathizer or not. I turned to the lighter pages and chuckled over Archie and Hagar, and I amused myself with the matrimonial ads, wondering what would happen if I were to write in to some of the "innocently divorced women from respectable families." I stopped at the color sections and felt a mild sense of depression. There was nothing to read, except about people propped up by the media, people promoted for a price. In between, I had refilled my mug, and now both the mug and the bottle were empty.

I rose to get more beer and realized I was tipsy. My mind was in a daze. I hadn't realized how fast I had been drinking. I thought of the woman who worked upstairs—she who had started a fire over my head, a fire that licked and teased—and I wondered what it would take to get to know her. Just then I heard a murmur, a collective sound from below. Like a rumble, it reached my ears—from the marketplace all the way up to my third-floor residence.

I went to the window and saw a crowd of people looking up, pointing over my head. I twisted my body and looked upward. I saw the *damarwalla*'s wife peering over the terrace wall, her breasts pressed erumpent against her blouse. She was flailing her arms, trying to explain something to the people downstairs, but they seemed reluctant to listen.

Soon there were thuds on the staircase . . . the sound of footsteps in a rush . . . and the doorbell rang frantically. It was one of those chirruping ones that thundered through your soul.

I opened the door and came face-to-face with angry people: lean, wiry youths in skin-tight jeans, vegetable vendors in white vests and striped pajamas, and some women in saris, who'd trudged up, their shopping bags full. There were about forty of them, and they crowded my staircase and my doorway, and all of them spoke at the same time. From their barrage I could gather some *damar* had fallen during application; it had scalded the neck and back of some poor woman shopping below. The woman had been rushed to Bhatia Hospital to get her burns treated, but the people who witnessed this were upset. They demanded an apology. They demanded justice. They wanted to meet the *damar-walla* who was responsible. "Call him," they said. "Just call him. We will show him to be careless. We will teach him a lesson he won't forget."

They were surprised when the woman appeared, she and her children, small, white, and terrified. The children cowered behind their mother, hiding their faces in the folds of her sari. From there they looked at the crowd fearfully.

The crowd turned to her and said, "Where is your man? Where is he hiding? What is he doing sending *you* down? Ask him to come down at once! Otherwise we will go up and get him. Then it won't be so good."

Speaking to them in Marathi, she said that he wasn't there, he was at work, and it was I who had insisted on the extra *damar* being done that day, so she had to come with her tots, who had homework actually, tests in school to prepare for. She told the crowd in a low, bitter voice about my visits, about my bringing the police, and slowly the crowd turned to face me.

An angry youth broke through the crowd. He came and stood close to me. I could smell his breath, the hot, incensed breath of youth. "*Kya,* sahib!" he said. "What sort of a man are you, making a woman work, making children do this kind of work? Now who will pay for this accident? You should have some sense, being educated."

Then an angrier voice from the back: "*Arrey,* what are we waiting for? Let's call the police; let's make a complaint about him exploiting little children, making them do dangerous work."

Then still more anger, and still more faces coming up in front, with their suggestions, with their breath and their sweat, which made me suffocate, made me dizzy, and at some point someone took my hand and, tugging gently, said I needed to see Varun Paoli, the local *dada.* It was unforgivable what had happened, and only he could settle the matter. My head spun. My mouth felt dry. The name brought fear to my heart, a clawing emptiness to my stomach.

I backed toward the door, trying to get a foothold in, but the grip tightened around my wrist. Sharp nails dug into my flesh, in the parts between the veins. A big pudgy face—rough, green, unshaven, with a handlebar mustache—came into sight and said not to worry: Varun Paoli would get it under control. No one was to say a word to me. No one was to decide what should happen. Varun Paoli knew what to do. He was the boss man of the area.

Some of the youths were not quite convinced. They felt that justice could be best dispensed by their hands. So they took their chances incurring Varun Paoli's wrath—they delivered a blow or two to my face, at the side, which got me squarely on the ear and made me blink in disbelief. In the midst of this, I saw the woman push through the crowd and drag her children away and the crowd give way respectfully.

I was led down the stairs, and on the way down someone delivered a punch to my ribs and someone a blow to my ear. It was a woman with her purse.

On the landings, I saw my neighbors look curiously. The men opened their doors partly and tried to peek. The women whispered to them, saying they shouldn't get involved. The children squealed and tried to push forward, but their mothers gripped them firmly and held them back.

When I reached the ground floor, I could smell the *damar* burn. I could smell the fumes thicken and spread as the tar boiled furiously in the vessel, which was abandoned like me. The level of the tar would sink lower and lower, I thought, and, approaching the bottom, it would boil, froth, and curl inward before evaporating, before disappearing once and for all, in a way faster than this incident would from my mind. I wondered how long that would be. I guessed it would depend on Varun Paoli. On the price he would set, the penalty he would decide, the punishment he would impose, as boss man of the area.

Held by my collar and wrist by the man with the mustache, I was led down the lane, through the bazaar where I had lived for forty years. The vendors clicked their tongues disapprovingly. The shoppers craned to see. The urchin boys twittered and ran behind the crowd. They had lost interest in carrying and fetching. This was Sunday entertainment at its best.

We turned into a side lane, to approach the place I knew as Varun Paoli's *adda,* his den where people drank hooch, played *matka,* and got their problems sorted out. There was a crowd of people standing outside the den; they were staring at a slate on the wall, on which the *matka* results would be scribbled in chalk.

Some people also waited at the entrance to the den. They sat tense and nervous on wooden benches in the portico. They were waiting for Varun Paoli's *adalat,* his court of instant judgment, a law unto itself.

Leaving me in the custody of two youths, the man with the mustache went inside the *adda.* The youths gripped me firmly, like I was quarry whom they'd trapped after days of pursuit.

After ten minutes—which seemed like a lifetime considering my embarrassment—the curtain parted and Varun Paoli emerged. He was a dark man of average height, with hair in a fringe across his forehead and falling over his ears. He reminded me of one of those villains from the Hindi movies of the seventies, the kind with sideburns and a sneer. I *namasted* him to show that I meant well, that I meant no offense. He nodded in a way I thought was extra friendly, extra respectful.

"What have you done, you fools?" Varun Paoli said, turning to the man who had brought me. "Who have you got here? I know this sahib well. He is from our gully. He has grown up here. How can you treat him like this?"

Taking me by the arm, Varun Paoli led me inside, saying he was sorry these louts had caused me so much inconvenience, but they didn't know a gentleman from a culprit. He said they were illiterate fools and that he was apologizing on their behalf, and then he asked whether I'd like a cup of tea. Without waiting for a reply, he snapped his fingers to a short, scruffy ruffian in baggy shorts: "*Do* special *chai. Jaldi!*"

The room was large and profusely lit. The walls were lemon yellow; the ceiling was a pasty white. There were thick white beams running across the ceiling. There were no windows, only fans whirring at high speeds and bulbs with green lampshades. We sat on a mattress on the floor, leaning against soft, round cushions with sparkling mirror work. On the far side of the room, some men sat at narrow tables, huddled over notebooks and pads of *matka* tickets. They were tallying some calculations and pretended not to notice us.

The tea came. It was served piping hot, in small white cups. Pouring it into saucers, we drank. Then, employing my most pleading voice, I told Varun Paoli about Raju Gondva, about his wife and his sister, who yelled at me like I was some common laborer. I told him about the many times I had requested them to send Raju Gondva to finish the job and how my trust was trifled with. Varun Paoli shook his head and said, "*Sala* Gondva, the bloody shirker. I will see why he didn't come. Working? Hah! He must be lying drunk in some gutter. Or in some whore's arms. Don't worry, sir; your job will be done. You will have no more complaints. But why you went to the police in the first place I don't understand. Next time, for anything like this, you come to me." He smiled, and I saw that his teeth were enormous, like piano keys with dark gaps in between.

Then he said, "You know, sir, I am thinking, there is so much good to be done in this world, so much work for people like you and all those waiting outside, that sometimes I think I should leave all this *kala dhanda,* this *matka-phatka,* and go into politics. Then I can be a public servant. I can truly serve the *janta.*" He paused. "You think I will win, sir, if I stand for election? You think I stand a chance?"

I looked at him. His face was solemn. Others in the room stopped their work. They looked at me in a peculiar sort of a way, as if my answer would decide something. It would decide either Varun Paoli's fate or mine. I gulped, nodded, and said, "Yes, most certainly." He had my vote for sure, and he'd get plenty more from the neighborhood.

"You are a good man, sahib," Varun Paoli said. "I wish I could be like you, but then my circumstances were different. No mother, no father, and four sisters to look after . . . and so many difficulties and no job. No money to go to school or to get a degree. Sometimes no money to eat." His voice tapered off and he looked sad. When he continued, he spoke slowly, as though he was sharing a long-borne burden. "So I fell into this line and met all sorts of people who changed my life, making me what I am. Otherwise, I would have been like you: educated, and a sahib." I clicked my tongue and looked pained, wondering what I had done to deserve his confidence.

"But now, sir, I am thinking: I *will* go straight. I *will* do some good, so people know that Varun Paoli is not all that bad. He, too, is decent."

He straightened from his reclining position. Drawing in his legs, he sat up cross-legged. "I will tell you one secret, sir, what I am planning." His eyes gleamed and his speech came in sharp, short breaths. "You see this *adda,* where people come to drink and gamble? I am going to knock it down. Not the full structure, but most of it. I am converting it into a temple—with a nice marble finish and bells that tinkle morning and evening, and a big *murti* with a crown of solid gold." He looked shyly at me and said, "You may not believe, no sir, that a man like me can be religious, but I am. I believe in him—totally." He raised a finger to the sky.

His voice dropped. He looked around furtively, as if he did not wish the others to hear him.

"I tell you what, sir. I have an idea. This is going to be a very holy temple. I will get learned priests to come and do *puja,* and for the opening I will get a film star or a politician to inaugurate it. But that is not the point, sir. What I want to say is I like you. You are a good man, a very decent man. So I want to give you a chance to contribute to this temple. Not much, whatever you desire, whatever is fine for your pocket. I know ten or fifteen thousand rupees is not going to make much difference to you. I know you will think of the blessings you will get and will contribute from your heart."

Here it was, I thought—the hit, the squeeze, the pretext under which I was being sacrificed, cut and bled like a goat on *Bakri Id*. Yet I found myself nodding, agreeing, saying yes, a splendid cause like this deserved support, I would be the happiest man alive to see a temple in the lane, a temple that would become famous. Despite the one we already had.

Varun Paoli rose. He gripped me by the shoulders and said he knew it; he just knew from the moment he saw me that I had been sent to help. Didn't he tell his men that? Didn't he predict that I was indeed a messenger of God? The others in the room raised their hands and agreed, saying they, too, had felt something as I walked in. Something like an aura, a presence, an inexplicable calm, soft, sweeping, and reassuring. And since I didn't know how to deal with my new Sunday status, my divine presence that shone and shimmered off me, and which brought me friends whom I had never expected, I looked down and delivered what I felt was my most absent and demure smile.

At that moment, I found myself thinking not of myself but of the African. How he'd have felt the first time people barged into his flat and emptied it out. Would he have been with his kids, telling them stories of heroic pursuit? Or would he have been with his wife—the kids away at their grandparents'—rubbing his warm snub nose against her smooth, tight night skin? Or would he have felt like me, reduced and violated, helpless in his own home, his own environment? I wondered how long he would have waited after the thieves left to laugh that hearty laugh of his. I wondered if he'd laughed at all, or had he simply saved it for another time, another country.

THE GREAT DIVIDE

✦　✦　✦

MRS. MULLAFIROZE'S HAND SHIVERED. She felt worried about it. Usually she wouldn't have given it a thought, for she was at an age where her limbs were honest enough to admit their deterioration; they gave gentle signs that told her she was dependent on the courtesies and kindnesses of the world. But this time the shivering sprang from an unsparing source: it was clearly fear that overtook her, made her bony hand convulse, as she clutched the morning paper disbelievingly. Her eyes fastened on the article in the center, on the headline that screamed: "70-Year-Old Parsi Woman Murdered. Manservant Absconds."

With the eyes of a hawk, which still mercifully allowed her to thread a needle in two attempts, she devoured the article:

> Jeanie Mariwalla, a resident of Jamas Baug and a retired school teacher, was found murdered in her one-bedroom apartment at Byculla. The body was discovered on Saturday, 17 November, by her nephew, Sohrab, and his wife, Angelina, who had dropped in to see her. At the time of her death Mrs. Mariwalla was living alone, her husband having passed away last December. The old teacher, a favorite with all the children in the Baug, is reported to have no immediate survivors. Inspector Pathare, who is heading the investigation, said, "While robbery

appears to be the main motive, the eighteen stab wounds inflicted on the victim's body are a serious indication of the killer's mind. He appears dangerous, possibly psychopathic."

The suspicion has fallen on a manservant employed two months ago. The suspect, a native of Bihar, used to be seen wheeling Mrs. Mariwalla through the Baug during the evening hours. He has been missing since Friday, the day of the murder. Led by Inspector Pathare, a high-level police team left this morning for Madhopur in Bihar, the suspect's place of origin. The murder comes on the heels of a spate of killings the city has witnessed in the last two years. The suspects— unemployed youths from Bihar and Uttar Pradesh—arrive in Bombay and take up employment with senior citizens who reside alone. Soon the youths take to demanding additional amounts of money from their employers and, if refused, don't hesitate to turn violent. Police commissioner Ravi Kulkarni has appealed to senior citizens to get their servants registered at the nearest police station. Dignity Foundation, a non-profit organization working for the welfare of senior citizens, has agreed to set up patrols to monitor and check on its members. All senior citizens are hereby requested to verify the credentials of their servants and to take necessary steps to . . .

Mrs. Mullafiroze could read no further. She sat clutching the newspaper with bloodless, wrinkled hands. The muscles in her throat pounded against the thin folds of her skin. Madhopur? Why, that was the place her manservant came from—that big *goonda*-looking man her husband, Dinsoo, had hired, despite her repeated warnings. Wait till she showed Dinsoo this, once he came in from his prayers, which were getting lengthier with age. He never listened to her—that man of hers. He always wanted his own way, thought everybody should obey him, just because he was an army man.

In reality, Mrs. Mullafiroze was very proud of her husband and his illustrious career. She had met him fifty-five years ago, when he was a young officer, handsome, rugged, with soft brown hair, bright green eyes, and a firm, even jawline. She expected all the spit and polish that went with the uniform, and he hadn't disappointed her. At times he appeared a little imperious, but that was understandable, for he was a born leader, almost always correct in his judgment.

His mettle had shone through in the 1971 Indo–Pak war, when he had led his troops against a formidable tanker unit. Employing a sagacious mix of brains and bravery, he'd outwitted the enemy and captured a post that was crucial to the war effort. For this he was honored by General Dorabshaw in the presence of two thousand soldiers. At the felicitation, Mrs. Mullafiroze, who sat in the front row, had glowed with inner radiance. She felt she had led the victory herself. Later, even an august evening spent in the presence of the General and his lovely wife hadn't served to elevate Mrs. Mullafiroze as much as the thought of being Dinsoo's wife, of managing his home while he served the country and kept it free from the advances of encroaching neighbors.

But this time her hero had made a mistake. He was growing old and careless, she inferred. All through his life he had looked after her, exactly as he promised he would, in front of the holy fire at the Banaji fire temple, where they had taken their vows. But now he was eighty and prone to making mistakes. He had hired this man Ram Kumar Yadav, so dark and fierce in appearance that he looked as though he could snap their throats with two fingers if he so wished. This man who had no relatives in the city and no past employers to recommend him, who said it did not matter what they paid him—work was work after all.

And murder was murder, and so easy it was these days—a life lived gracefully ending at the tip of a knife or waning under thick strangulating hands. Mrs. Mullafiroze shuddered. All the recent murders in the city were of senior citizens; it was like there was a conspiracy to eradicate them, a planned cleansing to make way for a more virile generation, a generation who took their chances, because that's how they saw life in the city—in resplendent blinding glamour. The city was being taken over; that was certain. Look at the numbers pouring in: hordes of migrants, parched for work, ready to live anyhow, anywhere. Look at them crowding the footpaths, the platforms, along the tracks, and under the bridges. Look at them sleeping, defecating, and washing in public places. What would they think of, if not murder?

And now the threat had crept into her home. Dinsoo would have to be warned. Eighteen stab wounds? she thought. I don't want to die looking like a shredded chicken. That's how people will remember me. And they will say, "Poor Silla, what a sight she looked all cut up!"

But would her husband listen, would he take her seriously, or would he nod his head with resignation and say, "Silla, my Silla, you are too suspicious. You must have faith in your fellow beings. You must learn to trust, so they can trust you in return. How do you know what Yadav is capable of till you give him a chance to prove himself? How will we understand our people, our countrymen—without opportunity, without trust?"

Opportunity? Why, she remembered how Yadav was hired. He'd been introduced by their gardener, the old *maali*. Yadav had arrived in the city with no contacts, no definite plans of where to stay, what to do. He had pushed a handcart for a fortnight and then looked for domestic work, thinking it would be easier and more respectable. He was used to staying with a family, he said.

"Like who?" Dinsoo had asked.

"Mother, father," he had replied. Father was retired now, an old soldier who had served with the Gharwals. He had lost both legs in the war, having led feetfirst into a minefield.

Dinsoo softened when he heard this. "Anyone else?" he asked. "Brothers, sisters?"

"Three sisters, all unmarried. My brother is there, but he minds his own family," Yadav had replied. He was reluctant to reveal more.

"Poor man, the onus must be on him," Dinsoo had said, and agreed to a salary of eighteen hundred rupees a month. He avoided Silla's eye when he did that, for his wife could be a *baniya* in matters of compensation. Besides, what good were his investments if they did not serve the heroes of the nation? One thing he told Yadav firmly: "Don't go squandering the money, okay? Make sure your father receives it at the beginning of every month." It sounded like an order and was intended to be one. It reminded Mrs. Mullafiroze of the times Dinsoo made himself responsible: Brigadier Mullafiroze taking charge of his men, their careers, their lives, their joys, and their sorrows. They had never minded not having kids, for their house—despite constant disbandment and resettlement in the course of various transfers—was always peopled with the lives of others. Over time, the regiment had come to mean family. Intimate details were known about the men who served under him, who jumped to his command, not because he ordered them to but because he deserved obedience at all times.

The confidence was such that cash-strapped *jawans* could approach him with their financial problems—a sister ready for marriage, a brother wanting a loan for further studies, a farm to be freed from debt—and Brigadier Mullafiroze would delve into his pocket without waiting for the wheels of bureaucracy to turn and do their bit. Or a captain in love could apply for leave, his excuse anything but that. And he'd be sure to get it, provided he was ready to withstand some ragging at the hands of his leader, a ribbing more vigorous than at the academy. Likewise, a soldier son could rush to his father's sickbed, no questions asked, no leave quota to worry about. "Just fulfill your duties as a son," was the only advice he would take with him.

It was common knowledge that the younger soldiers' marriages would come under strain, especially at the borders, when they were posted there and their wives were housebound, isolated, bored, sometimes even terrified till their husbands returned. At such times, Dinsoo and Silla would do their duty as senior officers, as stalwarts in the known battlefield of marriage. By cajoling, coaxing, or counseling, they'd get the couple to mix with other couples who'd been down that route, who'd been through a similar period of adjustment; this way they'd steer the marriage to calmer shores, where it stood at least a chance to endure.

Sometimes this excessive preoccupation with *others* ate into their own lives, when they got too involved, that is, when they took sides and stances: she for the wives, he for the husbands. But eventually the larger picture dawned. They used each other to understand the nuances of opposite-sex expectation, to grasp the finer unspoken things.

Themselves aware, they'd convey the answers to the dissenting partners, backing it up with extreme logic, rehearsed first in their own bedroom. They worked well as a team—antagonistic, fiery, squabbling, but fair-minded always.

But that was in younger, more alert days. Now she'd have to protect him, she thought.

There were things about Yadav that hadn't seemed right since day one. If God intended him to be a good man, why had he given him such fearsome features? His face seemed to protrude in a way that was simian. His eyes were beady, like sullen dots. His mouth was open; his lips drooped; his teeth were unusually big, like transplants. His skin was dark and swarthy, and there were shrubs of hair on his neck and shoulders. This drove her mad with repulsion. "I always feel," she said to her friends at the Willingdon Club, "that the brute was never washed as a child."

"But Silla," exclaimed Mrs. Adenwalla, thumbing through her cards during their afternoon flush session, "why don't you just dump him? Find fault with his work. Accuse him of keeping things dirty. Shout. Nitpick. So he leaves. It can be arranged, you know, without making it look like you have sacked him."

"I can't—even if I want to. Dinsoo is rigid about some things. You know how he feels about ex-servicemen. Says it is a privilege to support the family of a war veteran. Besides, I can't find fault with his work. In that he seems okay."

"What is worrying you then?" asked Mrs. Kashyap, scrutinizing her cards calmly. She knew Silla and her hysterical ways.

"I think it's the way he moves," said Silla. "He just kind of appears, slowly and silently. He never makes a noise, even when he is working. I never hear the sound of vessels, or clothes being washed, or the click of a door when he leaves. It's like having a ghost in the house, an invisible person."

"I would never tolerate that!" exclaimed Mrs. Kanga. Fat and voluble, she was Silla's closest friend. "I would ask him outright, '*Tum zinda ho ya murda?* Are you alive or dead?' I like human beings around me, huh, not some village zombie."

"But what can you expect from these villagers?" said Mrs. Adenwalla. "They are not used to employing their minds in the village. They come here all brain-dead."

"Oh, they may come that way, but they smarten up pretty soon," said Mrs. Pochkhanawalla, the well-dressed one. "Then they try and outsmart us."

"And how they succeed, huh? They take over our roads and our parks, and they don't pay taxes, and they build their slums all over, and soon our city starts looking like one big village, and soon we will be working for them. I tell you, that day is not far off, mark my words, you-all," said Mrs. Kanga. She threw her cards down in a gesture of resigned show.

The others laughed. All except Mrs. Mullafiroze. She wasn't listening. Her mind was racing. Her heart was keeping pace. What was the name of that movie she had seen in her youth? It had Audrey Hepburn as a blind girl holding out against a gang of housebreakers. *Wait Until Dark:* yes, that was the name! Well, here at least she knew the enemy; she *could* see him. It was just a question of anticipating his murdering mind. And outwitting it—in time!

That evening she left the club early. Usually she'd wait for the pastry shop to open and she'd take time choosing an assortment of éclairs and gateaux, which she and Dinsoo would savor after dinner. But now she had more important matters to attend to. And for this she needed the inspiration of single malt, a habit acquired during the years she'd wait for Dinsoo to return from the battlefront. With her first drink, she'd toast to his safety; with the second and third, their marriage and home. Once he was back, she'd given up the toasts and proceeded to knock back the whisky without preliminaries. Over the last two years she had stopped drinking, though. A sudden attack of colitis had brought about the abstinence. But now she was about to revive the custom. Colitis be damned! She had a husband to protect and a criminal to bring to book.

On reaching home, she realized she was nervous. She wondered whether the evil of Madhopur would choose to raise its feisty, murdering hand tonight. Eighteen stab wounds? She shuddered and let herself in through the main door. For a moment she flinched. At the entrance were Yadav's *chappals*. They were large and flared and had dark sweat stains soaked into the rubber. They reminded her of the feet that could bear down on them and crush them easily. She wondered whether she was being foolish by allowing this man to stay the night. It was Dinsoo's fault; her softhearted husband had allowed Yadav to sleep in the kitchen, rather than take his murdering intentions outside. How did other servants find places to stay: on the landing, in between floors, out on the porch? It was just a matter of making things clear from day one. But no, her Dinsoo had to go and welcome him indoors. "Poor man, let him feel part of the family. Why treat him like an outsider? Besides, where does he urinate in the night? We don't want him irrigating the garden." He was a trusting man, her Dinsoo, a great believer in natural goodness, in justice that restores dignity to men. There was no point talking to him. Operation Oust would have to be her baby.

She fixed herself a whisky, not a Parsi peg, four fingers clubbed, but a portion large enough to relax her. She had an hour before Dinsoo came in for his *chhota,* his small peg, and she wanted this time to work out the details of her plan.

First, she thought she'd photograph Yadav. She'd do so in the morning, for she wasn't sure he'd photograph well in the dark. And the flash wasn't working, either. But what would she tell him? What excuse would she give? She thought for a moment and brightened. She would say she wanted to get his ration card done. He'd believe this— the dumb ox! She strained to hear sounds from the kitchen. None. Depressing, she thought, and took a sip of her whisky. The sharpness of the malt paved the way for clear-sighted thinking.

She thought of two kinds of plans: one long-term, the other, immediate. The long-term plan would focus on getting Yadav registered, with all his details, at the nearest police station. For this she would rely on her nephew, Jamshed, a partner with Billimoria & Frazer, Solicitors & Lawyers Since 1924. Jamshed would look at Yadav with that sharp legal eye of his, and he would either convince Dinsoo to throw Yadav out or terrorize the brute into abdicating any unsavory intention.

As preventive action, starting tonight, she would keep an eye on Yadav herself. She would guard her husband and her turf. She took a sip of her whisky, then a gulp. Ah, she was feeling better already, more in control. Her lips puckered, her bony jaw tightened with resolve. The glass felt cool and reassuring in her hand. Her mind cleared and she thought calmly, This is going to be a working night; I might as well get started.

She walked across to the sideboard along the wall. Bending, she pulled one of the drawers at the bottom, slipped her hand in, and fumbled. She drew out a wooden box, long, rectangular, and dusty. Under the dust, she could see a gleaming coat of polish. Ah, she thought, how the workmanship of old lingers. She shook off the strands of dust that adhered to her fingers, then opened the box. A .32 pistol glittered.

As she raised the pistol and held it, the years seemed to slip away. She felt invincible, like she had in Amritsar, where Dinsoo had taught her how to use it, firing at old *Dalda* boxes till the logo was shot to pieces.

She checked to see whether it was loaded. It was. She needed a way to conceal it. Her eyes fell on a kettle cover: soft, thick, and embroidered, her grandmother's work of art. She placed the gun on the sideboard and neatly dropped the cover over it.

Then she went over the details. She must remember to keep their bedroom window open. If the brute tried to attack during the night they could scream for help. Of course, keeping the window open would invite mosquitoes, but then she could keep two mosquito coils burning. She made up her mind she wouldn't sleep in the bedroom. After Dinsoo went to sleep she would slip out and go into the room that preceded their bedroom, a tearoom with shelves of porcelain, large wooden cupboards, and carved sofas covered with bedsheets. Near the entrance of the room was a couch. She'd sleep on that and leave the door slightly ajar, alert to any passing footstep. She was a light sleeper, one of the benefits acquired with age.

She grimaced at the thought of the manservant attempting to sneak into their bedroom and cause harm to her darling Dinsoo. She wouldn't give him a chance. She would simply shoot him in the back. Once, twice, thrice, till she was sure he couldn't harm them. Ah, one in the butt, too, for effect. She wondered whether his blood was black; it certainly wouldn't be red. Nor blue, she thought poignantly.

Lightened by the malt, she reflected on her dream and whipped it to a conclusion: "Army man's wife stops killer in the dead of night." She saw her picture on the front page of the *Bombay Times,* erect on her Victorian couch, in a full-sleeved blouse, the edge of her grand piano showing. She saw the interview unfold. "I wasn't scared," she'd say. "I am an army man's wife, used to danger." Of course, she would give Dinsoo credit. She'd touch upon his bravery and the heroic deeds of his past, and his medal from General Dorabshaw.

She saw the sequel at the Willingdon Club: the ladies in rapture, guests nudging one another, darting glances of admiration as she passed, and the waiters hovering in attendance. She'd be called upon to tell her tale a number of times, and over ham and cheese sandwiches and mint tea and lemon cake her afternoons would be so much sweeter. She patted the kettle cover as if she shared a secret with its bulge. Later she'd take it to the tearoom.

Around 8:00 P.M., Dinsoo came in. He announced that he was ready to skip his drink and eat dinner. He looked tired, she thought. He'd had his friends over for bridge, and there had been a lot of chatter and ribbing, which excited him, tired him out. She rang for Yadav to serve dinner, and minutes later, as if by intuition, he wheeled in the trolley.

While the dishes were being laid, Dinsoo attempted conversation. "How is your father, Yadav? Does he see his friends from his old unit?"

"No, sir," came the answer, curt and uninterested.

"Why is that? Does he not miss them? All the talk about old battles, old officers, and old friendships?"

"All dead, sir," came the reply.

"All dead? But there must be some juniors who remember him, who remember his bravery. I know it is many years since he served, but things couldn't have changed so much."

"Dead, all are dead," came the reply flatly. The tone implied "don't ask me more. I am here to serve you, not to feed your sentimentalism."

A stony silence followed. Yadav stood at the side like a giant slave, mummified. He moved only when his employers pointed to the dishes. Then he'd glide in and serve expertly—with thick, hairy hands—and he'd remember to refill their glasses with water, without spilling a drop. That done, he would retire to the side, from where he would stare at the table with unflinching eyes—at the food but never at them.

Silla Mullafiroze glanced at her husband. He did not seem to mind this terrible silence, this precarious doom; he was content to chew his meat. She reached for her glass of water. Any man who could be so listless about his family was lying, or cold-blooded and dangerous, she inferred. But she was ready for him, this Rakshash of Madhopur. Three sips to that—yes, yes, yes!

After dinner, Dinsoo retired to the living room to watch the 9:00 P.M. news. A journalist was interviewing a Chief Minister, pushing him to take responsibility for the riots in his state. The Chief Minister was giving evasive answers, while in the background mobs with head-bands, swords, cans of kerosene, and gas bombs roamed. Places belonging to a minority community went up in flames. The mobs exulted. The police stood and watched, impotent. The Chief Minister spoke eloquently. He called it a backlash, the reaction of a few miscreants. This got Dinsoo incensed. He rose, his face crimson, his hand quivering on his walking stick, the blue veins on the back of his hand bulging. His head shook with disbelief, and pointing his stick at the screen, he yelled, "Bastards, how can you let this happen? In the land of Gandhi, how can you?"

"You shouldn't watch if it upsets you so," said Silla. He turned to look at her, and for a moment she saw something like defiance, fury, that old martial spirit roused but restrained. She noticed he was sweating.

He retired to bed as soon as the news ended. Mrs. Mullafiroze noticed he had forgotten to do the *diya*—the first time in fifty years. He was forgetting a lot these days. Some share dividends he hadn't deposited in the bank, and he had forgotten to pay the club fees and to tell Jamshed about the property tax. She didn't mind that; she reminded him twice and then did it herself. What was strange was, he never asked about these matters; it was as if he had relinquished his duties to her—man turning into child, child turning to woman, for protection. How well she understood him: her husband of fifty years.

After a while, she went into the bedroom, where she lit the *diya* and prayed. The wick burned encouragingly. She prayed longer than usual, taking care to utter the syllables slowly and clearly. In her religion, this was important; the right sound could move mountains; it could part the seas, split evil intent at the seams, and transform equations miraculously. At the side, Dinsoo slept, his mouth open, his chest rising and falling, punctuated by small throaty snores.

She stepped into the passage and saw the light in the kitchen was on. The door was ajar and the shadow of the servant was moving luminously. She could imagine those feet dominating her kitchen. She could see them coming down the passage, stopping outside the bedroom door, behind which her Dinsoo slept the sleep of old age. She shuddered, collected her thoughts, and disappeared into the tearoom, her watchtower. She took with her the kettle cover and the hard assurance within. Before entering, she stopped and arranged six walnuts on the floor of the passage. If Mr. Killing-Me-Softly brought his murdering footsteps their way, he would be flattened nicely. And now that shot in the butt didn't seem such a bad idea after all.

Pleased with her planning, she lay down on the Victorian couch. Its bright yellow satin upholstery was losing its sheen and tearing slightly. The largeness of the couch enveloped her, reminding her of her days as a girl, when she had to give up her bedroom to visiting aunts, uncles, and elder cousins. She had felt vulnerable and scared then, but now . . . she leaned over and felt the pistol under the kettle cover. It was close at hand, on top of a marble stool.

It was 2:00 A.M. when she awoke next. She woke with a start and a sense of guilt. Had she slept too heavily? Had she slipped at her duty? She shifted uneasily. She'd better check on Dinsoo, she thought. Just a peek would assuage her fears.

She took the gun from under the cover. Feeling powerful, she tiptoed barefoot into the passage, taking care to avoid the walnuts. She looked toward the kitchen. The door was open; it looked ominous in the dark. A crazy fear shot through her. The kitchen door was never left open. In the Mullafiroze house it was a rule that you slept with all doors shut. This applied to servants, too, and Yadav knew it only too well.

Her heart started racing. She tightened her grip around the pistol. Should she go and check? No! She realized she was scared. Oh, why had Dinsoo put her through this?

Dinsoo?

She felt a bolt of panic. Her heart pounding, her stomach in knots, she stole toward their bedroom. She pushed the door slightly and could see his sleeping form. He was on his side. A thick Chinese blanket covered him, from his neck down to his feet. Overhead, the ancient fan creaked. At the side, the curtains fluttered lightly. The sounds of night wafted in through the window, harmless and lulling as ever. She was tempted to pat Dinsoo's soft white head, to kiss and stroke his curls at the back, all this out of relief, but that would awaken him, so she didn't.

Her hand holding the pistol dropped to her side. There was no need to check the kitchen now, she thought. She would berate the Bihari tomorrow. She went back to the tearoom and made herself snug under the blanket. Maybe she was being foolish. Maybe Dinsoo was right after all. She settled her head against the cushion and readied herself for sleep.

When she awoke, it was with the silver light of morning on her face. It had found its way in through the long, thick curtains; it fell across the wall, the sideboard, the cupboards, and down on the floor halfway through the room. But what awoke her was not that as much as the breath and the presence of the Bihari towering above her. "What is it? What?" she spluttered, struggling to rise from under the blanket. She groped for the pistol, but the brightness in the room and something in the Bihari's eyes told her it wasn't necessary.

"Madam, oh, madam," the Bihari blurted, his eyes wide with fear. "It is horrible, madam, but sahib won't listen. He won't wake up for his morning tea."

In a jiffy, she was up and in the bedroom. Dinsoo's face was still, looking up at the ceiling. His mouth was wide open and there was a trickle of black foam running down the side of his stubbled jaw. Behind her, the Bihari ranted, "Oh, madam, what is wrong? Call a doctor please. Sahib will be okay, no?"

Stiff with shock, Silla Mullafiroze bent over the sleeping form of her husband. She stayed that way for a while, lingering, longing, waiting for a breath of air, for the click of a heartbeat that would tell her the *dhak-dhak* in her own heart was unfounded. When she was sure, absolutely sure, she brought her lips to his forehead and planted a deep, long kiss. His skin was cold but familiar and sweet as ever. "I am sorry," she whispered. "I am sorry, my darling, I wasn't there."

The arrangements took the rest of the morning. She called Dr. Jambhax and requested him to come over. He wanted to phone for an ambulance, but she assured him that it wasn't necessary. If he could call for the hearse instead, on his way out, well, she would be grateful.

While that was happening, she went into the bathroom, wet a napkin, and wiped Dinsoo's mouth. Gently she daubed over his forehead and cheeks, stopping to admire the peace on his face when the head tilted and sagged into her palm. With her other hand, she touched his skin under the neck and, finding it warm, for a moment thought *maybe*—but no, she was being foolish.

She opened his wardrobe and brought out a brand-new *sadra* and *kusti*: his shield and sword, according to the tenets of their religion. Worn under their clothes, it was meant to protect them—the Parsis—from any form of evil. The evil would be repelled instantly, back onto the evildoer.

Watched by Yadav, who followed her meekly, she packed a bag, just a few things—hairbrush, toothbrush, soap, perfume, lipstick, and towel—so that she could look her best at the funeral and at the evening prayers. She called the army headquarters and spoke to Major Singhal, who had served under Dinsoo. Would he arrange for some honors later, on any day convenient? Would he let her know? "Of course, of course, madam," replied the Major, and then softly he added, "If I may say so, madam, at the expense of stating the obvious, the country has lost one of its finest soldiers."

That done, she looked up the directory and called up the newspapers, and because they recognized the age in her voice they agreed to carry the obituaries. It was a miracle really, because they never did that. Too many April-foolers had had their way.

All through, the Bihari followed her. He kept looking at her mournfully, as if searching for some trace of emotion, some deep concealed grief. But Silla Mullafiroze was remarkably calm. It was as if all the sadness in her had been collected and locked away.

For the next twenty minutes she stationed herself at the phone, calling up family members and close friends. They had questions for her, not too many, just the odd one or two, which she answered briefly. "Yes, it was a peaceful death, thank you." "No, he didn't suffer at all. Thank God for that!" "Yes, I was by his side. I was sleeping, of course, when it happened."

The hearse arrived: a large van with scrubbed-out tires and a snout for a face. The pallbearers bundled out: men in white, with bloodshot eyes, scruffy mustaches, and bandaged hands. They looked like mime artists, but that's where the resemblance ended, for they made a great deal of noise drawing out the stretcher. Their breath smelt of liquor, their manners were rough and unruly, but that was expected, for after the funeral they would venture where stronger men feared to tread. They would take the body inside the *dakhmas,* the sepulcher towers of the Parsis, where vultures circled expectantly, waiting to lower themselves on the body and feed off its fullness. The pallbearers would walk in among the half-eaten bodies, the decaying flesh, and the progressive smells of life forsaken—and this would be their daily job, for which they needed to tank up, to deaden themselves, morning, afternoon, and evening.

When they trooped in to collect the body, Silla Mullafiroze waited outside, at the door of the bedroom. It was best she didn't see this: her Dinsoo unseated from their four-poster bed, where so many promises had been made and kept. She left the Bihari in charge. And from where she stood she heard him hiss at the pallbearers who were tying the hands and feet cursorily. "Be careful; show some respect. That is not anybody. That is Brigadier Sahib. He was a hero, a great soldier." Silla Mullafiroze was surprised at the animosity in his voice and the reverence behind it.

The funeral was held at the Towers of Silence, the burial grounds of the Parsis, at the foot of Kemps Corner, going all the way up to Malabar Hill. By late afternoon the prayer hall was full of condoling guests: relatives, friends, and admirers of all ages. They came in proper funeral gear, which is to say, white shirts, trousers, and caps for the men and white lace saris for the women. The younger women wore dresses, skirts of modest knee length, and their heads were covered with scarves of Chinese silk.

The priests entered: lush-bearded men with calm faces and learned expressions. They were dressed in white, their mouths covered by white masks, and standing at the door of the prayer hall, they began to pray softly, in rich, nasally resonant tones.

Silla Mullafiroze sat up front, a white sari draped over her head, watching them sway and chant over the shrouded body of her husband. Outside, in the sylvan surroundings, the birds chirped invitingly and a pleasant breeze stirred. Halfway through the prayers, a dog was brought in on a leash and the face of the deceased was shown to him. The dog sniffed and moved away. The guests released their breath, which they had drawn in sharply, for among the Parsis it was believed that a dog could tell if there were life remaining, some wisp of breath in some vein. Man's best friend could be trusted more than the coroner, for it was the dog who led the soul to heaven, he who helped cross the bridge between heaven and earth.

After prayers, four pallbearers hoisted the body onto a stretcher and began their journey uphill. The way to the *dakhmas* was lush and green. It was lined with bushes of *gulmohars*, jacarandas, laburnums, pink acacias, and roses, and occasionally a gangly peacock crossed with the air of a fearless landlord. It was rumored that when someone special died, the peacocks would dance in the thickets, dance spiritedly for the freedom of the soul.

Relatives and friends filed behind the pallbearers and followed the body in a quiet procession. The men walked in twos and threes, holding the ends of their handkerchiefs, to suggest they were united in their grief. The womenfolk were more circumspect; they held up their saris and trudged carefully, so that the embroidered borders would not scrape the ground.

Silla Mullafiroze chose not to go; her legs wouldn't take the climb. She stood watching till the procession disappeared. For a while she stood still, absorbing the stature of the trees, the white wooly clouds, the restful flight of birds, and the ominous peace of death, so final and definitive and without reproach. Behind her came sounds of life—of car doors banging, engines starting. Some of the guests were leaving; some of them were being offered rides.

From the side, a Parsi woman with a round sympathetic face, sorrowful eyes, and plump powdered arms descended and hugged her. "The priests prayed beautifully," she said to Silla. "Never heard them pray so well. The soul is sure to have begun its upward journey."

Without looking at her but with a faint tremor around her chapped painted lips, Silla replied, "Yes, but what about us, the ones down here? We are left alone, you see, in the trenches."

In the background, at a distance, stood the Bihari, head hanging, shoulders stooped, arms crossed, fingers entwined nervously. Around his chest was strapped a thermos of dark green felt. In it was the tea he had made for his memsahib, made just the way she liked it, strong, stirred, with strands of fresh mint and two teaspoons of sugar. Later, after the guests left, he would pour it for her, piping hot, and without a drop spilled. But that would be later, when there were just the two of them waiting, with no conversation, no words, no consolations, just the divide of class and community, sullen and almost always insurmountable.

Once they were gone and she, Silla Mullafiroze, was alone, sitting lost in thought, on one of those long wooden benches outdoors, then he, Yadav, would come up to her. He would stare at her wide-eyed, seeking to understand her minutest thoughts, seeking to fathom her loss. If only he could see some sign of collapse, then perhaps he could unload some of his own grief as well.

But that wouldn't happen. Silla Mullafiroze wouldn't collapse. Instead, seeing the confusion and torment on the Bihari's face, she would understand slowly what Dinsoo had stood for, why he had died—not from heart failure, as the death certificate had said, but from a national failure to dissolve differences, to overthrow biases, to bridge the divide and keep this diverse country as one. Having understood this, she'd take it upon herself to guard Dinsoo's legacy—his theory of trust, his motion of full confidence, reposed boldly and unconditionally in his fellow human beings.

She'd start by allowing Yadav to sleep with the kitchen door open, leaving her own bedroom door unlocked as well. She'd up his salary to two thousand rupees a month, allow him to circle an *agarbatti* over Dinsoo's photograph every evening as a mark of respect, and ask him to run to the bank every morning to deposit her share dividends and later to withdraw cash.

Over three years, she'd get Yadav's sisters married. Some of the money she'd recover from his salary; the bulk of it she'd waive. The last marriage she'd attend—traveling first by train, then by *tonga,* and over a *kuchha* road in a wooden palanquin feeling like the Maharani of Bliss. She'd bless the bride, who'd be adorned with flowers and gold and who'd refuse to look at her out of shyness. And she'd drink from their cups and saucers, which were small, chipped, and stained, rented from a tea stall at the railway station.

Through this induction into the national stream, the veins of Hindustan, as she termed it, Silla Mullafiroze would feel she had Dinsoo for company. "Onward, my love," she could hear him say, like he used to when they'd go out riding, or play a fierce game of badminton, or do thirty laps of the Naval pool together. Of course, when her friends at the Willingdon Club heard this, they shook their heads and said, "Poor, poor Silla. She is looking well no doubt, but her mind is certainly affected. Dinsoo's death has changed her so."

METER DOWN

✦ ✦ ✦

THROUGH SLEEPY, sun-soaked eyes Mohitram Doiphade looked at the slim, smartly dressed woman who sashayed down the carpeted exit of the Taj Intercontinental Hotel and clicked, in high metallic stilettos, toward his cab. Shutting his eyes firmly, Mohitram Doiphade began playing the about-to-be-enacted scene in his mind. He had been through it so often that he could visualize the confidence with which she would open the door, the marked disappointment when he refused her fare, the beseeching note in her voice while she pleaded her case, and the pout that came on when he adamantly refused her business. So often had he been through this pantomime that he chose to stay recumbent while she approached, his parched black feet, bare and swollen with corns, sticking out through the window.

"*Bhai* sahib," she purred, in a dainty sort of a way. "Famous Studio, *bhai* sahib."

Without opening his eyes, Mohitram shook his head curtly and flicked his hand in a gesture of annoyance. He could well have been shooing a beggar.

"Please, *bhai* sahib," she pleaded.

"Told you no, I don't want to go," he replied in gruff Hindi, opening his eyes slightly to show sleep and surliness.

"Take pity, brother. I have to get to a shoot."

"Go! Don't bother me," he snapped. "If you are a model, you should get yourself a car."

"But I don't know how to drive," she confessed charmingly, spontaneously.

"Good! Women shouldn't drive anyway," he replied, feeling satisfied for having aired a long-repressed bias.

"*Dukkar!* Pig!" she spat, and slammed the door vengefully, shaking him out of his stupor.

He sat up and glowered. "Your father's car or what?" he asked.

"If it were so, why would I have to ask a pig like you?" she retorted, and marched off heatedly.

Mohitram's eyes followed her tight buns swinging rhythmically. Temper in a woman was certainly desirable, he thought, awake now and reaching for the water bottle between his seat and the door. Uncorking the bottle, he let the water flow down his gullet. The water was warm from the heat of the flooring. Yet he drank greedily, splashing, in his hurry, some of it on his chest. He dropped the bottle to the side. It fell on the rubber mat, in between his *chappals.*

He shuffled in his seat to adjust his weight. The Rexene of the seat squeaked plaintively.

Flipping a greasy napkin over the open window, he leaned against the edge of the door and slept.

Soon he was snoring. It was a light slumber, as inert as one could hope to be on the streets of Bombay. A nice part of Bombay this was: breezy, lazy, touristy, nonetheless humid and scorching for those who worked outdoors.

It was twelve years since Mohitram Doiphade had arrived in Bombay. He remembered the rush of excitement he'd felt when the big brown engine with the dust of India stormed into the Victoria Terminus and settled with a hot, hefty sigh against its girders. Everyone had rushed to the door to catch the first impressions of the big city, where dreams could take shape, where fortunes could be built, if one persevered long enough. First, the city put you through the grinder, the *chakkhi,* as his uncle would call it. It pummeled you and pushed you, strained you and stretched you, and broke you in, bit by bit. Then, it would immunize you to its hardships. Once you were seasoned, it would reward you for your penance—lavishly, in a way no other city could.

It was Nathuram Doiphade, the younger, more serious brother of his father, Jagatram, who had given Mohitram this happy talk, sitting in a dark, cheerless hovel in a South Bombay slum. Nathuram had boasted about the city while black soapy water gathered and foamed outside and toxic fumes from frantically primed kerosene stoves rose and made Mohitram's senses swim.

"Bombay is a city with a great history," Nathuram said. "It has seen many changes, many rulers: the Arabs, the Marathas, the Portuguese, and the British. It has also seen many tragedies, faced many hardships. It has survived a fire, a riot, three bomb blasts, and a flood. It is not a city for slackers but for the strong. You will have to work hard, sweat, if you wish to succeed."

Twelve years hence, Mohitram Doiphade had come to some understanding with the city. He had worked as a canteen boy, a houseboy, a coolie, a handcart pusher, and had run a cab for a timber merchant who paid him a meager 30 percent of the profit. By holding two jobs and rationing his money—he sent some of it home and kept some for a little release in the livelier neighborhoods—he had saved up enough to buy his own black and yellow MMU 4977. With that he was accountable to no one—except of course to the traffic police, who threw their weight around because of the uniforms they wore. He smirked inwardly to see how the traffic constables caved in to his bribes, how ten-rupee notes slipped along with his license could help skirt over troubles like a broken signal, a wrong turn, and forays down one-way streets.

A thin voice disturbed him again. "K.C. College, Churchgate. Will you go?" The voice sounded urgent, like all Bombayites.

He looked up. The intruder was a boy in his teens, bespectacled, studious, with a soft face and mild, querying eyes.

"No," Mohitram snapped. "Meter down. Can't you see?" He closed his eyes in a show of resolution.

"Please . . . I've got my exams," the teenager pleaded.

"Said no, didn't I?" snarled Mohitram. These boys of today: how foolish they were.

The boy looked distressed. "Please, I am very late. I will miss my paper."

Mohitram gave him a long hard look. Raising a leg over the dashboard, he waved his foot at the meter. "Meter down, meter down," he mocked, grinning at the boy with *paan*-shot teeth.

The boy backed away in panic. He was convinced that Mohitram was an ill omen. Extended commerce with him would damage his prospects at the exams.

In a sense, the boy was right. Mohitram *was* a misanthrope. Specifically, he was a hater of all those who made him sweat and toil, who commanded him to *fly* them to their destination, who made him slave for his survival, driving him through narrow lanes and crowded spaces while they worked in plush air-conditioned offices and drew fancy salaries and went home at a reliable hour, knowing that their savings were gaining interest in the bank.

He hated them all: harried executives who told him how to drive; fat, slovenly housewives who clawed into their blouses for loose change; teenage couples who nuzzled and fumbled in the backseat like hypnotized calves; old men and women who took forever getting in and forever getting out—he was always worried they would fall and then he would have to rush them to the hospital and answer to a barrage of questions. More than he hated his customers, Mohitram hated the prospect of losing money. And right now, strange as his behavior was, he didn't mind losing out on some fares, the ones over short distances, which didn't amount to much. That's because today was an important day. He had to make decent money. And that kind of money didn't come from hoity-toity models or from breathless, panicky students. It came from, well, the man who came bounding across the entrance of the Taj Intercontinental Hotel. The man who was young, fair, athletic in his stride, and rich, as could be deduced from his clothes and from his demeanor.

Mohitram straightened up and wore his pleasant, most inviting smile. "Where to, sir?" he asked, his voice coated with subservience.

"Airport," replied the man. He opened the back door and threw his tan-colored bag on the seat. Mohitram's heart soared. The airport was at the other end of Bombay. Having rigged the meter that morning, Mohitram could hope to pocket nothing less than four hundred rupees. More, if he went into bottlenecks and traffic jams. The trick was to keep the conversation going while the digits flew and the meter reading rose steadily.

Mohitram wondered for a moment if he should demand a special fare from his passenger: six hundred rupees flat. He could say he'd get no business on the return trip; he'd have to drive back empty. He had done this recently with an Arab on Marine Drive, who appeared in a hurry to get back to his hotel, and—fool that he was!—the Arab had paid up.

But here it might not work. These foreigners were no fools. Mohitram started the cab. The ignition whined. The engine roared to life. Passersby recoiled to avoid the black fumes.

Mohitram studied his passenger's face in the rearview mirror. He looked pleasant and relenting, not the kind to begrudge some extra baksheesh. These *goras* usually carried five hundred rupee notes on them. So if he could arrange for the fare to touch around four hundred and twenty, he might just get to keep the balance.

The taxi hit the windswept stretch of Nariman Point, the beginning of Bombay's pride ride: the Queen's Necklace. The breeze made Mohitram happy. He could feel its moisture against his face. The city stretched out lazily, in a wide-arched smile. Mohitram thought it was the right time to start a conversation.

"You have seen our Mumbai, sir? What do you think? You like it? You come back?"

"Oh, I love it. It's got so much life, so much warmth," replied the foreigner graciously. Seeing Mohitram stare blankly, he amplified in simple English, "Very good, yes. I like it very much. Thank you."

Mohitram struggled, and began again. "Taj very good hotel, sir. But very expensive, no?"

"Yes, but very efficient and convenient." Again, seeing the look on Mohitram's face, he spoke simply: "Location good! Everything very near! Service also very good. I like it very much." The passenger might have found the broken English offensive to his own ears, but then what to do? This way at least he was getting through.

Mohitram smiled and nodded. He liked this fellow. It was a shame he would have to rip him off, but then these *goras* were so wealthy that even the poorest in their country made two thousand dollars, which was around one hundred thousand rupees. What was an extra hundred rupees, then? Mohitram would take it as a fee for putting up with a conversation in English.

"Our politicians very bad. All robbers, sir," Mohitram said, anxious to incur the foreigner's confidence.

"Oh yes, I read about Bofors. Amazing, how the crooks still haven't been brought to task."

"Bofors?" Mohitram looked puzzled. He was hoping to complain about the harassment to Bombay's *taxiwallas:* the threat of introducing harsh pollution norms, the expense in changing to CNG cylinders, the sharp increase in road taxes, and the ban on bar dancers, which had led to good nighttime business being wiped away. This Bofors was beyond his understanding. Besides, it had not threatened his pocket in any way. So it couldn't be anything serious.

"Bofors!" said the foreigner impatiently. He was getting fed up with this parenthetical conversation. "You know, the arms scandal?"

"No, sir, not in Mumbai," Mohitram said with a frown. Breaking into a smile, he continued, "Mumbai most important city, sir. No city like it. That is why all big robbery happens here. Harshad Mehta, Ketan Parekh, that Telgi-*walla ustaad*—all big *chors* work here."

"Wouldn't know about that, pal," replied the foreigner cheerfully. "I guess it's the same everywhere. Look what happened to Enron and Arthur Andersen."

Seeing defeat on Mohitram's face, the foreigner expanded, "Oh, robbery is everywhere. We have to live with it." He opened a newspaper, hoping Mohitram would get the message.

Mohitram grinned. Robbery everywhere, huh? Well, by his own admission, the foreigner had asked for it.

They were at Peddar Road now, slowing for a traffic jam. Mohitram switched off the engine and let his mind roll to the issue of the flyover, the overpass. The government wanted to construct an overpass over the main road, between the residential buildings, to diffuse traffic jams and keep the traffic flowing. It made sense, for so much time was wasted on this stretch, especially during the peak hours. The overpass would have been built had it not been for the bulbuls of Bollywood, India's nightingale sisters who joined hands with the residents and led a protest march. They threatened to stop singing, threatened to move out of Bombay, to leave the country.

The bulbuls were unassailable, a national treasure. Their songs were classics: they had made people fall in love, fall out of love, families rejoice, lovers reunite, prime ministers weep, and soldiers rise in nationalist fury. The matter of the overpass was suspended—for a while at least. And Mohitram waited in his taxi, sweating, swearing, while around him people in luxury sedans cooled themselves under the throb of powerful air conditioners and tapped away to soft, pounding music.

His passenger was buried in the newspaper. Through the mirror Mohitram studied him. His beige-pink suit was rich and expensive looking. His dark red tie stood out well against the white of his shirt. The tie had a long carved silver pin going across it. Mohitram decided to remember this detail. Not for any occasion but for when he would dress for the wedding of his sister, Meena, nine years his junior yet so close to his heart that it hurt just to think of her. Meena was the nucleus of his life. She was the reason he didn't want to take on smaller fares today. She was the reason he wanted to earn well, so that he could lavish her with gifts when she arrived later, at 8:30 P.M., on the 104 Mumbai Express. Oh, he couldn't wait to see her. He couldn't wait to hold her, hug her, his own flesh and blood. His foot tapped impatiently on the pedal and he drummed with his fingers on the steering wheel.

The traffic started again. This time it moved smoothly. Mohitram picked up speed and kept pace. He didn't want to slacken, lest he be late for Meena. He wanted to shave, bathe, buy flowers. He hoped that that rogue Ghasitram had used fresh flowers for the garland he'd ordered, not flowers from the graveyard. If Ghasitram did anything as inauspicious as that, Mohitram would wring his neck. He worried about some people in his *chawl*. Would they mention to Meena about his drinking? Or about his liking for *matka,* for street-corner gambling, which had become a habit? He didn't want Meena to know any of this. He was also worried about those loafer boys Kalloo Katela and Amol Lukha, who only planned how they could *patao* girls all day. Well, if they as much as approached Meena . . . Mohitram checked himself. He realized he was driving too fast. He had switched lanes twice. The foreigner was looking at him.

He dropped his speed and settled into position behind a speeding Hyundai and a sprightly Zen. The speedometer said sixty. The meter said twelve, which meant about one hundred and sixty rupees notched up already. They were at Prabhadevi now, Siddhivinayak, the temple of Lord Ganesha, benevolent lord of all good luck and favors. No new venture started without his blessings, without intoning his name or invoking his support. Mohitram ran a hand over his head deferentially.

The traffic lights blinked green. Mohitram sailed through. Soon he hit Mahim, where groups of beggars sat outside eateries, waiting for a rich man to stop and feed them. It was said, he who made the beggars eat would never go without his wishes being fulfilled. But such charity was not for Mohitram. All his money was saved up for Meena.

He planned to take her to places she had never seen or been to himself. He would take time off and they'd ferry across the harbor, to the Elephanta caves, where he'd buy her bangles and beads. He would take her to Manish Market and Grant Road—the shopping arcades, where she could buy pretty dresses, ribbons, perfumes. He would take her to Marine Drive and let her ride in a victoria, so she'd feel like a princess. They'd stop at Chowpatty and tuck into *bhel, sevpuri, ragda pattice,* and *malai kulfi*—yes, all the flavors of Mumbai. He'd feed her so well that when she returned to the village people would say, "*Arrey,* Meena, what has become of you? You are round like a vessel." And she would smile shyly and reply, "You know my brother. I am overfed on his love and generosity."

Over the last few days, Mohitram had planned everything to perfection. He would start early in the morning, run his cab until lunchtime, then hurry home and take Meena out for lunch and sightseeing. He would take her to nice restaurants like the *thali* place at Girgaum, the *pav bhaji* place at Tardeo, the fish places at Kotachi Wadi and Koliwada, and the kebab places at Mohammed Ali Road, where they could also slurp on the *malpuvas* and *phirni*. He would take her to Victoria Garden and show her the zoo and watch her feed the monkeys and the bears. He would drive her to Borivali National Park and show her deer and watch her pat and fondle them. And just when she thought she had seen it all, he would take her to Film City and show her some film shooting. Now *that* she would never forget. What luck he knew one of the light boys on that new Aamir Khan movie who would get them a pass. Oh yes, he'd take her to a movie every day, too, if he could help it. And he'd drive her all around Mumbai, its nicer parts. And if any customer flagged him down, he would simply point to his meter and say in his deepest, gruffest voice, "Can't you see? Meter down!"

They were passing the Mahim Creek now. "Yuck, this smell is terrible," said the foreigner, looking at the black marsh, a slime of subterranean neglect, and wrinkling his nose in disgust.

"This is actually a river, sir. The Mithi River. It runs through half of Mumbai and drains into this creek, but people here treat it like a gutter, throwing things in it, so it changed color. But don't worry, sir. We will soon leave it behind," said Mohitram, stepping on the gas. The cab shot past the crowded lanes, the jumbo billboards with discounts painted in eye-socking fonts.

It came to an overpass, which it climbed without a whimper. From here it was a straight run to the airport, along the highway, and Mohitram felt elated, as if his taxi had sprouted wings.

The bulbuls should be banned from using this flyover, he thought to himself. Then I'd like to see how they go overseas for their concerts? He giggled inwardly and made it a point to remember to share this with Meena. From now on there'd be nothing he'd keep to himself. He'd be having family here. Not cynical, city-spoilt family like

Nathuram, but a sister with her honest, rapturous love. He shot a look at the meter. It said fifteen, which meant around two hundred rupees earned already. Pity, though, the foreigner had no heavy suitcases. Mohitram could have charged extra for that.

"You travel light, sir?" Mohitram said, echoing what was in his mind.

"Oh, what?" replied the foreigner, startled. He had finished the newspaper; his attention was engaged elsewhere.

"Only one bag? And so small?" Mohitram asked. He hoped the foreigner wouldn't take offense at his asking. He didn't want to spoil things now.

"Oh yes! Only one," the foreigner said. "You see, I am not going anywhere. Just giving this to a friend who is flying out. It's for another friend, actually."

"You are not going, sir. Then you will be coming back? To the city? You will need taxi for that?" Mohitram hoped he didn't sound too hopeful.

"Of course I will want a taxi—your taxi—to come back," said the foreigner.

Mohitram soared. "Better, sir, better that *I* bring you back. These airport taxis: they are all *chors,* all cheats, sir."

The foreigner smiled warmly. "Oh, I don't mind if you want to bring me back. You are my friend, right? Why should I take another taxi, then?"

"Thank you, sir. You are most kind," Mohitram replied softly. What a nice fellow this was. He almost made Mohitram feel bad for overcharging him. But what to do? He needed the money for Meena. He wanted to fuss and spoil her.

The taxi flew past buses, rickshaws, scooters, and a row of factories that looked abandoned. Cars heaped with luggage honked sharply and whizzed past. Trucks came in close, then moved away, as if they had no intention of hurting this fly of a cab. On both sides of the highway were slums, where bare-bodied children played, running, squealing, stopping occasionally to scratch their black little bums, and where women with tired faces scrubbed and cooked while their men sat listless, jobless, smoking *beedis* and playing cards. Mohitram stuck to his lane, his bare foot squeezing on the pedal. He had never felt a better grip on life. He felt the highway belonged to him. He almost felt like singing.

A few meters away from the ice factory where he had to turn for the airport, Mohitram heard a familiar sound. First low, then sharp, but insistent and grating. It sounded like an ambulance, he thought, but as the vehicle approached he saw it was a police van in a hurry. He could see it in the mirror, darting, dodging, overtaking cars that were ready to give way. It came and slipped into the lane behind Mohitram—four cars behind him, then three, then just behind him, to his left, waiting to overtake him.

Mohitram moved to the right to give way. But the van held on. It stuck to his tail, the beeping maniacal in his ears. Mohitram slowed and peered into the mirror. There were cops standing on the footboard; they were beckoning to him furiously, and one of them waved a pistol.

"Some mistake, looks like," Mohitram murmured, and glanced at his passenger. There was no curiosity or surprise on his face. Just caged fury—like that of a trapped animal. He clutched his bag, the white on his knuckles resembling the pallor on his face. With a sigh, Mohitram began pulling over. The cop van followed like a dark, obstinate hound.

When the cops came rushing forth, pointing a gun through every window of the taxi, Mohitram said nothing. He maintained a look of studied helplessness, of solemn disapproval. What could he say? They grabbed at his passenger, manhandled him in that nice suit of his, slapped him, dragged him, cuffed and kicked him, all at the same time. There, in the open, along the side of the highway, they had him kneeling, a gun at his head, his mouth foaming with blood. He tried to say something about his rights, but they slapped him, challenging him to repeat that.

Later, at the police station, Mohitram caught a glimpse of him. Gone was the suit and tie; gone was the cool demeanor. His shirt was torn; his lips were swollen; his face—one side of it—was a nasty shade of blue. He looked sullen and defeated, yet he smiled at Mohitram and said weakly, "Sorry, friend. No return journey."

The cops heard this and misunderstood. They suspected Mohitram to be in league with the foreigner. His taxi might be a courier for the drugs. Three kilos of cocaine were found in the bag, beneath a cleverly concealed false bottom. At three thousand rupees a gram this was a sizeable haul. The cops couldn't let anything that hinted of a network or smelt like a clue pass. There'd be questions from the top. The press would get wind of it. The anti-narcotics department would move in and try to get mileage. Times like this, the cops weren't ready to listen about visiting sisters, kid sisters arriving in the city, full of hope. Before ruling you out, they wanted to know everything about you: about your life, your friends, your income, and your habits. Again and again they'd drill you, until they were convinced you were aboveboard, until everything was down in black-and-white, and they had your thumb impression as proof.

It was 11:00 P.M. by the time Mohitram was allowed to leave the police station. He left without his taxi, which would be stripped down to the chassis to complete the search. A panic tore at his heart. He fretted about Meena. She would have arrived three hours ago.

He took the nearest cab he could find. Along the way, he shouted at the driver, "Bloody bastard! I, too, drive a taxi. You are trying to waste time, huh, so you make more on the meter."

"No, son, I haven't done that in fifty years. Why would I do it now?" replied the driver.

Mohitram saw he was a frail man of seventy. His jaws were toothless hollows, his hands were thin and bony, like bird claws, and he wore thick foggy glasses, the kind that shield a patient after cataract surgery. Mohitram glared at him. What bad luck to be stuck with this old tortoise!

The taxi rolled into the Victoria Terminus. Without waiting to check the fare, Mohitram thrust a bunch of notes at the driver and rushed out. He tore through the hordes of passengers crowding the entrance: families shuffling with their luggage, kids in tow; coolies with muscular stacks on their heads, buckling at the knees. Skillfully he navigated his way past the upcountry travelers sleeping all over the foyer, their heads resting on pieces of luggage, while stray dogs came sniffing at their food baskets.

God, platform four—where was it? Mohitram thought. And where was the train? All he could see was tracks of cold steel with moonlight bouncing off them, tracks leading outward, into oblivion.

He grabbed a ticket collector, a thin, forlorn man in a black coat, and asked, "*Ek sau chaar* Mumbai Express. Was it on time?"

The collector looked at him indifferently and said that the train had arrived three hours before. Then slyly he added, "You will find it in the yard, if you are greatly interested."

"One girl: seen her?" Mohitram asked. There was a cold panic rising in his stomach, a sick feeling in his throat and chest. He could picture Meena arriving, all eager and excited, craning from her window to catch a glimpse of him. (She hadn't seen him since what, three years now!) He could see her getting off, nervous and mystified. What would she do? Where would she look? Whom would she turn to for help? And who would respond? Yes, who?

He had heard about unescorted girls finding men eager to help. He had heard about their reception on the first night itself. No—that couldn't happen to her. He must control himself. He must be patient. He *would* find her. Come what may, he would.

He clutched the ticket collector by his coat. "Speak up! Tell me!" he said in a choking voice. "Have you seen her, a young girl, afraid, and ever so pretty?"

The ticket collector looked at him as though he were mad. Through his eight hours of duty, he would have seen many girls, a hundred at least, maybe more. How to know who this madman was talking about? How to know who he thought was pretty? Best to humor him, get him off his back. "Ask the railway police," the ticket collector said, pointing to a room at the side. Outside the room stood a railway cop in uniform. He wore a navy blue cap pulled unevenly over his head, and he carried a *lathi* under his sweat-stained armpit. Mohitram saw he was grinding tobacco in his palm, back and forth, back and forth, increasing the pressure each time.

Mohitram ran up to the railway cop and started spilling his story. He described Meena, described her like the child she was, sweet flower of youth. He described her newness to the city, her tenderness of age, her excitement, her sprightliness, and her helplessness when she wouldn't find him there. Meanwhile the cop placed the tobacco strategically in his mouth, on the right side, pulling his cheek aside and squeezing it alongside the gums. Mohitram got a full view of his teeth, charred and chewed away by the habit.

With hands folded, tears streaming down his face, Mohitram blabbered on: "Please, sahib, please do something. Find her anyhow. She is only seventeen, a child, you see . . . my only sister. Please find her. I will be your slave for life."

A train hooted its departure. The announcer's voice broke overhead. It came rough and raspy over a cracking PA system. The cop signaled to Mohitram to be patient. The announcer went on about how some trains would be delayed. They would leave toward morning. A bridge had collapsed somewhere. Nothing serious, nothing lost, except the taxpayers' money.

Mohitram waited. He wore a pathetic expression. His heart threatened to leave his body; a frightful monster tore at his gut. If they couldn't care for a river, he thought, a sparkling, flowing river, what hope for a girl indeed, a lone trusting girl like Meena? The cop continued to fix himself a second dose of tobacco. He began playing with the powder, lifting it, crushing it, letting it fall, a sprinkling almost in his palm. Mohitram watched with a growing feeling that he was part of the fix.

The announcer went over the announcements slowly. All the trains delayed that night had to be rescheduled; the new timings were announced. The cop struck at the tobacco in his palm. To Mohitram's mind, it was like a gong going through his head.

A *chaiwalla* came by with his cart, making a rolling, clattering sound. The noise of the cart drowned the announcer's voice. Seeing them, the *chaiwalla* slowed, but the cop shooed him on.

Cupping his palm, the cop squeezed the second pinch of tobacco into his mouth. His face contorted as he shuffled to find the tobacco its rightful place, the perfect chewing position.

The announcements stopped. Mohitram began speaking again. This time he used a more subservient tone. "Oh, sahib, where do you think she is? Please help me look. What will I tell my parents? How will I face them? Oh, help me please, sir. I will be your debtor for life."

The cop wasn't listening. His attention was elsewhere—on a beggar girl who had walked past, a huge sack thrown over her shoulder, its bottom scraping the ground.

The girl couldn't have been more than eighteen. Her hair was long, brown, and caked with dirt. Her blouse was loose; it hung low at the back. Her shoulders were lean, dark, and smooth. Good bones, basically.

Mohitram looked, too. As if aware of them, the beggar girl turned. Her face was shapely, her eyes sharp with survival. She was searching for articles with resale value, anything she could find to sell: old *chappals,* old bottles, old magazines.

The cop fixed his eyes on her, staring suspiciously at first, then insolently. He chewed away, making smacking sounds with his mouth. The girl looked at him, as if reading his thoughts, and a strange vocabulary rose between them, a language of tacit understanding.

But for Mohitram there was no such understanding. "Sahib," he whispered to the cop, who now wore a peculiar expression. Not that of a captor but of a captive. Not that of a law keeper but that of one about to contemplate mischief himself.

The girl walked on, a faint smile on her lips. The sack trailed behind, making a dull scraping sound, leaving a track in the dust of the platform. The cop turned and followed her. He had pulled himself up smartly; the *lathi* swung in his hand.

"Sahib, please," Mohitram pleaded, knowing full well that he was losing ground.

The cop turned and stared at Mohitram. He stared at him with flat, glassy eyes and said in a tone that Mohitram knew only too well, "Duty *khatam, samjah*? My duty is over. You understand?"

LOVE IN THE TIME
OF AIDS

✦ ✦ ✦

I GOT UPTIGHT WHEN DR. DOONGAJI officially passed judgment on the scarecrow-thin woman who had minutes earlier sat outside his office shivering, her sari wrapped tightly around her shoulders. Bluntly his voice boomed over the swiveling half doors, "I have told you before, you have AIDS. There's nothing I can do about it."

In the waiting area, heads turned. Expressions of cold shock gave way to expressions of uneasiness. Feverish whispers were exchanged. An energetic young man in his twenties popped his head over the half doors. Standing on his toes, he stretched, peeped inside, saw the patient, sat down, and nodded gravely to the others. A fifties-something Parsi lady, with a flabby white face, short brown hair, plump arms, and a florid dress that showed her thick calves, shot instructions at her husband, who was old and hard of hearing. Without waiting for his reply, she pulled at their grandson, a frisky eel of six, and dragged him out of the dispensary. Her husband followed, blinking in confusion. A middle-aged lady in a sari, her hair done up in a bun, looked around for a camaraderie of outrage. Finding none, she took to looking down, severely, at the floor. A male patient got to his feet and asked the compounder whether it was his turn next. The compounder, a bespectacled man with frail shoulders and a listless expression, looked up from among the shelves of colored medicine bottles and said, "After him," pointing to where I sat, feverish and miserable, head, nose, and chest blocked with phlegm.

This was the summer of 1986, when AIDS was the new disaster on the horizon, the latest threat to mankind, and there were all sorts of theories being tossed around: God, displeased with man, sending down an epidemic to punish man for his wanton decadence; man being asked to find his own limits of permissible sexuality; man extinguishing himself, playing out his fantasies of being God by making way for a new generation of power clones, a few years away but expected nonetheless—none of which were true anyway, none of which we believed, yet felt excited about, in the way one feels about a new era of progress, a new threat, like an imminent world war or a terrorist strike somewhere.

I had been going to Dr. Doongaji longer than most of his patients, ever since I outgrew the pediatrician. As a doctor for minor illnesses there was no one better. Some might argue that he was old-fashioned, that he was not a medicine man of today, but I had faith in him. Besides, it was amusing to come to his *dawakhana* and find that nothing had changed. Nothing for twenty years! Still the entrance with long white folding doors. Still a railing at the entrance, polished brass, for the old and the handicapped to hoist themselves up. Still large dusty sofas that squeaked when you sat, their springs broken, their leather upholstery creased and crushed. Still armchairs of solid teak with sagging straw work. Still the oversized fan, which quivered and threw out air at astonishing speed. Still the walls with the paint peeling, the cement showing, and a placard that said: "Laughter is the best medicine."

Again the good doctor boomed, this time with the resonance of a man who wished to impact his environment. "This AIDS is a serious *bimaari*," he said. "Its treatment needs a lot of money. More than you can imagine. To afford it you will need to go to a government hospital."

We waited to hear her reply. If she said something, it was inaudible. A taut silence fell over the waiting room. The blades of the overhead fan made a slicing sound, which grew in our minds. We chose to look away, look down, anywhere but at one another. We had to grapple with the gravity of the statement we'd just overheard, a death sentence passed phlegmatically in our midst. An onlooker to the gathering would have thought we were at a funeral, mourning the loss of someone very young, who had been snatched away without warning.

Again, the firm voice of Dr. Doongaji: "Why don't you understand? I can't help you. I can't do anything. You please go to a government hospital, huh."

Silence again. Not a question or a doubt expressed. She was whispering, pleading, I thought. Maybe she needed a clue, some direction. Maybe she needed information, some time to think. Maybe she was stunned with shock and embarrassment. Maybe . . . she was just plain broken.

I knew Dr. Doongaji well enough to do what I did next: I charged into his office. The woman turned to the squeak of the doors swinging open. I saw her. No flesh—all eyes, bones, and teeth.

The woman stared at me with the face of a vulture. It was a face masked with confusion, ignorance, and terror, absent from the sequence of events it was being asked to understand. I trembled, as much with compassion as with fever.

Dr. Doongaji looked up. His glasses had slipped down his nose, which was large, oily, and smudgy. His face was rough and unshaven, peppered with white bristles. His eyes were dim with age. Shrubs of white hair sprouted from his ears. He looked more like a scientist than a doctor, a dissolute dinosaur forced into a world he did not care for.

"Ah, Pesi, what is the matter with you?" he said. "Are you dying or what, like this lady here? Look, her husband has died, leaving her a present. And she won't listen. Thinks I can save her."

"Sorry to barge in, Doc," I said, sniffing. "But maybe I can help. I know of an NGO, a non-profit organization that works with HIV patients. It helps them get treated in government hospitals. It offers counseling, support, and helps with their adjustment. Let me speak to them." I pulled out my wallet and began going through my phone list.

"Nothing can help these people, Pesi. Problem is, they don't listen.

They only want to fuck away. Fuck here, fuck there. Insert, insert everywhere. See where it gets them finally?"

The woman's eyes widened. Our language was alien to her. It was the language of the educated, the rich, and the powerful, whom she knew nothing about. The look she gave us said: berate me, but don't send me away, please.

"But Doc, it was her husband's fault. You said he infected her. So how can we blame her?"

"Blame her? Of course I blame her. The problem with these idiots is they don't listen. She came to me a year ago with her husband. He had tested positive, and I told her to take care, to make him always wear a condom before sex. No condom, no sex! I remember saying this ten times, and them nodding like goats. Now, he has kicked the bucket and left her with this *bimaari*. What can I do? I am not God. I don't have special powers. When they wanted to fuck, did they think of me? Did they even think of my words, my advice? And now she wants me to save her. What I can do, huh?"

Just then the woman whispered in a thin cracking voice, *"Bhook nahin hain, dawa do."*

"Look at the stupid woman," Dr. Doongaji said. "She wants me to revive her appetite. She wants medicine so she can feel hungry. Have you ever heard anything so absurd? Tell me, what do you do with such people? They don't understand. They just don't listen. Do you think this would have ever happened if the British were here?"

"Eh . . . what?" I asked, taken aback.

"I said, do you think this would have happened if the British were here, if they were still in power, ruling us?" His eyes narrowed, looking at me expectantly. For a change they weren't flickering.

"What have the Brits got to do with this, Doc?" I said, trying to grapple with the incongruity of the question. I wondered if the good doctor had taken leave of his senses, whether the years of practice and the company of illnesses had finally taken their toll.

"They wouldn't have tolerated it! They *would* have passed laws. They *would* have enforced discipline. They *would* have made condoms compulsory. They *would* have punished sexual offenders and made an example of them. That's what they would have done. You didn't know the British, son. They had a way of getting things under control." His eyes shone. His fists were clenched. The glasses were back in place. I saw there was a bubble of saliva at the edge of his mouth. Some bile had seeped through and lingered.

"But how would the British have managed to keep people from screwing around? How would they have controlled individual wills?" I said, feeling sore at this illogic.

"The problem with you, Pesi, is that you were born in the wrong age. You don't know what it was like under the British. We had discipline, cleanliness, prosperity . . . and no corruption, boy. There was no pollution, no disease. AIDS? Whoever heard of it? They would have made sure it never entered. They would have got it under control, like that uprising of 1857."

"But AIDS is a worldwide epidemic. The British, too, are grappling with it in their country."

"I don't know where you get your news, boy, but you had better not say things like this in public. AIDS must have come from the Africans, who are all the time fucking like monkeys, or from the Americans, who keep experimenting with different viruses to spend all those dollar grants they get, or from the Italians, those insatiable devils, who'd do their own sisters given half a chance. No, the British have a high moral code, son. They would never do something like that to their own country."

"But, Doc, it has nothing to do with countries. You can get AIDS from anyone: a partner, a syringe, a salon, a blood bank."

"Nonsense, you only get it from a weak will—that's what! How come we never had this when we were young? Don't tell me we didn't have urges, boy. We didn't get aroused? It was just that our morality was high. We chose our partners and stayed with them. And where did we get that from if not the British?" His eyes wore a faraway look, and the woman, too, seemed happy, for she thought our discussion was about her.

Exasperated, I picked up the receiver and dialed the NGO I knew. This was the one at Prarthna Samaj, which had visited our college campus during our annual festival and put up posters and banners and given out leaflets cautioning us against AIDS. The killer disease was here, they said, and what killed was not the disease as much as ignorance. Over two days, a human penis with eyes, hands, lips, covered in padded white satin-soft material, resembling an astronaut's suit, had gone around shaking hands, telling us males to be Condom Men, namely, real men who took responsibility for their actions, who protected themselves and their partners from risks. "Safer sex is better sex," Condom Man droned, in a deep voice that came out of a small microphone pinned to his suit. "Who says you can't feel pleasure through a condom? Who says you can't enjoy sex while wearing one? It's a question of what you feel in here," he boomed, pointing to his head with a pudgy white finger, his other hand on his hip. Accompanied by a group of helpers, Condom Man went around the campus, telling us to embrace him as a sign of our commitment to fight AIDS, to put the safety back into sex. If not that, then shake his hand at least, in a solemn lifesaving pact.

When the crowd scattered or eyed him warily from a distance, Condom Man would pick up a guitar and strum away to the words of a song that was deep and bluesy, in the tradition of John Lee Hooker or B. B. King. The song went something like this:

> You ain't so cool and you ain't so kind
> if you don't keep her safety in mind
> You ain't so hip and you ain't so hot
> if you can't be her man on the spot
> You ain't so smart and you ain't so clever
> if you don't get wise to her secret fear
> You ain't so fair and you don't really care
> If you don't carry no condom to wear
> O Condom Man, he's the real man
> O Condom Man, ladies' man
> He is the one who understands

Condom Man would shuffle and dance while he strummed away. He'd do so in the quadrangle or in the canteen, not hesitating to climb onto tables and chairs and deliver his message from there, and the whole act was so ludicrous, so Theater of the Absurd, that hearing him, the crowd would return: boys and girls so curious and amused that they'd lock arms across one another's shoulders and sing along happily. I must say Condom Man's enthusiasm *was* infectious. It made us feel united against a common, unseen enemy. I was so impressed by Condom Man's act that when his helpers asked for volunteers to join their campus program I decided—without hesitation—to enlist right away. I went to the staff room, and that's where I met the real Condom Man. She was gorgeously tall and fair, with warm brown eyes. "Hi," she said, smiling, extending her hand. She loosened the bun at the back of her head and let her hair cascade down her neck and shoulders. "Hi. I am Dr. Sayoni. But you know me as Condom Man." All I could do was nod limply and take her hand, which was softer than the satin-white outfit she wore.

THE PHONE AT THE NGO OFFICE rang for a while. I wondered if I had hitched onto the helpline. I was about to hang up when a woman answered. It was Suchita Shah, Dr. Sayoni's assistant, a grim-faced woman in her twenties who'd taken it upon herself to protect Dr. Sayoni's privacy. The doctor was always in demand. She was always being interviewed by the press, always in the news for rescuing minors from brothels or for taking up cudgels on behalf of some laborer who'd lost his job after testing positive. The more I worked with Dr. Sayoni, the more my admiration grew. I began to see her as a veteran of many battles, a woman who'd given up a promising medical career to follow her convictions.

Suchita Shah said the doctor wasn't in. She sounded cagey until I told her who I was. I inquired when Dr. Sayoni would be back and Suchita hesitated before saying, "Dr. Sayoni has gone to the police station. There has been a complaint against her by a political leader who thinks she is inciting trouble in colleges. The politician thinks Condom Man is vulgar. He says that Condom Man symbolizes free sex; he is promoting premarital sex, which is against Indian culture. He wants Dr. Sayoni to set down in writing that she will kill Condom Man, that

Condom Man will cease to exist from today. Only then will he with-draw his complaint."

"But that is absurd," I said. "Condom Man is so effective. He works; he sinks in. Research has proved that after meeting him students think twice about having sex without a condom."

"Yes, but you know these politicians. They want any opportunity to be heard. A bunch of party workers came this morning and started protesting outside our office, and then came the police van, and it was so humiliating, Madam being taken away like that, like a common criminal. I, too, wanted to go, but Madam said, 'You stay here, Suchi, and look after the office.'"

There was a pause and I don't know whether I imagined it, but I thought Suchita sounded like she was in tears. I had never heard her sounding so upset, not even while she instructed patients in terminal states, who would be lying in the NGO office, playing out their last-minute wishes on *gadlas*. There'd be a priest reciting passages from the Bhagavad Gita or a cleric reading from the Qur'an, and there'd be a strange look of wonderment on the patient's face, the look of a child.

Regaining control of herself, Suchita Shah asked me what my business was and whether she could help in some way. I told her my problem: a woman with HIV, all the symptoms, and nowhere to go. Suchita said I should send her to their office right away.

I thought for a moment. With Dr. Sayoni not being there, was there any point in me going to the NGO office? After all, I wasn't feel-ing too well myself. My cold was getting the better of me. My fever had taken up residence; it ate at my bones, my skin, my stamina, and my will. Drawing my chair close and resting my elbows on Dr. Doongaji's green felt-top table, I spoke to the woman with AIDS. I told her how to get to Prarthna Samaj, to the NGO office, where she'd be given food, medicines, and a place to sleep. She'd stay with others who had the same problem as her, and from them she'd learn how to cope with her sickness. Before that she'd be taken to a government clinic where she'd be checked. She thought "checked" meant "cured" and her eyes lit up. *"Kha sakungi?"* she asked. "I *will* be able to eat?" I nodded and turned away, unable to bear the smile on her cadaverous face.

I led her out, holding open the doors as I would for any lady more fortunate than she. People in the waiting area stared at me, as one might at someone who was foolishly ignorant. Only the compounder kept busy, separating colored tablets from white pills and pouring and shaking thick colored mixtures in large brown bottles. Occasionally he'd stick his tongue out, run a label over it, and slap the label onto a medicine bottle. Then he'd shove the medicine at the patient through a small arched opening in the partition.

I led the woman to a cab and instructed the cabbie where to take her. I slipped her the fare money and a five-hundred-rupee note. She took the note blankly and I wondered if she knew its value.

Then I returned to Dr. Doongaji in his office. On my way in, the compounder nodded at me, as if to say he approved of my action or simply to suggest he had safeguarded my place in the queue. It was difficult to fathom what he meant, his being the language of pills, powders, and potions.

"Well, now let's look at you, Pesi," Dr. Doongaji said, rising to his feet. "Let's see what you've come down with."

With a wave of his hand, he directed me to a room on the right. I knew the place only too well: the examination room with the raised bed, the Rexene mattress, the hard air pillow, the black wall fan swishing hot air over you while you were recumbent, the stool at the foot of the bed that I'd use to hoist myself up, and the green conical lampshade that dangled from the ceiling and had had a bulb missing for as long as I could recollect.

I lay down and Dr. Doongaji bent over me with a flashlight, saying, "Say aaaah." He opened his own mouth, showing me his row of gold fillings. He forgot to shut it.

"Aaaah . . . ," I went, holding my breath and looking up at the ceiling. I did that to avoid breathing in the doctor's musty breath. He peered inside my mouth, frowning, holding on to the flashlight like it would lead him to some rare, hidden treasure.

"Hmm . . . bad, very bad," he said, his eyes blinking. His eyebrows were gray and bushy, like foxtails, and as he came closer I got the smell of sour, fetid skin.

"Wait," he said, gesticulating with his open palm like he had just received a bolt of inspiration. He moved to the side, to where there were shelves along a wall. The shelves were lined with dusty old medicine bottles. He opened one of the bottles and, placing a finger over its neck, turned it turtle. He did this a couple of times, so that the liquid came in contact with his finger, and then he came over and said, "Now, Pesi, open wide, like the tunnel on the Khandala *ghat*. Imagine this is a big bus passing through, you are in the bus, and if you don't open wide you can't pass; you can't go to Khandala." I smiled. I'd heard these words since I was a boy.

He asked me to raise my head, which I did, and then he pushed the pillow below my neck, between my shoulder blades. He hooked two fingers round my upper teeth, and tilting my head back, he shoved his other hand—the one with the medicine—into my mouth, all the way to the uvula, which was sore and inflamed. Using his thumb and first finger, he caught the uvula and squeezed it hard, saying, "There . . . there go the viruses."

I began to choke and splutter, yet he squeezed away, rubbing my uvula like it were some inflamed evil that had to be snuffed out. My eyes filled with tears. My nose began to water. My mouth felt bitter. Whatever he'd applied was trickling down my throat. It was thick and burning, and I felt my uvula swell up. I thought it would burst.

Removing the stethoscope that hung around his neck, he placed it against my chest and said, "Breathe in; breathe out." He tilted his head and cocked his ears, as if he was trying to catch what the viruses were saying, as if he was trying to decipher their next move of attack, imminent in some zone somewhere. He blinked and wheezed, shifting the stethoscope to different parts of my chest. At one point, his eyes narrowed, and I thought I saw a slow, triumphant smile spread across his face.

My thoughts returned to the woman with AIDS. I wondered if she had reached Prarthna Samaj. "Prarthna," in Hindi, meant "prayer," and I wondered whether hers would be answered. Whether she would get her appetite back.

Holding the stethoscope to my chest, Dr. Doongaji asked me to cough three times, which I did. "Hmm," he said. "Bad chest, too. It's all this pollution, boy. It's settled in your nose, throat, and lungs."

"It's getting worse by the year, Doc," I said. "I wish the authorities would do something."

"Authorities? What authorities?" he snapped. "There is only lawlessness here. No one is working to improve things. No one is bothered. The other day my primroses died. You know the ones outside? Such nice flowers, so healthy they were. First they lost their color. Then the leaves wilted one by one, and finally they all died. If plants can't survive in this city, how do they expect human beings to live? Remember my words, Pesi; remember them well: *the price of progress need not be death.* That's what the problem with this city is. No respect for the living. No respect for life." He blinked. I noticed his eyes were watery, pools of misty regrets gathered over the years and locked away.

"Come," he ordered suddenly. "Remove your pants. It's time for Doongaji's *dhamakladoo.*"

Doongaji's *dhamakladoo*, as he called it, was nothing more than an injection, a savage poke delivered with such fury that it played hell with the viruses, ejecting them in twenty-four hours flat. That was Dr. Doongaji's guarantee, the patent by which he was known. No one knew why the *dhamakladoo* hurt so much or why it had to be delivered so viciously, like a deathblow, but it worked wonders, always did.

While he prepared the injection, I lowered my trousers and waited. My left hip was exposed. My face was on the pillow, which smelt odd. I raised my head and looked. The pillow had hairs and specks of dandruff stuck on it. I shoved it aside, and curling my hands into tight little balls, I placed my head on them.

From where I lay, I looked around the office. On the wall opposite were two large windows with thick green curtains. At the side was a glass *almari,* with shelves of old books and older forgotten medicines. From the top of a wall stared a giant-size portrait of Dr. Doongaji's father, Dr. Tehmurasp Doongaji, in a thick white overcoat and with a tall black *pagdi* on his head. He had magnificent whiskers and eyes brimming with hope. He, I was told, used to maintain an exquisite

collection of convertibles, which doubled up as ambulances for his patients. And more often than not, he ended up paying for his poorer
patients' medicines from his own pocket. And yet he had that look of
imperious pride, of fierce inapproachability, a refusal to bow down to
life's vicissitudes or its viruses. In the center was a 1979 calendar, its
pages buff with age, its edges curling inward. Above that was a grandfather clock, its pendulum swinging gently, rhythmically, its second
hand moving in fits and starts across its stolid white face.

I looked at the time and thought of the woman with AIDS. Her
clock, too, had started its final countdown. She'd be living on borrowed time. How long would that be? Months? Weeks? Days? Or
hours? Would her last days be comfortable? Would she have good days
and bad days? Would she laugh on good days and sleep through bad
days? And would someone tell her what they were about and why they
happened? And would someone be by her side, holding her hand
when she slipped into deep and permanent sleep? I wondered if I
should have found out more about her. About her poverty, her pain,
her real hunger. I wondered if she had family who ought to be informed. I wished I had taken her to the NGO office myself. I wished
I could know what was being done and why. Like the second hand on
the old clock, I had acted spasmodically, clumsily, to suit my own
rhythm, my own convenience.

Great doubt rose in me. Self-loathing and anger. I did not deserve
treatment. I did not deserve the cure. My self-worth was gone, gone
with the woman in the cab.

I felt a cool, stinging sensation on my hip and got the sharp smell
of an antiseptic. I saw Dr. Doongaji rub my hip with a wad of cotton.
In his other hand he held the syringe. "*Chaal,*" he said, his eyes gleaming. "Come, it will hurt a bit, but bear up."

I rose and swiveled myself off the bed. "Sorry, Doc, I need to go,"
I said, slipping my feet into my Docksides. As I tucked my shirt in, I
felt my mind triumph over my fever, my virus, my cold.

The doctor's forehead clouded with confusion. His hand froze in
mid-air. I noticed it was shivering. His eyebrows furrowed and he
said, "Come, don't be such a *bayla,* Pesi. Don't be such a coward."

"I'll be one if I stay, Doc. Sorry, but I need to go."

The half doors swung open easily. Holding the railing, I jumped over the stairs and rushed toward a waiting cab. "Prarthna Samaj!" I said to the cabbie. *"Jaldi!"* The cabbie knew by instinct it was a matter of life and death. In Bombay it was always like that. Someone's life hanging by a thread, someone's head at stake. The meter dropped instantly.

In the cab, I thought of Doongaji's *dhamakladoo,* the third-degree treatment for viruses. The syringe went all the way in, piercing flesh, piercing layers of tissue, blood vessels, and cells, into the bloodstream, into the heart of the enemy virus. What chance would it have against a hand like his? The hand of experience, which held down the syringe even after it had unloaded its contents and then along the same pathway made its way out, an axe of a needle with teeth. I tried to remember if I had seen the doctor change the syringe or the needle—if not on that day, then in the past—but there were no such recollections. I felt relieved to have ducked the *dhamakladoo.* At the same time I felt sheepish, for it was wrong to have rushed off the way I did, without an explanation. It was wrong to have taken the good doctor for granted, this sweet relic of a doc, who had served us well, in the time before AIDS, mistrust, and other progress-borne infections.

THE CAB HONKED AND SNARLED its way through the burgeoning traffic. Oozing past the Grant Road Bridge, we got stuck in a traffic jam created by pushers of handcarts struggling with their cargo. There was a lot of honking and under-the-breath cursing, but no one stepped out to voice their frustration, for everyone could see the struggle on the faces of the handcart pushers, their dark, spindly legs quivering, their knees shining with sweat, their gaunt faces melting under the heat of the summer sun.

A traffic cop came and blew his whistle hysterically. Gesticulating wildly, he bawled at the cabbies, who revved their engines and surged forward in a show of sullen hate.

On the bridge, brown sugar addicts pulled at lines of powder burning on silver foil, which coiled and hissed like baby serpents before disappearing into their parched lungs and throbbing, delirious minds. At the side, women cooked in burnt vessels, on small sooty kerosene stoves, while their children played with torn bicycle tires, which they tried hard to balance and roll. Under the bridge, hawkers of cameras, wristwatches, mobile phones, and transistors screamed, "Foreign, foreign," in a way importers of other viruses don't draw attention to themselves. Small gaudily dressed families, tourists from other parts of India, paused to consider the menu of choices, the glamour and glitz of a push-button city that knew all the right buttons to push, the right signals to send. Up ahead at the movie house, black marketers weaved a conspiracy of profit, whispering prices under bated breath, and farther up, on the pavement, out-of-work migrants stopped and pondered their chances over a wild, spinning roulette wheel. Where the wheel would stop, on which number, would determine who ate, who drank, and who got to live out his fantasy in the cages of untrammeled vice, Bombay's sleaze street built on the assumption that the road to hell is paved with good intentions.

Looking at this frenzy of life, I wished I could tell all these people what I had learned at Dr. Doongaji's. I wished I could repeat the wisdom of *the price of progress need not be death.* I wished I could say this in as many words—in Hindi, Gujarati, Marathi, Tamil, and all the languages of India. I wished I could put this on posters, banners, and billboards, across bridges, across highways, and of course at Mantralaya, where our leaders, our kurta-clad politicians, sway the people for their votes. But for their lives? No, never.

Until that happens, until a dream of such waking proportions is possible, I thought I would search for some recognition in Dr. Sayoni's eyes. I would save lives, collectively, individually, as if my own life depended on that. And I would sing along with her, side by side, shoulder to shoulder, sing spiritedly, heartily, from some place deep down in my gut, from where I would try to match her enthusiasm, her conviction, her flow of beauty and sacrifice. I would sing at the police station, in colleges, in *maidans,* in places of high-exposure risk, where fools, as they say, fear to tread. And under my breath, I might change the words to sound like this: "O Condom Man, give me your hand, for I am the one who understands." And I hoped that she would understand, too. She would find the pitch I was trying to reach.

Having come to the conclusion that Dr. Sayoni was more on my mind than the woman with AIDS, I tapped the cabbie on the shoulder and instructed him to take a right to Lamington Road, to the police station, where my Condom Man fought charges of indecency. And while the cabbie grunted and protested, asking why I couldn't make up my mind from the beginning where I wanted to go, I chose to observe an expression of tight-lipped, well-guarded silence. For how to explain to him—a man who toiled under the scorching sun, shifting gears and switching lanes a hundred times a day—that I myself had no clue to my own journey or my destination, that I was just one of those for whom the call of *love* had triumphed over the drone of *death*—one being the assertion of life; the other, its prompt denial.

BABU BARRAH TAKKA

✦ ✦ ✦

GOING BY APPEARANCES, Madhulikar Srini was taking a tea break over an afternoon newspaper. His office wore the usual signs of a public sector undertaking: pale, gray blinds shutting out the light; a large, rickety steel desk with an off-white Formica top; an old desktop computer covered with a plastic jacket, tucked away in a corner; a calendar hanging off the wall, the year's theme being unity in diversity, expressed by birds and bees flitting over a field of sunflowers whose petals were upturned in an eager pollinating smile; at the side, a Godrej cupboard, a last man standing, in steel, memories of a day and age when steel was not yet deemed a designer metal. A tall floor fan threw a concentrated breeze in Madhulikar's direction; it formed a wrinkled coating over his tea. On a chipped plate, next to the teacup, were two plump *vadas,* around them a moat of thick orange sauce meant to pass as ketchup. The *vadas* had gone soggy from being soaked too long in the sauce. All the items on the table were lying untouched, and this spoke of Madhulikar's state of mind, which was disturbed, terribly, terribly disturbed.

Strange it was that Madhulikar should be like that, for at the place where he worked—the National Petroleum Resource Corporation— few employees could be found dispirited. Most of them enjoyed their work for the reason that there was very little work; they could leave at 6:00 P.M. sharp. You should see them scurrying home, shuffling into the ample bus designated to reach them to the railway station, their faces bright and beaming, their jokes friendly and prodding, their twos and threes decided as schoolchildren might: "*Ithe Sonwalkar, ithe.* We got much to talk about."

Yet Madhulikar was disturbed. The newspaper was frozen between his fingers. Its front page was unturned; its edges flapped noisily under the fan. Madhulikar tightened his grip and stared remotely at the news. The murder of a social activist, the arrest of an income tax commissioner who was found to have assets worth rupees thirty crores, and the entry of an underworld goon, Varun Paoli, into politics—these seemed like trivial happenings compared to his own problems. He read without the usual relish.

Like all problems in their state of incipience Madhulikar's problems appeared insurmountable. They occupied him, distracted him, bore down on him, and left him feeling crushed.

It had started with Disha, his elder daughter, wanting to marry a boy she had chosen. The two had met at management school. For twenty months nothing had happened. Just group outings, laughter, a common sympathy for the environment, and a certain fondness for the Mumbai Film Festival, for which they had cut lectures together. Then, during the last seminar, having muddled heads over a project that required marketing the state of Maharashtra to non-resident Indians, they had fallen in love. In between coffee breaks, burgeoning data, and PowerPoint slides, they felt something confusing and real. They emerged dazed from this revelation. Wonderful thing, love! It made you feel foolish and inspired in the same breath. At times, they worried, too: would this wave of emotion dislodge them from their careers, which were important to them? But as they shared views and drew closer, they realized their love could lead to a mutual striving; they could build something strong together. Their dreams took on a new meaning. Their resolution showed on their faces and in their smiles. Madhulikar saw this and his heart opened up. By God, all he wanted was for his daughter to be happy.

Where was the problem then? Nothing really, nothing initially! The boy's side met the girl's; they enjoyed an evening of laughter and

snacks. The boy's father was short, fidgety, and laughed a lot. "Ha, ha,"
he went like Santa Claus, dangling his stubby legs from the sofa. The
boy's mother smiled with her cheeks and facial muscles. With her
eyes, which were small and riveting, she ripped loads of information
from the girl's family—from their gestures, manners, clothes, conversation, all that slipped casually and unconsciously in the course of an
evening. The boy was to study in the United States. Twenty-five lakh
rupees were being spent in a nudge, which could have been averted by
opting for a not-so-expensive university. "But then, what is money
when it comes to a child's future? Don't you agree, sahib?" the boy's
father had said, leaning over and extending a tray of sweetmeats to
Madhulikar. "Of course, of course," Madhulikar had said hurriedly,
helping himself to a piece of *mithai*. When he bit into it, he found it
wasn't as sweet as it looked; it was sticky and difficult to chew, a nuisance, in fact, to his public composure.

The first few weeks went by in meeting relatives from the boy's
side. Aunts, uncles, cousins, elder cousins, elder aunts, elder uncles, oldest living aunt, oldest living uncle: they were all eager to see the girl.
So lunches and dinners were organized. Hearty introductions took
place. The girl was adorned at the door, her feet rather—with long
grains of rice and vermilion. When they did that, she blushed and her
cheeks mirrored the glow in her heart. Inside homes, on large, copious
sofas, family roots were dug out and discussed; connections were
traced and established. The state of the country, too, was discussed: the
upswing in the stock market, the real estate boom, the foreign investment pouring in. Madhulikar's job was envied. How lucky to be
working for the government; the government looks after its own. He
smiled, wondering whether there was an insinuation of lethargy, of
corruption and decadence. Either way, they'd be right.

Jokes were bandied about how in the old days wives were chosen
by the boy's parents and no one questioned or challenged the logic.
Some grooms—now uncles, gray and potbellied—had gone in blind-
folded, without even seeing the girl or her picture, and they'd done well,
from the looks of it. A smart-aleck uncle cleared his throat and asked
Disha if she could trust her man to the US of A—to its blue-eyed,

white-skinned femmes fatales? She laughed. "Where will he get the time for mischief, Uncle? He will be busy working overtime. He has to save, to bring me over."

The boy's mother stiffened. The girl was impractical. Where would Jai have time to work? They weren't spending twenty-five lakh rupees so that he could work in some lowly cafeteria or in some gloomy library. She put on her most charming smile and said, "*Beti*, why not stay with us—here in India? Let us be parents to you, while Jai is away. Give us the opportunity to look after you. What do you say, *bhai* sahib?" she asked sweetly, turning to Madhulikar.

"Of course . . . of course," he replied softly, sadly. He realized Disha's absence *was* imminent. In India, a bride's place *was* with her in-laws, and he didn't have the money to send her overseas.

Late that night, when her mother was putting away the dinner leftovers in the refrigerator and her sister was plodding at her homework, Disha said to Madhulikar, pouting, "I don't want to stay with them, Papa. I want to be with Jai. During my best years of marriage, I don't want to be away."

"I know, love," Madhulikar had said, noting her expression and thinking, God, he'd miss her. "But your presence will distract him, and besides, it's only for two years. He will be back soon, and then you can be together for a lifetime!"

"But don't you see?" she said, sitting up, looking at him like he were the only man in the world who'd understand, who'd do something to change her situation. "I don't want Jai coming back to his parents. Their wealth will spoil him. I want him to have his own life, his own money, his own future. Our life, our money, our future."

Madhulikar sighed. What do you do when your offspring sounds exactly like you? When she echoes that strain of gene you've passed on to her. And you know it's being played right back at you. Hugging helps, or so he believed. He did just that. Without saying a word, he held her tight.

From that day on, the boy's parents took to looking after Disha the way they said they would. "We must shop for our daughter soon. Nothing less than a Paithani sari, mind you. And jewelry from Khubchand

Amirchand, head to toe, so all can see. One set for the engagement, and one set for the wedding, and one set for later, when she attends important functions with us. And one set for Kahini. Who knows? She might find a nice boy at the wedding. Yes, such things happen," the boy's father would say, looking at his wife, who would add with a smile, "And why only for the girls? One set for *bhabhiji* and something for *bhaiyya*. And anyone else in your family, near or distant, who needs to be pleased, just let us know." "Yes, sir! Just don't hesitate," the boy's father would say, beaming. Then he'd break into that loud, uproarious laugh of his.

Madhulikar had blushed and protested. He said all this expense wasn't necessary; they were getting a gem of a boy; what more could they want?

"*Arrey,* what are you saying, sahib?" the boy's father would retort. "Give us a chance to show our feelings. She is *our* daughter now, and you are *our* family."

"Of course, sir, but you needn't be so generous," Madhulikar would say.

To which the boy's father would reply, "What is money, sir, I ask you, in front of children's happiness?"

"What is money? What is money?" Madhulikar saw the full face of it over the next few weeks. He saw a fortune being spent on astrologers, one lot from the north, one from the south. The pundits pondered over their charts, discussed, debated, and finally agreed that the sixth of December (three months from then) would be the ideal date, so auspicious a day that even the Gods would attend. The boy's father glowed. "Worth it, no?" he asked Madhulikar. "Calling these men of God. They know how to make a marriage work."

Priests were appointed. They would arrive shaven headed and bare chested, in cloudy white *dhotis,* looking aloof and sanitized. Naturally, such purity would come at a price. And since money was never discussed in matters of the heart, it was invited in the form of a donation to the temple. On this arrangement even the Gods would smile; they'd confer their blessings on the young couple. And, for a more temporal angle, there was tax relief under Section 80CC of the Income tax Act: 100 percent exemption for such donations.

Madhulikar brooded over the amount to the priests: twenty-five thousand rupees, payable in advance, cancellation not allowed. Later, there'd be plane tickets for them, their accommodation, their food, car hire, special clothes, special footwear, shawls, *chappals,* visits to other temples, and *daan,* which was charity in armfuls, not alms, like in the old days. "Of course, we will share everything," the boy's father had said. "Right now I will pay through my company, and later, we can do the accounts. So I am going ahead, huh, and no compromises on the ceremonies, on their new life about to begin?"

"Yes, please," said Mrs. Srini, Madhulikar's wife. She didn't see the look her husband gave her. Or perhaps she chose to ignore it.

When it came to choosing the venue, the boy's father suggested they book two gymkhanas, side by side. "In business, one has so many obligations, so many commitments, that leave out one person and you never know when you will need him."

Madhulikar wondered what this was going to cost him, whether he'd be expected to pay half the amount for the boy's guests as well. His own guests wouldn't be that many: no more than two hundred or so—so why should he foot the bill for this man's extravagances? On second thought, might it not look cheap if he refused? Might it not be an admission of inadequacy, of small-mindedness? All these thoughts assailed him. He carried them to work. And back again.

Planning the *mandap,* the backdrop, was another event. Sitting with the boy's family in their Nepean Sea Road flat, sitting on the terrace, facing the sea, sipping *chai* and chewing on chutney sandwiches, they flipped through a book of designs. The *mandapwalla* sat on the floor, on his haunches, rubbing his knees. They glanced through the designs, ranging from floral and geometric to graphic and symbolic. They lingered over some of the designs and flipped through others cursorily. They stopped at a design of Rama and Sita in exile, exulting in each other's love. The God and Goddess looked wide-eyed and radiant, joyous and inspiring. The *mandapwalla* had to stop himself from whistling out with excitement. "This will look beautiful, sahib," he said, "but so much time and labor will go into it that I will have to hire four men to work full-time."

Anxiously Madhulikar spoke. "Yes, but do we really need this? Seems such an extravagance, don't you think?"

The boy's parents exchanged looks. The father said curtly, "Ha, sahib, it might be expensive, but it's like having a *murti* at the wedding. It's out of respect—for the Gods."

"Besides," said the boy's mother, drawing herself up. "It will be inspiring for the priests. They will be reminded to chant their best. And if there's a problem, we can . . ." Her voice tapered off. She looked at her husband, who said yes, they could spend if money *was* an issue.

Madhulikar blushed. "Nothing like that, sir. I just thought . . ."

"*Arrey*, sir, don't think. I always say, at a time like this, we parents must give up thinking. Money goes like water. But what to do? All our life we have done so much for the children, and then, to hold back at the last minute . . . let no parent be guilty of this."

Madhulikar murmured that he felt the same way, but to his own ears his voice sounded hollow and insincere. He felt a kind of a dread, as if, through some act of betrayal, he had let himself down.

The boy's father began to speak of the in-laws of his elder son, Jai's brother, who had married and left for the United States the previous year. "I tell you, sir, what a heart that family has. Forty lakh rupees they put down without a thought. Even the couple's air tickets they bought, right down to the airport transfers!" His voice dropped. "They even did a *havala* transfer. Moved rupees into dollars, all hush-hush and illegal, and used that money to set up the couple. At first, they were nervous. Not used to it, you see. But I told them how in business we do it all the time. We know all the tricks. In fact, I got it done for them—through my contact, Mussabhai. And now the couple is so happy, they can see it was worth it. First, even I used to wonder: why are they spending so much money? But then I realized this is not money we are giving; these are blessings. How to deny that to our children? How to steel our hearts?"

I must be a fool, fool, fool, Madhulikar thought that night. He was sitting on the living room floor, surrounded by a bunch of fixed deposits and share certificates. Next to him were two dusty box files with their clips open. In front was a pad with calculations: with columns, scratches, and revisions. Some of the share certificates were old and discolored; they were cracking in places where they'd been folded, and the staple pins on them bled rust.

He glanced at the sum on the pad. Had he missed anything: an extra zero, a carry-over digit? It could make all the difference. But, no, *this was the truth.* After thirty-four years of service, the sum of his savings was eleven lakh, eighty thousand rupees. That would be how much he'd get if he were to liquidate everything.

He glanced at a paper lying next to him, sticking out from under the pad. It was a longer list, with longer figures and more zeroes. His tab for the wedding came to sixteen lakh rupees. That would include the costs for the ceremony, the priests, the venue, the *mandap,* the food, the flower decoration, the lights, the tables, the chairs, the carpets, the music, and the buses—strictly air-conditioned, he had been told. Roughly, it would also take care of the outstation guests. "You will like our people from Jaipur," the boy's father had said. "They are like Rajputs in matters of enjoyment. You do this much for them," he said, showing a pinch, "and they will do that much in return." And he had thrown open his arms wide and smiled a lush, broad smile.

Madhulikar understood he was being called upon to prove his capacity, his strength. It was the kind of game people played during marriages, when requirements of splendor outweighed reason, when every purchase made is a statement about your status, and any departure from custom is seen as shallowness, deserving condemnation.

And society was so warped and so lopsided that the burden always fell on the girl's family. Madhulikar sighed and stretched out. He'd been sitting cross-legged a long time now. He looked at the list before him. The amount still did not take care of gifts for the boy's side: for Jai's aunts, uncles, cousins, Jaipuri guests, and so on and so forth. What were they expecting from him? What did they like? Then, what about his own family? he thought. He hadn't even gotten around to them yet. He had to get his wife a new set of jewelry, some saris at least. God bless her, she deserved it—the noble woman! She had never asked him for anything all these years, not like other women, hinting, cajoling, moping, sulking, even nagging about material things. And Disha and Kahini—he'd have to get something for them, too. Something elaborate, because the boy's side would be watching and they would judge his heart by the size of the ornaments. And, of course, he'd have to give the boy something, too, something substantial. Not just the trousseau, but something like a settlement, to help him get started. It would be better if he did it in dollars. But how did this *havala* thing work? No point thinking about that, because he wasn't going to be able to afford it. And no point dealing with underworld goons, because that was unthinkable. *"Hey Bhagwan,* spare me that," Madhulikar said to the idol sitting in the corner of the room. The idol continued smiling, as it always had, one hand raised in hope. Madhulikar searched its face for a trace of sympathy, some sign of response. He'd known miracles to happen—just like that.

For the first time in his life, Madhulikar felt lonely and abandoned. He felt the burden of his years, all fifty-five of them. His heart went *dhak dhak,* as if intending to leave the shell of his body, as if wanting *out.* He felt a drop of sweat run down his face. He noticed that his palms were moist; they felt stiff, like his shoulders, and there was a dull pain in his left side. Could he be having a heart attack? he thought. Quietly he waited for the grinding pain, the seizure that would force him to lie down, knock him cold and kill him perhaps—there, on his life's achievements. They would think he had died of shame. They would not see the relief, the sweet, subtle triumph of escape on his face. Out of contempt for the struggle he had undertaken, he'd lie facedown on the certificates and dribble a little spit onto them—his life's achievements that had proved inadequate. Yes, death would spare him the humiliation of begging, borrowing, or stealing. Or maybe he could just take the bribe.

THE *BABU BARRAH TAKKAS,* they used to call them: the ones who took the bribe. *Babu barrah takka* because *barrah takka,* or 12 percent, would be the minimum bribe for the officials at the NPRC—the clerks, the head clerks, the field staff, the engineers, the supervisors, the inspectors, the managers, the regional heads, the directors, the management, et al.

How did the system work? Well, it was all about an apex body of the government empowered to make decisions, using the taxpayers' money. The NPRC was the direct representative arm of the petroleum ministry. It was established to disseminate resources that would fuel the growth of the oil industry. It was there to subsidize products, to promote awareness, and to usher in progress. It had great powers and budgets to back it but little or no accountability. No one had to carry the can, and no one ever felt the heat, which explained why its employees took their jobs lightly, why corruption reigned unchecked, why risks were taken and deals were struck with magnanimous regularity, and why no one was alarmed: because everyone was involved. Well, almost everyone, save a few employees like Madhulikar.

So far, he hadn't felt the need to take a bribe. No, it was a lot deeper than that. There was his family and a history of honesty. And when your roots are solid—as they were with him—it's not easy to tear yourself asunder, to be the one who succumbs, shamelessly.

Hadn't his grandfather given up land given to him by the government in favor of needy farmers? Hadn't his father vacated their three-bedroom flat, handing over the keys to the landlord, because of a commitment made years ago? Hadn't his uncle—the one who'd run off to Kenya at eighteen—made his millions and then given them away to starving children in Somalia? With this kind of a lineage, what chance did Madhulikar have to become a *Babu barrah takka*? How would he face his father, his grandfather, his God Almighty, before whom he sat in *puja* one hour daily?

No, not possible. Not till today, at least, when he was beginning to think seriously, think differently. Besides, it was just once. For his daughter's sake. For her happiness. Wasn't *that* important? No, most important! "But what do I have to give my daughters besides character and education?" he used to say. And now he was getting educated by life. The expenses were mounting. The shopping knew no limits. The boy's parents were doing a lot for Disha. They had bought her expensive saris, shoes, jewelry, and designer dresses from Ensemble, where the prices, it was whispered, began at forty thousand. Unfortunately, they expected twice as much. "We will look after our daughter, you look after your son," the boy's father had said. And Madhulikar knew what that meant. They would take care of their son's education, but he, Madhulikar, would have to do the rest. And he didn't earn in U.S. dollars—unfortunately.

But the bribe would take care of that. Didn't all bribes come in cash, in *rokda,* as they called it? And this *rokda* would be a huge amount, huge enough to make a transfer, a *havala.* Madhulikar's heart ached. Truly, how miserable he was that he was even thinking of it. And really, it was true what Chaggan Babu, his college professor who taught him ethics, used to say, "One act of deception leads to another; one rotten cell infects another; kill it before it kills you." It killed Madhulikar to think what it would do to Disha if he fell short in his obligations. She'd have to live with the boy's parents. She would have to hear their taunts later.

He sighed and leaned back in his chair. It squeaked but held his weight. The late-afternoon silence fell around him. He flicked the newspaper to page 2. His eyes fell on a headline that screamed: "Housing Board Fails to Rehabilitate Displaced Tenants," and below that: "Old couple at Goregaon Bludgeoned to Death." The phone rang. He answered it.

"Srini!" the voice from the other end screeched. It was Archrekar, his boss. He always called Madhulikar by his surname, and for some reason that irritated Madhulikar. "What have you thought, Srini? Have you gone through the proposals? Have you decided?"

"No, sir, but I will, before the evening is up. And I will have my report ready by morning. I hope that is okay with you, sir? In such an important matter, we don't want to rush. We don't want to regret our decision later."

There was a pause. The voice at the other end sounded cold yet restrained. "No, of course not, Srini, but if you ask me I would go with Lodha. I have met him personally. A good man, a capable man, like you, Srini. Why don't you meet him and see? You will like him."

By God! thought Madhulikar. The stakes must be high this time, for Archrekar to come on so strong. But, of course, a gas station on the expressway was no small business. It would mean crores of rupees of business. The payoffs would be huge. Everybody would be looked after.

What's more, this was to be a model gas station, which meant that the company could invest in it, too. The company could set it up for the owner. And in this there'd be further moneymaking opportunities: Tenders invited but vendors signed indiscriminately. Kickbacks on everything, from construction to design, from food companies to soft-drink manufacturers, from equipment providers to kiosk makers, from the guys who sold computers to the guys who would maintain them, from ATM operators, card operators, Internet providers, advertisers, and of course, the adulterated gas—a cash cow that could only be maintained with the connivance of partners like Lodha. Madhulikar remembered him: a short, obsequious man, with a double chin and patchy skin.

"Certainly, sir, I will take into account what you say," Madhulikar said. "Once I have read the proposal, I will discuss it with you. Then maybe we can call the party and have a meeting. I am sure it will be to *our* advantage." He winced. His ears felt like they were on fire. Had he really said that? Had he crossed the line, broken his code, put out his hand like a *Babu barrah takka*?

There was a sharp silence at the other end. Then Archrekar spoke. "That would be nice, Srini, very nice, the correct way to approach it. In fact, just do it your way, and let me know if you need anything—any information, that is."

Every man has his price, or so the pundits of greed believe. For Madhulikar it was his daughters. First or second, it did not matter. He loved them both equally. In their presence, he became young, unfettered, joyous; he could listen to their banter for hours. When he looked upon them—their sweet faces, their trusting eyes—his heart would expand like it was being called upon to store some mammoth, impossible joy. Some men felt that way about sons, about continuation and lineage. Madhulikar wasn't one of them. He liked his two girls and their dependence on him. They looked up to him, listened to him, gave him so much respect and love. For them a thousand cynics he would bear, a thousand expenses, too, and not for anything in the world would he do anything to risk their happiness. Having decided thus, he took Lodha's call without his usual frostiness. It came at 5:00 P.M. sharp, just as he had finished going through the proposals, and he knew even before he picked up the receiver who it was—the death knell of his conscience.

He spoke to Lodha and endured his unctuousness. It hurt to think that he was bending his own rules, for in his books tendering parties weren't allowed to call before a decision was made. It would amount to disqualification.

They decided on a meeting. 7:30 P.M. the following day, at the clubhouse on Marine Drive. "If you are not comfortable, please say so, sir. We can always meet at some five-star hotel. Or perhaps you would like drinks and dinner at the Rooftop? I can come and pick you up. It's no problem, sir. I am always at your disposal—always."

Madhulikar put down the phone with a trace of disgust. How low would the man stoop? How much would he grovel for a piece of the pie? And where did the pie end, where indeed? Well, he himself was no better, he thought, picking up the file with the proposals. He would have to prepare his report, come up with an analysis, give his recommendations, an eyewash and a farce, but it would have to be done as a matter of bureaucracy, for that's how the NPRC operated.

There were three tendering parties: the Lodhas, the Seths, the Kankadias. Each owned property along the expressway. Each wanted the NPRC to develop it and allow them to manage it for a share of the profits. Each felt theirs would be a feasible and lucrative location. It was for Madhulikar to decide who was right. He held the key to their future.

Strangely, he did not see it that way. In his thirty-four years with the NPRC he had figured out how things worked: how under a veneer of impartiality individual pockets were lined and personal fortunes were built.

There, on a hot sunny afternoon made more oppressive by his own downfall, Madhulikar Srini tried to picture the sequence of events if left to a *Babu barrah takka.*

Ten minutes would have been spent on the proposals, weighing the capabilities of each party. No analysis would have been made, no queries raised. The preferred party, the one most amenable, would have been summoned to a club or a restaurant of standing. Expensive liquor and exotic snacks would have been ordered; lavish tastes and habits would have been discussed. The host party would have been supplied with ample hints. Then the conversation would move to other topics: the state of the share bazaar, the new economic policies, the onslaught of competition in the petroleum sector and its impact, in the midst of which the soliciting party would nurse but one question at the back of his mind: am I getting the license or not?

After a while, the *Babu barrah takka* would declare, "I have been through your proposal. [Pause.] I think it holds merit. [Pause.] Of course, there are a few questions, but in principle it looks okay. To me it does."

If the host party is a seasoned player, which in all probability he is, he will intervene and say, "Look, sahib, I don't know your company's policies. I just know I want this license anyhow. You be my guide, sir, and help me get it. I am ready to follow *all* your instructions."

At this stage, the *Babu barrah takka* would pretend to look reflective. In reality, it was probably the third drink in his system that brought on that look. He has worked out his calculations earlier and has been primed by his bosses as to what size of deal to strike. Yet he must pretend, he must playact, he mustn't make it look too simple.

"I don't know," he'd say doubtfully. "I would love to see you get this order. I would love to see you succeed, but it is my boss . . . he is close to one of the other parties. I don't know whether he will listen, or if he will agree."

Dropping his voice, the host party should then say, "You tell me, sir. Is there some way we can get around your boss? I am prepared to do whatever it takes—in my power."

"See," the *Babu barrah takka* would say, "my boss is not alone. There are others over him. They will question him. We have to do this carefully, very, very carefully, so no one is upset."

This is the cue for the party to make his pitch. The door has been unlocked; now it's up to him to open it, by loosening his purse strings, by showing his willingness to invest. Deferentially he must say, "I understand, sir; we cannot afford to ignore anyone. Please tell me how many people need to be covered. And for what amounts."

The *Babu barrah takka* will do some calculations, plucking at his eyebrow. Then he'd suggest a figure. Meanwhile, out of nervousness, the host party would have gulped down his drink, and yet his throat would feel itchy and dry.

Once the amount was specified, a fresh round of drinks would be ordered. A natural ease and friendliness would set in. Both host and guest would now warm and expand to each other, and the *Babu barrah takka* would lower his voice and say, "After this license, I will show you how we can look at other opportunities. This location is a gold mine. I hope you realize what you are getting?"

"Of course, of course, sir," the party would say. "I can't thank you enough—for your help."

And the *Babu barrah takka* would open up and say, "See, I have nothing in my heart, I tell you. I help everybody. But sometimes people don't appreciate. They forget what I have done. Then, I also wait my time. When the opportunity comes, I show them."

Drunk on all the foreign liquor he had imbibed, the *Babu barrah takka* would launch into a tirade about ungrateful people, an ungrateful world, and the ungrateful place he was employed. The party realizes he has made a friend he didn't want.

But this was never Madhulikar's situation. He never met suppliers socially. He never allowed them to entertain him. He never took their calls, and if they managed to get through, he would write out a report and disqualify them. To date, he held a strong contempt for the *Babu barrah takkas,* which showed in his eyes, his face, and his stiff, haughty manner when he spoke to them. They, in turn, thought him foolish and impractical, one of those foolish idealists who'd go broke to his grave. Their aversion suited him, for his faith in his thinking was deep and unshakeable.

But this time there has been some change, a mellowing of sorts, a willingness to blend. Maybe he was getting practical, now that he was close to retirement, Archrekar thought, after his chat with Madhulikar. Who can resist the Goddess of Wealth when she comes knocking at your door? Good, then, that Srini had come around.

Out of habit, Madhulikar went through the proposals carefully. He took an hour over them. As he had anticipated, Lodha's case was the weakest. For one, his location was half a kilometer off the main road, which meant that it could easily be missed by the passing traffic. For another, the ground there was stony; it would be expensive to lay the pipelines. This made the yellow slip on top all the more amusing. "Worth considering!" Archrekar had inscribed in lavish blue ink. Worth how much, and for whom? Madhulikar thought wryly.

It was 7:00 P.M. by the time he finished his report. In between, there had been some distraction. His father's words had appeared loud and clear in that small room: "Your office is your temple. It feeds you, clothes you, maintains you. Do not abuse this generosity ever."

But things were different then, Madhulikar thought. Society was clean and incorruptible. Honesty was the rule, not the exception, and there were great examples all around—leaders like Gandhi, Nehru, and Patel, men of impeccable integrity. But one must adapt, however late. And even as Madhulikar told himself this, he felt foolish. He felt his life had been a waste. All these years he had carried the illusion of character, of it being something solid, which you carried inside you and which carried you in return, holding you upright for the rest of your life.

After work, he decided not to return home. He walked—from his office to Flora Fountain, seeking anonymity among the hordes of men and women returning from work. Usually he would have paused and browsed at the books on the pavement: the *Teachings of Vivekananda,* the *Lives of the Saints*, the *Autobiography of a Yogi*, *The Gospel of Sri Ramakrishna,* and though he owned all of these—they sat in his bookcase at home—he would have picked them up and mulled, taking care to flick the traces of dust that had settled on the pages. But today he just wasn't in the mood to do so. Instead, he walked through the Oval *maidan,* past the groups of boys playing cricket with tennis or season balls. He noted the excitement of the players and their focus on the ball, which got hit all over the place and rolled away, hiding itself in tall shoots of grass. Coming on to Churchgate Station, he stood with the crowds at the signal and waited patiently while the traffic flowed past and a constable retained them with a rope and a whistle. It was only fair that he should wait in line, he thought. For who was he to go against the traffic?

Deep in thought, he reached the seafront. The sweet, fresh air of Marine Drive did nothing for his mood. He envied the couples who sat with their backs to the city, their shoulders hunched, gazing at the sea. He stared at the people in their cars. How comfortable they looked, how well looked after, like they knew where they were headed. The walkers, too, he envied. They had nothing to shed but physical weight. Not the weight of a troubled conscience.

Reaching home, he made up his mind to have a light dinner and retire. It was important that he go to sleep early, before the demons of regret came knocking, before they came to taunt him, making him realize there was no other way he could have chosen.

His wife received him at the door. "Why are you so late? Where have you been?" she asked agitatedly. She brought him a glass of water, and as he drank, his eyes fell on the furrows above her eyebrows. He realized there was something nagging at her mind.

After he'd showered and changed into his home clothes, she began speaking to him, her words spilling out in a flurry. "*Bhabhiji* called this morning. She wanted to know when we could take them shopping—for jewelry and for saris. I thought she meant just her and her daughter, but she was talking about all their aunts, nieces, and cousins. She said they were one close-knit family, so they'd expect gifts as well. *Hey Ram,* I thought. So much expense: how will we afford it? We are not business people like them. We don't have black money hidden in our cupboards. Of course I didn't tell her that. I just said I would check with you and let her know. I don't know what to say. I am so worried. This wedding will wipe us out. And we still have Kahini to think about."

She started crying, and instinctively his arm went around her.

"Sudha, my Sudha," he said. "Don't worry. We will manage. We will cope. I have made some arrangements. We can't let Disha down, in front of her in-laws. Trust me, we will manage."

The sobbing subsided, and after a while Sudha looked at her husband. "I know you are clever, but I can't help worrying. I know how hard you have worked for this money, how carefully you have invested it. And, now, it will all go—just like that. It's not fair, not fair at all."

"No Sudha, it *is* fair, if it's for our little girl. We have to give her a chance. Things are not what they were in our days. Today everything is measured in terms of money. Later no one should say to her, 'Your parents scrounged; they cut corners.' Let us do our best for her. That's the least we can do for our child."

And because Sudha was touched by her husband's thoughts, and because she knew him to be a proud, doting family man, and because she had a world of faith in him, she started crying again. But this time she wore a smile, an embarrassed sort of a smile. "So, what do I tell them?" she asked, wiping her tears with her sari.

He thought for a while before saying, "Saturday is fine. I will have the money by then."

Next morning he went to the office early. He opened a new file in his computer and slowly and methodically typed out his report. He printed it out, using two sheets of paper, and placed these in a plastic folder. With this and the proposals under his arm, he walked down the corridor. He stood outside Archrekar's door and knocked. He didn't wait for a reply; he just walked in.

There was someone else with Archrekar; he had his back to the door and was slumped in his chair with the familiar air of one used to the place. It was Rathod, head of retail. Madhulikar despised him, for Rathod was a lazy intellectual who had sold his soul to the devil. It was rumored that Rathod's personal wealth stood at rupees six crores. He had bungalows in Lonavala and Matheran, a farmhouse in Panvel, and a beach house in Alibaug. All this had come from heading retail, from deciding how much of fuel was gas and the rest, well, additives.

"Why, sir, if you are busy—" Madhulikar said, backing toward the door.

Archrekar rose. "No, Srini, come in. Mr. Rathod was just leaving."
Rathod looked surprised. Stiffly he excused himself and left.

Madhulikar seated himself and began. "I have been through the proposals, sir, with a fine-tooth comb, and from what I see, it is an open-and-shut case. In fact, there is no question about it."

"Yes, go on, Srini."

"You see, sir, it's not as if we are favoring one party over another. . . ." He paused. "But we have to be fair."

"Yes, of course, but what is your opinion, Srini? I want to know!" Archrekar was frowning heavily. Could he have misconstrued that last chat with Srini? Would the fool follow his conscience, like he had all these years?

"Ah, my opinion, sir? It is based on many factors. Location, space, bank securities, creditworthiness, experience, but mostly, there is one factor that is most important." He noticed that Archrekar was sitting on the edge of his chair, leaning over. His palms were locked, he was grinding his thumbs, and under his desk one leg flickered nervously.

"Yes, yes, Srini, I am sure you have done your homework, but have you taken into account what I said?"

Madhulikar pretended to look shocked. "Of course, sir. You are my senior. I must give careful consideration to your suggestions. But like I was saying, there is one important factor, the main factor in choosing the party. Without this, all other factors are useless." He smiled at Archrekar, who for some reason did not smile back. The fool! The bastard! He was going to double-cross them. He was going to cut them out of the biggest deal of the year. Archrekar knew he shouldn't have trusted Madhulikar.

"Safety, sir! Safety is the most important factor. No point having a gas station if it is not safe. That is why I think Lodha is the best. His location is inside. No chance of a calamity there. Imagine if there is an accident close to the highway, near a gas pump, what a disaster it can be. That itself disqualifies the others."

Archrekar leapt up. "Excellent thinking, Srini. Excellent! By God! It never struck me, but, yes, safety is so important. That should be the main factor." He looked at Srini admiringly. What a fine fellow, what a good mind, and what a strong line of reasoning. If only he would work with them more often. Oh, what a waste he had been—all these years.

"I have prepared a full report, sir, explaining why this proposal is ideal. If it is off the highway, people can stop, relax, and take lunch. Maybe there can be a cafeteria at the side, or a restaurant . . . some restrooms, some recreation for children, like a cybercafe or video games. So much scope for expansion, sir, as the traffic increases. We can even have a garage, with a separate section for trucks and a separate section for cars and light vehicles. And a motel, which would be lucrative."

"Perfect, Srini, perfect. I think it makes so much sense."

Now was the time to make his pitch, Madhulikar thought. He dropped his voice and spoke.

"I hope Lodha appreciates this, sir. I hope he respects our confidence and lives up to our expectations."

Archrekar looked astonished. Why, yes, Madhulikar was soliciting. There was no doubt he was ready to play ball.

"You are meeting him today, aren't you? At his club?" Archrekar said slyly.

Now it was Madhulikar's turn to look astonished. "Oh, you know about that, sir. I thought, just to clarify—"

"No harm, no harm, Srini," Archrekar said softly. "You have taken so much pain with the report, nothing wrong if you put a price on it. It's good work, I can tell you that, and I wouldn't ask for anything less than five lakhs if I were you."

Madhulikar coughed. "Well, sir, I was thinking more like ten. After all, he is going to benefit lifelong."

Wow, thought Archrekar. Srini sure was making up for lost time. Well, good for him—always place for a good mind on their team.

"I am sure he will see it that way too, Srini. I know Lodha to be most accommodating. And don't worry, not a word of this will leak out. We have dealt with him in the past."

Madhulikar wondered about the "we," all who were involved—Archrekar, the directors, Rathod of course, the Regional Head, the

Surveyor, the General Manager, and, most likely, the Chairman. He wondered why the Chairman needed to be corrupt. At his level, everything was paid for: car, house, trips abroad, club expenses, children's education, medical expenses, etc. Enough is never enough, Madhulikar thought, and mankind must always hunger for more, want more than what their stomachs could take. Well, in his case, the first bribe would be the last.

He went back to his desk and tried to examine his feelings. Strangely, he felt nothing. Just emptiness, a deep, dark vacuum beyond a sense of loss. He also felt a little puzzled. Was it really that easy? What use education, struggle, toil, manners, diligence, hope, planning, refinement, realization, if eventually that was all there was to it—to fall in line and progress?

The day dragged on. He busied himself with various matters: arranging a dealer conference in the North, where sales had dropped, the sponsorship of a cricket match where engine oils could be advertised, planning a sales promotion for coolants, all the activities that went with it.

He did things listlessly, feeling that everything he did was contaminated.

Soon it was time for lunch, and Chandrashekar, his friend from accounts, came to call him. Over lunch, they would whisper about the syndicate, about the *Babu barrah takkas*—their latest deals, payoffs, trade-offs; their out-of-turn promotions, postings, and transfers, which they bought. When they'd tire of that, they would talk about investments, safe ones in banks and mutual funds, which could get them that additional .5 percent or 1 percent, depending on the period of maturity. They'd be content with that—clean talk about clean money, without the easy 12 percent, without the games and machinations of the *Babu barrah takkas*—and they'd walk tall and proud, indifferent to the slime all around, indifferent to the sneers that would follow, the voices that would hiss, "Fools, backward fools!" behind their backs.

But that day there was no appetite—not for chitchat, nor for food. Madhulikar was grappling with a big gloom in his mind, and it seemed to have spread to his stomach, for he asked Chandrashekar to proceed without him.

His friend was persistent. "What, Srini? Come no, for my sake. I have so much to tell you."

It was hard to refuse his affable friend. So Madhulikar accompanied him to the lunchroom, where the executive cadre ate. Standing in line, waiting to get to the buffet table, Madhulikar felt a sense of monotony. Again he felt part of a crowd: no different, nothing special.

The lunchroom was crowded and noisy. Over the rattle of plates and cutlery, there were the sounds of laughter, chatter, and chairs being dragged.

A long, white table lined the side of the room. On it were dishes of food, with burners glowing underneath, and stacks of plates and cutlery at the side. The dishes had been uncovered and were smoldering with aromas. The NPRC employees waiting in line peered into the dishes curiously and, lifting the spoons at the side, served themselves generously.

Madhulikar took a plate and filled it sparsely: a little dal, a spoon of *sabji,* a splattering of curd, and two small chapatis. He moved to the side and was waiting for Chandrashekar to serve himself when he felt a friendly prod. He turned, and to his horror he saw Archrekar and, behind him, Rathod. Both were smiling broadly. Both looked like evil apparitions without their horns, searching for the perfect trinity.

Helping himself to a mountain of rice, eyes fixed on his plate, Archrekar smiled and said, "Eat well, Srini; eat well. Why is your plate so bare?"

And not to be outdone, Rathod added, "Ha, ha, and don't forget the dessert. I believe today's is extra sweet."

Then, to Madhulikar's horror, they both winked at him, the broad wink of friendship, of acceptance. And as Madhulikar smiled back weakly, he felt a churning in his stomach. His hand that was holding the plate went limp. The water from the curd rushed to the side, to the edge, and some dal spilled and mingled with it, and the mixture threatened to spill over and stain his nicely ironed trousers. But Madhulikar didn't seem to realize this. He felt like a *Babu barrah takka:* small, insidious, and unworthy. He mumbled something about what there was being enough. Eat less, want less, stay healthy, live longer. Now where did that come from? he wondered. His father probably!

Quickly he dragged Chandrashekar away—to a table in the far corner of the room, out of the noise and commotion. He sat there like a recluse, plucking at his chapati, dipping it into the dal and curd, tasting nothing, hearing nothing. He kept thinking how he would face Chandrashekar once he'd taken the bribe—how he'd sit through those conversations, pass judgments on others, judgments cast in steel. Could he cancel out those years of friendship just like that? Could he opt out of conversations, making some excuse that he himself did not believe in? And was it just friendship that had brought them together? Or something more precious, more binding, something that shone like a piece of coral in this sea of slime?

In between mouthfuls, Chandrashekar kept jabbering, "Be careful, Srini; be careful. I don't trust those two. They are up to something, I tell you. They will stick something onto you. Please be careful, my friend."

Looking at his friend, wide-eyed and frantic, Madhulikar stopped eating and said with a smile, "You care so much, Chandu. Sometimes I wonder why I am worth so much affection. What is it that makes you care?"

In his heart, Madhulikar knew the answer. It was probably the same answer his wife or his daughters would have given. Or any of his nephews and nieces who came to him for advice. Any of them could have told Madhulikar what he wanted to know. But it would be nice to be reminded who he was, what he stood for, and what he meant to the world he lived in. Sometimes that made all the difference.

JAMAL HADDI'S REVENGE

✦ ✦ ✦

JAMAL HADDI WAS FASCINATED by the wall in front of him. He was impervious to the noise behind, which came out of drunken conversation, drunken ribbing, and drunken oaths from men who had no other purpose but to down their grievances in the watery brown brew that was served to them with mechanical indifference by overworked, tyrannized boys between the ages of fifteen and twenty.

In the cramped, squalid liquor den that was his daily refuge, Jamal Haddi focused his attention on the wall and its occupants. A translucent oily brown lizard fastened its eyes on an unsuspecting baby moth no more than four inches away. The moth was ignorant; the lizard was still, very still. The beady eyes of the reptile were riveted on its winged quarry, and occasionally a flickering tongue spelt out its poisonous intent. Jamal Haddi was rooting for the lizard. With the full brunt of his drunkenness, he wanted the lizard to get its prey.

"Go on, *chipkali*," said Jamal in his mind. "Eat to your belly's full. Don't spare the moth. Don't spare it your fury. Don't let it live a second longer than it deserves." The moth had no business being there. It was too thin, frail, and out of place in a place like this. It should have known that. Besides, the moth wasn't a survivor. In Jamal's book of life, only the strong would prevail; only they had the right to live. Now, the lizard was a survivor. You could tell. By the way it looked: unflinchingly hungry. By the way it clutched the wall: with crocodile legs. By the way it moved in and destroyed: caring not for beauty, nor for justice. Ah, what pleasure Jamal felt when it finally lurched forward. In one swooping motion, it sprang at the moth and crunched it away with eager, imperceptible teeth. Ah, how he enjoyed that; how much personal triumph he felt, for he, Jamal Haddi, hated all things of beauty, especially when they forgot their place.

It was good that the lizard came into his mind and distracted him, for he, on his sixth glass of hooch, was grappling with a monster in his mind. Kunta, his wife, was cheating on him. No, "cheating" was too good a word. If that's what it was, it would have proved at least that she had some respect, that she wished to protect him from the truth. But here she was shamelessly giving herself away. She didn't even care to hide the ritual, the preliminaries of seduction, the slow doing up of herself that, stroke by stroke, broke Jamal Haddi down.

Evenings, the lipstick would come on, then the eye shadow. From behind the curtain in their dingy hut she would emerge, having adjusted her sari to display more of her flattened stomach and portions of her dark hips. God, how much navel would she show? Be reasonable, woman; be reasonable! Jamal would think. Okay, he needed the money she brought home. He needed it after he had lost his job with the municipality. In one sweep, they had gotten rid of all the temporary sweepers, like they were rubbish on the streets, the same rubbish that Jamal Haddi used to sweep before the city awoke, sometimes dislodging it with his leg and with a silent curse.

In his own way, Jamal had been proud of his work. He made the city livable, and sometimes, with a little luck, he found something in the garbage that was worth selling. Dumri, the pawnbroker, gave him a standard two rupees for it, which bought Jamal an extra half glass at Gulabi's *adda,* the liquor den at the end of the slum. With the retrenchment, the money had stopped coming in. His support system had been cut off, and Jamal Haddi found himself at home, useless, ineffective, craving alcohol and release from a crushing reality.

The first few days at home were difficult. Two demons rose in his mind: the demon of poverty and the demon of addiction. Both demons fought for precedence and expressed themselves as fits of savage anger:

anger against the municipality for dispensing with him, anger against Kunta for wasting money schooling the children. Educating the boy was understandable, but why the girl? What good would the education be if it led her to the kitchen?

He cursed Kunta and her parents. He cursed her for coming to his house empty-handed and his own foolishness for accepting her. That brother of hers—working for the railways—could he not get Jamal a job cleaning the station? Maybe he didn't want Jamal Haddi to learn how corrupt he was. They all were! Why, there were sahibs in the municipality who had made so much money taking bribes that they could build bungalows in their villages. It was said when they had a marriage in the family they filled up their wells with alcohol—so much money they had.

Despite his poverty, Jamal would make it a point to visit the *adda* every evening. He would get the money from Kunta, who would give it to him without a word. Part of her earnings would go toward the daily rations, part toward buying her peace from Jamal's ranting.

Kunta had found work at a local hospital. She washed vessels and linen and did odd jobs like helping in the sickroom when the nurses failed to turn up or cleaning up after aged patients who had lost control of their bowel movements. It was a thankless job and she hated it, but it kept her from Jamal Haddi and his slow, leering persecution.

The money wasn't much—eight hundred rupees a month: four hundred for the house, four hundred for Jamal Haddi. Being practical, Kunta knew how to scrimp and cope with expenses. She made a deal with Pramilabai, who lived three *kholis* away and sold vegetables grown along the railway tracks. Every two days Kunta would buy stale vegetables at one-eighth their original price. These she would boil, reboil, and serve as broth, a meal rounded off by a solid crust of bread. There was no money for milk, but she was sure the broth would sustain the children.

One day, five months after Jamal Haddi had been discharged from the municipality, Kunta lost her job at the hospital. She did not tell Jamal why or how it happened, but he heard her crying one night to herself. That stirred something in him. He moved forward to touch her, but she became cold and resentful as soon as his hand touched her face. He felt the presence of a stone wall, hard, cold, and unavailable to him. He thought it prudent to roll onto his side and sleep, his back to her.

With Kunta at home, things became worse. Jamal Haddi sneered and spat insults at her. Useless, so useless she was, that even her employers had gotten rid of her. In his case, it had been a retrenchment drive, a policy decision, but she was singled out for expulsion. Maybe he should get rid of her, too. It was *his* goodness that had kept her, and for this he was now paying a price.

Day in and day out, Kunta heard his insults without a trace of retaliation or a flicker of emotion. If there was suffering, she did not show it. Not even when he called her a slut or hit her. When things got too much, she would take the children out and leave them at the neighbors'. The blacksmith's family was nice. They remembered to feed the children before returning them home.

Jamal Haddi had not known when Kunta's alternate life had begun, when she had first taken such a step, canceling out the restraining angels in her mind. All he knew was the money had started pouring in: twenty, thirty, even forty rupees a day. He didn't need to fight for it, get abusive, or wrench it away. Morning and evening, the notes would appear in his shirt pocket. He would wait for a day when it wasn't there so he could spit abuses at her, but she never failed him. That suited him, for he could drown himself and his demons at the *adda,* his back to the crowd, his face to the wall.

Jamal Haddi recalled there was one other woman in the slum where they lived who had turned to the convenience of an alternate income. But she was a widow with two young mouths to feed. She had an excuse, and Jamal himself, returning one night from the *adda,* drunk and staggering, had offered her two rupees to jerk him off. After an hour, the woman had flung back his limp cock, spat her disgust, and walked off, leaving Jamal feeling exposed and incomplete. For a moment he had wondered if that was the reason that Kunta had turned to other men but then quickly—by the alchemy of self-deception—convinced himself that his impotency was born of her wrongdoings, her faithlessness. He hated her all the more.

Thinking about Kunta and her indifference, Jamal downed the hooch in his glass and almost instantly felt a burning in his gullet, a spinning sensation in his head. He hoped that Gulabi wasn't mixing anything into the liquor. Last year, two youths from the slum had died of poisoning, but that was because they had drunk at one of those unfamiliar *addas,* where they weren't known. At Gulabi's, things were different. He usually came up and cautioned Jamal Haddi when he had drunk too much. He also extended credit to Jamal and once or twice had dropped him home.

Jamal hadn't liked the way Gulabi had looked at Kunta. It was sly, coaxing, and loaded with a message of desire. Although Kunta hadn't returned his interest, Jamal had, in his mind, blamed her for arousing the *adda* owner. Bloody whore, she affects men, Jamal thought, because men know that she is available. She throws sex at them—the fucking whore. The blood rushed to his face, and he felt a wrench in his chest, as though it were exploding. The poison was spreading, searing different parts. Jamal massaged his chest, glad that he was sitting with his back to the crowd. This was his favorite spot: the lone bench, facing the wall. The wall was his best friend, his mirror. It never changed countenance, never made demands; by its sheer presence it discouraged others from sitting with him. Jamal was not the best of company. He preferred to drink alone, drink quietly, facing nothing but the brooding sandstorms in his mind and the fits of vengefulness he felt, during which he contemplated the many ways by which he could murder Kunta. Petrol, axe, the grinding stone, the gunnysack—he had been through every method. If he had delayed the decision it was because he hadn't found a way that was satisfying enough.

That day itself Kunta had been particularly bad. She had disgraced him by allowing two men to call on her. Both were tall, broad built, and flashy. Both wore sunglasses, white starched shirts, and gold watches and looked, at first sight, like cops. This scared Jamal Haddi, who kept himself out of sight. It was only when he heard her laugh, lightly, flirtatiously, as she joined them outside the hut that he realized they were her paramours. For the evening? Or the night? he wondered. How would she be? came the next thought. Warm and responsive? Or passive and reluctant? He felt a stab of jealousy as she got into a white Ambassador and drove away with them.

Painfully, with tears blinding him and the sullen brick wall for company, Jamal realized that Kunta didn't "go" just for the money. It was gratification she was after, a rebellious celebration of her revived youth. He saw her riding one of the men, her fingers digging into his shoulders, her dark, heaving figure soaking in his manhood, deriving strength from it, deriving power. Because Jamal knew her well, knew how she grew with her own sexuality, he saw her take control of the second man. She'd do it rhythmically, naturally, without guilt or clumsiness, because her dark, foaming beauty allowed her that much power and that much grace. She was the universe when she copulated, and Jamal hated it that she had shared this abandonment with others. Sometimes, when he and she were together, her passion had scared him, because he wasn't sure he could take all of it himself. Now he knew he wasn't enough. He remembered how in their early days she would continue to sway and rock, taking her own pleasure, learning her own lessons, claiming her own fulfillment, as if in a dream. Jamal looked down and saw he had an erection.

He didn't know whether to feel angry or elated. He was a bit of both actually, more elated because it was a long time since he had felt aroused. All these months, the booze had made him *ineffective,* and frankly, Jamal had ceased caring. The notion of sex had barely crossed his mind, except in the form of ugly memories of Kunta. So the strain and throb that plagued him now, in his khaki trousers, came as a surprise and a revelation. He decided to borrow money from Gulabi and vent his frustrations on an economically priced prostitute in the red-light district.

THE LIGHTS OF KAMATHIPURA TWINKLED mischievously and Jamal felt excited as he approached the cages that housed the ladies of pleasure. The time was past midnight. The area was abuzz with activity. A late-night show had ended, and hordes of animated youths walked out of the theater. Jamal paused to look at the billboard over the entrance. Being illiterate, he could not read, but the picture said it all. A busty woman in a bra and petticoat, her hair loose and flowing, looked down at a man who adhered to her midriff. This merged into a collage of the same woman being made love to by a man who was nuzzling her neck. Jamal stared at the points of her brassiere. His eyes wandered to the swell of her breasts and followed the man's hands, which were just above her crotch. Jamal made up his mind he would take a woman who looked like that. And he would punish her.

He approached the cages and saw the first bunch of whores— Nepalis. He didn't like them. They had flat faces and flat chests. Besides, they seemed so inexpressive, so remote. He walked farther and felt excited. There, sitting on the steps outside the cages, were the kind of women he liked. They wore thin, strappy dresses that ended above their thighs, boldly showing their legs. There were four such women, standing cockily, and as Jamal stood and gloated at them, one of them lifted her leg and showed him the underside of her thigh, right up to the butt. This made Jamal want to rush in and relieve himself, but he knew that he must be patient. He must find the face he was looking for. Then he could afford to get carried away.

As he walked away, the whores taunted him. They challenged him and his manhood, and Jamal flushed, because he knew that they were laughing at him. This made him angry. All whores laughed, he thought. It was their way of protecting themselves against the world. He sneered, because just then he thought how Kunta had laughed when she went off with the two men. The bitch—she was a born whore. Well, he would show her. Soon he would.

The next cage had dark women from the South. They had thick legs, voluptuous bodies, and black wavy hair left loose for effect. One of them who was standing stretched languidly, deliberately. She wore black hot pants that cut into her thighs and a sleeveless top that showed her shaven armpits and a tubular stomach. Sexy, she looked, thought Jamal, as he felt a stirring in his blood. There were two whores sitting on the steps; one was running a comb through the hair of the other. Jamal preferred the one standing. He thought she came closest to the woman on the billboard. He asked her her price, but she quoted high. Jamal laughed and walked on. The whore called after him, "*Arrey*, I was only joking. Come back. That was the full night rate. One time is only twenty rupees, and you can take your time." By then Jamal had rejected her. The booze inside made him feel light and powerful. He liked this feeling. He had a choice. He could take whom he wanted, how he wanted. He could be unkind and merciless. He would show her that a whore had no right to enjoyment. He would teach her how whores deserved to be treated. Why, in a single night he would punish all the whores of the world.

That's when he saw *her*—alone, on the steps, outside her cage. There were sounds of laughter from inside. But she sat alone, a radio to her ear. A song was playing—*"Jiya bekaraar hain"*—but it was hoarse and cracking. She kept trying to adjust the tuning. She did not see Jamal looking at her. She was slim and dark. She wore a petticoat and a blouse—no sari to cover her. She ran a finger through her hair, and Jamal saw the full sweep of her face. It was young, sensual, slightly sad. The song added to her sex appeal. Jamal wondered why she was alone. He peeked inside the cage. Saw customers and whores there. The customers were being fed; they were being teased. One of them had his shirt off. The room was divided into small cubicles by long, moldy curtains.

The girl saw Jamal looking at her. She put the radio down and smiled at him. It was a bleak, famished smile, one of forced labor. Jamal pretended to look indifferent. "How much?" he asked. "One time first—then, later, maybe more."

"Ten rupees," she said. "Want to come?"

Jamal was stumped. She was the best-looking girl he had seen so far, and her price—so reasonable! He couldn't believe his luck. He swelled with masculine pride. "Don't talk about one time," he said. "Talk about a full night. How much?" he asked.

"No full night," she replied fiercely. "Only one time."

Jamal was taken aback. He felt rejected. He wanted to walk on. There were many more cages to see, many more women from different parts of India. He didn't need to suffer this girl, who acted as though she was doing him a favor.

He looked at her and saw that her waist was showing above the petticoat. It was flat, smooth, and inviting. Her hips were slim. Her breasts were firm and beautifully proportioned, kept in place by a low blouse, which was buttoned with a single button and a straining safety pin. Jamal knew that he wouldn't be able to walk away from those breasts. They were too real, too potent. Like Kunta's body, they had a language of their own.

By then the girl had lost interest in Jamal. She was fiddling with the radio and humming along. Jamal liked the song, too, so he felt an affinity with her. On an impulse, he began to dance to the song. Not too fast, not too abruptly, he twirled to the tune. The girl looked up and giggled. Her laughter came naturally, infectiously. Girls from other cages began to point at Jamal.

Jamal felt free and liberated. He knew that all eyes were on him, but he did not care. After a long time he was making someone laugh, and he liked the laugh, for like the song, it rose from the gut. Jamal danced some more. Passersby thought him mad and stepped out of his way. "*Wah,* Meena, you seem to have won yourself an admirer," said a voice from inside. "Hush, don't call her that," said another voice abruptly, sharply. "She is Sunaina now, remember."

As she heard this the girl's eyes narrowed and clouded with pain. Some past brought to the surface, thought Jamal, despite his own liquor-soaked senses. Quickly he wooed her, distracted her, gesticulating like a courting hero. A ripple of laughter followed. Jamal quivered youthfully to the rhythm. His eyes fastened on the girl in front of him. He was dancing for her, for her happiness only. Eventually, she raised her hand to her face and laughed. It was a gushing bridal laugh, not the laugh of a whore, and it convinced Jamal that, be it one time, he would go with her.

The song ended. The whores clapped. An announcer's voice on the radio announced that the program was over; it would resume the next day at the same time. On the street, a small traffic jam had occurred. People leaned out of their cars, their eyes devouring the women who called out to them. The women blew kisses and beckoned. The onlookers looked away.

"*Chalo andar!* Come inside!" Jamal whispered to the girl, his throat parched partly with passion, partly with lack of refreshment. She shook her head. She didn't want to go with him.

Jamal pleaded, "*Chalo,* please. I won't bother you. Only once."

"No," she said fiercely. "I won't go with you. I am tired. Take someone else. Anyone but me."

"I can't," said Jamal. "It's you I want. You I fancy. I don't come usually. So don't refuse, please."

She wavered and looked at him. Then suddenly she said, "You are nice, but don't insist on me. Don't! You will hurt yourself."

Jamal was puzzled. He spoke through his confusion and his liquor, which now made his head feel heavy. "How can you hurt me? I am already hurt, damaged. You can't hurt me. No one can hurt me. I am beyond hurt."

"Then go away; leave me alone," she hissed.

Jamal felt sad and defeated. This was unexpected, but he knew he couldn't walk away. There was something about the girl that held him. The way she had given herself to the song: she had belonged to it, to its romance. She did not belong here—on the streets of Kamathipura.

"Why should I go? What's wrong with me? Am I deformed? Distorted? Too ugly for you? Is it a lover you are expecting? Give me a reason, and I will leave," said Jamal sullenly.

"It's not that," she said. "It's just . . . just that I am not well, not clean. I don't want to contaminate you. Please understand."

Jamal stared at her disbelievingly. From inside the cage came a light curse—"*sali bewaqoof*"—that made Jamal angry. It seemed unfair to him that Meena or Sunaina—whoever she was—was being cursed for her ignorance, her honesty. Jamal looked at the girl before him. She had lowered her eyes, out of sadness, out of shame. It made Jamal want to do something for her, something heroic. In that moment all the liquor left him. He looked at her soberly and said, "I still want you. I won't go away till you agree. I will wait till morning, if I have to."

She looked at him despairingly, as if he were mad. She was convinced he was a lunatic; the doubt showed itself in her eyes. "Okay." She shrugged. "If that's how you want it, it's your funeral."

"No, not mine." Jamal smiled. "Many others', but not mine," he added cryptically as she led him into a stench-ridden room at the side.

BREATHLESS IN BOMBAY

◆ ◆ ◆

ARINGDHAM BANERJEE SURVEYED THE SCENE with clinical satisfaction. Everything was perfect, just the way he liked it. The band—sharp and peppy yet pleasantly restrained—played the music at a pitch that encouraged genial conversation and left room enough for the occasional squealing reunion. The lawns glowed with warm orange lights; the trees from which they hung were dark and self-effacing; the waiters were clean, white, and smiling, all of them; the bar was ample and expansive, manned by three bartenders, young, restless, and anxious to set a jolly pace.

The guests were discerningly dressed. The older men in *sherwanis* and Nehru jackets, the younger ones in jeans and jackets—jeans tucked into boots or flowing over soft *mojris* curled at the tip. The women wore designer labels. Their look was crisp, elaborate, self-conscious, capable of inviting and sustaining conversation and brazenly or subtly calculated so that flesh would show: a planned ripening, you could say. The women threw one another sharp glances from afar and compliments from near. Under their breath they hissed or burned. If they became too competitive, they downed their feelings with cool, colored cocktails and with a flick of their hair changed the subject to other matters. Expertly they skirted from topic to topic and bubbled with revelations sharp and high-pitched, lending to the occasion an all-too-fantastical grace, a fierce bonhomie that was brittle, brewing, and bombastic at times.

This was Aringdham's wedding party, his way of celebrating a higher love, of crowning his reputation as the Gatsby of Bombay. He had prepared for it weeks in advance.

"THE LIGHTS? NO, NOT THESE; something more subdued please. I'd go for warmth, subtlety, and the moonlight. Yes, let's work with the elements. Let's not forget it is outdoors! What, no valet parking? Rot! I want six at least: two at each entrance. And while we are on about parking, could someone look at how the traffic will exit? I don't want the guests getting stuck in a traffic jam, honking away in a drunken frenzy. Timing? No, there should be no limit on how long the party would last. Pay off the cops, if necessary. Work it into my bill, and if they still hassle, slip them a bottle of Black Label."

Aringdham's bride, the lovely, exquisite Ritika Trilok, was sure that the club manager—a bald, red-faced, billowy-whiskered Anglo-Indian by the name of Keith Rosario—was going to throw his hands up, make some excuse not to rent them the premises, no matter that Aringdham was a privilege-class member, that he'd forked out half a million in cash to acquire his membership and had conveniently forgotten to take a receipt, knowing full well that some of the money would be diverted into individual pockets. Sitting in Rosario's office while Aringdham mulled over the arrangements, Ritika could sense the growing peevishness of the manager.

As Aringdham considered the cuisine, he couldn't choose between Punjabi, Goan, Hyderabadi, or Continental, so he decided to have them all, on separate serving tables. Chinese and Thai couldn't be ignored. The first was bound to go down well if delivered in the Cantonese style; the other had the scope to spring forth surprises and provide the exotica essential to maintaining the reputation of the host. The danger in these Oriental menus was that the flavors could coincide, could appear repetitive, so two whole days were spent deciding on the dishes, just in case the guests decided to try both. On the third day he went through some turmoil wondering whether skipping Mangalorean seafood would create a serious gap in the menu. A dinner without

Haryali clams, butter-and-garlic squid, black pepper pomfret, and tandoori crab was, well, slipshod. But, as Ritika pointed out, half the gourmet set lived off dinners at joints like Mahesh and Trishna when they weren't into their fit-for-life diets and their Spartan yogic obsessions, so he decided he could live with the omission.

Aringdham wanted the chefs to preside at each table. Many of the guests were devotees of fine food. They'd be curious about the ingredients. They'd want to know how the dishes were prepared as a matter of form or courtesy and surely as a conversation piece for the next social gathering, which would probably be the day after or, at the most, a week later. If they didn't ask, the press surely would, especially that freeloading critic Anna Paul Singh—with her loud laughter, her garish clothes, her false smile, and her social-climbing ways. But she wrote at length, covered space, and said some nice things in the hope of being reinvited, so all in all it was worth enduring her.

Those who served had to wear costumes that looked their part; otherwise what difference would there be between this bash and any other, between this level of refinement and that of the cursory weekend do? It was decided that the Punjabi chefs would wear bushy black beards, flowing kurtas, and fiery sun-gold turbans studded at the crest. These would be hired from the fathomless trove of Shabbirbhai Dresswalla, Costumers, Disguisers, & Fabricators Since 1927. The Goans would be in cloudy white vests and checked cotton *lungis* rolled up to look like those worn by fisherfolk; later they would change into three-piece suits with spotted bow ties and pink flowers stapled to the breast, and some decent money would be spent on getting them tailored at the Best of Fonseca Tailors, Byculla.

The Hyderabadi chefs posed a problem: what could they wear that was traditional? After much debate Aringdham decided on Pathani suits. "Dark blue, not black," Ritika cautioned, revealing a childhood superstition about black. The chefs of the continent were fitted with buccaneer trousers, white button-down shirts, and suede waistcoats; their mustaches would be trimmed, their hair jelled, and they would apply no coconut oil lest it interfere with the aromas of the fine food.

Before leaving the manager's office, Aringdham suggested a rehearsal: two days before the event the chefs would make a mock presentation. There was no avoiding this if they wanted the party to rock. *They?* Keith Rosario checked himself from raising his eyebrows. He nodded instead and said, "Why not? Good idea!" But under his snowwhite whiskers he simmered and made up his mind to speed up his retirement plans; the congested hills of Nainital were preferable to the vagaries of the Bombay elite.

But ask Aringdham that—ask him to confess to his eccentricities—and you'd be met by stiff, sullen silence. To his mind he was a perfectionist, a man who saw to minutiae. He couldn't bear the idea that others might find him lacking. What if the upper echelons of society, to whose comfort and opinion he was catering, dismissed him as unfinished? What if they discovered his origins, which were not like theirs? The planning and precision camouflaged the reality; it threw a deft security blanket over his past, the shame of being born poor, of having led a life of grim, unyielding misery.

THROUGHOUT HIS CHILDHOOD AND TEENS, Aringdham had brooded about how he'd been raised. In the decrepit *chawl* where he grew up, he cried out against the penury and misery many times over—mostly at night—in the silence of his mind. Against the severity and squalor of the one-room apartment in which he lived he learned to shut his eyes, hoping that when he opened them the harshness and poverty would have disappeared. Against the loneliness—in the company of a sullen, overworked mother and an aloof, traveling father—Aringdham turned inward and pensive, determined that one day people would seek him out, that one day he'd attract them in hordes and unreservedly receive their admiration.

To numb himself against the loud quarrels that erupted from neighboring rooms and poured poison into his childhood, Aringdham buried himself in his books. Math, science, history, geography, general knowledge, any knowledge. Most times it worked like a mantra, gave him hope that there was a wider world outside. But there was an equal number of times that his hopes collapsed before an invading tirade of domestic violence, before fights more emotionally than physically brutal, before the indignity of waiting outside a common toilet, can in hand and fighting to keep your place in the queue, then, coming face-to-face with someone else's shit.

The feuds of the next-door neighbors that spilled through thin plaster walls taught Aringdham about life, about a world where relationships did not survive, nor niceness, nor dignity, where all that was good was forgotten in a daze of myopic blindness and where limits were crossed with unpardonable ease. From the prison of his childhood Aringdham learned how money, or the lack of it, could shatter families, how husbands could turn into wife-pounding savages, how wives could cheat and run out on husbands, how brothers could arrange to have sisters felt up, how sons could take to easy money and daughters to lives of easy virtue. He vowed that he'd never let that happen to his children; he'd build a wall high and solid till he could no longer see the squalor, no longer hear the shouts, the curses, and the screams of denial. Eventually he'd forget their existence altogether.

To make sure he achieved what he wanted, Aringdham worked as if he were possessed. On reaching college he took a part-time job with a consumer research company, and with the money earned he moved out of his parents' home and took a room in a hostel. He went without meals, shut himself to the temptations of parties, pubs, and girlfriends, and spent more time in libraries than in the canteen. He worked at his grades and received them, too: the As and A pluses, good enough to secure a seat at the Indian Institute of Management, where he procured a rank at the end of two years and was recruited off the campus for a salary that made his head spin. He chose an Indian company over the multinationals, an old Gujarati group with a global presence. He thought he would rise faster there, attain more respect, and learn about privately held wealth, which was always cumulative and enormous.

By then he had distanced himself from his parents almost completely. It was not that he turned overly proud; it was just that he ceased to have anything in common with them. They had no clue about his work; they never asked, and he never volunteered. He felt his relationship to them was a pure accident. He was comfortable in this opinion and saw no reason to change it.

From an early age he had felt contempt for his mother, but he learned to tolerate her whining ways, her stories of deprivation, and her sagas of life's extended betrayals. She'd grumble away while stirring the veal in the pot, or the liver, which was just as bad, for it filled the room with pungent smoke and made his eyes water. "Too young I was when I married your father. Didn't know then what I was doing, what I was getting into. And how was I to know he was married to the bottle? That's all he cares for, over you and me. Now, in my family, no one was even allowed to take a drop. If any of your uncles came home that way, you know what your grandpa would do?"

When she was so far gone on self-pity, it didn't matter that Aringdham was trying to study, to imbibe a store of knowledge that was real and absorbing. Her diatribes would end with some stricture— against his freedom, her perception of it. "Stay away from those Jhun-jhunwallas. Their mother's into black magic." Or: "If ever I catch you with those Lobo boys, I will break your skull. Don't think I don't know. All sorts of drugs they are taking."

Toward his father he felt plain, rising anger: his was a life steeped in despair. Money had always been a problem that remained unresolved. He worked for the Indian Railways as an assistant driver, which meant that as soon as he took his place in front he stripped to his waist, took three swigs from his hip flask, and began to feed the engine with heaps of coal. Only when the train exited from the city, only when the fresh air and the smell of plowed earth would cool his senses would he feel he'd left his demons behind—demons of poverty, failure, and regret— and to make sure, he'd fling in some more coal, urging the train to go faster, to burn away the tracks, and his past, till the driver would curse him for his foolishness and remind him that they still had a long way to cover.

Strange was the life his father had chosen. It was as if he dreaded coming home. Just after returning he'd often say he was going to the station to check the work charts, and then he'd slip away. He'd drink till nightfall, check the *matka* closing results, and, if enriched by a few hundred rupees, walk along the railway tracks singing the songs of his childhood. He'd make it a point to get home when Aringdham and his mother were asleep. Otherwise their faces would remind him of his poverty; the gray, crumbling walls would crush in on his consciousness; his wife's demands for extra income would infuriate and torture him; the scream of a passing train would mock him, its tremor reminding him of the frailty of his own life; and the news on Doordarshan, relayed in black-and-white, would reinforce those feelings. Nevertheless, he'd eat his dinner before the television set, and then before the tiny sink in the passage he'd gargle ferociously as if to flush the booze out of his system, as if to eject the bitterness he felt at not being a part of them. The bitterness would follow him to his pillow and leave faint green dribble stains for the next morning, reminding him that the bile was part of his history, his routine, and, inadvertently, theirs.

What did his father know of success? What did he know about what went into achieving it: the sweat, the strife, and the struggle? Every so often Aringdham would ask himself those questions. To succeed one *had* to make hefty sacrifices, abandon an entire youth to fulfill a dream, which was what he did.

For six years Aringdham worked for the Gujarati group. He handled their garment export business and whipped it into a 480-million-rupee cash cow. Traveling frequently, living in hotel rooms, out of a suitcase, he developed markets, launched collections, appointed franchises, and envisaged trade shows and events that put the company's brands center stage. His work came to be recognized, and he was spoken of as a rising star in the field, the man with the golden touch. At twenty-eight he served as a consultant to the Ministry of Textiles, helping to shape trade policies. At twenty-nine he represented India at global forums. At thirty he was cut down to size by the Gujaratis, who felt he was rising too fast for their liking. They transferred him to another division, loss-making retail, which was in shambles.

Aringdham called their bluff and resigned. He took some buyers with him and used his goodwill to persuade others to defect. He started his own company, Banwagon, and the first deal he negotiated was with Woolcot of Spain, worth four hundred thousand U.S. dollars. Three years later he was supplying to some of the biggest houses in the world: Texspin of Holland, Spindles of the United States, and Viva Mariola of France. He opened three factories: two in the south, in Coimbatore, and one in the north, in Gurgaon. He had twelve hundred people working for him—three shifts daily, holidays included—and branches in nine countries worldwide.

Eventually he got where he wanted: a world where the stars shone warmly, where everything appeared brilliant and perfect, where achievement had no limit, beauty no boundaries, and poverty and coarseness no place whatsoever. Like his party and its enchanting guests, everything shone for him and for him alone.

Yet he had to make a painful decision. His past had to be buried with resolute deftness. While he housed himself in a six-bedroom bungalow at Carmichael Road in the upper end of Bombay and placed himself in the care of one cook, three other servants, and two drivers, his mother was left to spend her days in a one-bedroom flat in Borivali, a distant suburb. There she sat in a wheelchair, thumping her knees every so often, hoping to beat out the arthritis that had taken root. Her only companion was the *bai,* a derelict servant with buck teeth and gray hair, who jabbered non-stop in Marathi and whose words she lapped up because she was amazed that someone so old had so much to report and share.

Aringdham's father had become an alcoholic by this point. After numerous ins and outs with Alcoholics Anonymous, he finally succumbed to a liver infection and died, vomiting, one summer afternoon, on the floor of the general ward at the Vinesh Gandhi Hospital. Although they'd cleaned him up, trussed and wrapped him in a white sheet so that only his jaundiced face showed, it had taken days for Aringdham to clear his nostrils of the stench of a puke that had been building up since God knows when.

At the funeral his mother whimpered like a hurt pet dog, which angered Aringdham. What was she crying about? What had she lost? Her husband had brought her no joy; he had, in fact, denied the woman in her. He had denied her a life, if all that she'd moaned and whined about when he was alive were to be believed. And her arthritis had begun long back, a stiffening of the heart and soul, for which he was responsible. She should have buried him years ago.

Try as he did Aringdham could not offer the right consolations; he could not find the right thoughts, let alone the right words. Eventually it was the old *bai* who consoled his mother. She'd come with her two sons and daughter, and together they'd wailed and sobbed like professional mourners. This made Aringdham suspicious: Were they doing this in the hope of a settlement? Or did they have designs on the flat? After the funeral it was the *bai* who took his mother home. Aringdham noticed how his mother gripped the *bai*'s hand and how the *bai* cupped his mother's head helping her into the taxi. Of course he provided the fare, but found it strange that the *bai*'s two sons and daughter climbed into the taxi as well. It was the wrong time to say anything, but he made a mental note to keep an eye on them. Right now their support suited him well. He had a wedding coming up—the wedding of the season. He had to excel. And deliver.

HE LOOKED OVER THE LAWNS. The guests—somewhere between their third and fifth drinks—were hearty and relaxed; the snacks circulated and disappeared; the lights, as he had instructed, had been dimmed; and the music, which had turned to dance music, engaged the younger guests. People everywhere immersed themselves in conversation. Everything was bright and sparkling; it was a feast of success, a power bash getting livelier by the minute. The stars shone overhead, and he felt warm and happy.

Over the buzz of voices, Aringdham heard a light, rippling laugh that chimed and tumbled across the lawn and touched him in the center of his heart: that sacred space reserved for only one. The voice belonged to Ritika, his darling bride, in whose honor he had arranged this party. Well, not quite. The fete was for their union, their love, higher than the Himalayas, purer than its peaks.

◆　◆　◆

THEY HAD MET LAST NOVEMBER at the National Convention for Wool Exports in New Delhi. She had no business being there, but she was. She had come to ask for *daan,* for charity, as he'd later joked. She had begged her way into his life and heart. She said it wasn't like that. She could think of no better place to make her point than the convention. She needed the woolens to clothe *her* orphans in Kashmir. Their plight was miserable, so very miserable. He believed her, for she looked miserable when she said that.

It was on the second day of the convention, toward the end, that she made her entrance. She sprang onto the stage, grabbed the mic, and urged conventioneers to stay and listen. He had just left the podium, which he'd shared with the minister of textiles, the minister of industries, and the commissioner of exports. "Wait, please . . . ," she said, and they turned to face her, a slim, animated woman in her mid-twenties. "Please wait and hear me. Even while you plan great progress in exports, forays into new world markets, I urge you to look at those who are losing their lives."

Another of those damn animal conservationists, Aringdham thought, and was about to call for security when she held up pictures of children frozen to death, their faces blue and stiff with neglect.

"We are trying to do all we can, but it's obviously not enough," she announced in a discernibly cracking voice. She introduced herself as working for Sahayta, a non-governmental, non-profit organization that focused on rehabilitating children in Kashmir whose parents had been killed in terrorist attacks. And, she explained, because they could not accept foreign funding (being in a war-sensitive zone, they did not wish to invite allegations of alignment), they were lean on cash. She requested that the wool manufacturers pitch in—with clothes and blankets, whatever surplus was available. Anything more would be an act of kindness.

When Aringdham heard her, felt her dedication, and evaluated the sacrifice of youth and beauty she was making for her cause, something broke in him. It was as if all that he and the others had discussed—all the plans, the policy making, and the global alliances—were insignificant.

He felt a flame of respect for the young woman, and with it a stirring that the situation didn't give him scope enough to analyze.

"Please be assured, Miss . . . ," he fumbled, "that our association will do its best to understand. Send us a proposal of your requirements, and we will see how we can help."

The next morning the telephone in his room rang. At first he couldn't place the name, but the desk clerk said, "She says it's urgent, something about children in Kashmir—you know about it."

Aringdham was not a morning person—usually he was surly and incommunicative till the first cup of coffee had gone down—but that morning he found himself alert and edgy. He tried to feign an exuberant "hello," while he searched his mind for a way to see her before he departed. Her voice—soft, deferential, and apologetic—sounded like a bell in a monastery. Sweet and exhilarating, that ringing voice worked better than coffee. He wondered whether he should sound more officious, but when she told him she'd stayed up all night to complete the proposal he melted. He agreed to see her at eight that evening.

Two hours after the call, Ritika did something she hadn't done for some time: she bought a new outfit, exquisitely tailored and expensive. She told herself she was being ridiculous. She did not even know him, this Aringdham Banerjee. All she knew was that he was the founder of Banwagon, a big fashion-wear brand, a success story in its own right. She had seen his picture in the papers, read about him and the high-profile parties he attended in Bombay with models, fashion designers, hoteliers, social swingers, Bollywood stars, and the who's who of corporate India. Ritika did not care for these tinsel town bashes; they belonged to a world far removed from hers, a world that was hollow and staged, unlike hers, which was real, so terrifyingly real that you could not afford to playact for a second. There were so many challenges, so many hurdles, when you were working with children affected by terrorism and poverty. Everything seemed to be against you: terrain, weather, public ignorance, governments, and life itself. She hoped to impress this on Aringdham. He looked like the sort who'd understand.

Before she met Aringdham, Ritika spent extra time at the mirror. She accentuated her hair, eyes, lips, and cheeks, and she added some silver jewelry to show that she could be interesting. She chided herself for being specific. For heaven's sake, she told herself, you need to interest him in the project, not in yourself. And to reassure herself of her motivation she picked up her laptop, a hard copy of the proposal, a calculator, a pad, and hung a pen-on-a-chain around her neck. Yes, that looked professional enough, she thought.

They met in the lobby of the New Meridian. He looked dapper in a black T-shirt, black designer jeans, and an olive blazer. He wore mocha suede shoes and a belt to match, and this made him appear younger than at the convention, where he'd worn a suit.

They sat at a corner table in the cocktail lounge. It was early, so the lounge was empty. Ritika felt his eyes taking in her outfit, a mauve short-sleeve pantsuit, and she was glad to have taken such care over her appearance. With his trained bachelor eye, Aringdham continued to notice things about her while he spoke. He liked her subtle use of makeup, her unpolished nails on slim fingers unburdened by rings, and her hair, which fell persistently over her eyes and which she brushed back slowly, luxuriously, as if bracing herself to make a point. Unspoken, in silent appreciation of each other, an unplanned intimacy sprang between them; the heart and mind of each opened to what the other had to say. They expanded as two people who knew they were young and attractive and, if not that, then with some worthy business in mind.

He ordered the drinks—a Singapore sling for him, a strawberry daiquiri for her. She hoped it wouldn't be strong; it was a while since she had indulged, and she wasn't sure of her tolerance now.

Ritika began her presentation by showing him the conditions in which they found the children: burns, missing eyes, torn limbs, and mostly always paralyzed with shock. There were four workers at Sahayta who made up the rescue team; two were locals, not even trained social workers. They took turns: two would retrieve the children, while the other two stayed at the shelters. She rattled off statistics: the number of children orphaned every month, the number wounded, impaired, partially treated by hospitals and mistreated or unwanted by relatives who were themselves poor. She spoke of deaths—from tuberculosis and typhoid and often from malnutrition or frostbite. Those below the age of four were most vulnerable, and the babies, they hardly ever survived. Of course the newspapers never reported this. As she spoke Ritika noticed that Aringdham hadn't touched his Singapore sling.

She showed him slides, but toward the end of her presentation her laptop stopped working. "It's an old model," she apologized.

"How old?" he asked, trying to gauge Ritika's age.

"A 486," she replied sheepishly.

"Well, that's not too old," he said generously, forgetting he owned a Pentium 4. He suggested she continue her presentation using the hard copy.

He heard her out. "It's obvious clothing is not the only issue," he said. "The problems are fundamental and persistent—food, shelter, clothing, and medicine. The unfortunate part is you can't expect aid from the government. Everything is being diverted into security. Your organization's size makes you all the more insignificant. So the aid has to come from a private source—and on a sustained basis."

"Yes," she said eagerly, understanding what made him a tycoon but seeing also the workings of a fine heart behind the quick, grasping mind. "Yes, sustainability is important. We do need a steady inflow of funds—to heal the children, to rehab them, to educate them, to teach them sports and real-life skills. Some therapy, too . . ." Her voice tapered off. She watched him taking in all this with his hands folded, cupped before his mouth. His fingers were long and articulate, like those of a saxophonist. His mouth, she decided, was firm, warm, and sensitive.

"You like this?" he asked suddenly. "This private war of your own?"

"What do you mean?" she replied, not sure whether he was being audacious or skeptical.

"Do you believe you can change these kids' lives? Give them hope, a future, a bright and honest future?" he asked.

"I wouldn't be telling you this if I didn't. I wouldn't have traveled from Srinagar—by bus," she said.

"The best way to win a war is to become the side you are not," he said. "Think yourself the winning side, think you have all the resources you need and that success is round the corner."

"How do I do that?" she asked, incredulous and a little annoyed at his pat response. "Every moment we are dealing with realities. We are dependent on people's kindnesses. We can barely afford to keep our heads above water."

"I know," he replied sympathetically. "I know. I've been in a war, too."

Ordering a fresh round of drinks, he asked a few questions. How did they conduct rescue operations? What kind of terrain did they cover? Were there any paramedics for support? Not relief workers but trained paramedics who knew how to get in and get the victims out? What kind of doctors looked after the children? Was there any psychiatric help available? Round-the-clock nursing? What was the children's routine? How were they schooled? How were they entertained? How was their progress monitored? She answered slowly, painstakingly, and all the time he scribbled on the pad he'd borrowed from her. He rested it on his lap, under the table, and she could see his hand move zigzag, zigzag, like he was marking charts, a flowchart. He stopped when his cell phone rang.

He excused himself and left the table to take the call. She wondered whether there was a girlfriend. Minutes passed. She felt an urge to see what he was scribbling. She could take a peek, but it would be embarrassing if he were to walk in on her. Three times she fought the urge, but the fourth time she raised the flap and opened to the page he'd scribbled on. Staring back from the paper was a near likeness he had sketched of her. Just the face—with words such as "worry," "fear," "tension," "anxiety," and "obsession." At "obsession" she fumed. So that's what he thought of her, that she was a bundle of nerves. This talk and sympathy was one big joke. Her eyes filled with tears.

When he returned, she exploded. He hadn't just fooled her but also the program, the children, their condition, their future—all that she stood for. He listened to her quietly. Meanwhile he noticed the movement of her lips and he wished that he could silence them by bringing his mouth upon hers. He would like to kiss her, just like that, without warning, while she was venting, and her lips twitched like a sweet little goldfish; he would like to show her how they could be in rhythm—her anger, his desire—and how fire could quench fire and transform it into a mutual collective yearning. He was surprised at himself and at her for inspiring this in him. At that moment he wanted her more than anything else, more than any goal or business ambition. He would remove everything unnecessary—her fear, concern, anger—all that interfered with her beauty, her inner sanctity. If only she would give him a chance to prove he could take control of her and her life.

He listened to her and spoke simply: "Will you give me time to change this picture? Once you are confident about survival, everything will change. Trust me."

There was something about the way he said that. Something earnest. There was also a darting vulnerability in his eyes, which made her feel she was wrong to have doubted him. She'd worked long enough in harsh terrain to realize when the harshness was suspended; she was also intelligent enough to know when she had made a miscalculation. But desperation *does* make you thin-skinned, she reasoned, and she'd been out of mainstream society so long that maybe she'd lost her sense of humor. She drew in her breath and said weakly, "I don't know, I really don't know what to say."

"Then don't say anything!" he said, taking her hand.

She felt a load leave her, a spring uncoil in her heart. The blood rushed to her face and she wished he wouldn't let go of her hand. He did so reluctantly, but the magic didn't disappear. A connection had been made, and fears had been dispelled. Thereafter, she sipped her daiquiri and struggled with the uncanny attraction while he spoke of his work, his beliefs, his travels, his dreams, and his knowledge of programs in developing countries. She was impressed by his store of knowledge; rapt and relaxed, she allowed herself to get drunk. She also allowed herself to eat what he ordered, allowed herself to be coaxed into a nightcap and to be led out light, silly, and laughing on his arm. She was happier than ever, happier than she'd been in a long, long time, and less worried now.

In the morning she woke up beside him, very embarrassed and contrite. "Please, please don't misunderstand," she said. "I didn't do this to win you to my cause. It's not for the aid."

"I should hope not," he said sternly. "I should hope not, considering you've professed love at least ten times during the night, and wrenched a similar confession from me an equal number of times. I hope to God, Miss Trilok, that you don't extend this liberty to all your donors."

At that she had blushed and flung herself at him. His eyes shone, making him look like a boy on graduation day. She melted into his arms and forgot about guilt and responsibilities and matters of aid and sustenance. All was well. No, it was perfect. So complete she felt—and protected.

She spent the day with him. They made love before breakfast and after; they clung to each other in the shower and outside it. There was a meeting with the exports commissioner, which Aringdham almost canceled but later decided to attend because the industries minister was also going to be present.

He could barely concentrate at the meeting. His mind kept going back to Ritika, to her soft, melting body, her bath-fresh fragrance, her lissome, responsive form—soft, ethereal, almost unreal—which seemed to morph into something warm and engulfing, something to suggest that all barriers of time and distance were being removed, were being replaced with something wonderful in anticipation of better times to come.

That night Aringdham proposed. There was no point fighting it. He couldn't live without her now that he'd found her. How was he to manage, though? With her tucked away in the Himalayas and him in Bombay?

"Why, with the help of my picture," she replied. "Unless the face has changed."

And they both laughed, realizing how ridiculous it had been in the first place. What could it have been—that outburst? Something like nervous energy, a sexual, chemical dread building up before release. Everything was fine now. Everything was acceptable. Everything made sense.

The next day they caught separate flights out, he to Bombay, she to Srinagar. Soon they reverted to their routines. His buyers visited, yet he found time to call once a day, when the lines were clear.

Three weeks later Aringdham called to say he was coming to Srinagar. He had some work in Delhi. She was ecstatic at first but turned nervous later. Would he mind the bare shelters, the sullen kids, the steel beds, the torn mattresses, the broken ceilings? Would he mind the meager meals, the chipped crockery, the toilets with poor drainage? She called him to ask whether she should book him into a hotel? "Heck, no! Not unless you are ashamed of me," he said.

Two days before his arrival, a bomb went off near the shelter, shattering two of its windows. The explosion set a ration shop on fire. Worse, it snapped something in the head of eleven-year-old Altaf Hussain, who had lost his parents in a similar blast. Crying, he ran out into the street and fell to a burst of gunfire. Ritika, who rushed after him and held his shredded body, wept uncontrollably. She lost her will to eat and sleep and could barely concentrate on her work. A feeling of worthlessness, of waste, of the inane fallibility of life, began to dawn on her. When Aringdham arrived, she clung to him and cried, and this gave him the opportunity to speak about her taking a break, to persuade her to go with him to Bombay. Of course he knew enough of her to know she wouldn't abandon the children; hence he made the aid the excuse. He had many ideas now on how they could rejuvenate Sahayta. He wanted to share them with her, wanted her to be part of the momentum that made it a reality. She thought it sounded too good to be true.

In Bombay he told her about a plan to start a trust and register it with the commissioner of charities. The commissioner was an old friend; he could be persuaded. She found that kind of thing shocking and told Aringdham so, but he shrugged and said, "Business realities— can't be avoided."

Contributing a sizeable amount himself, Aringdham convinced two friends—Sarabjit Nagpal, a pharmaceutical baron, and Arup Sen Gupta, an investment banker and financier—to invest in Sahayta. Both were ideally positioned to strengthen the trust. Nagpal provided the medicines and contributed a four-wheel-drive truck and a driver. Sen Gupta brought in a generous cash component and spread it out across low-risk interest schemes to make the trust self-reliant. Aringdham took on the costs of reinforcing the shelters and provided the clothing, blankets, beds, and boots. As part of the *new thrust,* as he called it, he added a laptop (a Pentium 4) and a cell phone with roaming. He also added funds to the budget for two extra staff members. "You are going to need them," he told her. "I don't plan to keep you single for long."

The wedding was planned two months later. Using the excuse of the trust, Aringdham managed to hold Ritika back for three weeks. During this time she built up a high guilt load but admitted that for the first time in years she felt young and alive. Though she didn't like the congestion of Bombay—its traffic, pollution, and hectic impatience with anything that wasn't commerce, anything that didn't smell of opportunity—she felt at home in its libraries, its theaters, and its bay-view restaurants, especially the Sea Lounge at the Taj.

To make sure she could take time off for the wedding, Aringdham hired a social worker by the name of Lalitha Desai. She had ten years of experience and was a gold medallist from the Tata Institute of Social Sciences and passionate about giving damaged children a future. She had been through a bad marriage, was childless, did not have much money, and was looking to escape memories of the past. The job with Sahayta came as a boon. And Aringdham was not the kind to pinch pennies, especially if it freed time for his love.

Thus he cleverly and skillfully plotted his own happiness. He brought Ritika down to Bombay a month before the wedding and plunged her into a whirlwind of parties, dinners, and social engagements. It appeared that every evening someone wished to meet her or he'd want her to meet some friends, clients, people in the industry, or people in the ministry. After two weeks she wondered how he could keep this up, be his charming self night after night and work the next day. She wondered how he could see the same faces, endure their stories, their bragging, their repetitive jokes delivered with hearty aplomb. She missed her routine in the hills; she thought of the children and wondered if they missed her. The reports were encouraging. Lalitha Desai had taken well to the kids. She had introduced new games, made changes to the syllabus, was teaching them Hindustani music and yoga. Reconstruction on the shelters had started. The back portion was going to be extended, and once complete, it would house the social workers, who would no longer have to bunk with the kids. Ritika smiled. Good thought, but the kids wouldn't sleep alone. They were babies at heart. The four-wheel-drive truck was a big hit: the children rode in it to the lakeside every evening, and this brought some color to their cheeks.

ARINGDHAM'S EYES ZEROED in on the entrance. An important guest had arrived. Rajendra Singh Parmar owned an airline and one of the largest television networks in the country. He knew little, if anything, about aviation or television, but he was politically connected and known to help his friends. Aringdham moved to receive him.

On the way Amie Kanga, an elderly Parsi lady, stopped him. "Ah, Aringdham, there you are," she said, reaching for his face with flabby white arms. "Where have you been, you bad boy? Here, let me kiss you, before you get hooked, booked, and cooked." Aringdham politely offered her his cheek and she delicately kissed it. Then, pulling him down to where he could see her dazzling white pearls and smell the perfume that rose off her powdered breasts, she snapped her fingers against his temples, the Parsi gesture for good luck, and said, "*Bahut, bahut tandurusti, dikra*. A lifetime of good luck, son." Normally Aringdham would have stood and spoken to her, for he was fond of Auntie Amie, but right now he thanked her and moved on. He had to get to Parmar Sahib quickly. He was too important a guest to be left unattended. Besides, Aringdham didn't want any of the other guests—especially his competitors—to collar him.

Aringdham walked along the edge of the lawn. Thankfully there were no lights here, nor people. A waiter offered him a drink. He picked a whisky, took two gulps, and placed the glass back on the tray. "That's it!" he said to the waiter, and, wiping his mouth with a tissue, walked away. He couldn't meet Parmar Sahib with a drink in his hand. It was important that he make the right impression, for though Parmar Sahib was a recent acquaintance, he'd be a good man to know. No one knew his past, where he came from, or what his core business was, yet many of the bigwigs of India, including some film stars, media barons, industrialists, and cricketers, enjoyed a place on his board. Aringdham felt pleased that Parmar Sahib had bothered to come. It spoke to his own standing among the elite.

He came to a part of the lawn where the tables were being laid. By the dress of the chefs he could tell this was the Oriental spread. The soups and starters had been laid out, and the burners had been lit, the blue of the flames contrasting nicely with the orange hues from the trees. The night had taken on an ephemeral quality, a shimmering buzz, metaphysical and unreal. A medley of aromas rose from the trays. Aringdham would have liked to have stopped, but Parmar Sahib couldn't be kept waiting.

Just then, without warning, the lights went off, plunging the party into darkness. The guests went, "Ooh," wailing their disappointment. A pallid gloom fell over the lawns; it was as if someone had hurled a thick woolen blanket over them. It felt warm, too, as if the breeze had fallen. From afar the guests appeared more like birds of prey, like people dressed to enjoy but now frozen because their fun had been arrested. Aringdham cursed softly and looked around. It seemed like a uniform collapse—all over the city—some fluctuation in the grid, perhaps. He proved right, for seconds later the lights were back. And they seemed brighter now, harsher perhaps, because of the moments of deprivation and the transition to light so sharp and definite. The guests cheered. And Aringdham noted the clarity with which he could see them now: details of what they wore, how they smiled, the snacks they eyed, and spouses not their own. He could see hips swaying, not for the music but for eyes that would blink and absorb. And he could hear laughter that was meant to flatter, that suggested wavelengths in progress or dates for later.

The manager, Keith Rosario, stepped in his way. He gripped Aringdham by the arm, his face redder than usual, his voice embarrassingly loud. "Everything satisfactory, sir, I hope? All the guests are happy?"

Aringdham got a strong whiff of alcohol. Rum. He could tell by the smell. He looked coldly at his arm, and instantly Rosario's pinkish white fingers withdrew.

"You see, sir, I like to keep my word," Rosario spluttered. "I had promised you a party to remember, so I hope nothing is lacking, sir. I hope it all meets your expectations?"

"Yes, Mr. Rosario, all is well. A little less attention on the bar, though," Aringdham said before he walked away. Rosario blushed. These rich blokes couldn't bear to see anyone enjoy. Not like people in the hills, who opened their hearts and doors to all. No simplicity left, that's what the problem with this city was! Not like in the old days when everyone was free and open. He sighed and grabbed a drink off a passing tray. Then, on second thought, he called to the waiter and replaced it.

Aringdham saw that Parmar Sahib had joined a group of youngsters. He was smiling in their midst—that same indulgent smile he had seen on page 3 of the *Bombay Post*. Aringdham wondered if the smile was real. Did it spring from some inner source, genuine and spontaneous, or was it induced and cultivated? Did it harbor secrets of how wealth could pour in unexpectedly? How it could multiply overnight and find its way into mysterious banks outside the country? Did the smile say it knew how the country ran, and where and when it stopped running, and where funds were diverted, like a river dammed, to its rulers and their pockets?

Parmar Sahib seemed relaxed with the youngsters. He would! thought Aringdham. They were all highflyers, achievers, crossover filmmakers, fashion designers, runway models, painters, musicians, writers, producers, television stars: the future wave of India. Brand India, as they were calling it now in a recent tide of optimism. Parmar Sahib would want to be part of them. They gave him what he lacked—glamour, glitz, and social panache.

Aringdham was surprised at his thoughts. What had happened to him suddenly? He looked around and drank in the shining pockets of goodwill, the clever talk, the ribald bonding, the chemistry of the moment, which he had himself drawn on earlier to feel young, successful, and superior. But now were people looking out for him? No! Were they missing him? No! Wishing for him, toasting him, drinking to his health? No, no, no!

Did the conversation and the bonhomie cease because he wasn't around? Not a chance! Would it stop if he were to stay here in the dark or if he went away or dropped dead quietly at the side? Would anyone miss him besides Ritika and a few genuine friends like Nagpal and Sen Gupta? No. It would just spread to another lawn, another party. Same faces, different venue. It was all a game of self-reflection and self-promotion, a Ferris wheel of illusion that never stopped, because if it did people wouldn't know what to do with themselves, their lives, their wardrobes, and their manners, all so carefully cultivated for occasions like these.

This was interesting; he'd never seen it this way, in this light. He was intelligent enough to know he was going through some transformation, an awakening beyond a lightbulb moment. He stopped a waiter and picked up a glass. Any glass, it did not matter now. Then he retired into the shadows where no one could see him but from where he could see them all. What a chance this was to play voyeur, to observe and evaluate equations, to take stock of the world he had built and of the people who were drinking and feasting off him tonight.

In the midst of this, he spotted Ritika. A rare diamond, she sparkled for him and him alone, because in reality she was where she did not belong. She was here because of her love for him. The guests were polite to her and she to them. She exchanged pleasantries, said the right things, saw to their food and drinks. Patiently she listened to their views on child-aid programs, their jargon about generation next: "The child is the future of man. We love the child so much, we'll drink some more. Don't mind us, for that's how we are. We can't change the world, so why change ourselves?"

Ironically, none of them had ventured out of Bombay to parts of India affected by a catastrophe—neither to Latur when it shook and collapsed, nor to Bhuj when it reverberated and ruptured, nor to Gujarat when it burned. Yet they spoke of their love for children, their social commitment, and notions of good corporate citizenship. As Ritika listened to them, she smiled and only volunteered as much as they needed to know. By their short-lived conversations Aringdham could tell that they didn't know what to make of her. "He could have married better," he imagined them saying. Or, "She's not a Bombay girl; she won't last." "Big deal," someone else would say. "She will become one. I have never seen anyone hold out against the city. The city has a way of taking you in. You can't help but get swept off after a while."

Aringdham looked toward Parmar Sahib. His circle had increased. Nimesh Pai, the Bollywood producer, had joined in now. He looked funny in a fluorescent yellow shirt straining at the paunch, his side-burns flowing down his cheeks. The shirt had a limelight of its own; it shone and revealed shrubs of hair flattened by perspiration. Pai's mannerisms implied an attempt at shaking off his years. But what about his failures—the flop movies he had made in the last ten years? Aringdham could guess what his pitch would be: he'd be trying to build up a case for his flops—how they had fared well outside the country; how within India the timing was bad, there were too many big-budget films released at that time; how the big markets lay outside India; who'd imagine otherwise that Amitabh Bachchan would get so big in France? And so on and so forth, Pai would pontificate—how Bollywood must reinvent itself, shed its dependency on Hollywood plots, attract better scripts, consider collaborating with foreign studios, and summarily look at the world as its market. Occasionally he'd drop names like Ted Turner and Rupert Murdoch—to keep Parmar Sahib interested. And Parmar Sahib *was* interested. Anything to do with the media and celebrity fascinated him. Like most of India's business gentry, Parmar Sahib was starstruck, and Pai was still a big name.

Aringdham took a sip of his rum. Exquisite, this Jamaican stuff. No wonder Rosario had been going at it. Aringdham thought of his conversation with the manager and felt ashamed. What was the difference between the manager and Nimesh Pai? They were both doing the same thing, availing themselves of an opportunity and juicing it. Rosario, grabbing at booze he would never normally taste, and the producer, trying to make a channel sale for his movies.

"Television is any day a better medium than cinema," Nimesh Pai would say to Parmar Sahib. "Cinema doesn't have that kind of reach. Nor the sweep and the impact."

"*Nahin,* sir," Parmar Sahib would reply quickly, "the investment in television is too high. Too much money has to go in, and it takes years to recover."

And Nimesh Pai would immediately talk about *Kaun Banega Crorepati,* that one big break that put Star TV at the head of the ratings. At the same time he'd comb Parmar Sahib's face for signs. When would be the best time to sell him a television show?

A good dance number had started: Nancy Sinatra's "These Boots Are Made for Walkin'." A group of women cheered. All forty-plus, they were the beauty queens of yesteryear, salvaged and restored by endless face-lifts. They descended on the male models at the bar and dragged them to the floor. The Swapnil sisters led the offensive. In private they were known as the sisters of swap, because at different times they'd been married to the same guy, Prem Swapnil. Sangeeta Swapnil got to keep him; Naina Swapnil had to back off. Yet they were one big happy family, with Naina Swapnil refusing to give up the surname. It had its advantages. On the guest list of the rich and famous, names could be forgotten but not surnames.

Some of the guests had started to eat, holding plates in one hand, drinks in the other. Aringdham could tell they were from the consulates. Next to them was Pat Trivedi—French-bearded and brown-eyed—who wrote a weekly column for the *Bombay Post.* A superficial knowledge of jazz and a deep understanding of same-sex swinging made Pat popular with the foreigners. Another socialite, Bhisham Malkani, had tried to break into this circuit for years, but he didn't have the panache to give his sexual leanings an intellectual varnish. So he had to be content with married Indian bisexuals whose wives were into swinging with younger men.

Some of these wives were on the dance floor; they were gyrating with the male models in a spirit of pelvic synchronicity. From a distance the female models looked on and whispered to one another. What they said couldn't have been flattering, for their minds were soaked as much in envy as in alcohol. Yet when they'd meet, they'd exclaim, "Darling, what energy! Where do you get it? Just looking at you, I feel so wasted." And the elder beauties would wink and say, "Exercise, dahling—all kinds! It's *the* elixir, you know?"

Aringdham watched all this as he sipped his rum. A wisp of a breeze lightened his mood, made him feel refreshed and truantlike.

His eyes fell on Sam Bakshi, the shipping tycoon of India, prince of socialites, and playboy of the Eastern world, around whom a large number of men and women had gathered. Bakshi was holding court, and Aringdham could guess what he was saying. He'd be talking about a course, on the art of spiritual rejuvenation, that he'd taken recently, how he had awakened to a world outside fast cars, fast horses, and fast women. Ever since Bakshi had become "awakened," his life's mission was to press people into taking the course. His guru was Swami Kaviraj, a half-bald fakir with strands of long ropey hair, kohl-rimmed eyes, and a faint smile transfixed permanently. He gave the impression of one who knew he was going to hook you sooner or later.

Aringdham had attended one such course. Bakshi had cornered him at his New Year's Eve party when Aringdham was on his fourth drink and too polite to refuse. Because Aringdham was well-read, he had seen through the sham—the spiritual rejuvenation course came out of Vipassana, the Buddhist technique for self-realization, practiced over ten days of self-observed silence. Clever, crafty Kaviraj had distilled it down to two days; he had packaged it into a dull, watered-down version, a quick fix that worked at the physical level, inducing a little lightness—relief, not realization—and this way he made it easy for the spiritual wannabes, the idle rich bored with their toys. "Of course you can do what you want—enjoy! You can continue to indulge in the material, but don't get attached, that's all," he cautioned, smiling, while participants in the course sighed ecstatically and agreed to leave the distribution of their wealth to him. They agreed to it as a precondition critical for spiritual growth. And he helped them all he could.

Aringdham didn't tell Sam Bakshi he'd seen through this, for Bakshi wouldn't take kindly to a dissenting view. Besides, that wasn't the way to get by in Bombay's socialite circles. You had to nod when the mighty spoke. You had to show interest and open-mindedness. You had to scratch the other's back, so the other would scratch yours in return, and by mutual consent you progressed and prospered, were invited to parties and featured in the papers, and would have the rest of Bombay envying you. It was a society full of icons, and more dangerous than the icons were those who made them and those who sustained them by their adulation.

Aringdham felt a sense of embarrassment. He realized how deeply he had craved this attention. How important it had been to get here, to stay and scintillate once he'd arrived. Well, he was tired of this game of pretense and performance, all the silent one-upmanship calculated to make an impact, to reflect his wit and reflexes, and to feed some illusion of superior refinement, which was never fulfilled and always growing. He was surprised at himself. It was as if he had donned a new identity, had gained a new power—calm, curious, and self-assured. He hoped the feeling would stay; he could live with it easily.

There appeared to be some stir at the entrance. Jay Chawla, the industrialist, and his wife, Shaheen, had arrived. They were in their twenties and quite a favorite with the party set. Jay wore a transparent black shirt, sleeveless, which showed the serpentine tattoos on his chest and arms. Shaheen did the same with her belly; it was tattooed colorfully and her navel was pierced with a diamond stud. Their hair was blond and jelled, and through their eyes a piercing vitality showed. It was rumored that the two were using Colombian white, the purest you could get off the streets of Colaba, but that was a rumor spread by people who'd seen them disappear into the restrooms together. There was no proof of it, none whatsoever.

Aringdham thought the Chawlas would hunt for him, would come to congratulate him and Ritika, but no, they headed straight for the dance floor. The crowd parted and welcomed them with shouts of, "Oh ho, here they come," and "We will, we will rock you." Shaheen blew kisses and rolled her eyes—oh, she'd stay and talk, but when Jay wanted to rock, she had to roll. "Later, dahling, later—I promise!" she told them. "The night is young, and so are we."

Jay leapt onstage and fired instructions at the bandleader, Joe Braganza, or Jazzy Joe as he was called. The crowd went, "Yes, yes, yes," and Jazzy Joe nodded. He was here to entertain, here to please. He shot instructions to his musicians, and the music switched to a popular Hindi tune, the remix of a classic song. The beauty queens went mad. They shook their boobs and hands vigorously. After a while they lifted their arms to reveal thick green underarms and they danced *bhangra*-style, pouting their lips and swinging their hips expertly. Jay was center stage. He bent his body backward and, with a well-rehearsed motion, jiggled a part of his chest, fingering a make-believe guitar in mid-air. The beauty queens surrounded him and screamed hysterically. Shaheen grinned with achievement. Wasn't he too much, just too much? She drew closer and stuck her tongue out—at his quivering chest, his flattened stomach, his arched groin, which came into sight. "Isn't he too much, girls? Isn't he a real pacesetter, a real party animal, a real floor burner?" The crowd squealed in agreement. "Oh take off your shirt, Jay. Let's see those muscles; let's see that chest." By cheerleading for the Chawlas, the people on the floor earned their approval and an invitation to their parties.

Aringdham sighed. He looked for Ritika. She was talking to Parmar Sahib, who was without his coterie. The film producer Pai was on the floor, cutting a lewd number with a model, a wannabe actress six inches taller than he. Ritika was listening to Parmar Sahib, who spoke softly, but her eyes were roaming, searching the lawns beyond the lights. From where he stood Aringdham could read her mind. His wife was missing him; she needed his presence, a touch, a smile, to reward her for her patience. Aringdham stepped out of the shadows and set off at a pace. She saw him and her face lit up.

"Where have you been, Aringdham?" Ritika asked reproachfully. "Look, Parmar Sahib is all set to leave, and he hasn't eaten yet."

"No, no, how can that be, Parmar Sahib? We can't let you go so soon."

"I have been here for some time. But you have been absconding." Parmar Sahib looked at Aringdham with warm eyes that twinkled and saw through him—as if they knew his secret, as if they knew Aringdham had been watching him.

"I was getting a few things organized. I didn't expect everyone to make it, but they have," Aringdham said. He was anxious to stress his popularity with Parmar Sahib, but no sooner had he said that than he felt ashamed.

"That they have," Parmar Sahib agreed. "Who'd want to miss a party like this? Especially when it's *your* wedding party."

With the authority of a man who had built an empire, Parmar Sahib said, "Anyway, I must go now. I have an early flight to catch, and before that, tonight, I have to stop at the CM's." He said it so plainly that it didn't seem like he was showing off. Besides, Parmar Sahib didn't need to boast of his proximity to the chief minister. His connections were well-known.

"But, sir, some *khana* at least," Aringdham offered.

"Nothing! I will come, I promise—for *bhabhi*'s home-cooked meal."

"But I can't cook, Parmar Sahib!" exclaimed Ritika, horrified.

"Doesn't matter. You will learn. I know. You will be a good cook and a good wife. He is a lucky man," Parmar Sahib said, pointing to Aringdham. His eyes fastened on Aringdham, as if they were trying to convey more, as if they had guessed his detachment.

Just then Rosario came up to Ritika. With the air of a soldier on duty, he asked whether she'd like the rest of the dinner served and whether the vegetarian and non-vegetarian tables should be separated. Ritika excused herself and went off to see to the arrangements.

"Come, Parmar Sahib, let me walk you out," Aringdham offered. "I wish you could stay, but since you've promised to come home, we are letting you go—on the basis of this promise."

"I will," Parmar Sahib replied, and Aringdham wondered whether he was being facile.

As they were walking out, Nimesh Pai came running from the dance floor. "Parmar Sahib, Parmar Sahib, please," he spluttered breathlessly, sweating at the forehead. "Can I call you next week—at the office? I think I might have something good, something bigger than *Crorepati*."

Parmar Sahib stopped. He looked at him hard and then said softly, "There are many ideas bigger than *Crorepati,* but for that you will have to go into politics." At this he burst into laughter. Aringdham laughed, too, and the producer also—slowly at first, then uproariously, and then to a whimper when he saw that Parmar Sahib was walking away toward his car.

Near his Lexus, Parmar Sahib stopped and spoke to Aringdham.

He had regained his softness. "I am sorry," he said. "I didn't have the time to bring you a gift. I just got in from London this evening. Do you know we are buying four new aircraft? We had an option to lease, but we preferred outright purchase."

"Why, that is splendid!" exclaimed Aringdham. "But you don't have to apologize about a gift. Your presence itself was that."

Parmar Sahib put an arm around him. "Do you know what is the greatest gift you have today?" He didn't wait for an answer. "Your wife! She is pure gold. You know, in our kind of lives, we have to endure a lot. Do things we don't mean, say things we don't believe. We have to do this all the time, be onstage where we shouldn't be. But all that is okay if you can come home to one fundamental piece of honesty. One truth to remind you of who you are, where you belong. I think that is what you have achieved today. You have brought your conscience home and are just beginning to realize it. You have built your base. Now you will see how far it takes you." Parmar Sahib got into his car and disappeared, leaving Aringdham convinced that he *had* indeed seen him in the shadows.

Aringdham didn't feel like going back to the party yet. He knew that Ritika would be busy with the dinner. That was their deal: his planning, her supervision. She wouldn't back out on that. In fact, she might even prefer it to exchanging pleasantries with people who hadn't scratched the root of human existence, who hadn't fathomed its responsibilities and its sorrows, who were too busy enjoying it sunny-side up.

He lit a cigarette and walked down the driveway, a dark stretch shaded by luxuriant trees on either side. Here no one could see him; only the sporadic gleam of his cigarette gave away his presence. As he watched the tip glow, he thought of it as a dot of enlightenment, a center that dawned and disappeared, as he would one day. And he found the solitude comforting, complete. For some strange reason he'd never felt like this before. He had always needed company, friends, a circle to reflect his success and his well-being. He wondered about Parmar Sahib. He seemed genuine, not the dark, controversial figure he was made out to be. People can be jealous, Aringdham thought. You can't believe all that they say. But then again, Parmar Sahib had risen from obscurity. He'd just appeared—with interests in two of the most capital-intensive industries. What was his secret? What was his past? What were the ashes he had left behind?

Whatever it was, Aringdham knew that Parmar Sahib had been an intelligent and sensitive guest. He'd listened more than he had spoken. He'd seen through the facades, as his comment to the producer had indicated. Significantly, Parmar Sahib had liked what he'd seen in Ritika, the same quality Aringdham had seen—the true expression of womanhood: a woman not afraid to follow the callings of her heart, not afraid to draw strength from it and live by her conviction. Maybe Parmar Sahib had also stood in the shadows a long time ago or once in a while he still did.

Knowing that he had made a friend, one that might benefit him, or not—and little he cared for that—Aringdham returned to the party. At the side where the food was spread, the lights had been made brighter. At the bar alcohol fizzed and flowed; there was a crowd of men and women caught up in conversation. Confidences were being shared and violated. New equations were being negotiated delicately—either for business or for personal development. Nimble-footed waiters scurried across the lawns, maneuvering their loaded trays. They tempted the guests to break from their conversations.

The society queens said, "No, how could I eat dinner after this?" "Feel how fat I've become," they'd say to the male models, who would grope them with strong, willing fingers, hug them with knowing arms. The queens would sigh and lurch. "Here, not there," they would say, and feel the warmth through their dresses, a warmth that would flush their cheeks. Bodies would burn; mouths would run dry. The husbands would look away with practiced ease. In the eye of a storm keep your lid; go home and tear it off. Or plan a hush hush rendezvous on Sam Bakshi's yacht. Men would be men, God's irascible creatures. Though, God knows, the women were catching up.

Behind the food tables the chefs had taken up their positions. On the dance floor the crowd was going mad. Jazzy Joe poured hot lead from his guitar; he was playing *Dum Maro Dum,* the hippie song of the seventies. Jay and Shaheen had disappeared. It was whispered that they had retreated to the restrooms.

Aringdham stopped at the bar. He picked up a bottle illustrated with a pirate. The label read: "Jim Brady's Double-breasted Rum," whatever that meant. He nodded to the bartender.

Someone thumped him on the back and said, "Hey, dude, great party." Aringdham recognized him as Anant Ghosh, an upcoming actor who starred in art and crossover films. Someone at his side quipped, "Yes, great bash, but don't tell him to do this often, or his wife's gonna kill you!"

Aringdham smiled and raised his glass. He looked at the man whom he placed as USA-returned—someone's guest brought in uninvited—and he said, "You bet! She's seething already because of the gatecrashers."

"Hey, what's your problem?" the man with the fake accent drawled. "You having a bad trip?"

Aringdham chose not to reply. Sometimes it was correct to be cold.

At the other end of the bar, Pai was swaying on a barstool. He looked drunk, and occasionally he would glance at the dance floor and hiccup. Aringdham saw that his model friend had found a new partner, a younger man with whom she was dancing fluidly.

The bartender served the rum and Coke, which Aringdham stirred absentmindedly. His friend Arup Sen Gupta approached. He was leaving, for he was an early riser and a stickler for yoga and morning walks. He promised Aringdham that they'd get together soon—he, his wife, Nileema, Aringdham, and Ritika—once they'd come back from their honeymoon. "Where are you off to anyway?" he asked. "Not Kashmir, I hope."

Aringdham saw his friend to the entrance. On the way he was stopped by people who told him how wonderful the food was, how unprecedented the experience, how gorgeous the costumes, and how spectacular the music! "Like the host," someone said, and Aringdham smiled and said he was glad they'd come, gladder still they'd enjoyed it. In his mind he was thinking, Why, why not Kashmir? Why not Srinagar? Just a stopover to see how things had progressed.

He realized that his mind was ready for more alcohol; it was at that stage when anything surplus would be inspiration, because it had figured itself out; it had mapped out his concept of the future. He stopped at the bar before the same bartender, who smiled with understanding. While his drink was being prepared, he looked out for Pai. What a fascinating fellow he was, so bare and transparent, whether chasing skirts or opportunities.

It appeared that Pai had found company. He was trying to make conversation with Rosario, who stood tall, red-faced, and disapproving. Aringdham took his drink and inched forward. Pai was trying to explain to Rosario the reach of television over cinema. He stretched out his fingers, thrust them at Rosario, and said in a slurred rush, "Television, many households! Cinema, just one." To which Rosario replied, "No offense, sir, but you won't catch me before the idiot box. Not with the kind of soap they show these days. As for cinema, it's not the same. Where are the movies like *The Bridge on the River Kwai, Where Eagles Dare,* or *Hornets' Nest*? That was cinema."

"Wait . . . ," said Pai, almost swaying himself off the stool. "Wait till you see my next film. It's about an older-man-younger-girl romance."

Rosario found it imprudent to reply. He'd rather contemplate rum than romance. As for escapism, there was nothing to beat the lofty slopes of Nainital.

Glass in hand, Aringdham moved from the bar. He mingled with his guests, accepting their compliments on an impeccable evening, certainly the party of the year. He found A.K., the photographer, posing for a picture with girls on either side of him, wannabe models with their heads on his shoulders, arms around his waist, the hope of a break alight in their eyes.

"Hey, A.K., you are safer this side of the lens," Aringdham said, and continued walking.

The girls howled with laughter, and A.K. shrugged good-naturedly and admitted to a touché. One of the girls came running after Aringdham. "Oh, Mr. Banerjee, please," she said. "I need to know, will this be on page three . . . the bash, I mean?"

Aringdham looked at the white face, the anxious eyes, the cheeks and lips moist with makeup, and he was tempted to say, "Sure, look for it in the obituaries, for that's where you belong—all you brain-dead people, all you soulless wits, who've come without even knowing me, because you knew someone who knew me and because I, in turn, am known for my parties and not for what I am or have been through." But of course he didn't say that. He just said, "Wait . . . wait and see," and began walking away, and she stamped her foot and whined, "But that's just what I can't do. I need time to inform all my friends."

Thinking of all the people there who relied on his hospitality and whom he had come to be associated with, Aringdham shivered. He missed Ritika, missed her poignantly. The rum, too, was beginning to take effect. He imagined himself as a stalker in a deadly game of virtual reality. The lights were virtual, the people and their actions, too. The reality was what he had married, what he had become, and what he craved now.

He came across Puru Raj Singh, popularly known as P.R. Singh for his pleasant disposition and his willingness to befriend all. The cool restaurateur was with his wife, Ravina, who clung to his arm. They had been married six months and had only just finished with their introductions and parties. Ravina was to make her professional debut soon, something that would keep her shining on the social circuit, a complement to P.R.'s public image.

"I knew she had it for fashion the moment I saw her with the wedding clothes," P.R. said to Aringdham. "I've spoken to Nats and she agrees. She's going to let Ravs work on her summer collection—under supervision, of course. You know Nats—she loves to guard her turf. Though once she sees what Ravs can put out, she's going to walk, I tell you."

Nats was Natasha Saigal, the famous designer, and out of politeness she might let Ravina, or Ravs, as she was now known, work with her. P.R.'s restaurants catered to her shows; his clients were hers as well, and there was an unspoken contract of mutual interest between the two. Aringdham felt he was no one to disturb this, so he beamed at Ravs and said, "Well, going by what you're wearing, Nats has some hot stuff coming."

And Ravs purred, patted her shoulders and said demurely, "Oh, just something I put together overnight."

And P.R. added, "She didn't want to outshine the bride, you see."

On this pleasant note Aringdham parted with P.R. He knew not why, but it was almost as if he were taking leave of all these people, saying farewell to these stars of Brand India, these icons who kept polishing their own halos, toasting their own success, and who'd burn out eventually because they'd confuse excess with success, wealth with achievement, and opulence with taste.

He saw her at last —talking to Charu Sinha, the socialite columnist who wrote about people she knew and people she didn't. Charu Sinha didn't believe in research or in the tedium of a personal interview. It was her opinion she gave—saucy, brassy, and indignant—and women of a traditional background who did not have the luxury of having a say in their lives would lap her up. Here was a woman ready to shoot from her hip, able to plunge through doorways uninvited and hurl black invective at whomever she pleased. How much catharsis can one expect in a morning paper?

"I was just telling your wife," Charu Sinha said, with a flick of her new haircut, "that I'd love to write about the good work she's doing. It's so inspiring—to find a woman in a man's territory, doing her own thing."

"Oh yes," Aringdham said, wondering if relief work could be called her thing, her or others'. Instead he said, "You should see her with those kids, Charu; an angel she is."

"Oh, it's not just me," Ritika said hurriedly. "I get a lot of support—from him."

"Really?" Charu Sinha exclaimed, flicking her hair again, her bangles jangling, her eyes averted, scanning the crowd. "I must hear about this, this new-age metrosexual who allows his woman to stay in the hills, kicking through snow, enduring the cold, the hardships, saving kids who'd be burning up with revenge otherwise. It's so utterly cool and renegade. Why, Arie, we must meet next week, over lunch, and you must tell me about this very mature arrangement of yours. How is it going to work—with you here, and she there, and a whole country between?

"And hey," she said, looking at him sternly, "talking about support, I am expecting you to buy a hundred copies of my new book. It's coming out next week, and it's a real scorcher. You must give copies to all your buyers and clients."

Aringdham promised and said what a wonderful idea that was; he hoped the publisher would print five thousand copies at least. What, only two thousand! What a shame, what a crying shame indeed. How depressing that no one promoted literature seriously enough in this country. Now, if she were published in the West, like Lahiri or Roy, she'd have gotten places by now.

Charu Sinha drew herself up. She pulled her sari tightly around her shoulders and spoke in a voice unlike that of a forty-year-old woman, unlike the steam that crackled and hissed off her columns in the morning papers. "Well, everybody can't have Jhumpa's or Arundhati's luck, I suppose!"

Near the dance floor a song ended. The crowd cheered and roared their requests. Voices cracked with drink and desire. Jazzy Joe beamed. He looked short and happy. Someone had offered him a drink, the first of many to come.

The food was out in full array: hot, delicious, and enticing. The servers' costumes were bright and arresting. People noticed them and flocked to the tables. They came again and again, trying out new dishes, heaping their plates and sighing wistfully.

A glass broke; no one seemed to mind. Keith Rosario dreamt of the bottle in his desk. Charu Sinha dreamt of a publisher in the West. Ritika dreamt of her kids. Aringdham dreamt of making a call. Bombay-Srinagar-Spain: could that be possible, at this time of the night?

IN A QUIET LANE behind the club, a police van cruised up silently. Its doors slid open, and its occupants tumbled out. They stretched. They yawned. They clicked their heels and came alive. Some of the waiters rushed out with whisky and glasses, sodas, plates, and trays of snacks. The cops opened the door of the van, revealing the depth and darkness inside, the netted windows like cages.

They put the food inside the van and opened the whisky. The streetlight illuminated the bottle and the grim, anxious faces of the men who waited, hands outstretched, glasses raised.

Rats, sniffing at the gutters, stopped their forays. Their beady eyes glinted. A dog, asleep on the pavement, rose from his slumber and approached the cops, wagging his tail and beating it against their legs. Later they would throw him chicken bones and pieces of *naan* with chilies inside, and they would howl rapturously when the dog went away yelping.

A car screeched by, its speakers pounding. The cops looked up and then away. Some drunken youth celebrating his father's wealth. Too much effort to catch and threaten, and for what when the needs of the night had been met?

The moon emerged from behind a cloud and illuminated the empty stretch of street, the tall, proud Gothic buildings. The fencing around the club—sharp, iron spokes, flat and rusted—drew a clear line of demarcation between those inside, who reveled and feasted, and those outside, who slept on the jagged pavement, their faces brown and placid, their hair damp with sweat, their bellies round and distended, their ribs gleaming under a velvet sky, and their arms and feet stiff like the branches of a fallen tree.

Yet they snored and slept peacefully, for theirs was not the vice of music, or of fine food, or of dance, or of clever conversation. Theirs was the vice of deep abysmal sleep, rising and falling, rising and drifting and feeding off the cool night air, the will of fate and the stars above, blinking uncertainly and sheepishly. And theirs was the vice of a single dream, an unchanging dream: to prepare for another day of labor, another day of toil, another day of survival, which would allow them to sleep on a half-empty stomach, or half-full, if they were that lucky, that is.

1. How has the book changed your understanding of Bombay? Does it make you want to visit?

2. Who are the characters you felt most drawn to? For what reasons were you drawn to them?

3. If you were residing in Bombay, how would you—as a responsible citizen—go about addressing these issues: unplanned development, corruption, encroachment, poverty, and class divide? If you were to start a nonprofit organization, which cause would you take up?

4. What role has the author intended for the women in the work? Please discuss in relation to Ritika in *Breathless in Bombay*, Silla Mullafiroze in *The Great Divide*, the three ladies in *A Different Bhel*, Shyla in *Haraami*, Kaveri in *The Maalishwalla*, and Vicki in *Traffic*. Which of the women captures the true essence of the Indian woman?

5. With temptation having set in at the ghat, what do you think happened to Mataprasad after the end of *Dhobi Ghat*?

6. Do you think Bheem Singh from *The Maalishwalla* returned to his village? Bearing in mind that going against tradition was to invite the wrath of the entire village, what course of action would you advise for Bheem Singh in his marriage?

7. Do you feel trading off his sense of ethics makes Chacha in *The Queen Guards Her Own* any less heroic?

8. Which portions of the work did you find most shocking, touching, humorous, and/or thought-provoking?

9. Did Madhulikar Srini in *Babu Barrah Takka* take the bribe eventually? If you were in his shoes, what would you do? How would you justify your actions to your wife and your to-be-married daughter?

10. Does the author's approach to his work remind you of any American author, past or present?

11. By the author's own admission, his work has one overriding goal—to sensitize the haves to the have-nots. Has he succeeded in his purpose? What feelings does the book leave you with?

For more reading group suggestions, visit
www.readinggroupgold.com.

St. Martin's
Griffin